WINGED HEROES

By Mya Thompson
Illustrated by Virginia Greene

The**Cornell**Lab Publishing Group

Design by Brian Scott Sockin and Shan Stumpf
Edited by Jill Leichter and Caroline Watkins

ISBN: 978-1-943645-21-3

10 9 8 7 6 5 4 3 2

The**Cornell**Lab
Publishing Group

Published by:
The Cornell Lab Publishing Group
An imprint of WunderMill, Inc.
321 Glen Echo Lane, Ste. C
Cary, NC 27518
www.cornelllabpg.com
www.wundermillbooks.com

To Anya and Niko—and to
all birdkind.
— *Mya Thompson*

To Mom and Dad—and every
creature, great and small.
— *Virginia Greene*

WunderMill
www.wundermillbooks.com

WINGED HEROES

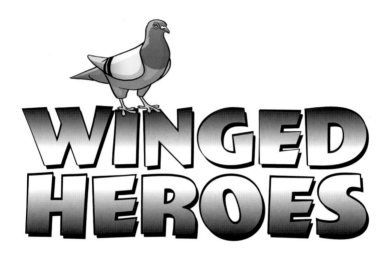

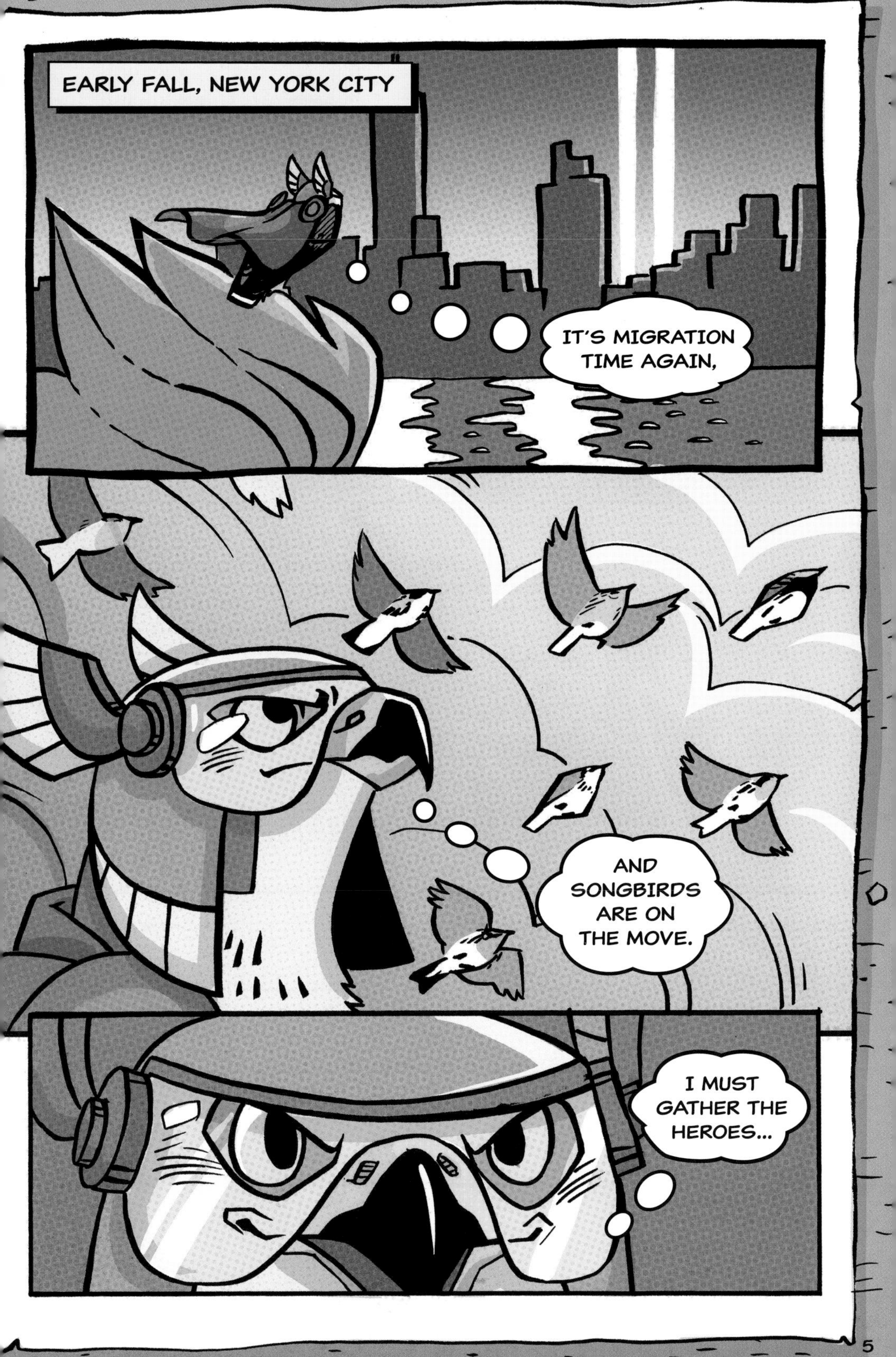
EARLY FALL, NEW YORK CITY
IT'S MIGRATION TIME AGAIN,
AND SONGBIRDS ARE ON THE MOVE.
I MUST GATHER THE HEROES...

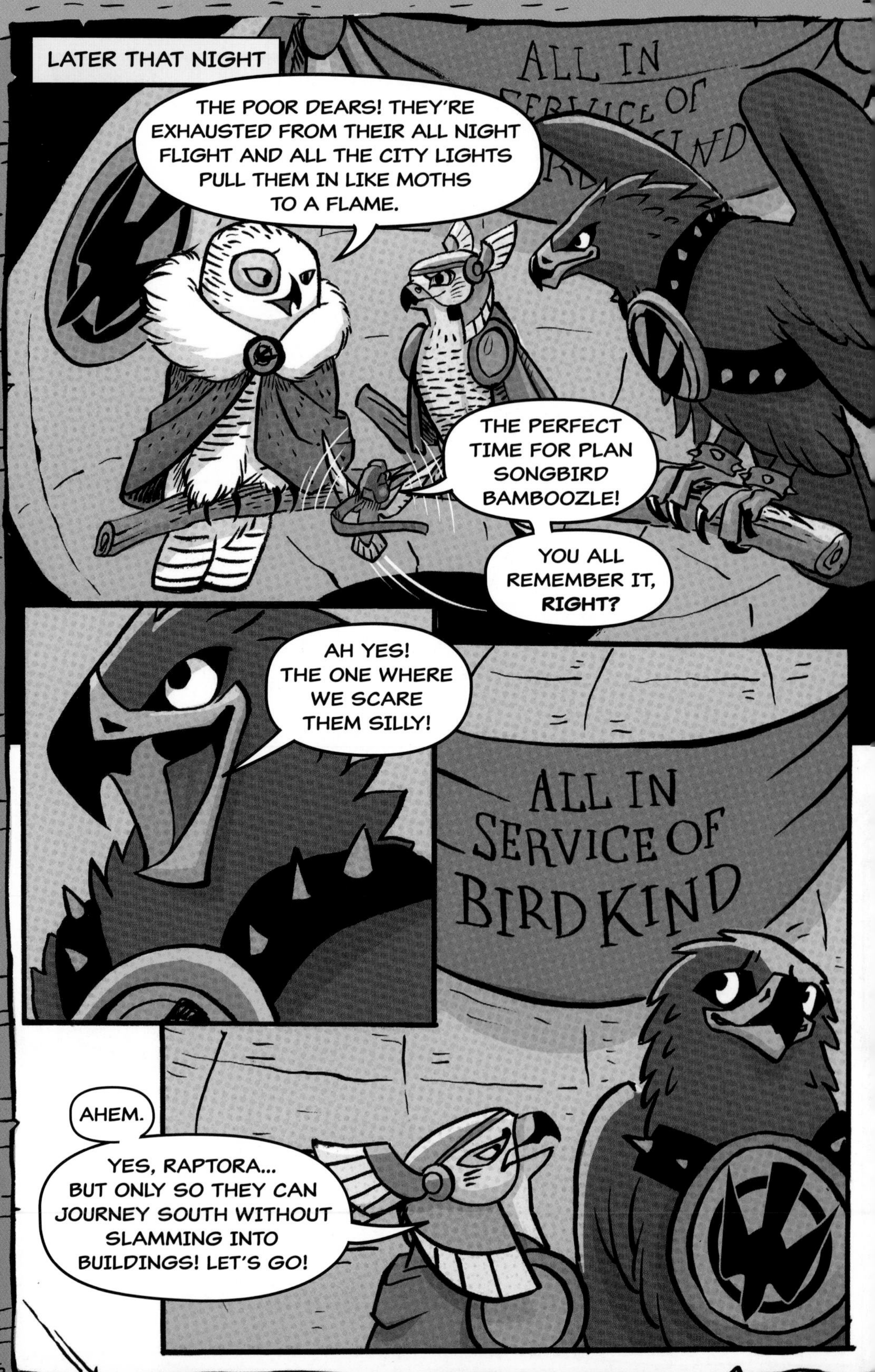
LATER THAT NIGHT
ALL IN SERVICE OF BIRD KIND
THE POOR DEARS! THEY'RE EXHAUSTED FROM THEIR ALL NIGHT FLIGHT AND ALL THE CITY LIGHTS PULL THEM IN LIKE MOTHS TO A FLAME.
THE PERFECT TIME FOR PLAN SONGBIRD BAMBOOZLE!
YOU ALL REMEMBER IT, **RIGHT?**
AH YES! THE ONE WHERE WE SCARE THEM SILLY!
ALL IN SERVICE OF BIRD KIND
AHEM.
YES, RAPTORA... BUT ONLY SO THEY CAN JOURNEY SOUTH WITHOUT SLAMMING INTO BUILDINGS! LET'S GO!

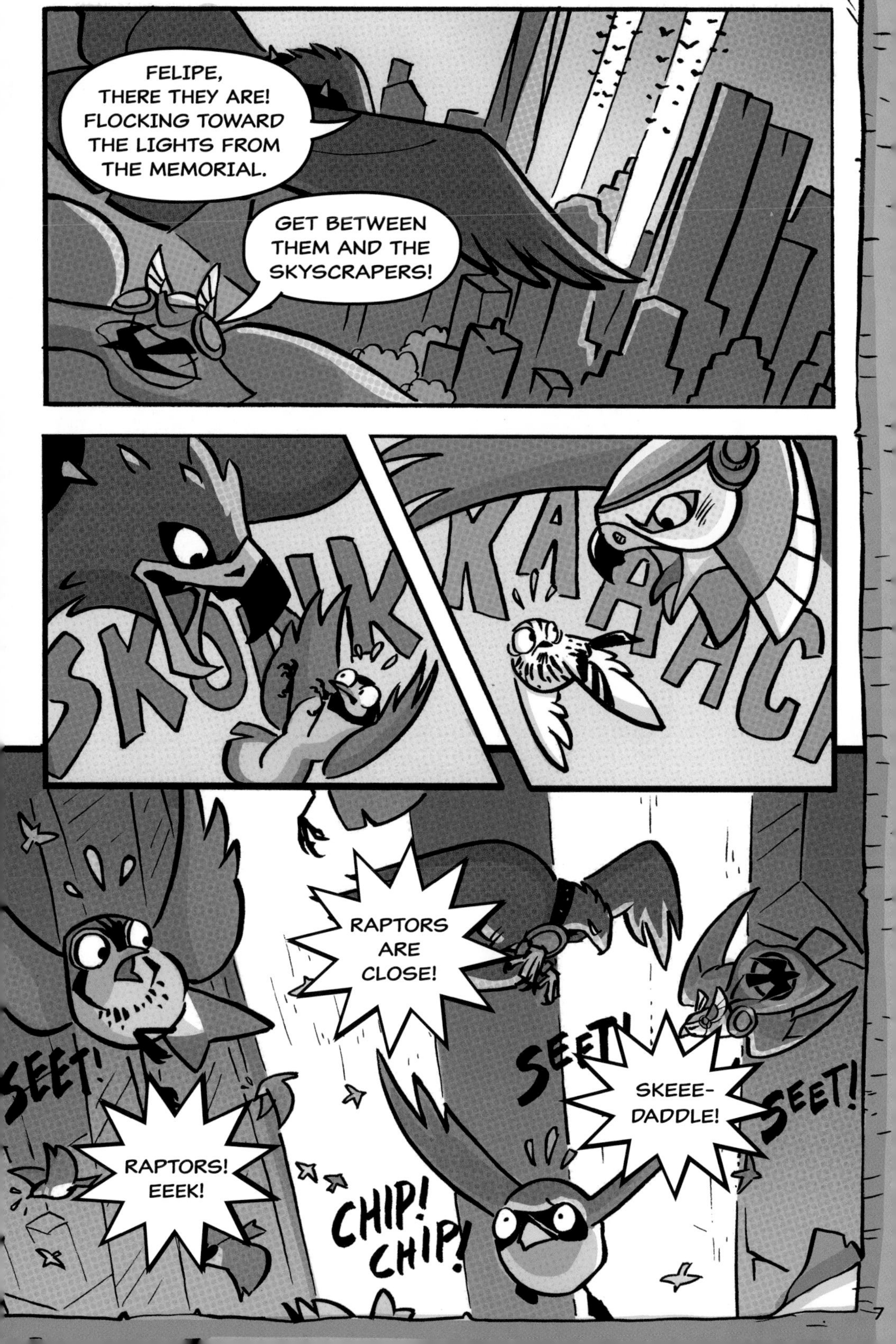
FELIPE, THERE THEY ARE! FLOCKING TOWARD THE LIGHTS FROM THE MEMORIAL.
GET BETWEEN THEM AND THE SKYSCRAPERS!
SKOUK
WAAACK
SEET!
RAPTORS ARE CLOSE!
SEET!
SKEEE-DADDLE!
SEET!
RAPTORS! EEEK!
CHIP! CHIP!

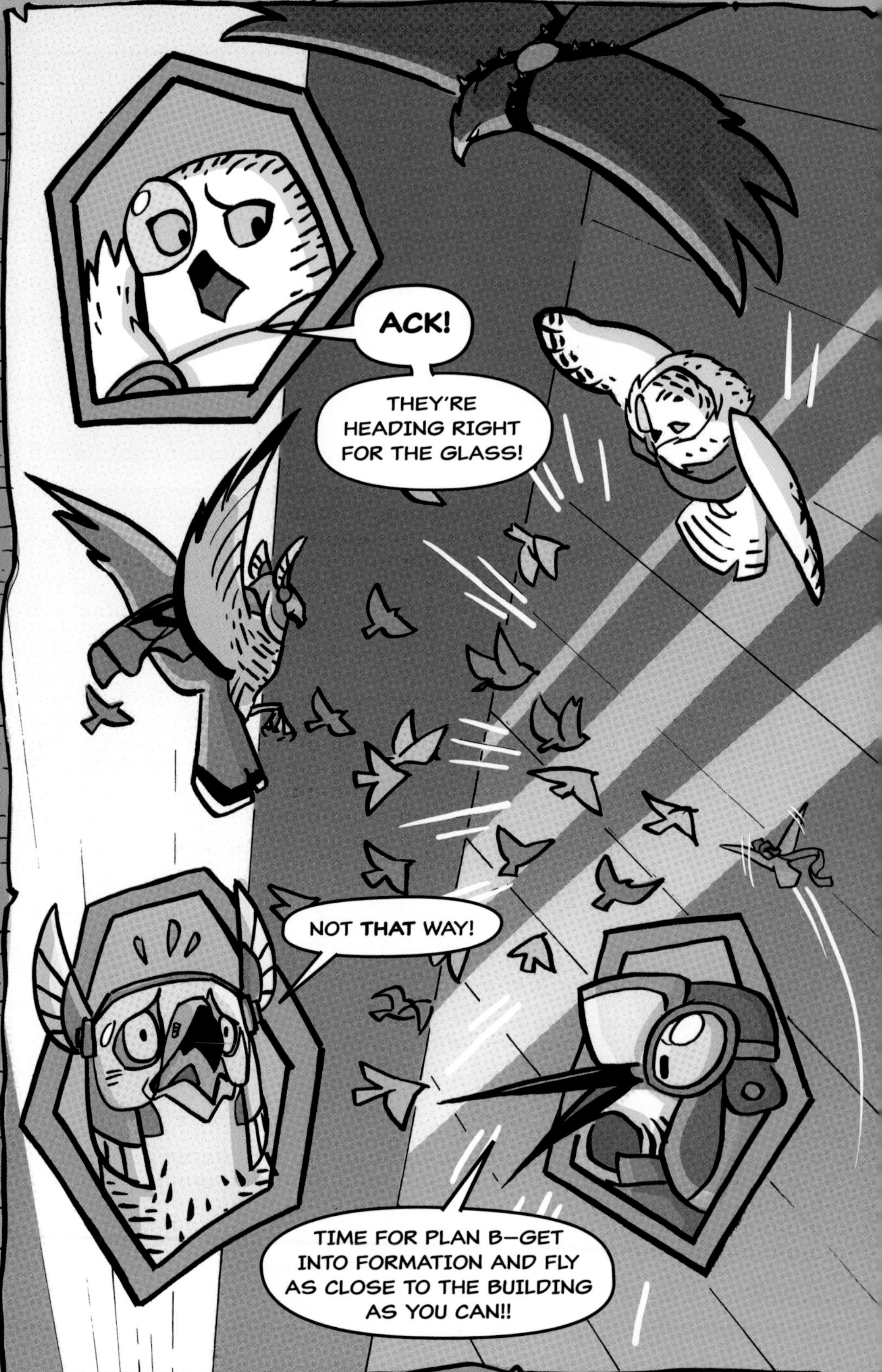
ACK!
THEY'RE HEADING RIGHT FOR THE GLASS!
NOT THAT WAY!
TIME FOR PLAN B—GET INTO FORMATION AND FLY AS CLOSE TO THE BUILDING AS YOU CAN!!

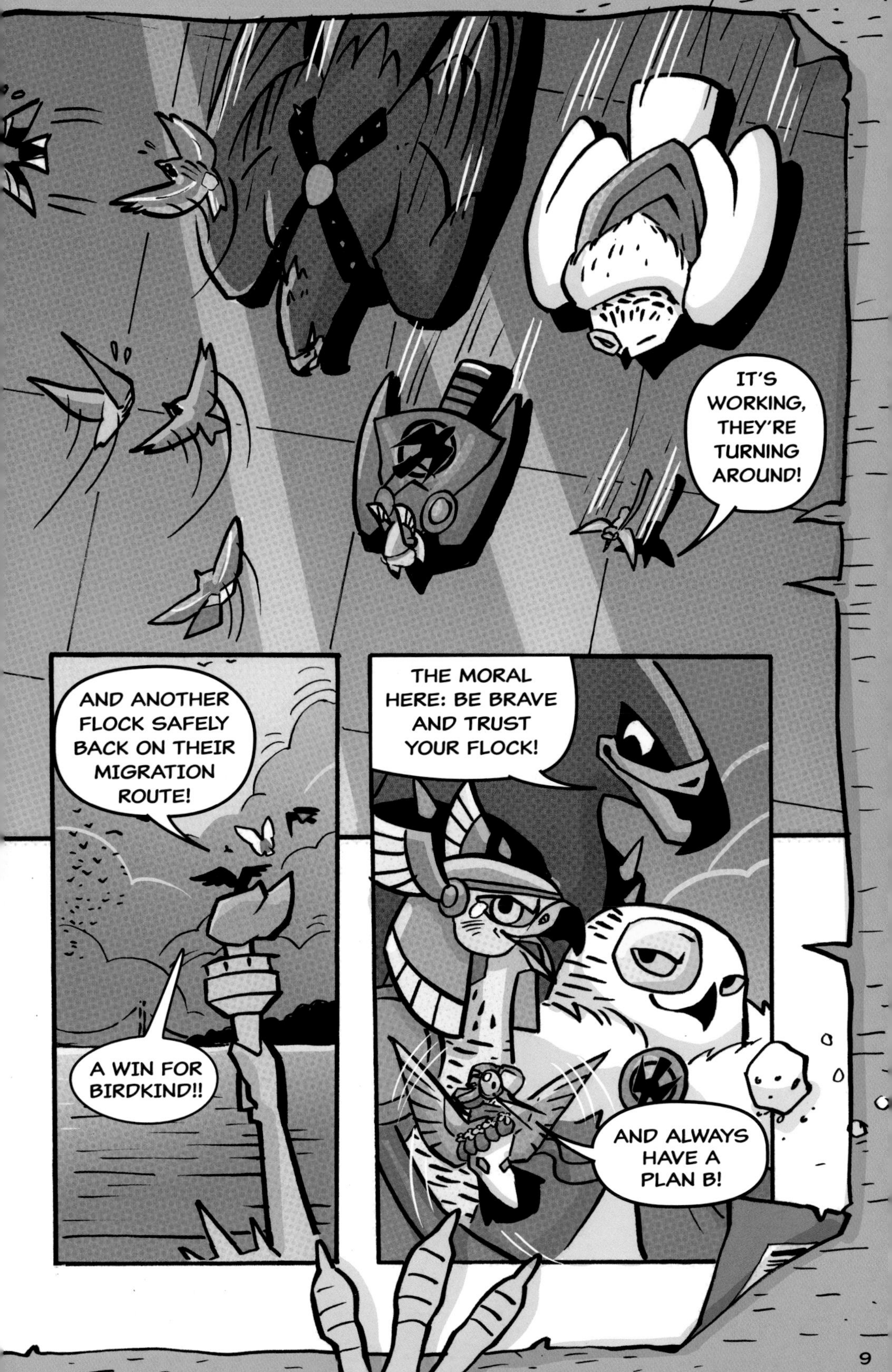
IT'S WORKING, THEY'RE TURNING AROUND!
AND ANOTHER FLOCK SAFELY BACK ON THEIR MIGRATION ROUTE!
A WIN FOR BIRDKIND!!
THE MORAL HERE: BE BRAVE AND TRUST YOUR FLOCK!
AND ALWAYS HAVE A PLAN B!

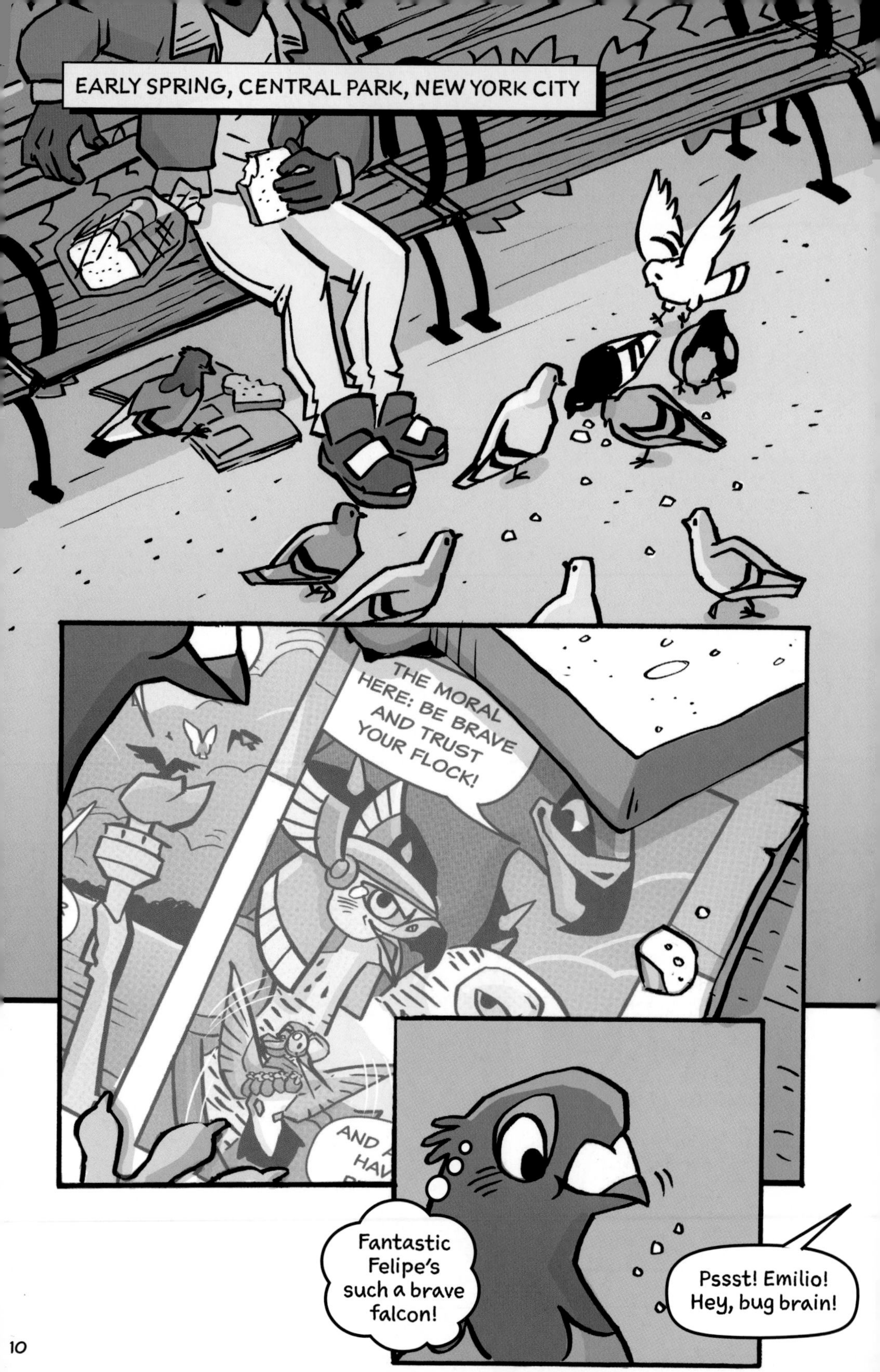
EARLY SPRING, CENTRAL PARK, NEW YORK CITY
THE MORAL HERE: BE BRAVE AND TRUST YOUR FLOCK!
Fantastic Felipe's such a brave falcon!
Pssst! Emilio! Hey, bug brain!

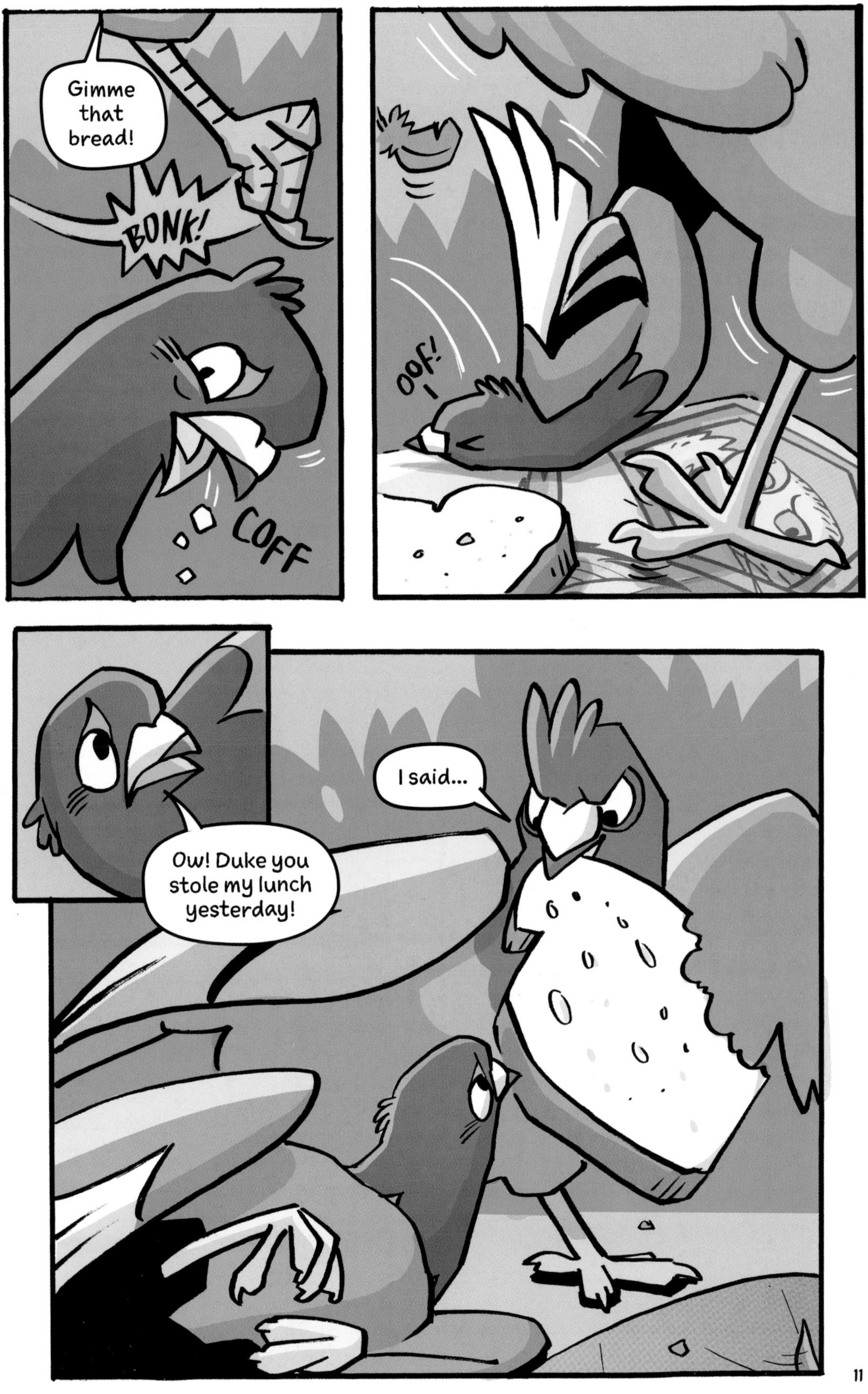
Gimme that bread!
BONK!
COFF
OOF!
I said...
Ow! Duke you stole my lunch yesterday!

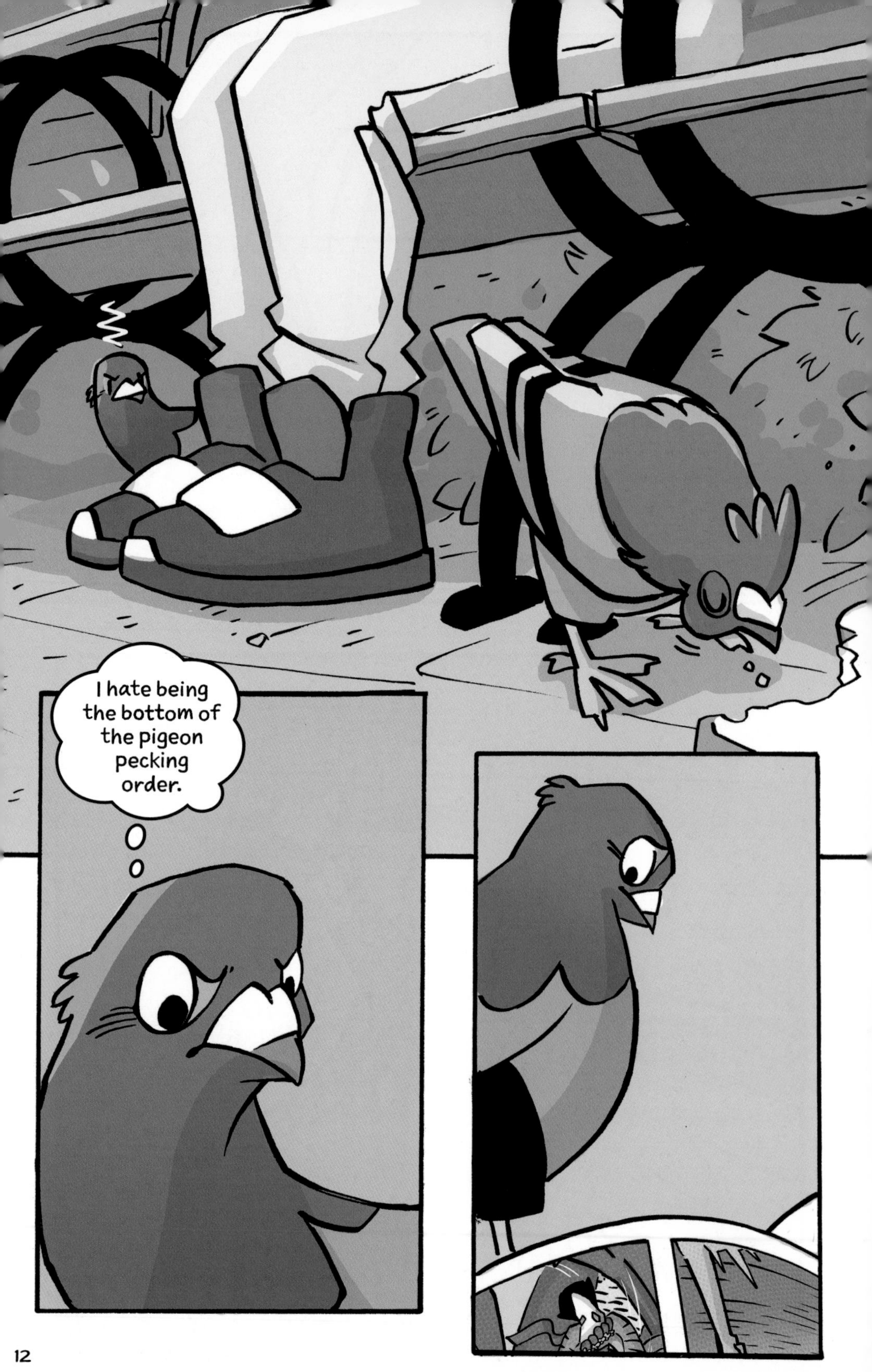
I hate being the bottom of the pigeon pecking order.

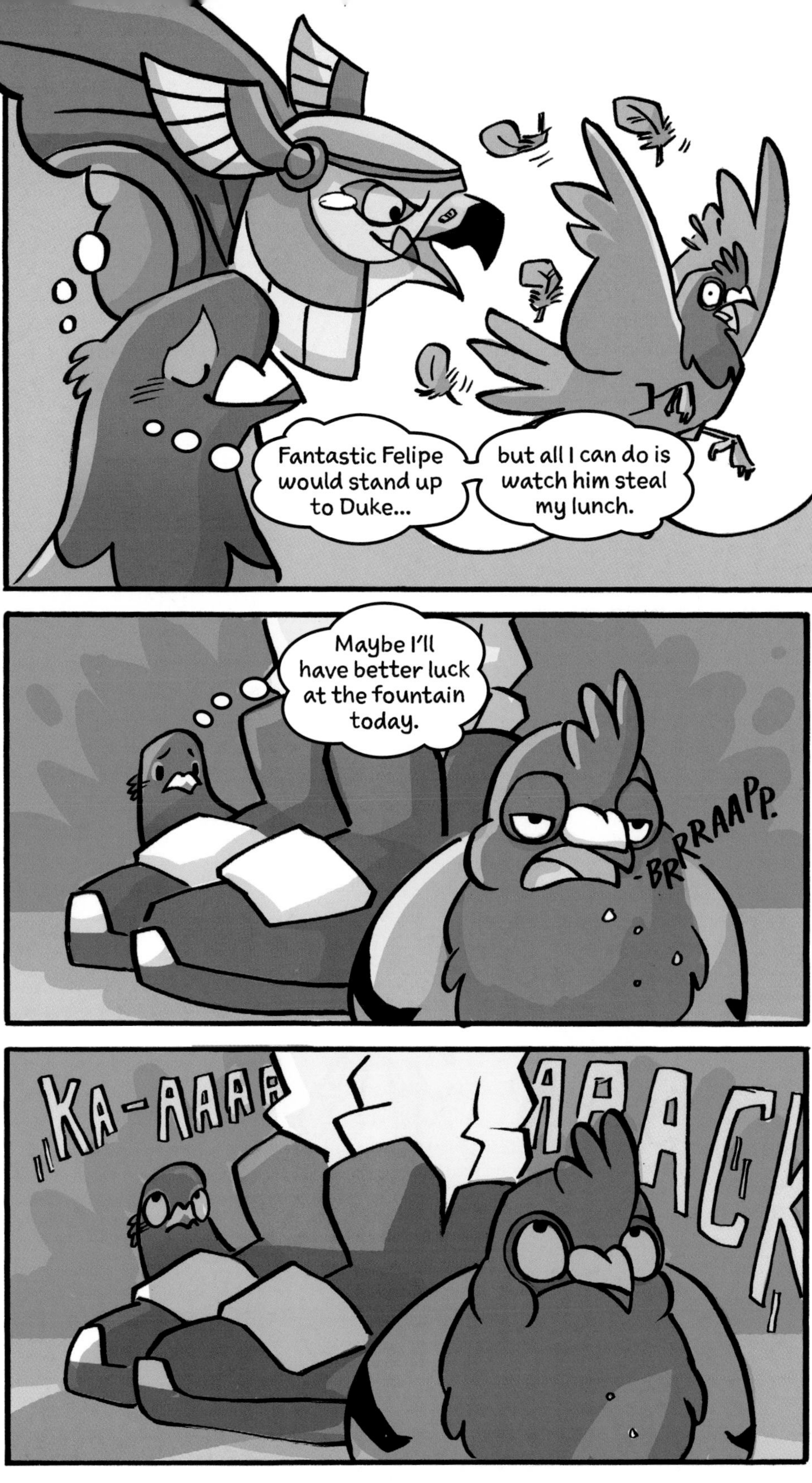
Fantastic Felipe would stand up to Duke...
but all I can do is watch him steal my lunch.
Maybe I'll have better luck at the fountain today.
-BRRRAAPP.
KA-AAAA
AAACK

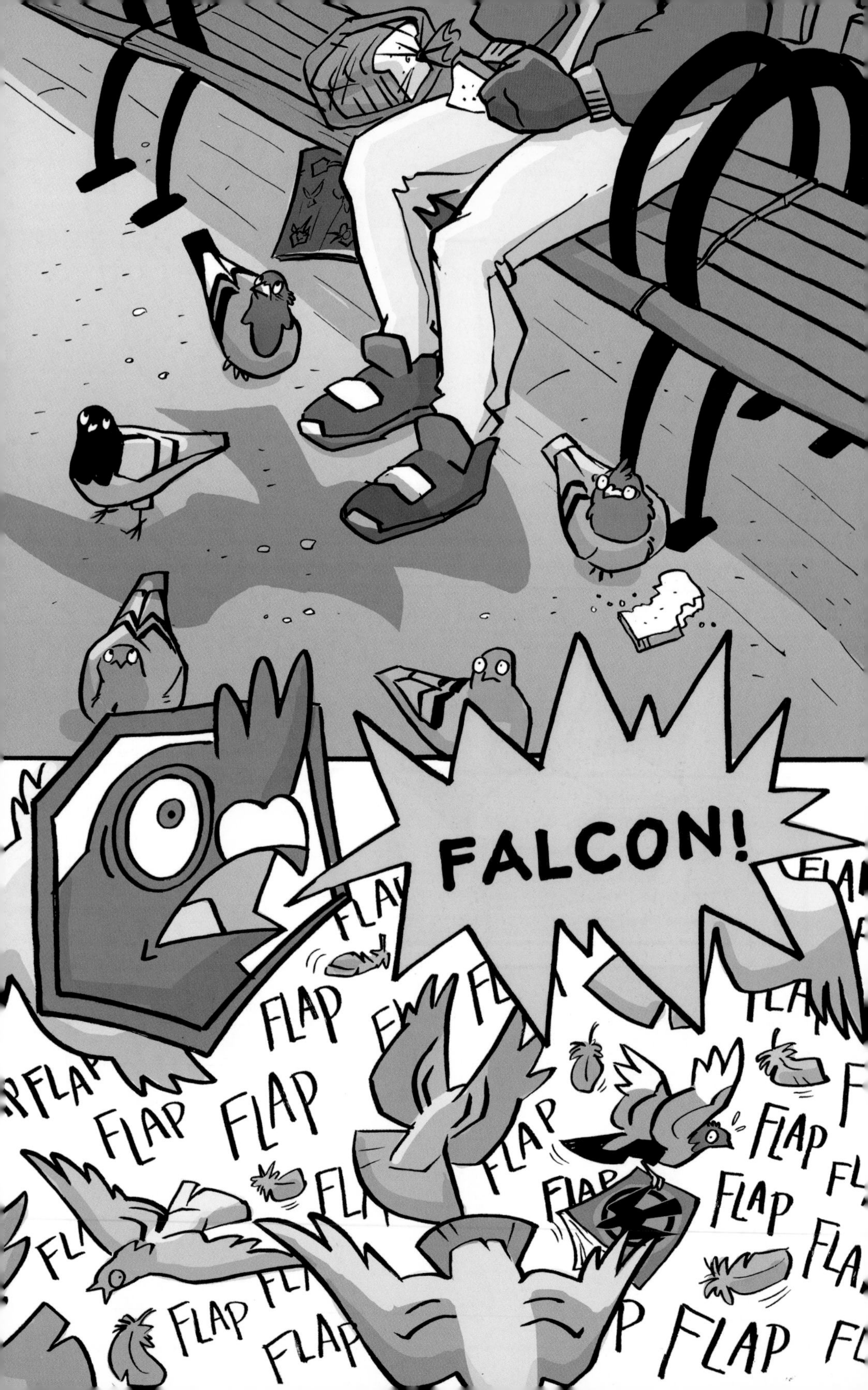
FALCON!
FLAP
FLAP
FLAP
FLAP
FLAP
FLAP
FLAP
FLAP

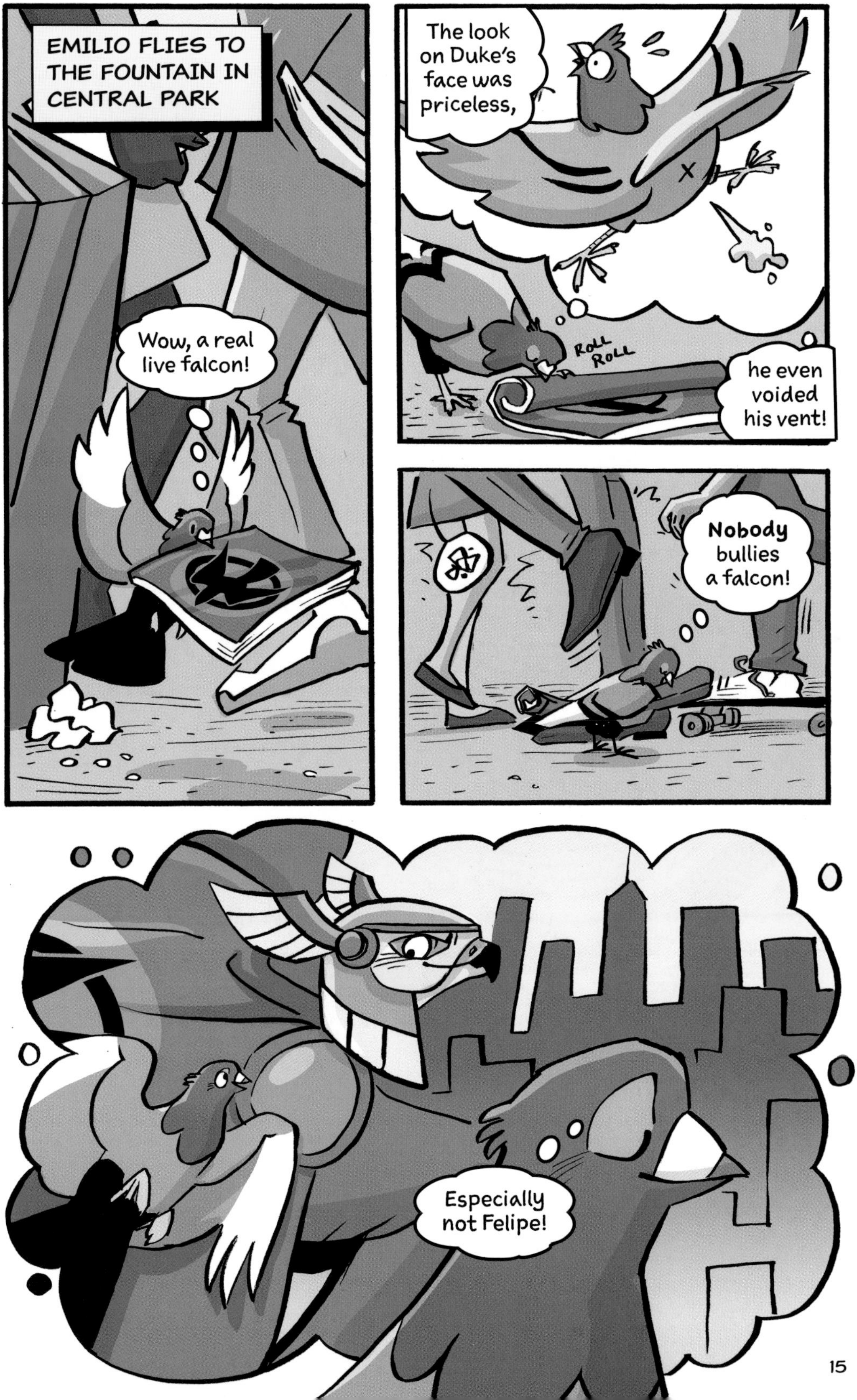
EMILIO FLIES TO THE FOUNTAIN IN CENTRAL PARK
Wow, a real live falcon!
The look on Duke's face was priceless,
ROLL ROLL
he even voided his vent!
Nobody bullies a falcon!
Especially not Felipe!

WINGED HERO: FANTASTIC FELIPE —THE FEARLESS

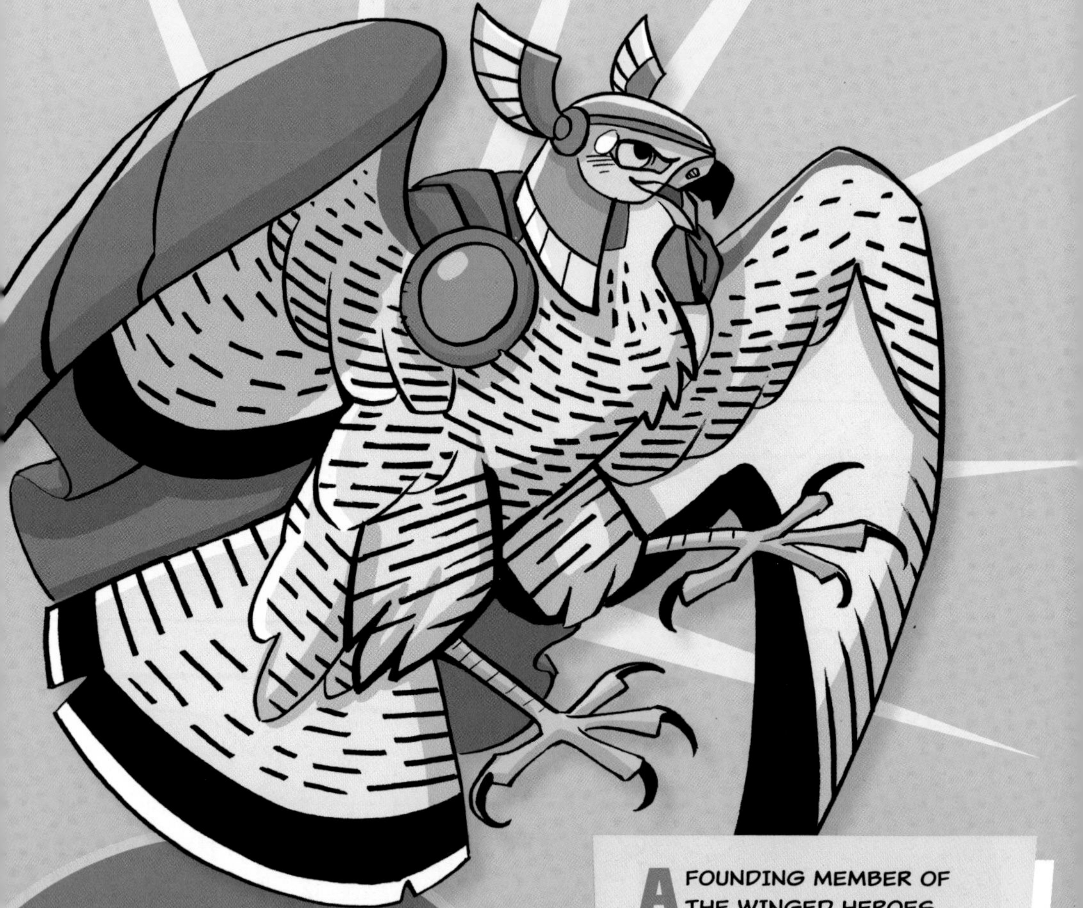

JOB DESCRIPTION

CO-FOUNDER OF THE WINGED HEROES

POWERS INCLUDE

- FASTER THAN ALL OTHER BIRDS
- AWESOME EYE-TALON COORDINATION

WEAKNESS

- SOMETIMES ACTS TOO FAST WITHOUT THINKING IT THROUGH

A FOUNDING MEMBER OF THE WINGED HEROES, FANTASTIC FELIPE IS DARING AND FAST, BUT THIS FALCON'S CHILDHOOD WASN'T EASY. AFTER HIS PARENTS WENT MISSING, FELIPE WAS RESCUED AND RAISED BY HUMAN WILDLIFE REHABILITATORS. ONCE HE WAS STRONG ENOUGH TO SURVIVE ON HIS OWN, HE WAS RELEASED INTO THE WILDS OF NEW YORK CITY TO FEND FOR HIMSELF.

THE REAL PEREGRINE FALCON
(FALCO PEREGRINUS)

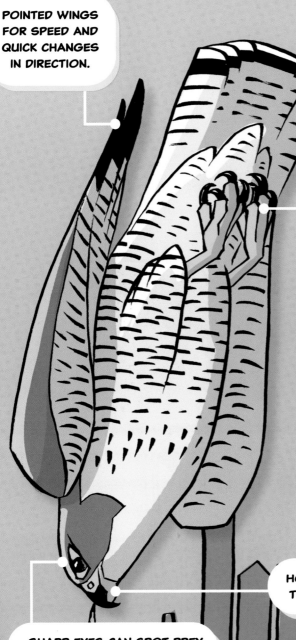

POINTED WINGS FOR SPEED AND QUICK CHANGES IN DIRECTION.

SHARP TALONS CAN SNATCH PREY IN MID-AIR!

HOOKED BEAK SNAPS THE SPINES OF PREY.

SHARP EYES CAN SPOT PREY 13 SOCCER FIELDS AWAY!

DIET
- BIRDIVORE! EATS 450 SPECIES OF BIRDS INCLUDING PIGEONS.

NATURAL HISTORY
- PEREGRINE FALCONS PERCH UP HIGH AND ATTACK FROM ABOVE, DIVING AT HIGH SPEEDS AND SNATCHING PREY IN MID-AIR WITH THEIR TALONS.

- IN THE WILD, PEREGRINES HUNT FROM HIGH CLIFFS. IN CITIES, THEY USE THE TOPS OF BUILDINGS AND BRIDGES.

NATURAL SUPERPOWER
- PEREGRINE FALCONS ARE THE FASTEST BIRDS IN THE WORLD. HOW DO WE KNOW? KEN FRANKLIN MEASURED HIS PET BIRD NAMED FRIGHTFUL DIVING AT 242 MILES PER HOUR (390 KPH) WHILE PARACHUTING NEXT TO IT.

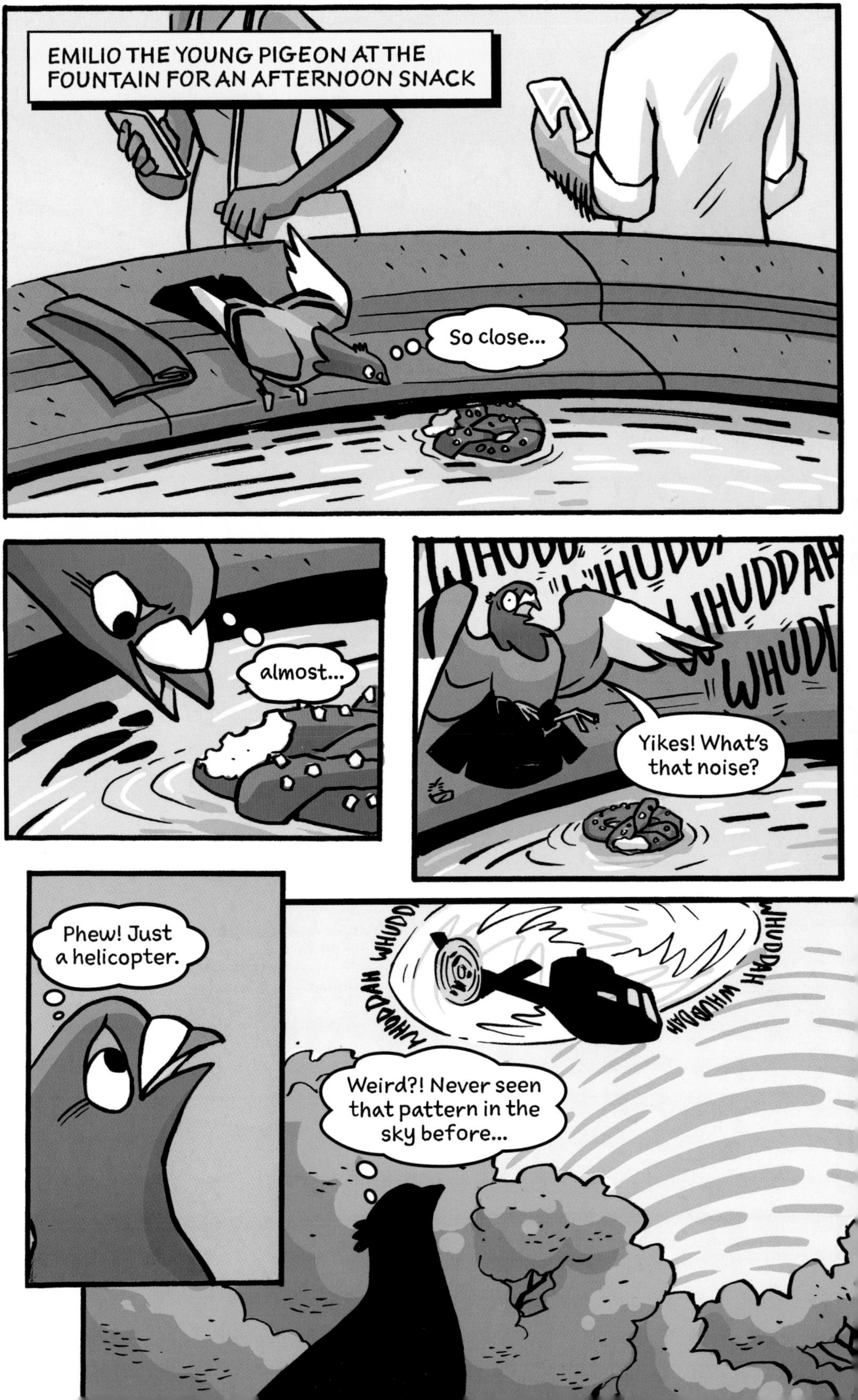

EMILIO THE YOUNG PIGEON AT THE FOUNTAIN FOR AN AFTERNOON SNACK
So close...
almost...
WHUDDAH
Yikes! What's that noise?
Phew! Just a helicopter.
WHUDDAH WHUDD
WHUDDAH
WHUDDAH
Weird?! Never seen that pattern in the sky before...

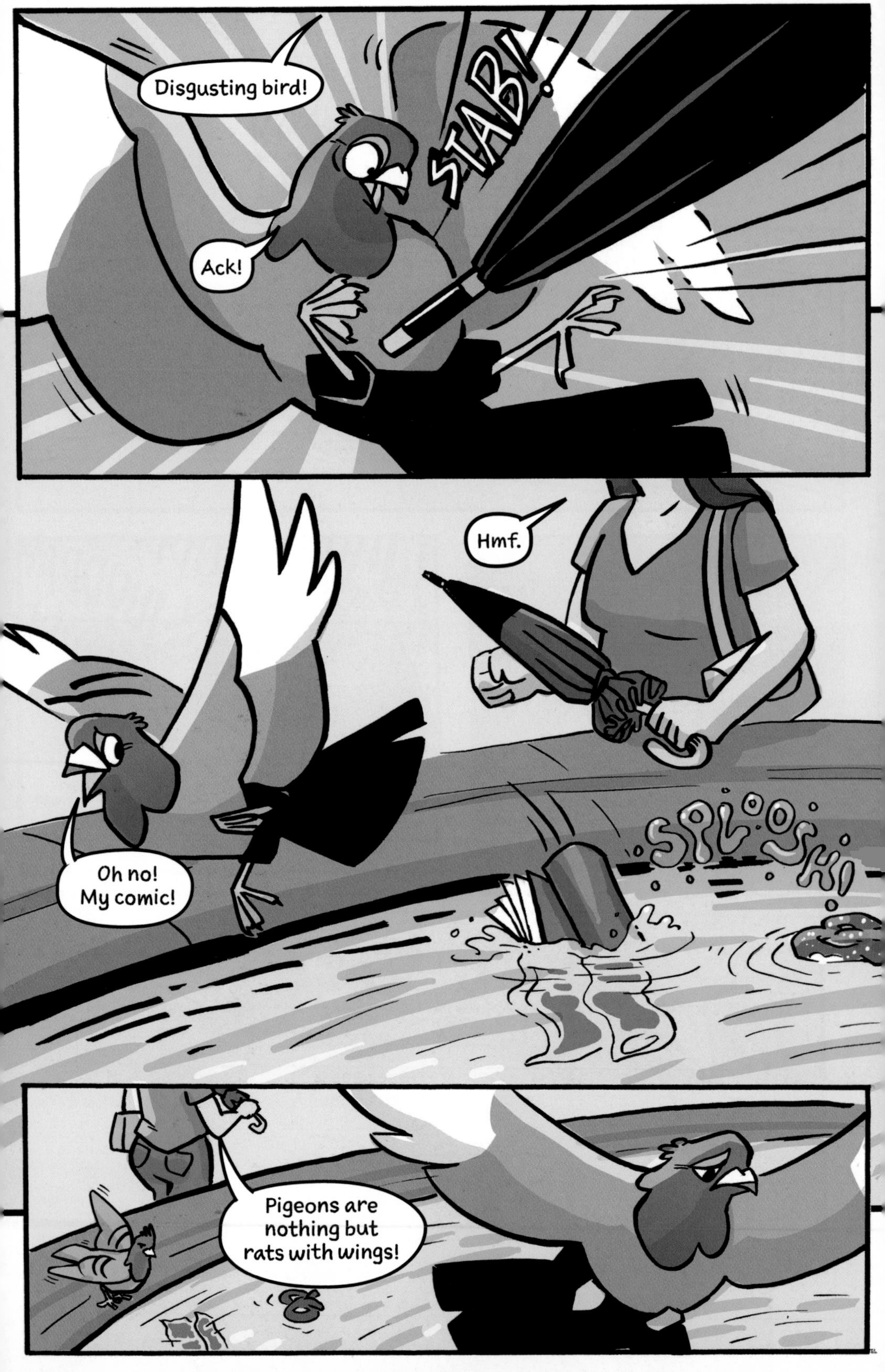
Disgusting bird!
STAB!
Ack!
Hmf.
Oh no! My comic!
SPLOOSH!
Pigeons are nothing but rats with wings!

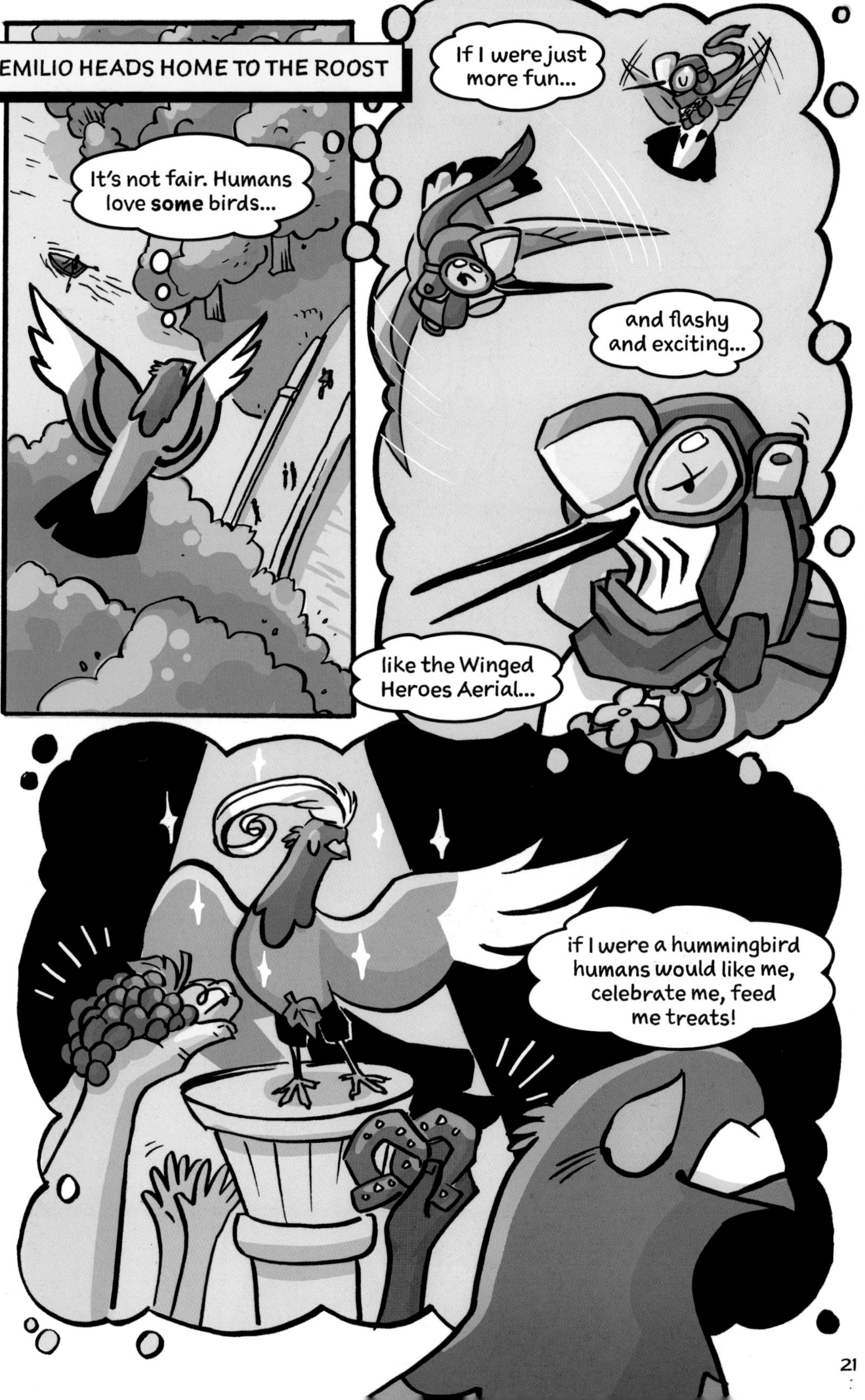
EMILIO HEADS HOME TO THE ROOST
It's not fair. Humans love **some** birds...
If I were just more fun...
and flashy and exciting...
like the Winged Heroes Aerial...
if I were a hummingbird humans would like me, celebrate me, feed me treats!

WINGED HERO: AERIAL—THE SEEKER

LOVED FOR HER ENERGY AND ENTHUSIASM, AERIAL KEEPS THE WINGED HEROES ORGANIZATION HUMMING.

AERIAL IS CLEVER AND OPTIMISTIC. SHE DOES NOT REST UNTIL SHE GETS THE JOB DONE—AS LONG AS SHE HAS PLENTY OF SNACKS.

HATCHED IN THE SUBURBS OF NEW JERSEY, AERIAL TRULY BELIEVES THAT BIRDKIND CAN HAPPILY LIVE SIDE-BY-SIDE WITH HUMANKIND.

JOB DESCRIPTION
CHIEF OPERATING OFFICER

POWERS INCLUDE
- BACKWARDS FLIGHT AND HOVERING
- EXTREME AGILITY AND ENDURANCE

WEAKNESS
- REQUIRES FOOD OFTEN, OTHERWISE SHE COLLAPSES WITH HUNGER

THE REAL RUBY-THROATED HUMMINGBIRD

(ARCHILOCHUS COLUBRIS)

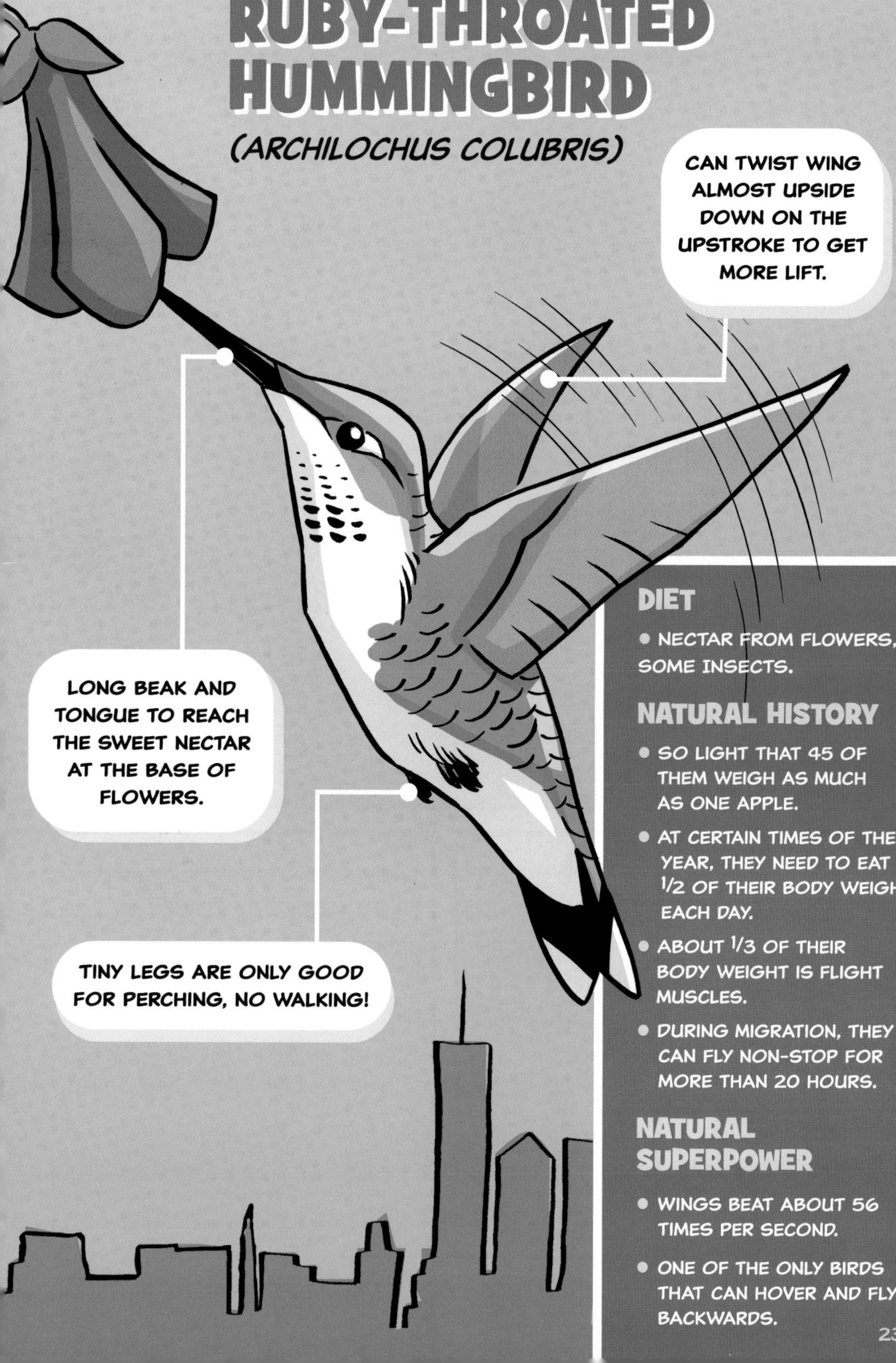
CAN TWIST WING ALMOST UPSIDE DOWN ON THE UPSTROKE TO GET MORE LIFT.
LONG BEAK AND TONGUE TO REACH THE SWEET NECTAR AT THE BASE OF FLOWERS.
TINY LEGS ARE ONLY GOOD FOR PERCHING, NO WALKING!

DIET

- NECTAR FROM FLOWERS, SOME INSECTS.

NATURAL HISTORY

- SO LIGHT THAT 45 OF THEM WEIGH AS MUCH AS ONE APPLE.
- AT CERTAIN TIMES OF THE YEAR, THEY NEED TO EAT 1/2 OF THEIR BODY WEIGHT EACH DAY.
- ABOUT 1/3 OF THEIR BODY WEIGHT IS FLIGHT MUSCLES.
- DURING MIGRATION, THEY CAN FLY NON-STOP FOR MORE THAN 20 HOURS.

NATURAL SUPERPOWER

- WINGS BEAT ABOUT 56 TIMES PER SECOND.
- ONE OF THE ONLY BIRDS THAT CAN HOVER AND FLY BACKWARDS.

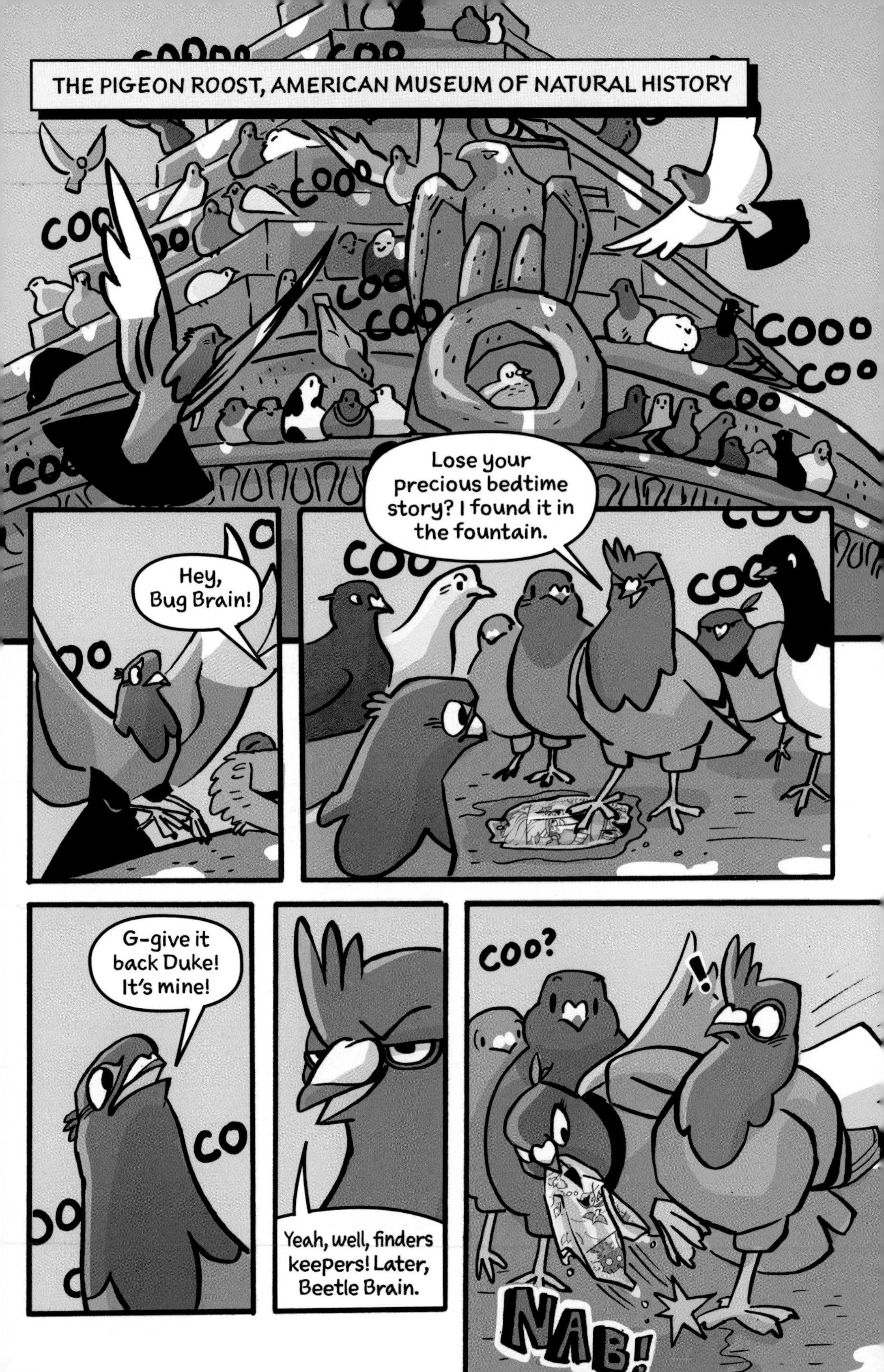
THE PIGEON ROOST, AMERICAN MUSEUM OF NATURAL HISTORY
COOO
COO
COOO
COOO
COO
COO
Hey, Bug Brain!
Lose your precious bedtime story? I found it in the fountain.
COO
G-give it back Duke! It's mine!
CO
Yeah, well, finders keepers! Later, Beetle Brain.
COO?
!
NAB!

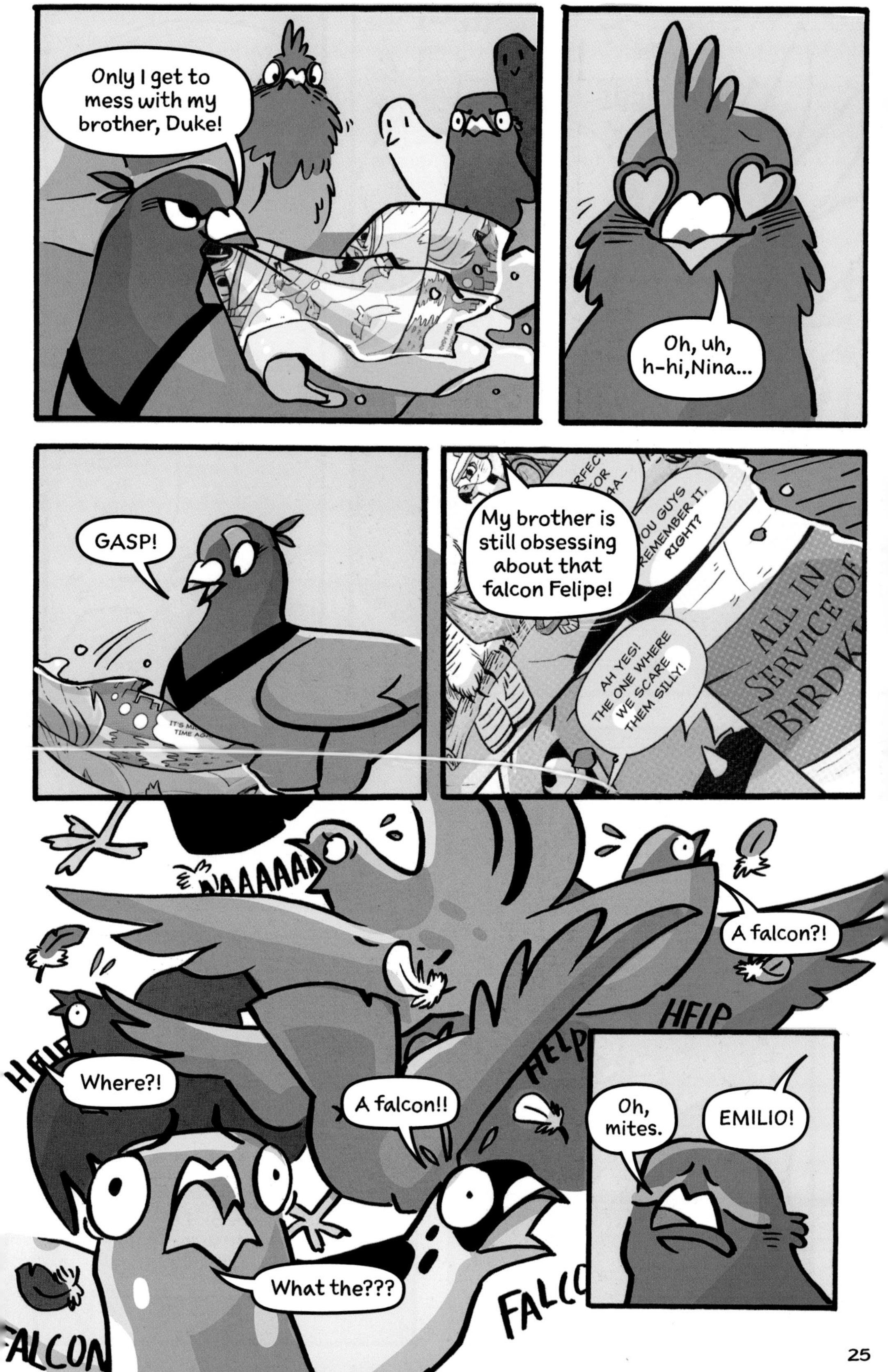
Only I get to mess with my brother, Duke!
Oh, uh, h-hi, Nina...
GASP!
My brother is still obsessing about that falcon Felipe!
AH YES! THE ONE WHERE WE SCARE THEM SILLY!
ALL IN SERVICE OF
A falcon?!
Where?!
A falcon!!
What the???
Oh, mites.
EMILIO!

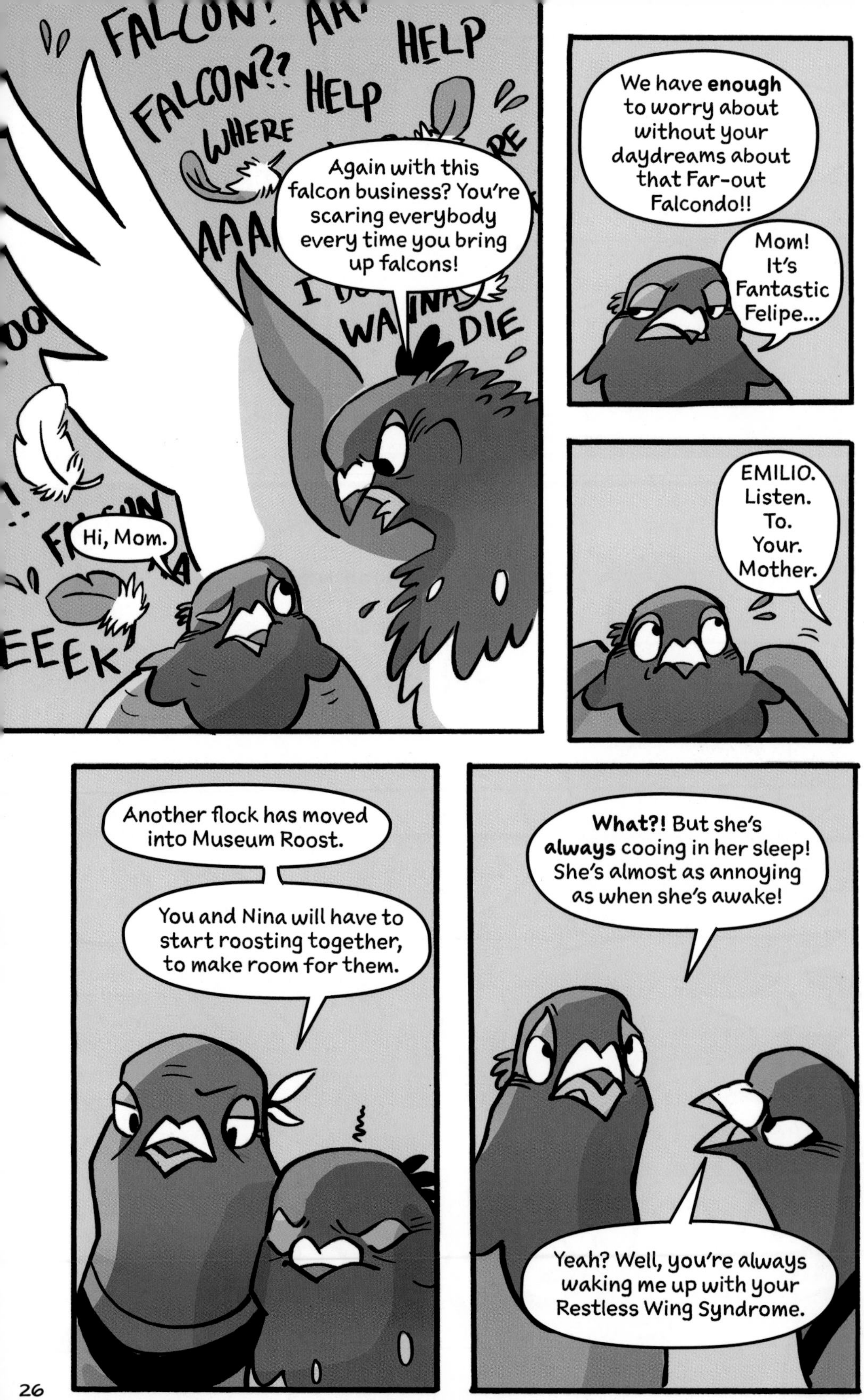
FALCON! AH
HELP
FALCON??
HELP
WHERE
AAA
Again with this falcon business? You're scaring everybody every time you bring up falcons!
WA DIE
Hi, Mom.
EEEEK
We have **enough** to worry about without your daydreams about that Far-out Falcondo!!
Mom! It's Fantastic Felipe...
EMILIO. Listen. To. Your. Mother.
Another flock has moved into Museum Roost.
You and Nina will have to start roosting together, to make room for them.
What?! But she's **always** cooing in her sleep! She's almost as annoying as when she's awake!
Yeah? Well, you're always waking me up with your Restless Wing Syndrome.

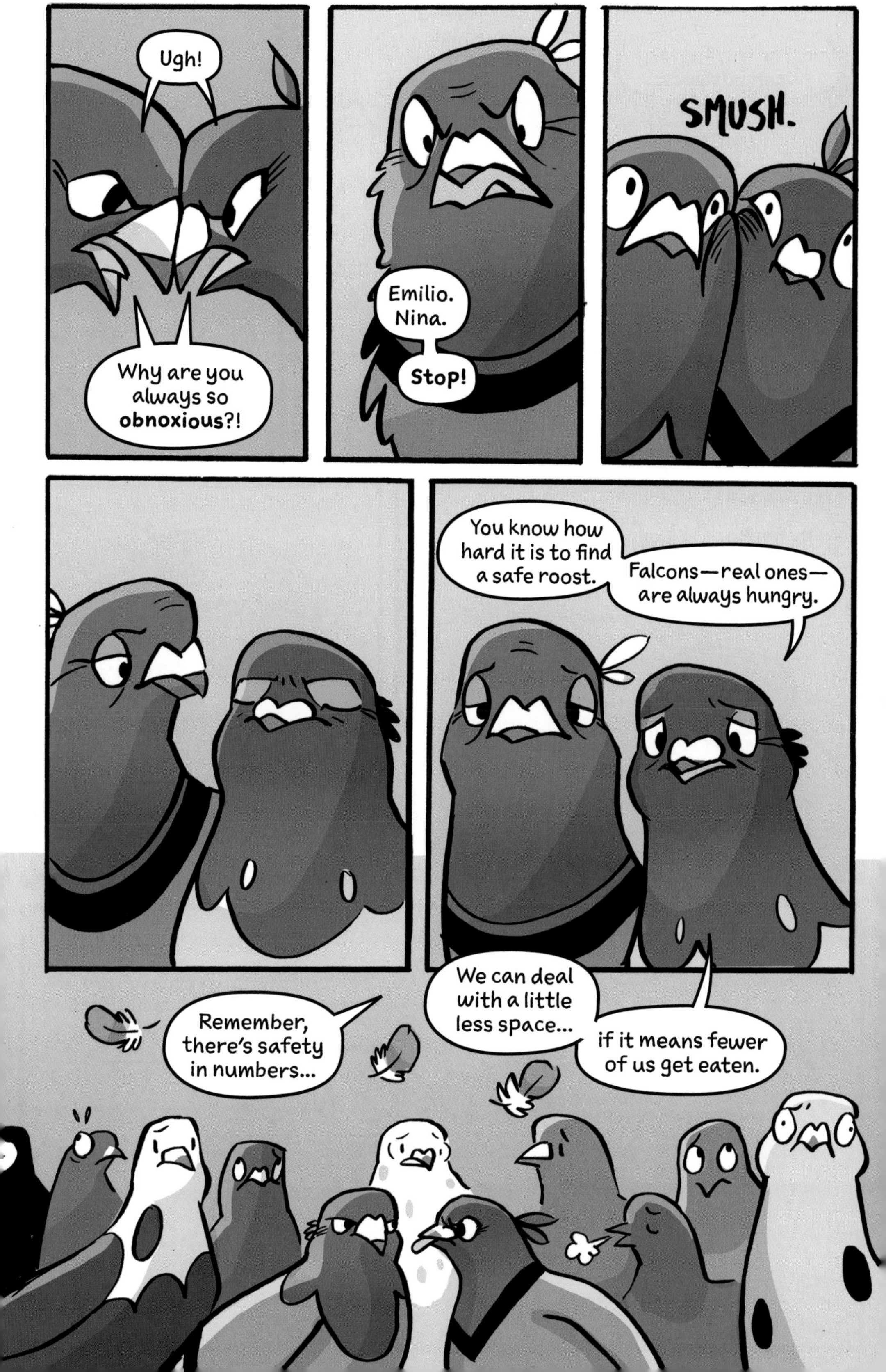
Ugh!
Why are you always so **obnoxious**?!
Emilio. Nina.
Stop!
SMUSH.
You know how hard it is to find a safe roost.
Falcons—real ones—are always hungry.
Remember, there's safety in numbers...
We can deal with a little less space...
if it means fewer of us get eaten.

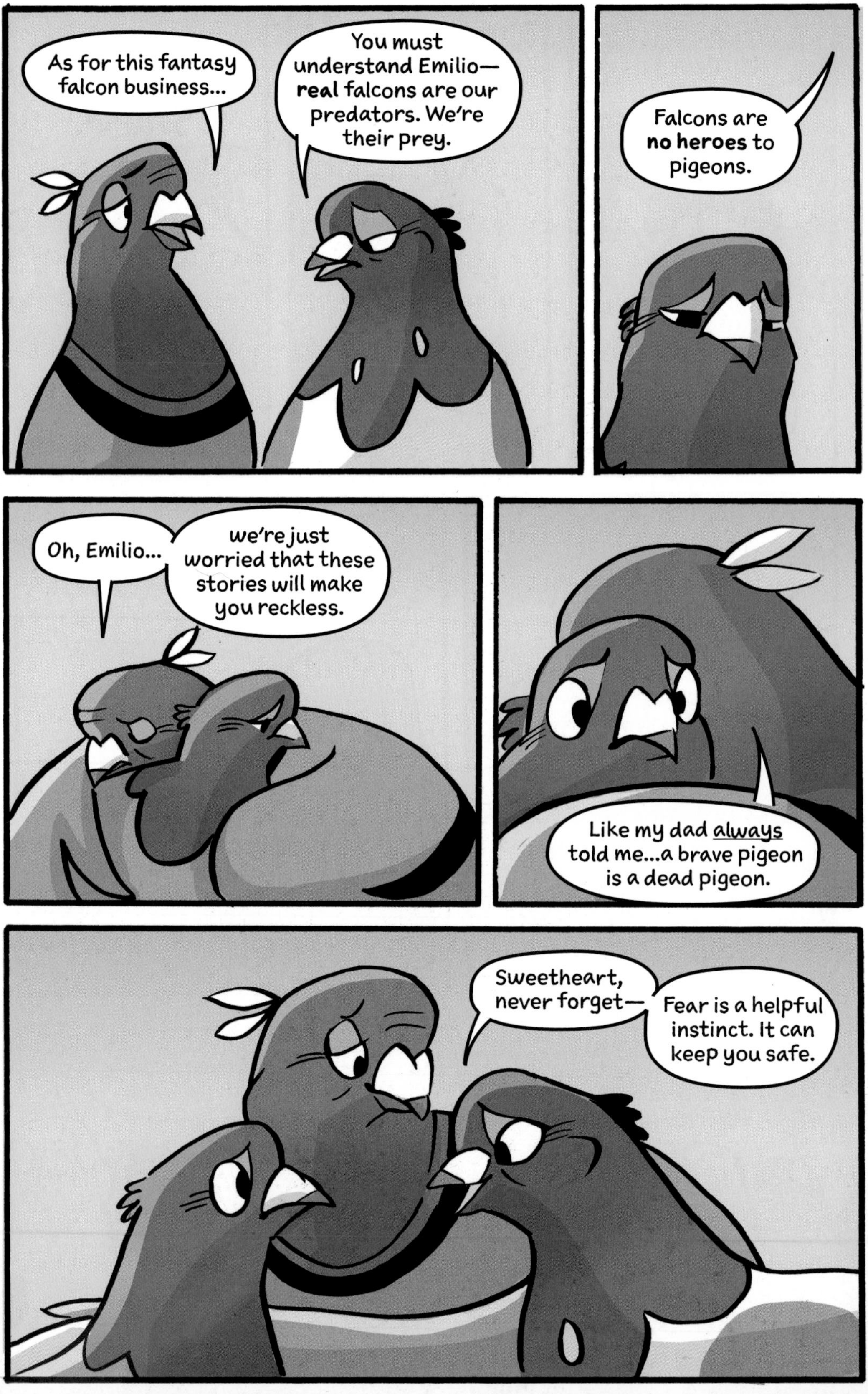
As for this fantasy falcon business...
You must understand Emilio—**real** falcons are our predators. We're their prey.
Falcons are **no heroes** to pigeons.
Oh, Emilio...
we're just worried that these stories will make you reckless.
Like my dad always told me...a brave pigeon is a dead pigeon.
Sweetheart, never forget—
Fear is a helpful instinct. It can keep you safe.

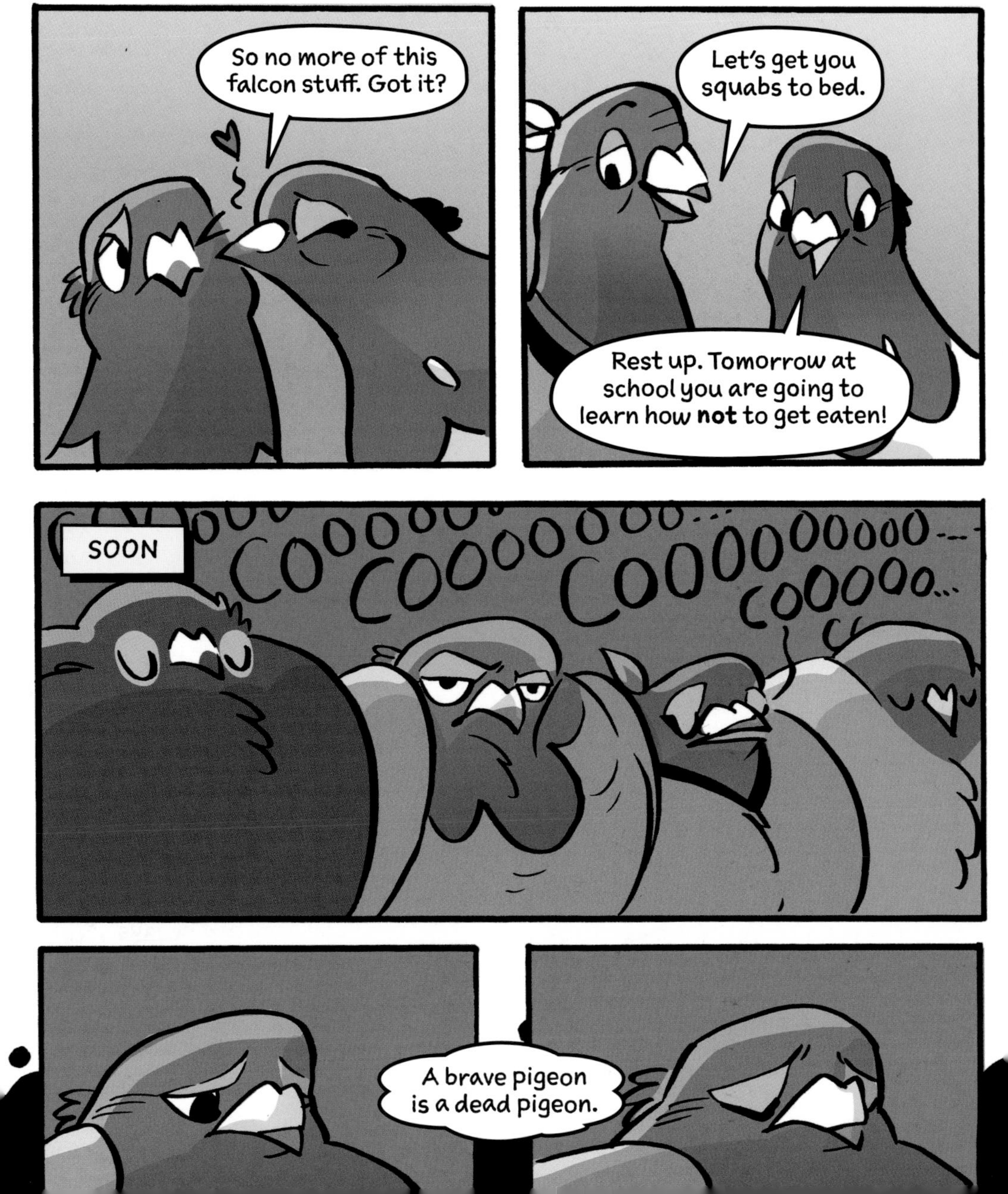
So no more of this falcon stuff. Got it?
Let's get you squabs to bed.
Rest up. Tomorrow at school you are going to learn how **not** to get eaten!
SOON
COOOOOOOO... COOOOOOOOO COOOOOOOOOOOO--- COOOOO...
A brave pigeon is a dead pigeon.

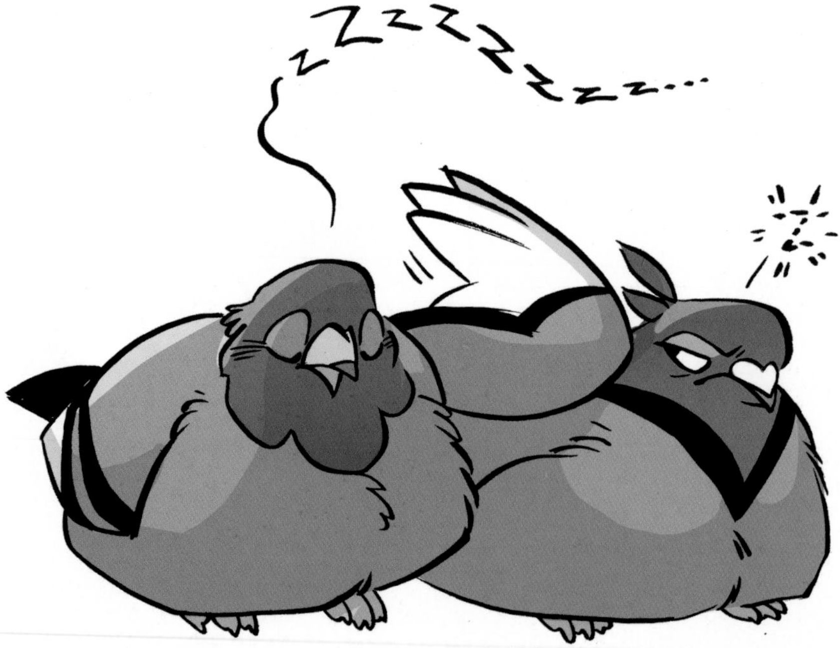
zZZZZZzzzzz...

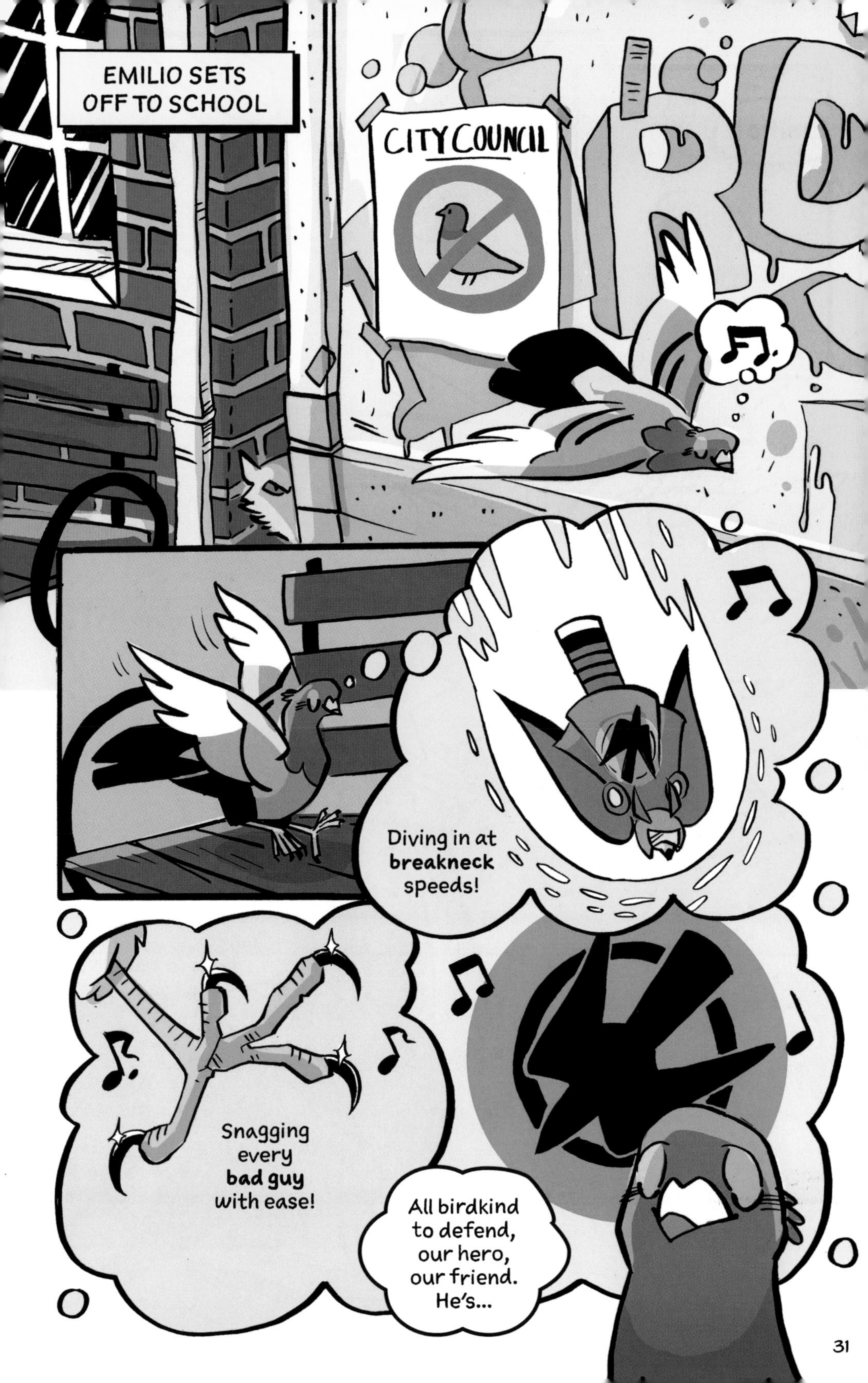
EMILIO SETS OFF TO SCHOOL
CITY COUNCIL
Diving in at breakneck speeds!
Snagging every bad guy with ease!
All birdkind to defend, our hero, our friend. He's...

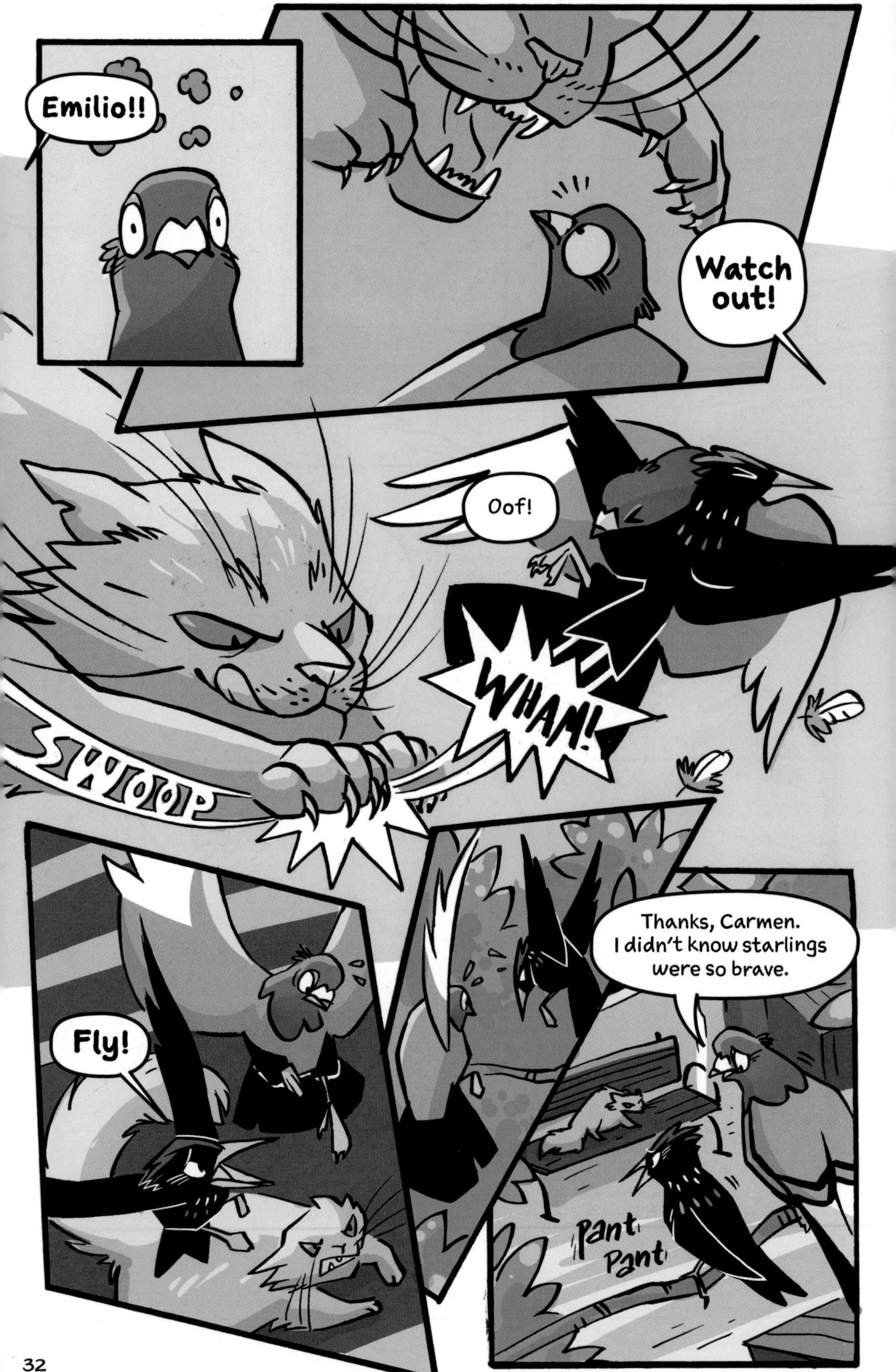
Emilio!!
Watch out!
Oof!
WHAM!
SWOOP
Fly!
Thanks, Carmen. I didn't know starlings were so brave.
Pant Pant

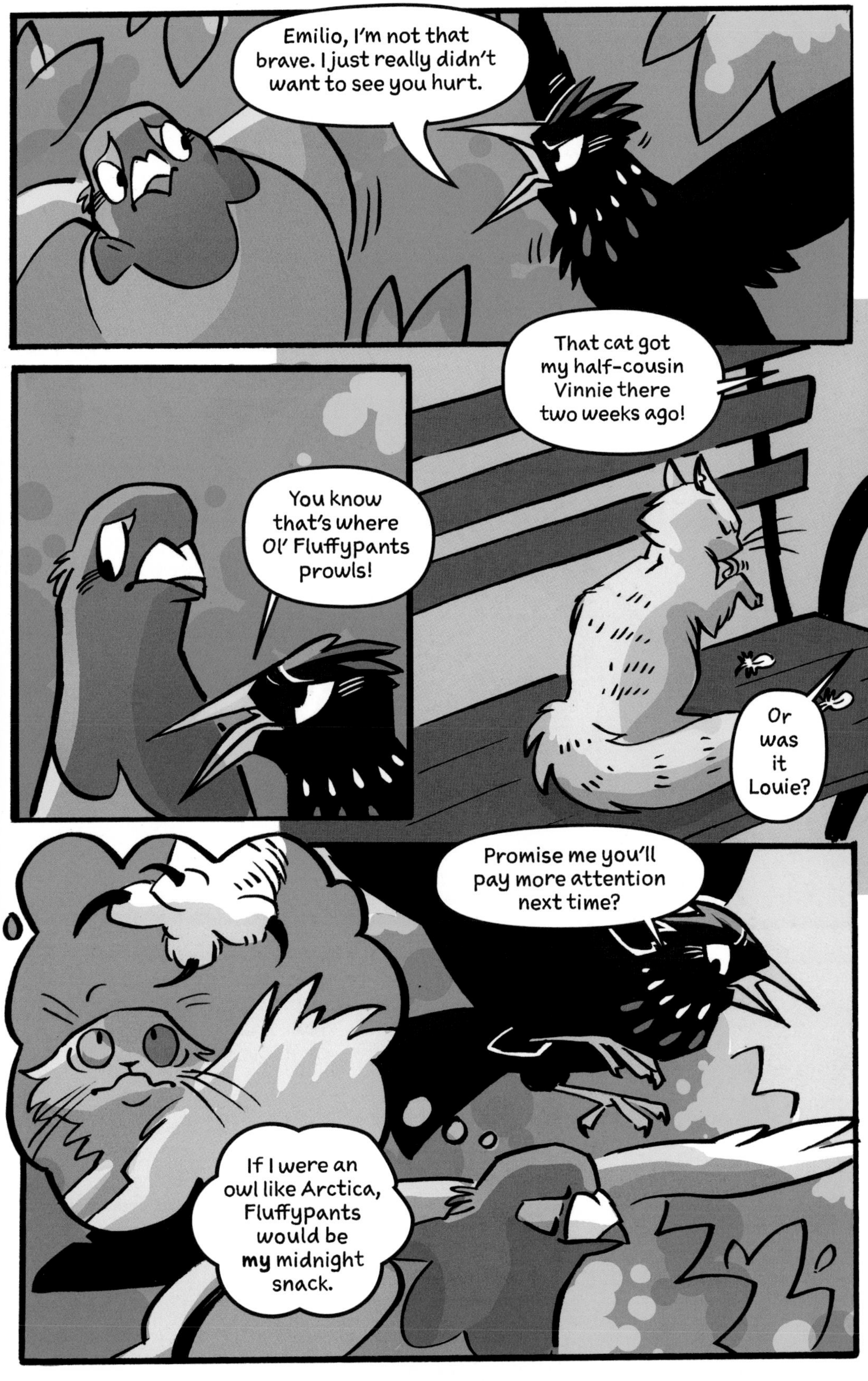
Emilio, I'm not that brave. I just really didn't want to see you hurt.
That cat got my half-cousin Vinnie there two weeks ago!
You know that's where Ol' Fluffypants prowls!
Or was it Louie?
Promise me you'll pay more attention next time?
If I were an owl like Arctica, Fluffypants would be **my** midnight snack.

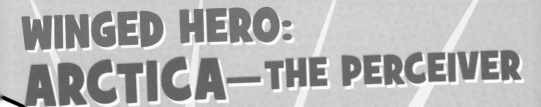

WINGED HERO: ARCTICA—THE PERCEIVER

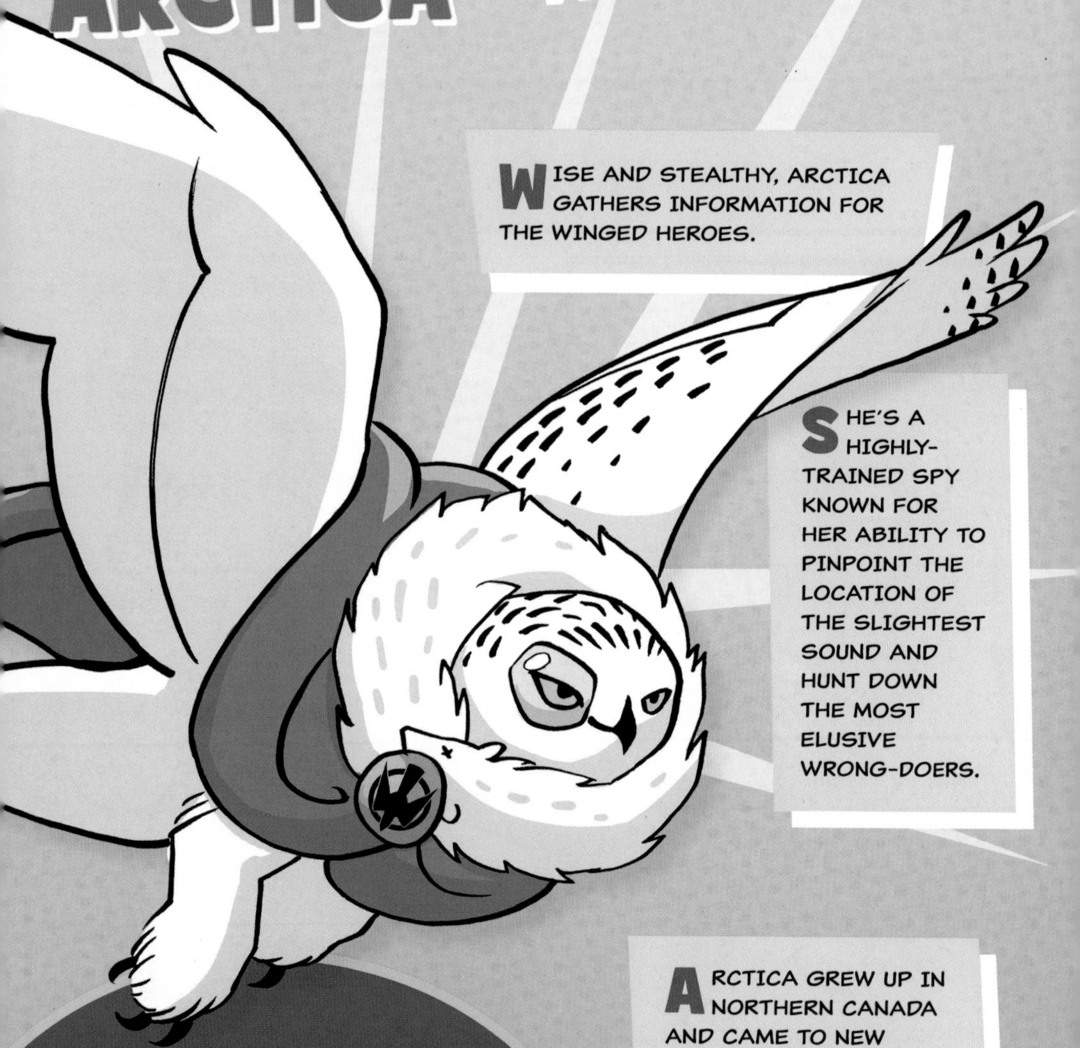

WISE AND STEALTHY, ARCTICA GATHERS INFORMATION FOR THE WINGED HEROES.

SHE'S A HIGHLY-TRAINED SPY KNOWN FOR HER ABILITY TO PINPOINT THE LOCATION OF THE SLIGHTEST SOUND AND HUNT DOWN THE MOST ELUSIVE WRONG-DOERS.

ARCTICA GREW UP IN NORTHERN CANADA AND CAME TO NEW YORK CITY IN SEARCH OF FOOD. THE HEROES RESCUED HER FROM ONE OF THE BUSIEST AIRPORTS IN THE WORLD.

JOB DESCRIPTION

CHIEF SPY

POWERS INCLUDE

- PRECISE LOCATION OF SOUND
- ATTACKING WITHOUT DETECTION

WEAKNESS

- THIS SENSITIVE SOUL IS EASILY OFFENDED AND WILL HOLD A GRUDGE

THE REAL SNOWY OWL
(BUBO SCANDIACUS)

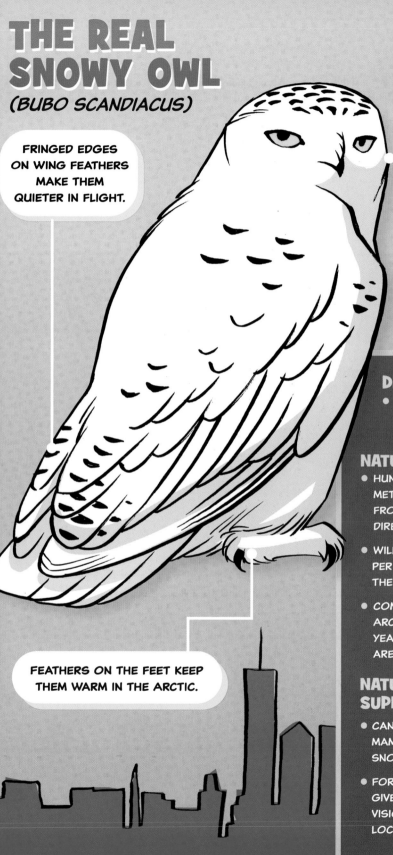

FRINGED EDGES ON WING FEATHERS MAKE THEM QUIETER IN FLIGHT.

SENSITIVE EARS ARE WELL HIDDEN UNDER FEATHERS.

FEATHERS ON THE FEET KEEP THEM WARM IN THE ARCTIC.

DIET
- SMALL MAMMALS LIKE LEMMINGS AND MANY KINDS OF BIRDS.

NATURAL HISTORY
- HUNTS USING THE WALLOP METHOD—ATTACKING FROM ABOVE AND LANDING DIRECTLY ON PREY.
- WILL EAT 3-5 LEMMINGS PER DAY WHEN THEY GET THE CHANCE.
- COMES SOUTH FROM THE ARCTIC ONLY ON SOME YEARS, PREFERS OPEN AREAS LIKE AIRPORTS.

NATURAL SUPERPOWERS
- CAN LOCATE SMALL MAMMALS UNDER DEEP SNOW JUST BY LISTENING.
- FORWARD-FACING EYES GIVE THEM THE BINOCULAR VISION THEY NEED TO LOCATE SMALL PREY.

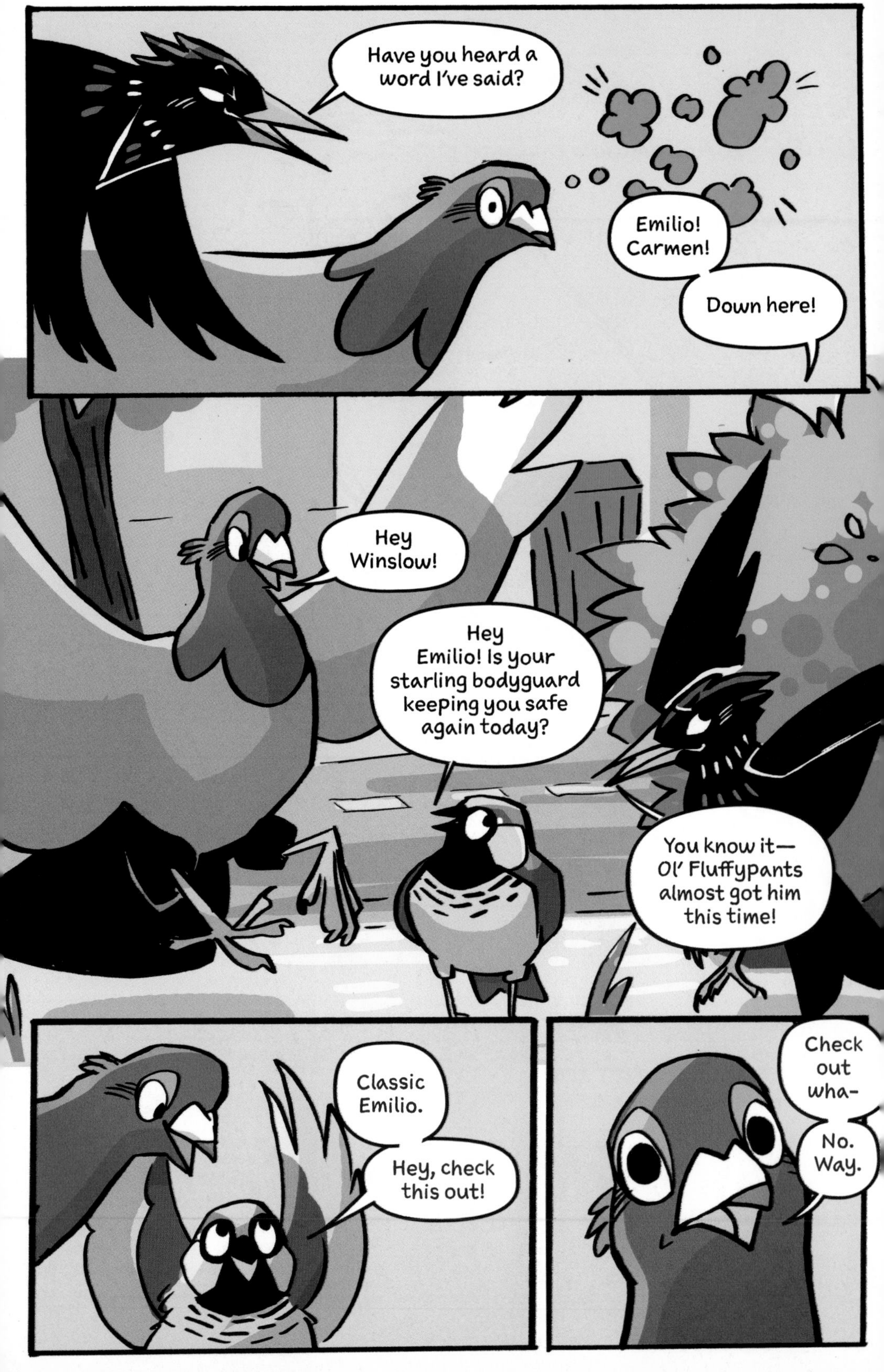
Have you heard a word I've said?
Emilio! Carmen!
Down here!
Hey Winslow!
Hey Emilio! Is your starling bodyguard keeping you safe again today?
You know it—Ol' Fluffypants almost got him this time!
Classic Emilio.
Hey, check this out!
Check out wha-
No. Way.

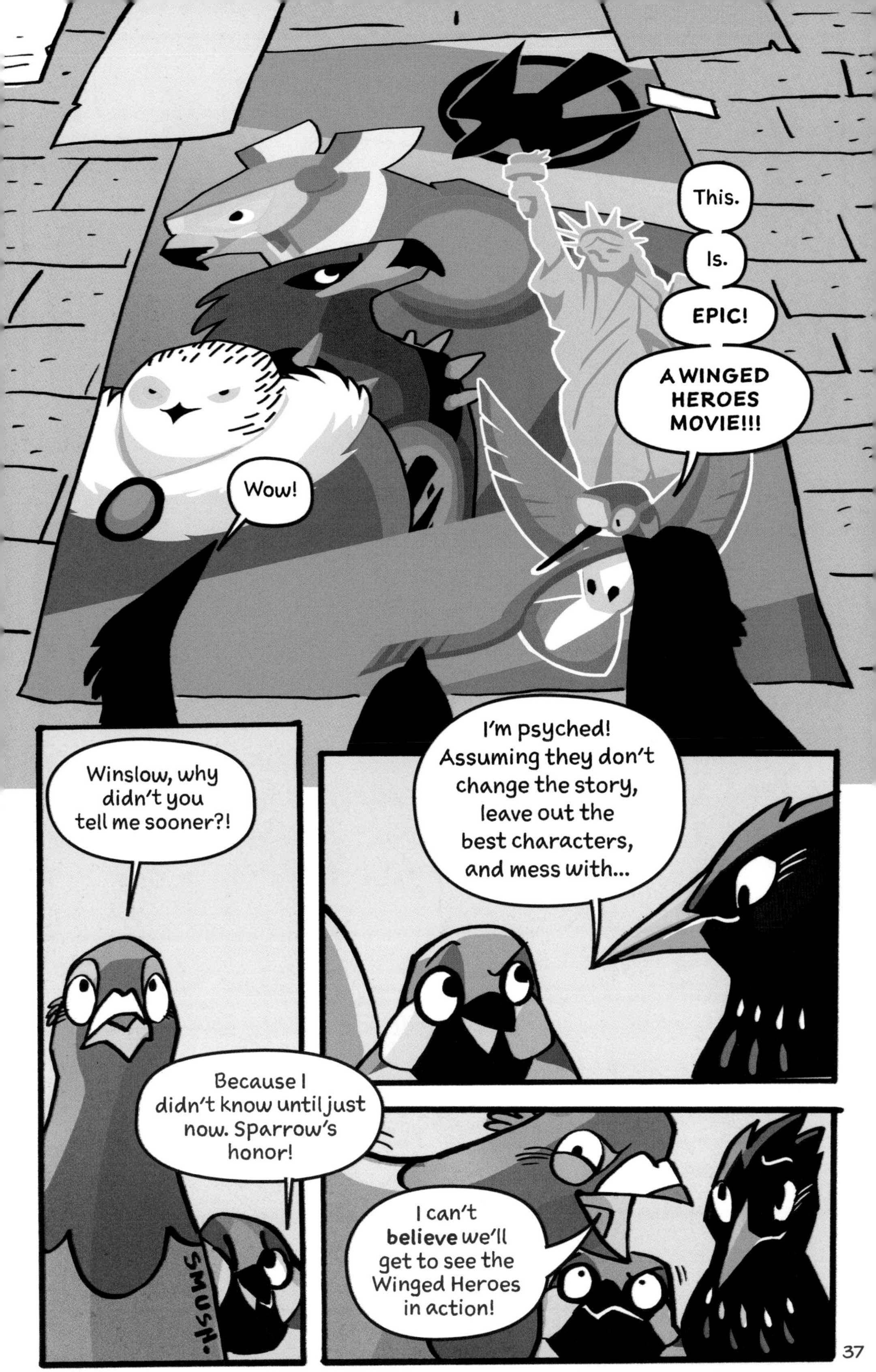

This.
Is.
EPIC!
A WINGED HEROES MOVIE!!!
Wow!
Winslow, why didn't you tell me sooner?!
I'm psyched! Assuming they don't change the story, leave out the best characters, and mess with...
Because I didn't know until just now. Sparrow's honor!
SMUSH.
I can't **believe** we'll get to see the Winged Heroes in action!

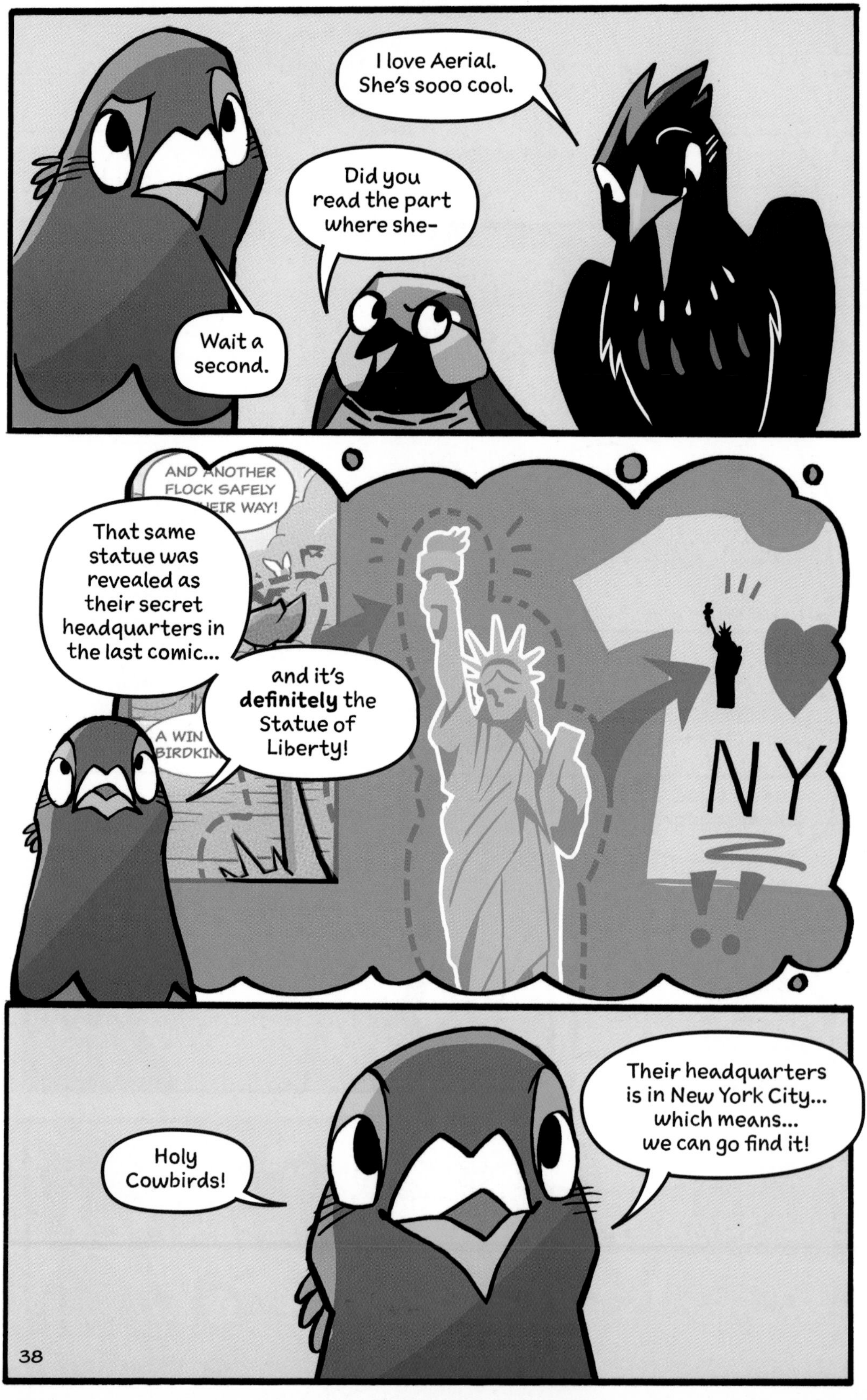
I love Aerial. She's sooo cool.
Did you read the part where she-
Wait a second.
AND ANOTHER FLOCK SAFELY
That same statue was revealed as their secret headquarters in the last comic...
and it's **definitely** the Statue of Liberty!
NY
Holy Cowbirds!
Their headquarters is in New York City... which means... we can go find it!

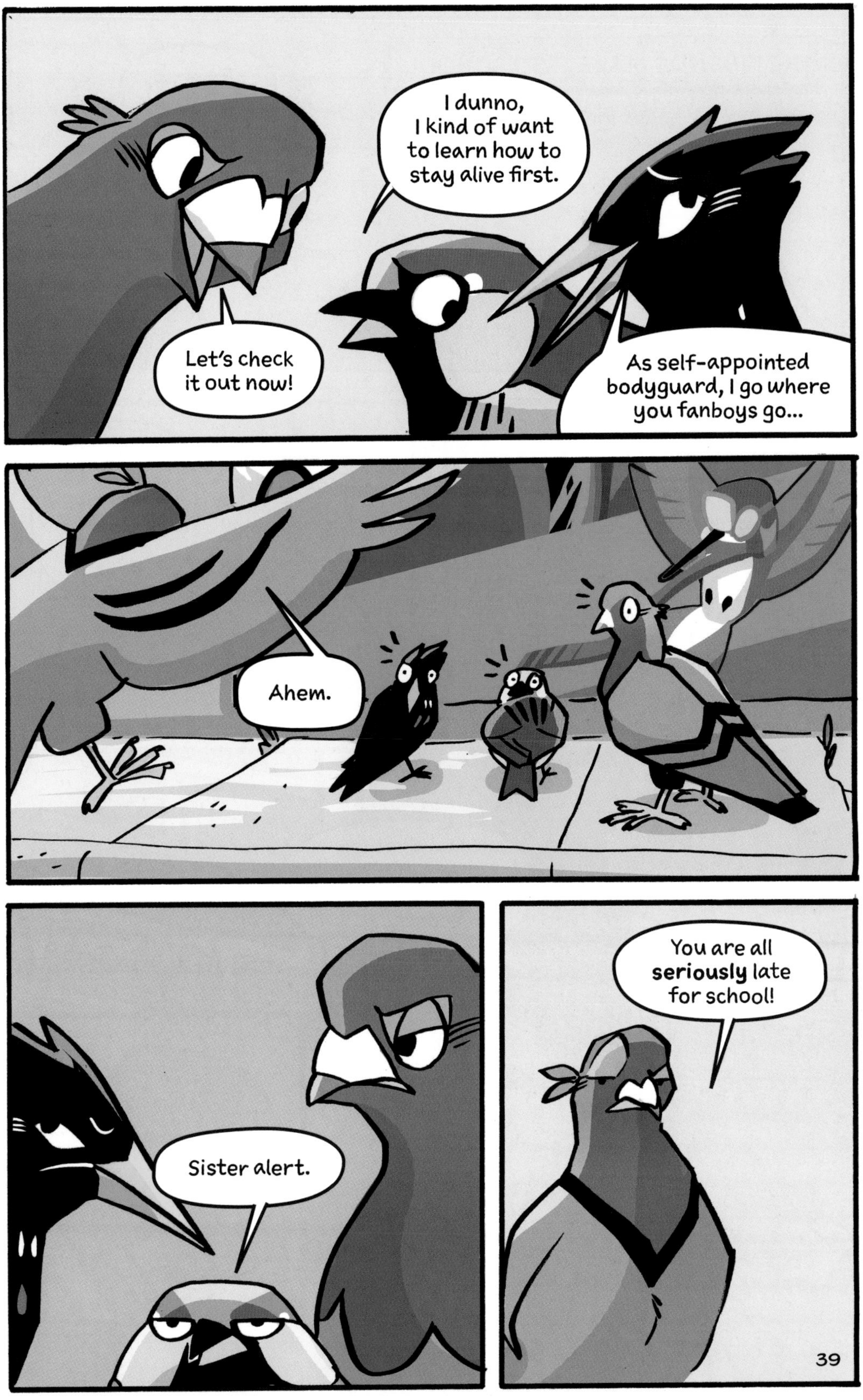
Let's check it out now!
I dunno, I kind of want to learn how to stay alive first.
As self-appointed bodyguard, I go where you fanboys go...
Ahem.
Sister alert.
You are all **seriously** late for school!

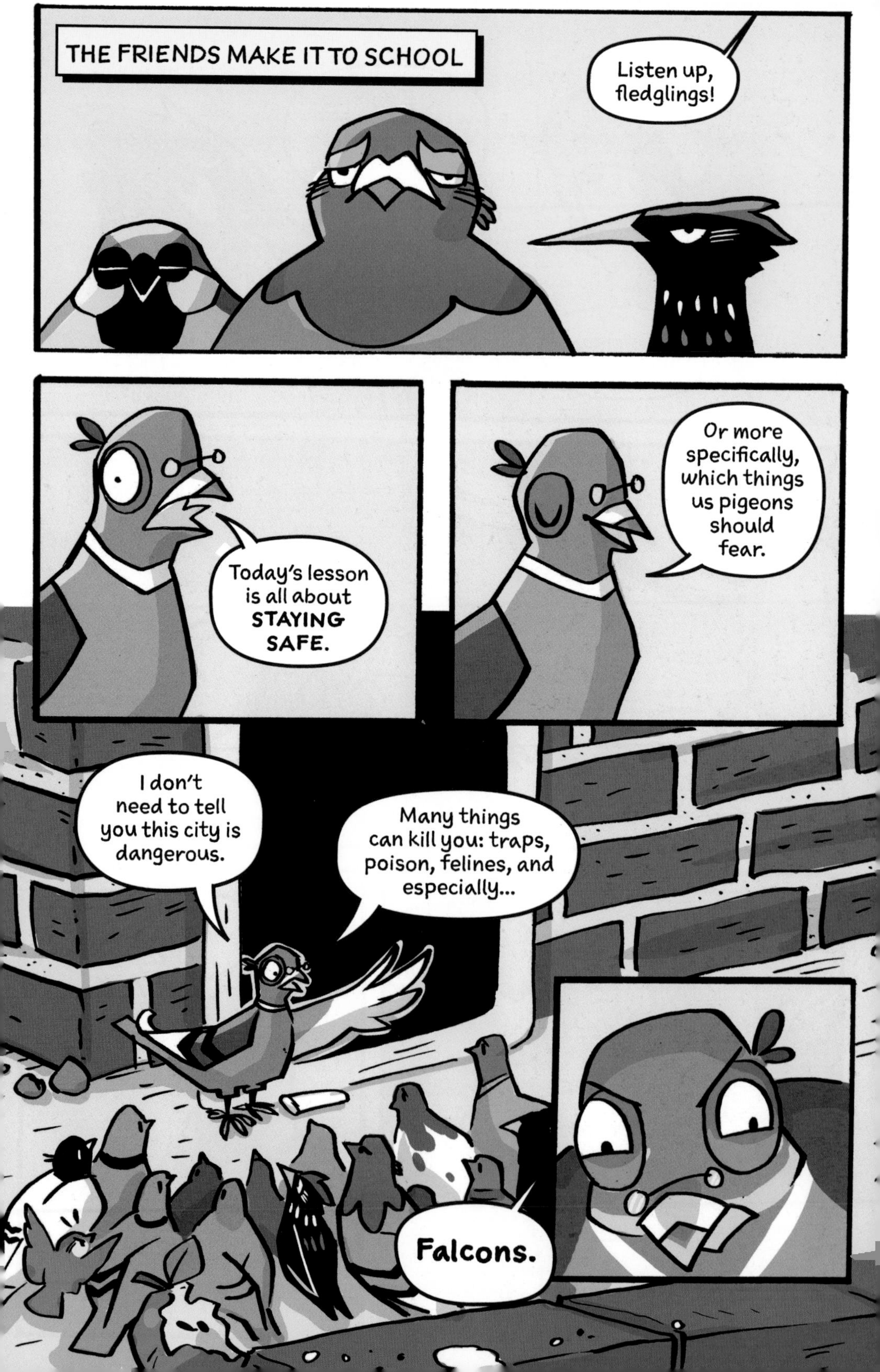
THE FRIENDS MAKE IT TO SCHOOL
Listen up, fledglings!
Today's lesson is all about STAYING SAFE.
Or more specifically, which things us pigeons should fear.
I don't need to tell you this city is dangerous.
Many things can kill you: traps, poison, felines, and especially...
Falcons.

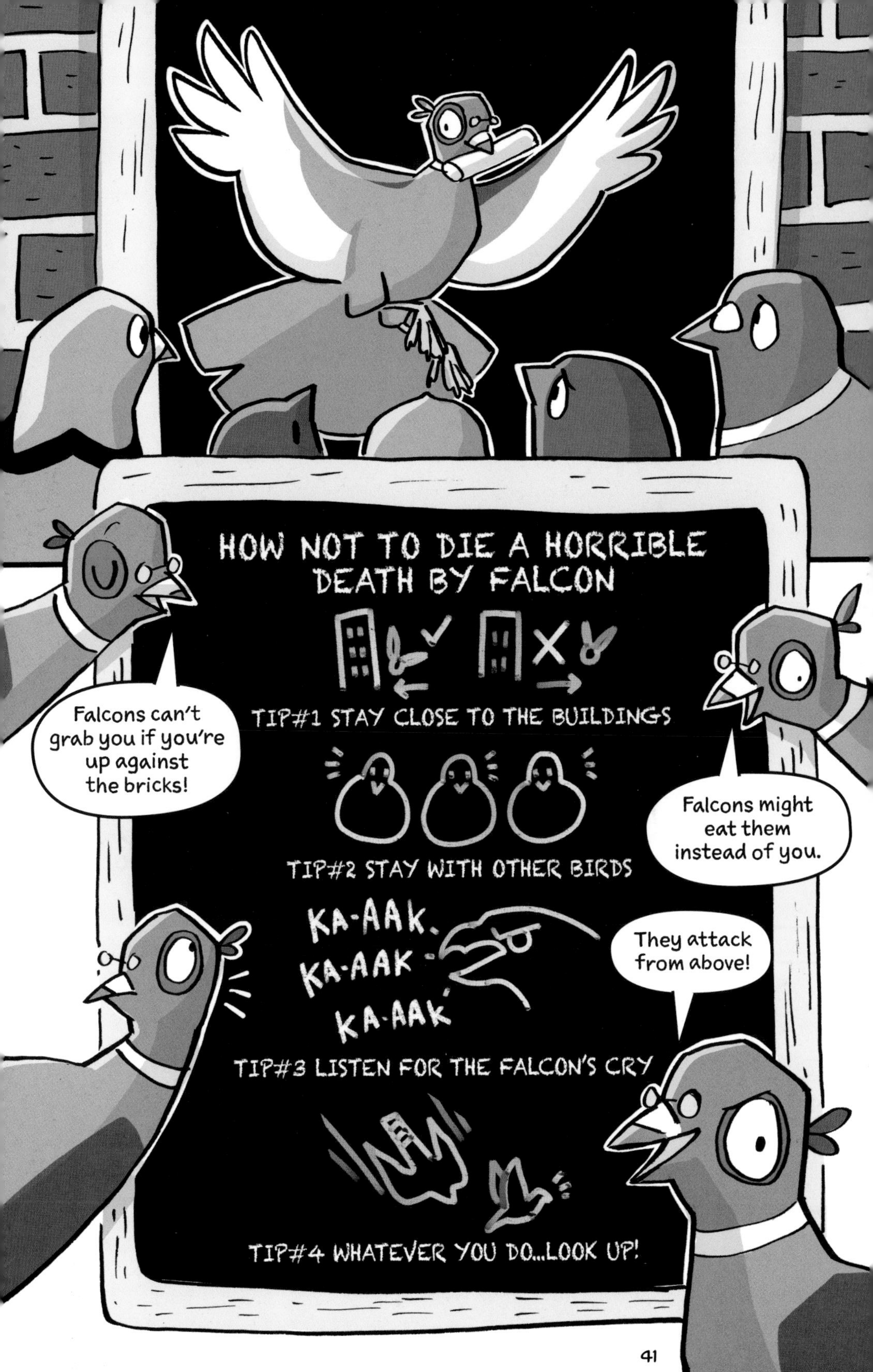
HOW NOT TO DIE A HORRIBLE DEATH BY FALCON
TIP#1 STAY CLOSE TO THE BUILDINGS
Falcons can't grab you if you're up against the bricks!
TIP#2 STAY WITH OTHER BIRDS
Falcons might eat them instead of you.
KA-AAK. KA-AAK KA-AAK
TIP#3 LISTEN FOR THE FALCON'S CRY
They attack from above!
TIP#4 WHATEVER YOU DO...LOOK UP!

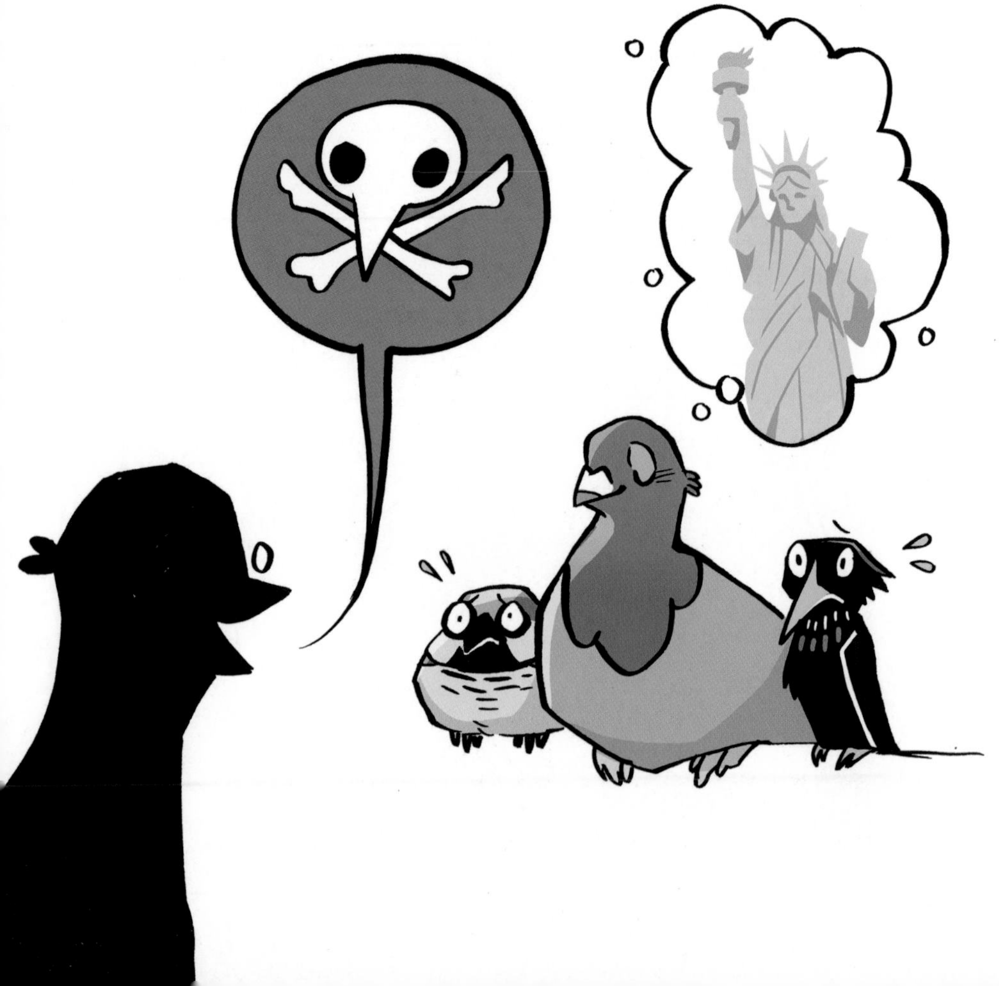

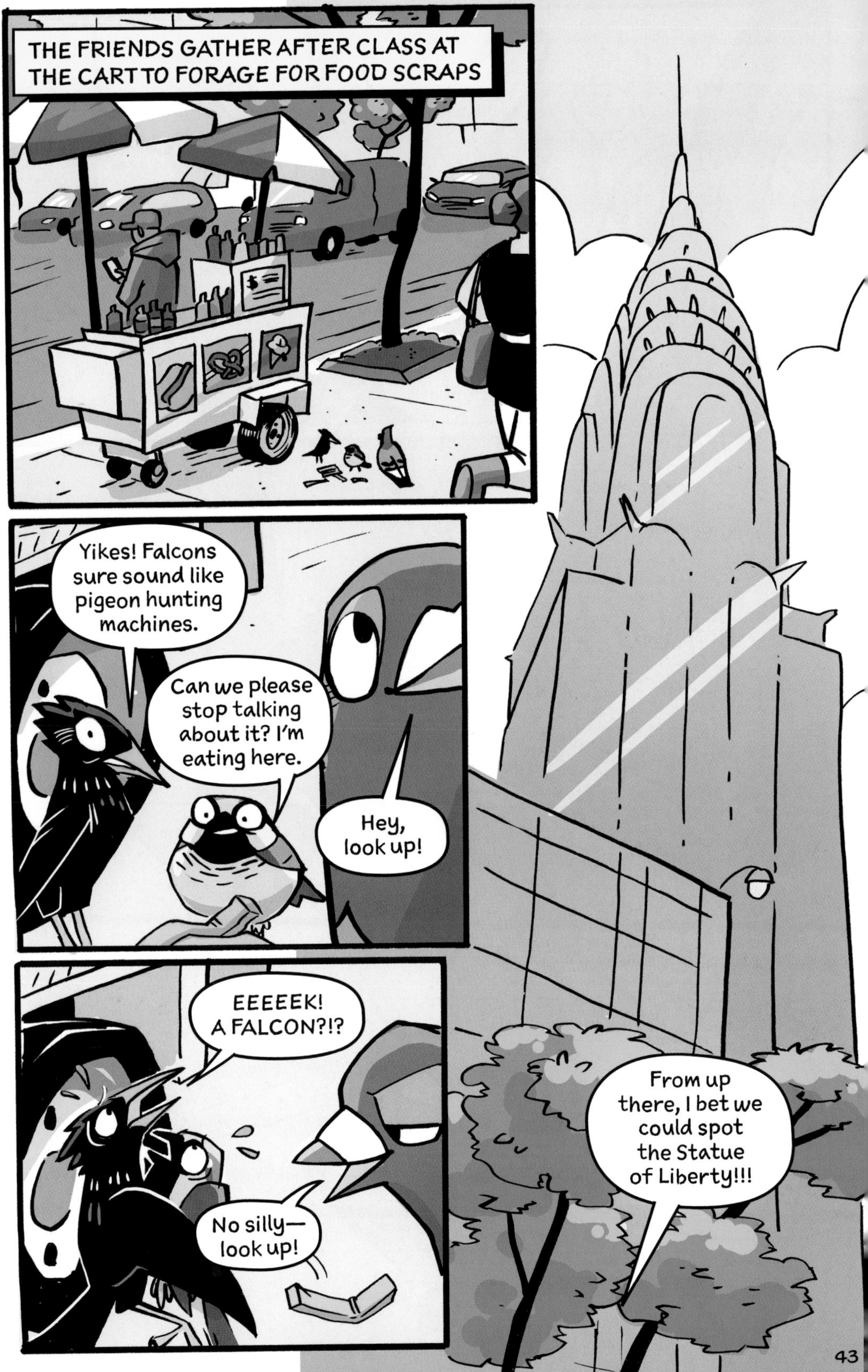
THE FRIENDS GATHER AFTER CLASS AT THE CART TO FORAGE FOR FOOD SCRAPS
Yikes! Falcons sure sound like pigeon hunting machines.
Can we please stop talking about it? I'm eating here.
Hey, look up!
EEEEEK! A FALCON?!?
No silly— look up!
From up there, I bet we could spot the Statue of Liberty!!!

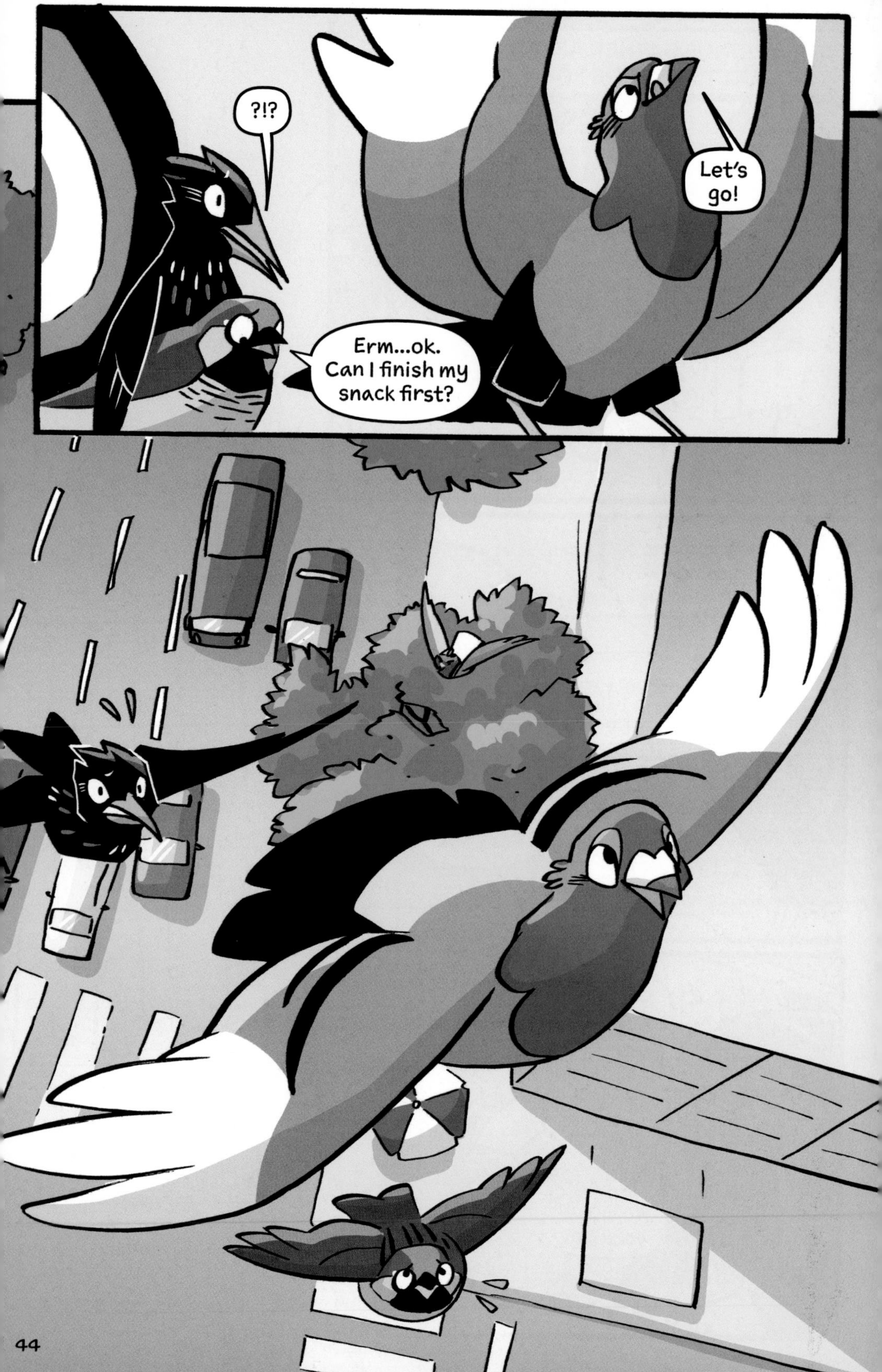
?!?
Let's go!
Erm...ok. Can I finish my snack first?

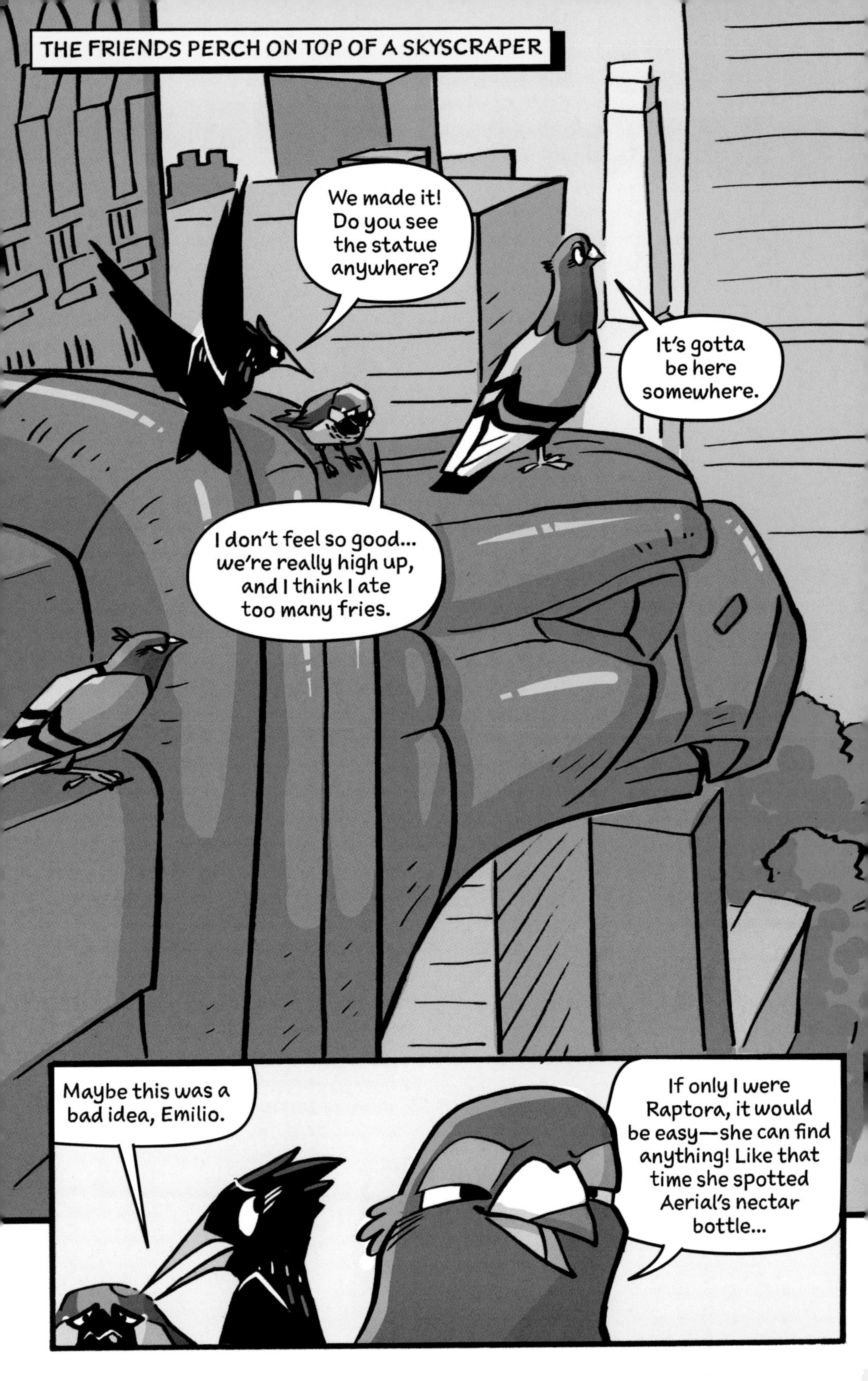
THE FRIENDS PERCH ON TOP OF A SKYSCRAPER
We made it! Do you see the statue anywhere?
It's gotta be here somewhere.
I don't feel so good... we're really high up, and I think I ate too many fries.
Maybe this was a bad idea, Emilio.
If only I were Raptora, it would be easy—she can find anything! Like that time she spotted Aerial's nectar bottle...

WINGED HERO: RAPTORA—THE VISIONARY

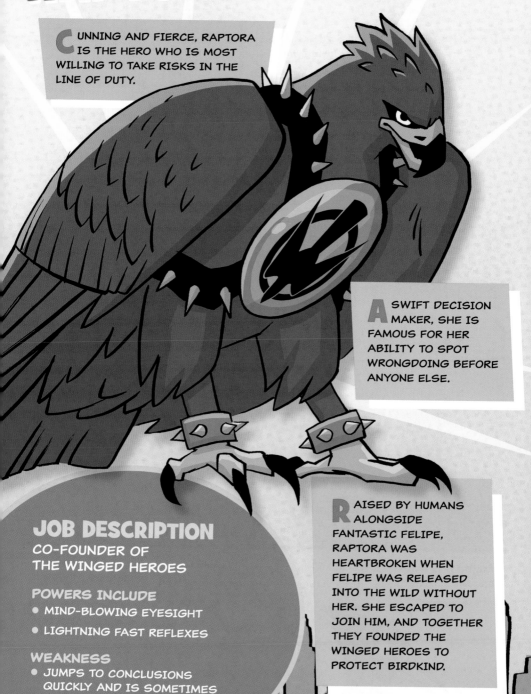

CUNNING AND FIERCE, RAPTORA IS THE HERO WHO IS MOST WILLING TO TAKE RISKS IN THE LINE OF DUTY.

A SWIFT DECISION MAKER, SHE IS FAMOUS FOR HER ABILITY TO SPOT WRONGDOING BEFORE ANYONE ELSE.

RAISED BY HUMANS ALONGSIDE FANTASTIC FELIPE, RAPTORA WAS HEARTBROKEN WHEN FELIPE WAS RELEASED INTO THE WILD WITHOUT HER. SHE ESCAPED TO JOIN HIM, AND TOGETHER THEY FOUNDED THE WINGED HEROES TO PROTECT BIRDKIND.

JOB DESCRIPTION

CO-FOUNDER OF
THE WINGED HEROES

POWERS INCLUDE
- MIND-BLOWING EYESIGHT
- LIGHTNING FAST REFLEXES

WEAKNESS
- JUMPS TO CONCLUSIONS QUICKLY AND IS SOMETIMES WAY OFF BASE

THE REAL GOLDEN EAGLE

(AQUILA CHRYSAETOS)

DIET

- RABBITS, SQUIRRELS AND OTHER MAMMALS. SOME BIRDS TOO!

NATURAL HISTORY

- ACROBATIC FLYERS WHO SOMETIMES DROP STICKS AND THEN DIVE TO CATCH THEM—HUNTING PRACTICE!
- FIGHTS IN MID-AIR BY LOCKING TALONS WITH AN INTRUDER AND TUMBLING DOWNWARD.
- HUNT TOGETHER IN PAIRS TO BRING DOWN DEER AND OTHER LARGE MAMMALS.

NATURAL SUPERPOWERS

- EYESIGHT AMONG THE MOST POWERFUL OF ANY ANIMAL—CAN SEE PREY MORE THAN A MILE AWAY (1.61 KM).
- CAN SPEED MORE THAN 100 MILES PER HOUR DURING A HUNTING DIVE—ALMOST AS FAST AS THE PEREGRINE FALCON!

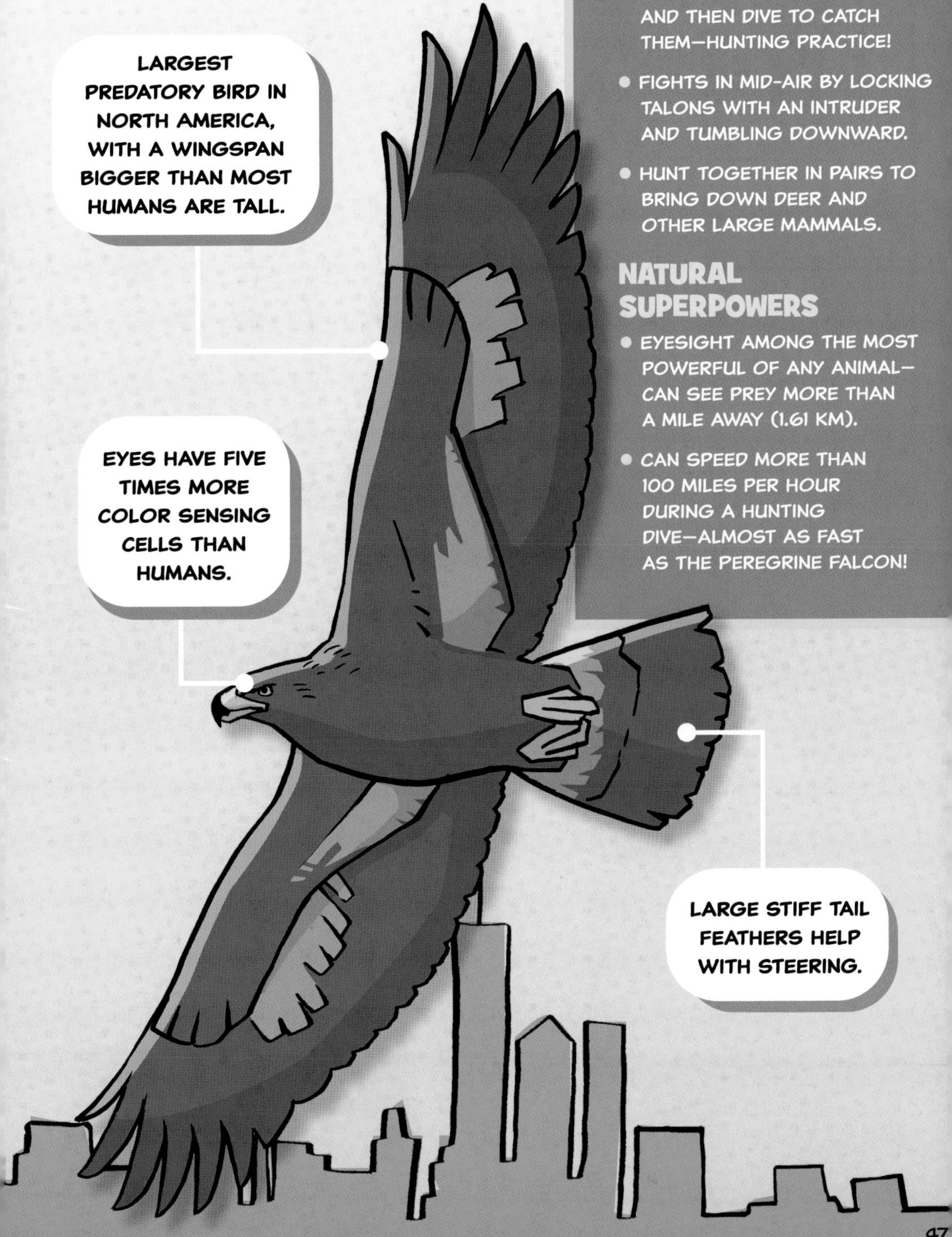
LARGEST PREDATORY BIRD IN NORTH AMERICA, WITH A WINGSPAN BIGGER THAN MOST HUMANS ARE TALL.
EYES HAVE FIVE TIMES MORE COLOR SENSING CELLS THAN HUMANS.
LARGE STIFF TAIL FEATHERS HELP WITH STEERING.

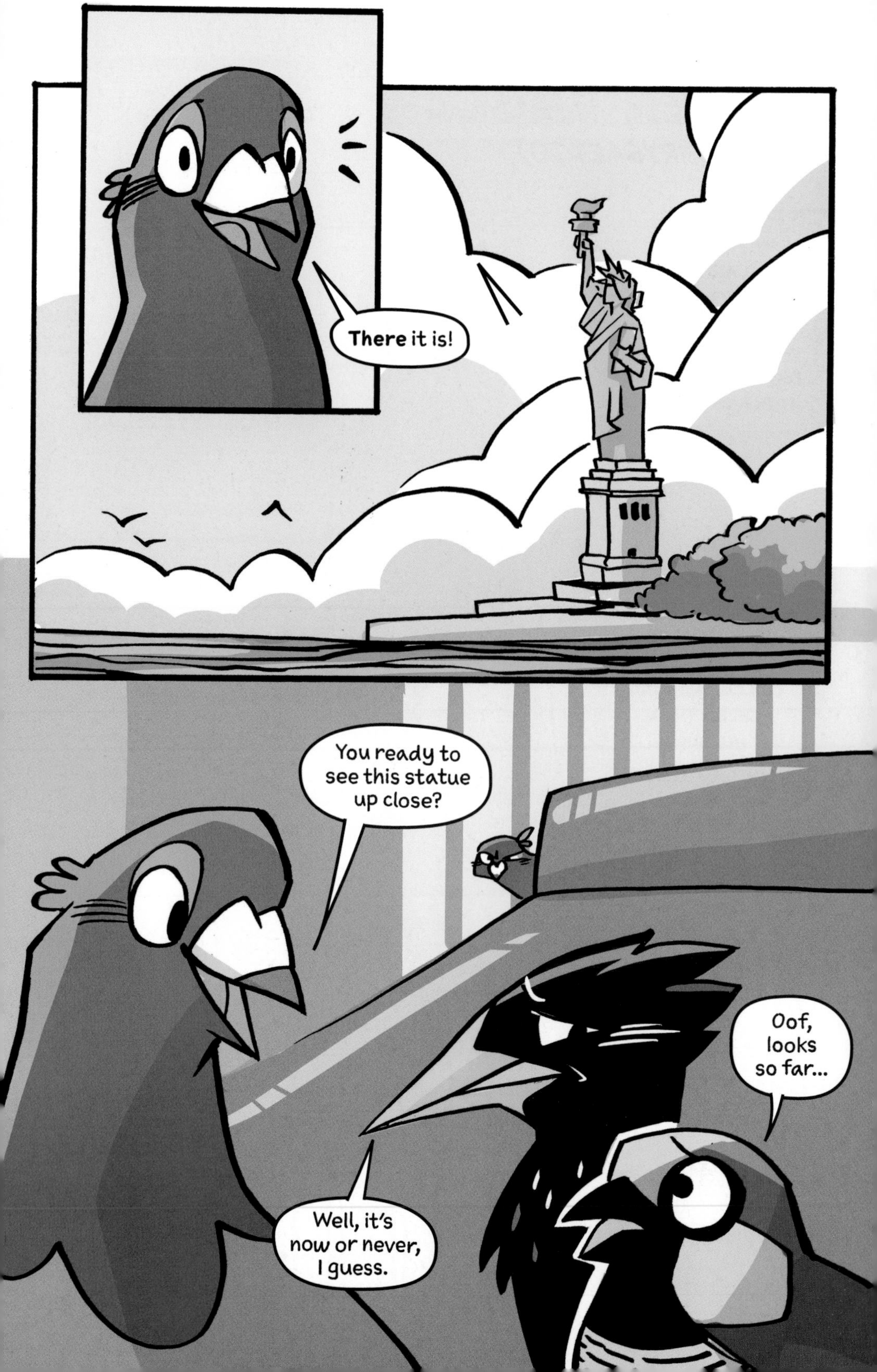
There it is!
You ready to see this statue up close?
Oof, looks so far...
Well, it's now or never, I guess.

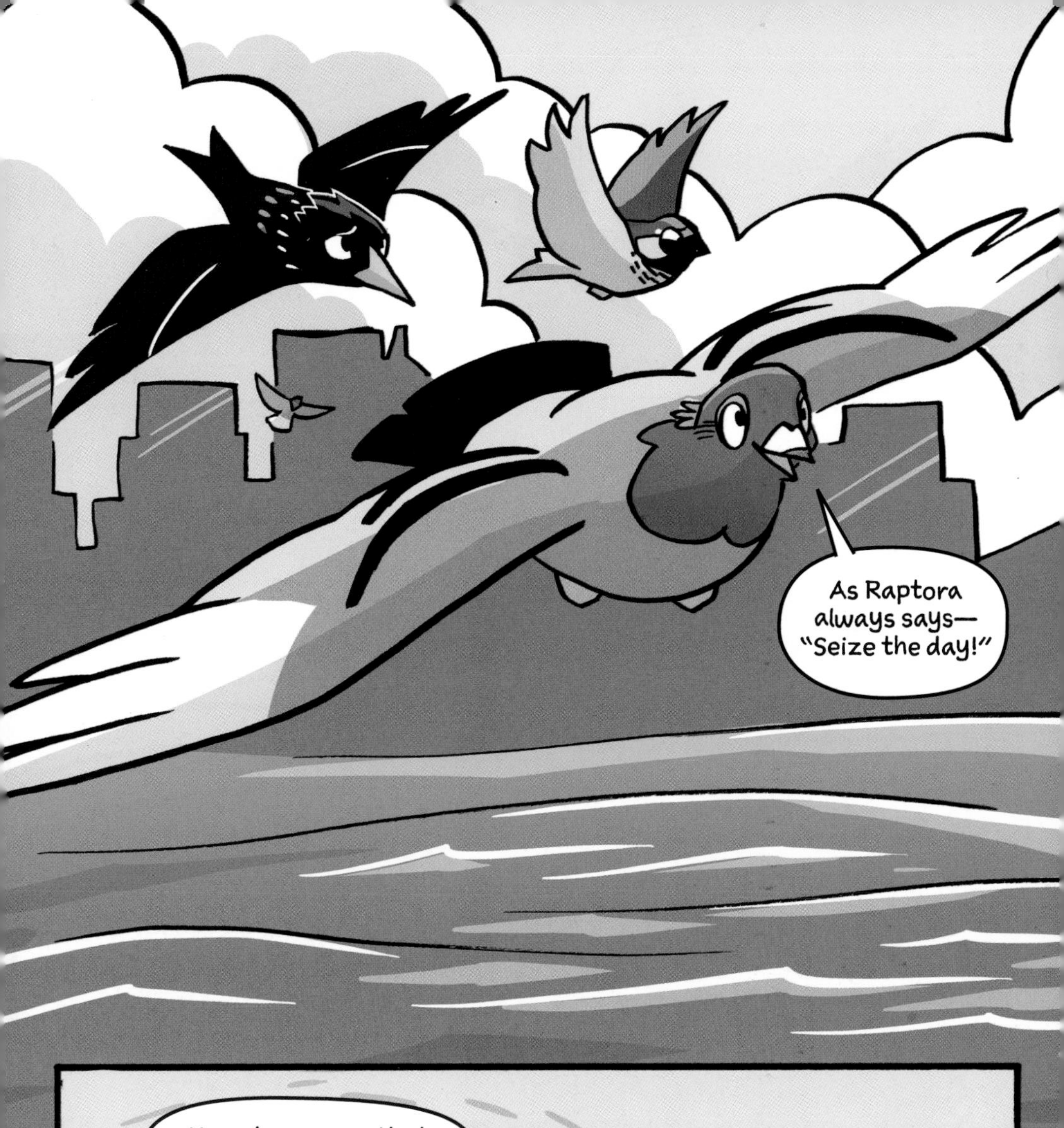
As Raptora always says— "Seize the day!"

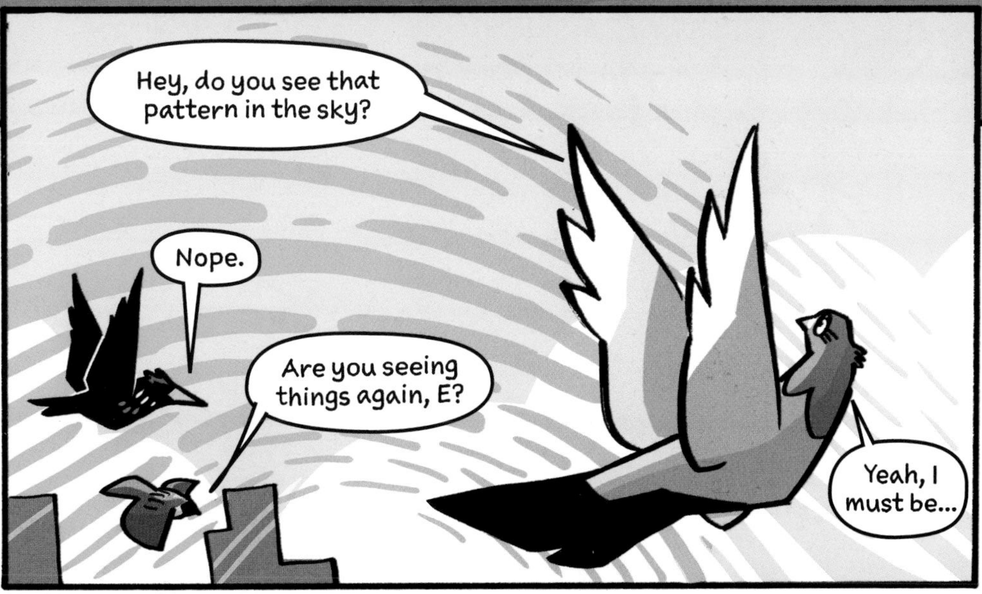
Hey, do you see that pattern in the sky?
Nope.
Are you seeing things again, E?
Yeah, I must be...

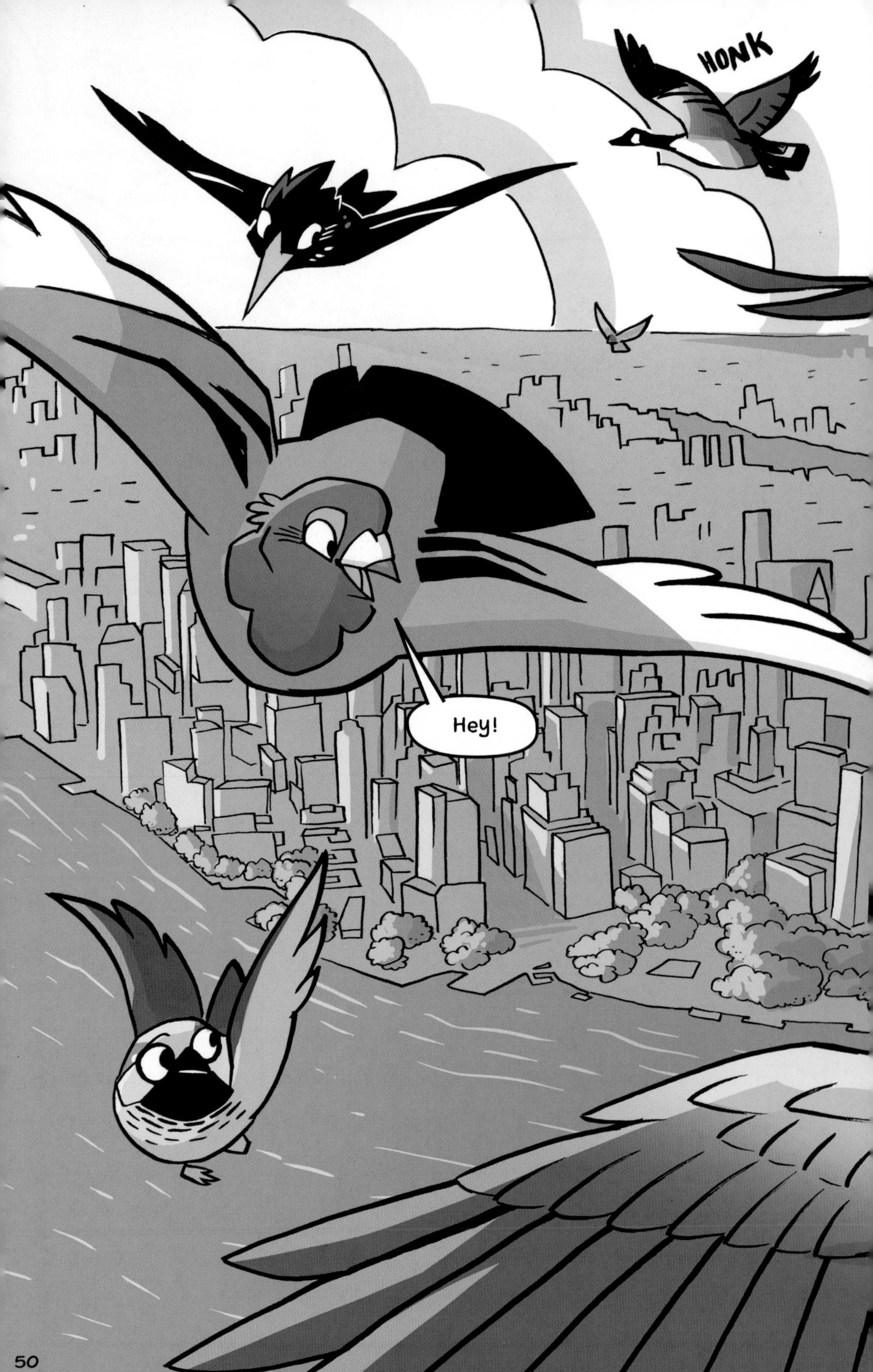
HONK
Hey!

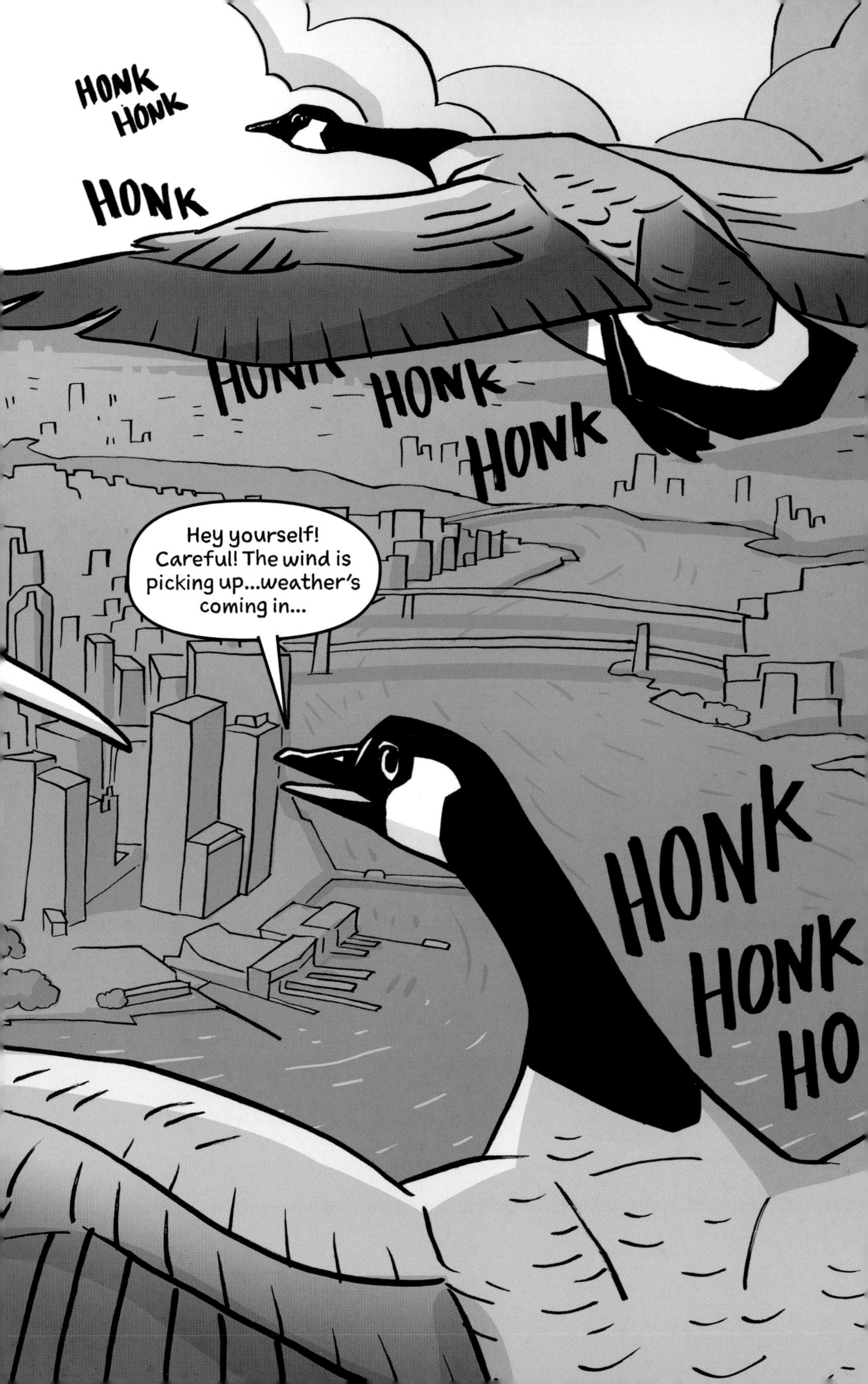
HONK
HONK
HONK
HONK
HONK
HONK
Hey yourself! Careful! The wind is picking up...weather's coming in...
HONK
HONK
HO

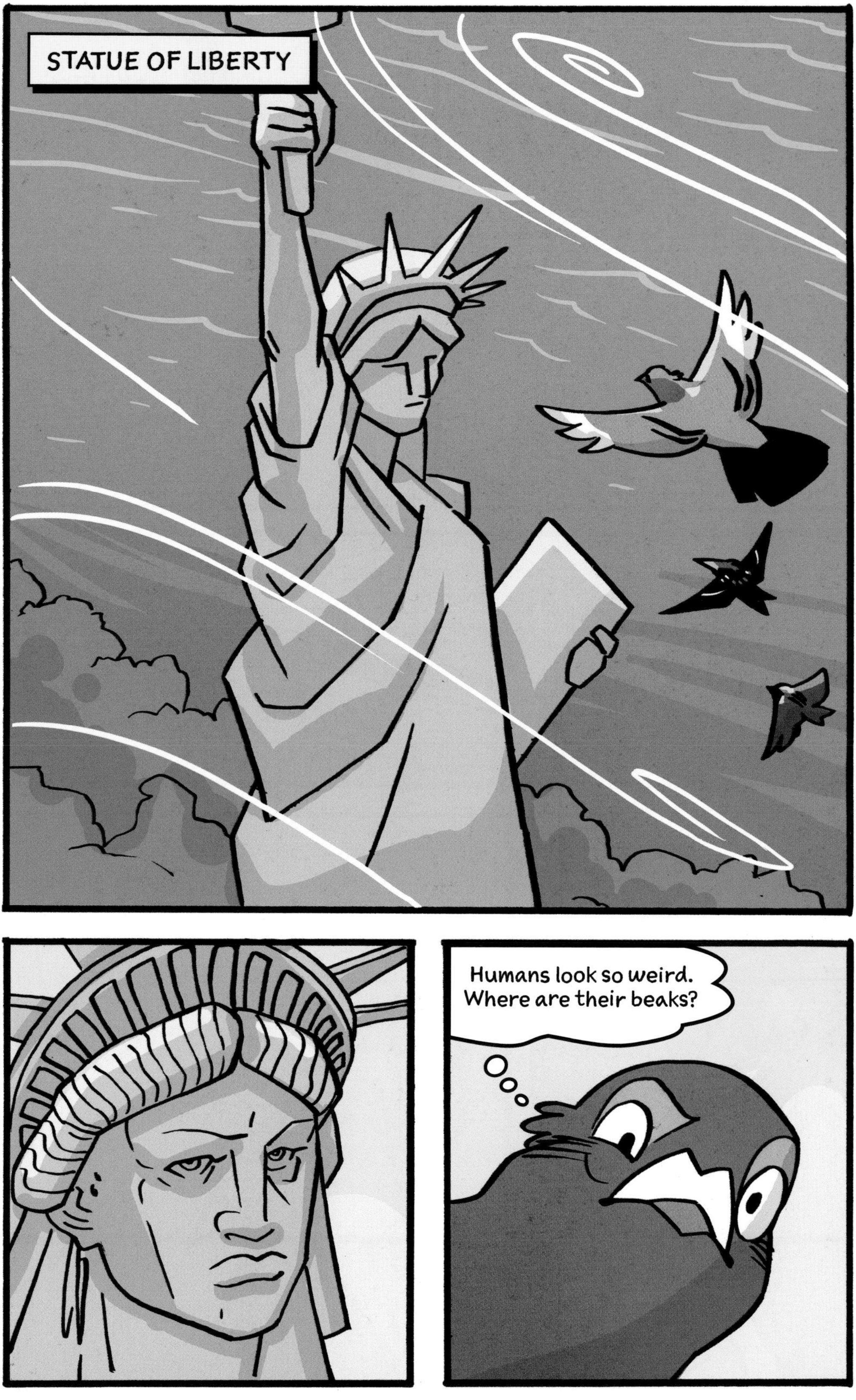
STATUE OF LIBERTY
Humans look so weird. Where are their beaks?

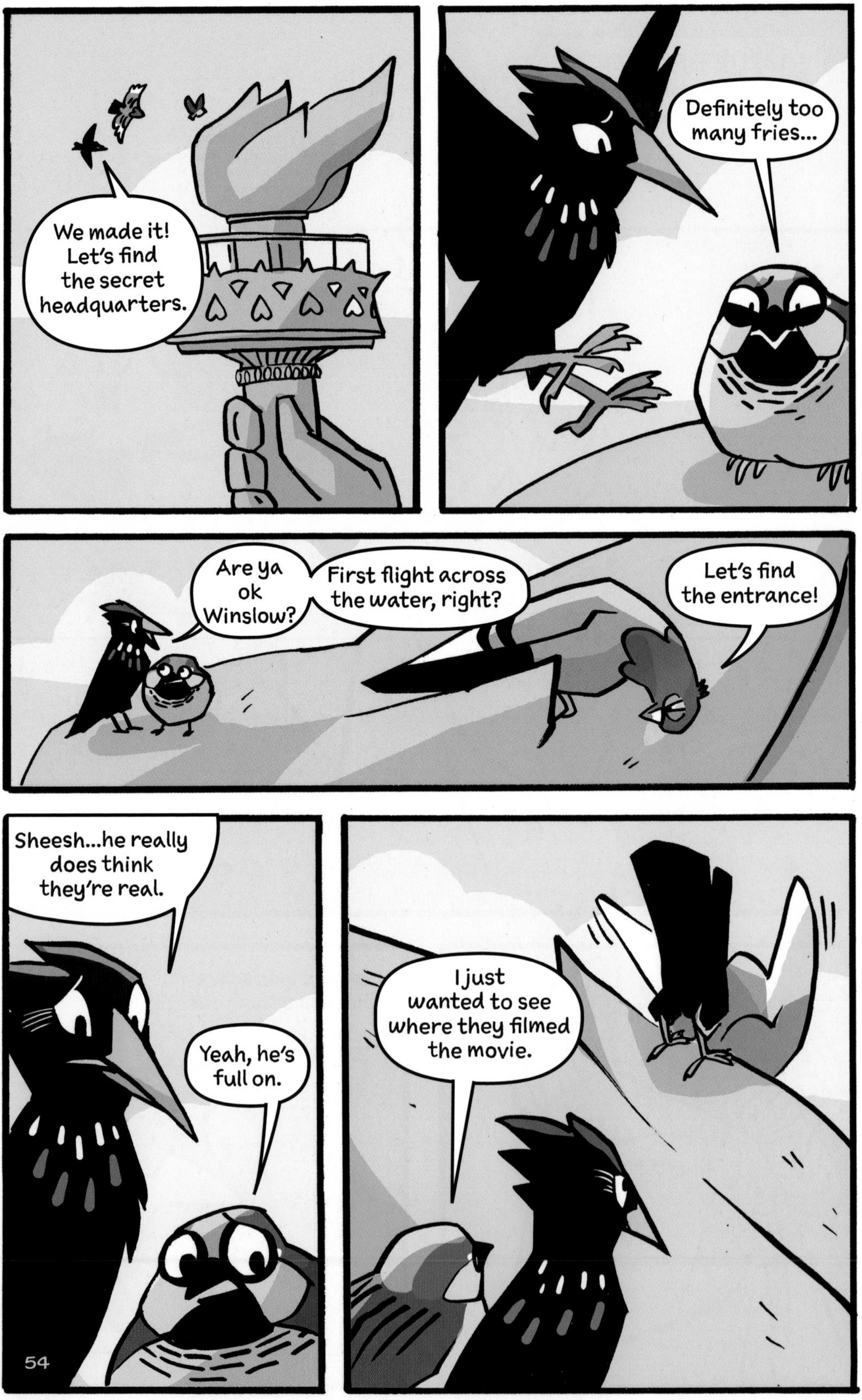
We made it! Let's find the secret headquarters.
Definitely too many fries...
Are ya ok Winslow?
First flight across the water, right?
Let's find the entrance!
Sheesh...he really does think they're real.
Yeah, he's full on.
I just wanted to see where they filmed the movie.

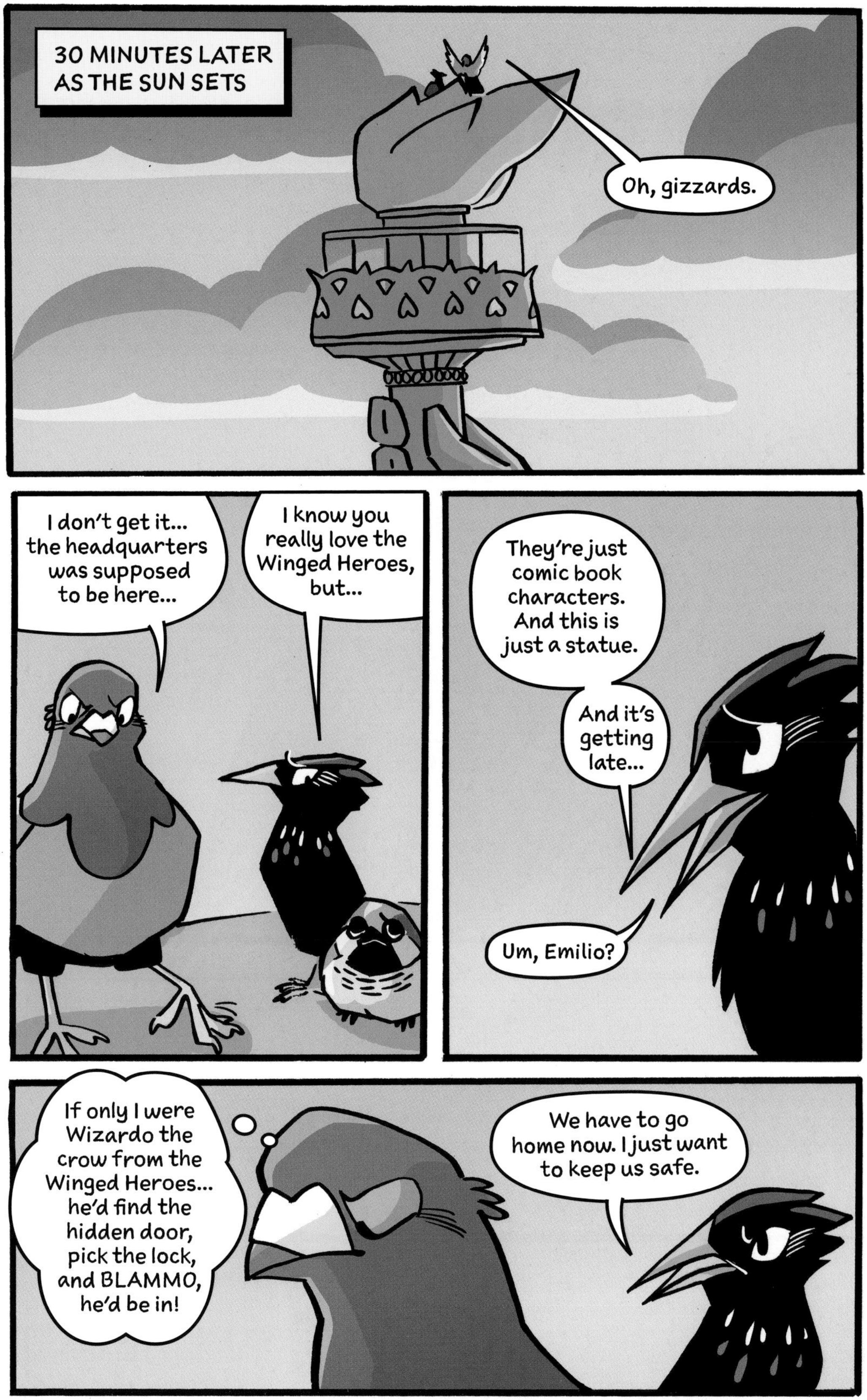
30 MINUTES LATER AS THE SUN SETS
Oh, gizzards.
I don't get it... the headquarters was supposed to be here...
I know you really love the Winged Heroes, but...
They're just comic book characters. And this is just a statue.
And it's getting late...
Um, Emilio?
If only I were Wizardo the crow from the Winged Heroes... he'd find the hidden door, pick the lock, and BLAMMO, he'd be in!
We have to go home now. I just want to keep us safe.

WINGED HERO: WIZARDO — THE PUZZLE MASTER

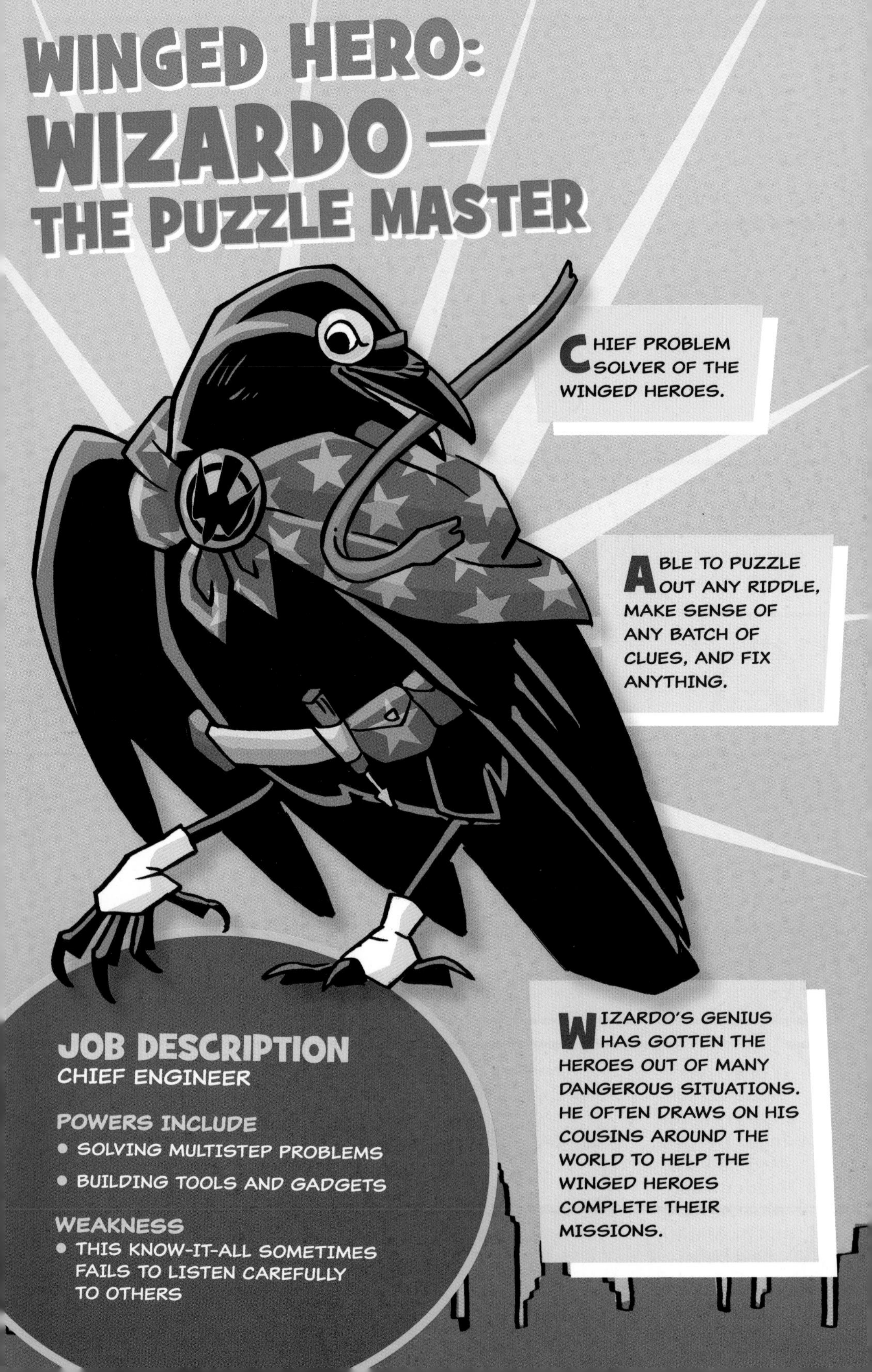

CHIEF PROBLEM SOLVER OF THE WINGED HEROES.

ABLE TO PUZZLE OUT ANY RIDDLE, MAKE SENSE OF ANY BATCH OF CLUES, AND FIX ANYTHING.

WIZARDO'S GENIUS HAS GOTTEN THE HEROES OUT OF MANY DANGEROUS SITUATIONS. HE OFTEN DRAWS ON HIS COUSINS AROUND THE WORLD TO HELP THE WINGED HEROES COMPLETE THEIR MISSIONS.

JOB DESCRIPTION

CHIEF ENGINEER

POWERS INCLUDE

- SOLVING MULTISTEP PROBLEMS
- BUILDING TOOLS AND GADGETS

WEAKNESS

- THIS KNOW-IT-ALL SOMETIMES FAILS TO LISTEN CAREFULLY TO OTHERS

THE REAL AMERICAN CROW

(CORVUS BRACHYRHYNCHOS)

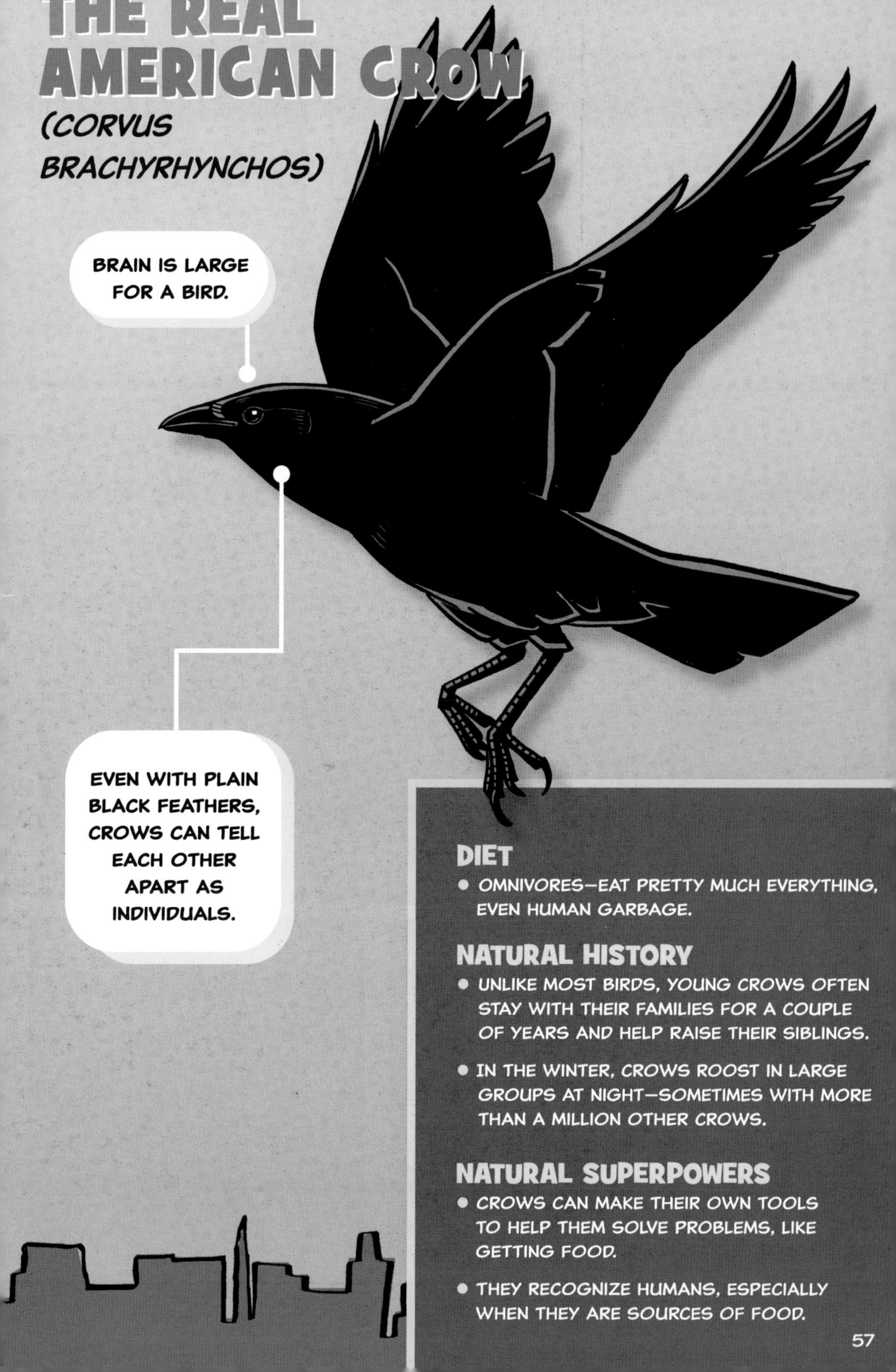
BRAIN IS LARGE FOR A BIRD.
EVEN WITH PLAIN BLACK FEATHERS, CROWS CAN TELL EACH OTHER APART AS INDIVIDUALS.

DIET

- OMNIVORES—EAT PRETTY MUCH EVERYTHING, EVEN HUMAN GARBAGE.

NATURAL HISTORY

- UNLIKE MOST BIRDS, YOUNG CROWS OFTEN STAY WITH THEIR FAMILIES FOR A COUPLE OF YEARS AND HELP RAISE THEIR SIBLINGS.
- IN THE WINTER, CROWS ROOST IN LARGE GROUPS AT NIGHT—SOMETIMES WITH MORE THAN A MILLION OTHER CROWS.

NATURAL SUPERPOWERS

- CROWS CAN MAKE THEIR OWN TOOLS TO HELP THEM SOLVE PROBLEMS, LIKE GETTING FOOD.
- THEY RECOGNIZE HUMANS, ESPECIALLY WHEN THEY ARE SOURCES OF FOOD.

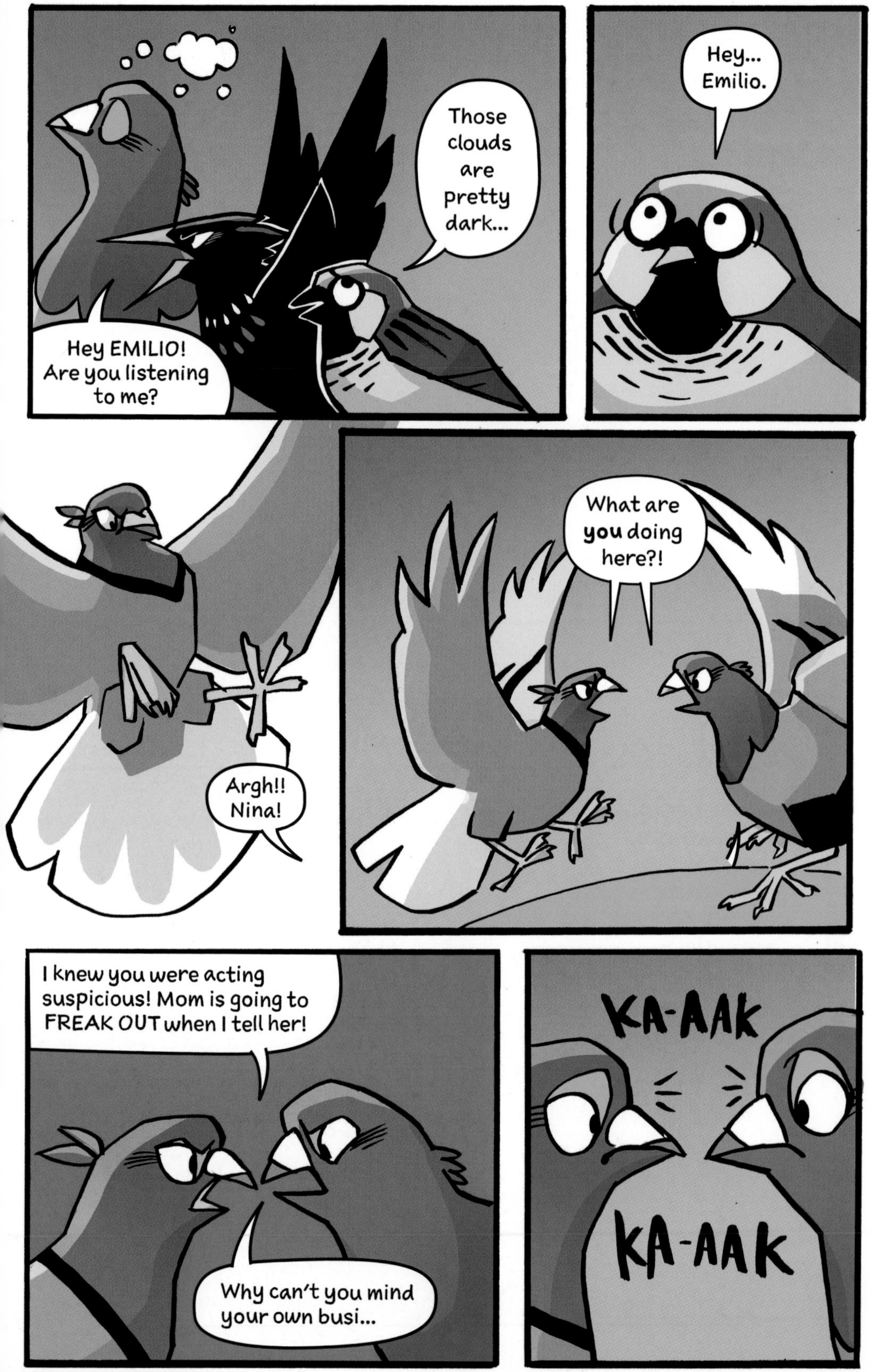
Those clouds are pretty dark...
Hey EMILIO! Are you listening to me?
Hey... Emilio.
Argh!! Nina!
What are **you** doing here?!
I knew you were acting suspicious! Mom is going to FREAK OUT when I tell her!
Why can't you mind your own busi...
KA-AAK
KA-AAK

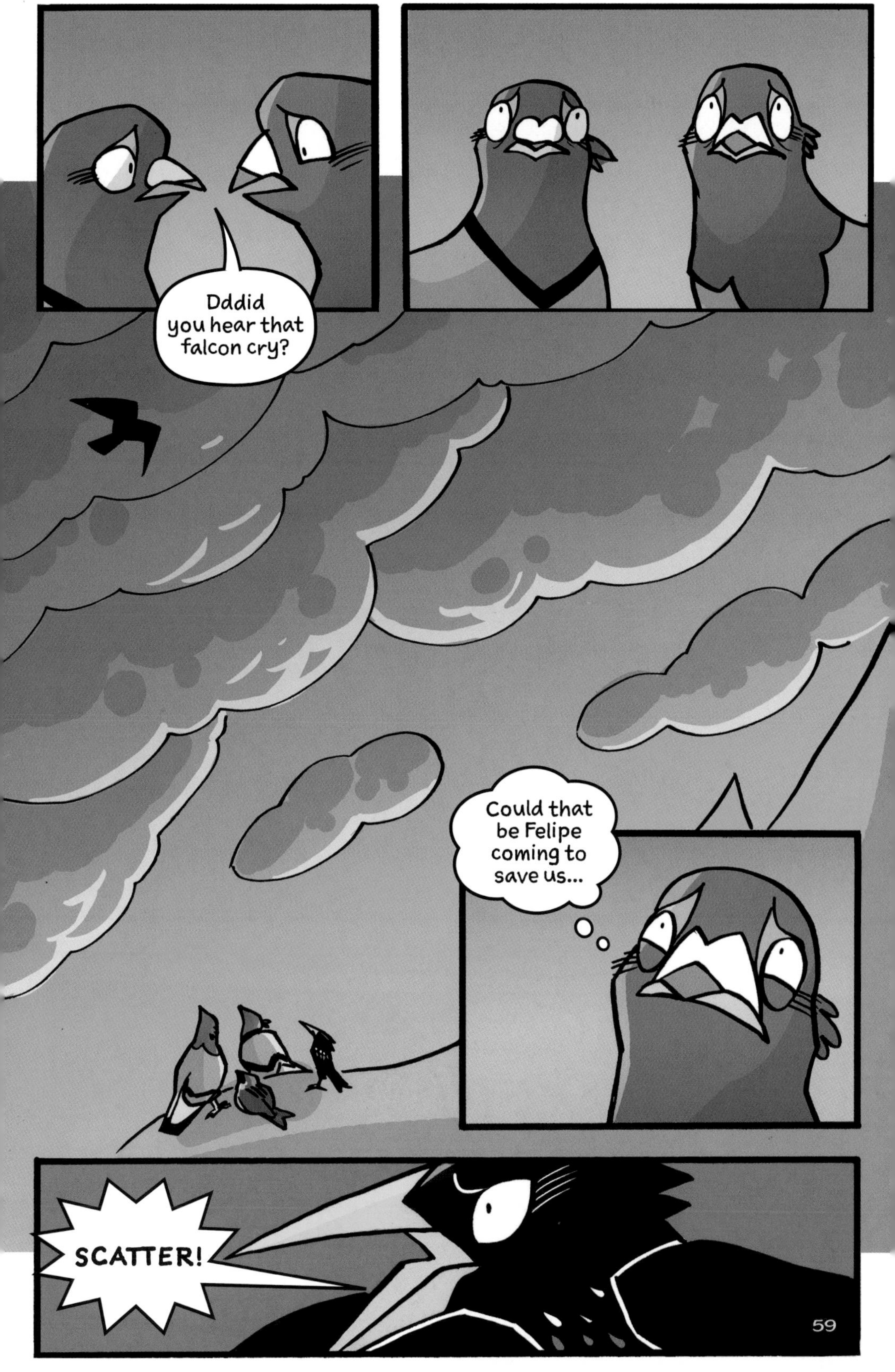

Dddid you hear that falcon cry?
Could that be Felipe coming to save us...
SCATTER!

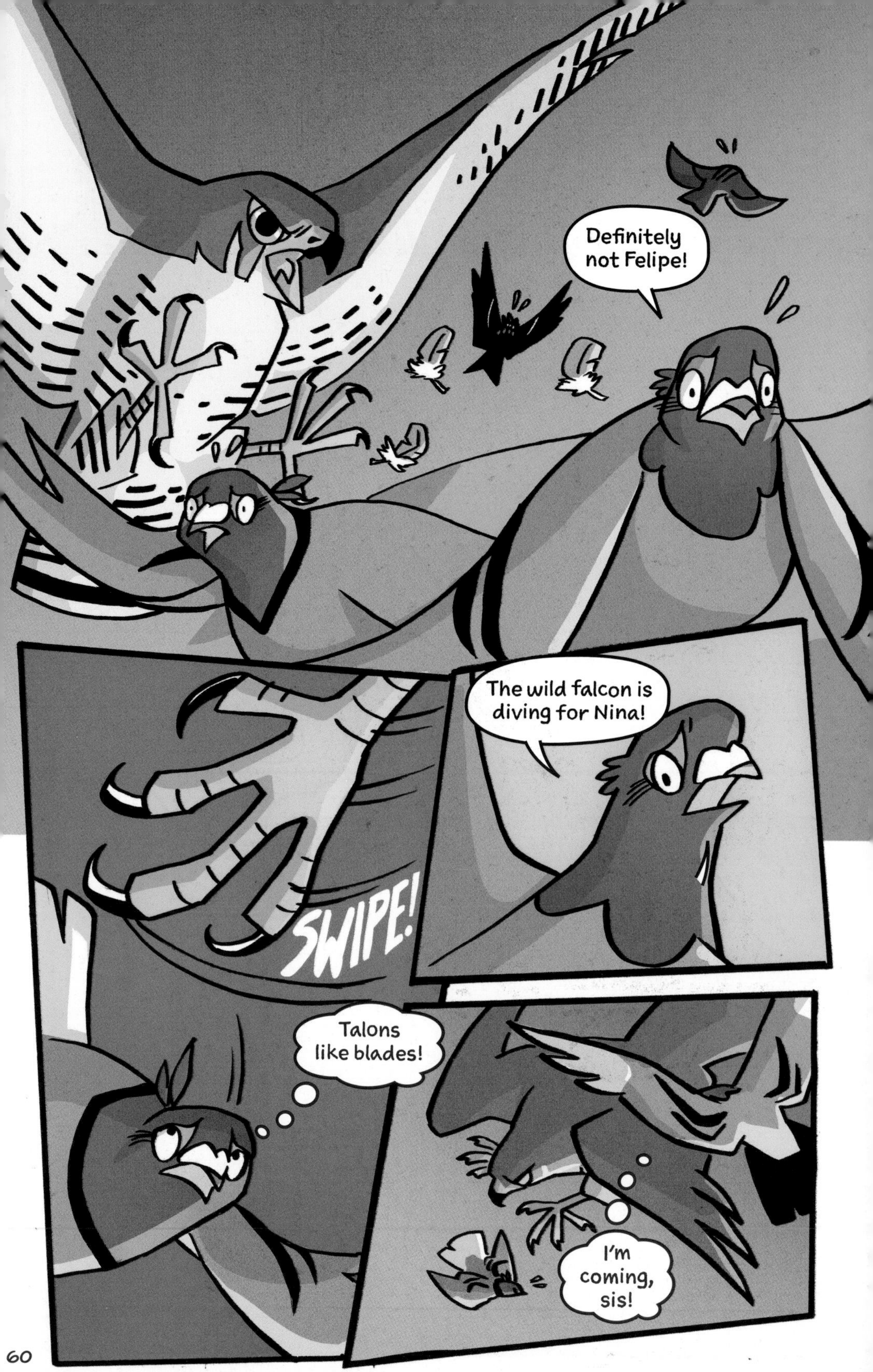
Definitely
not Felipe!
The wild falcon is
diving for Nina!
SWIPE!
Talons
like blades!
I'm
coming,
sis!

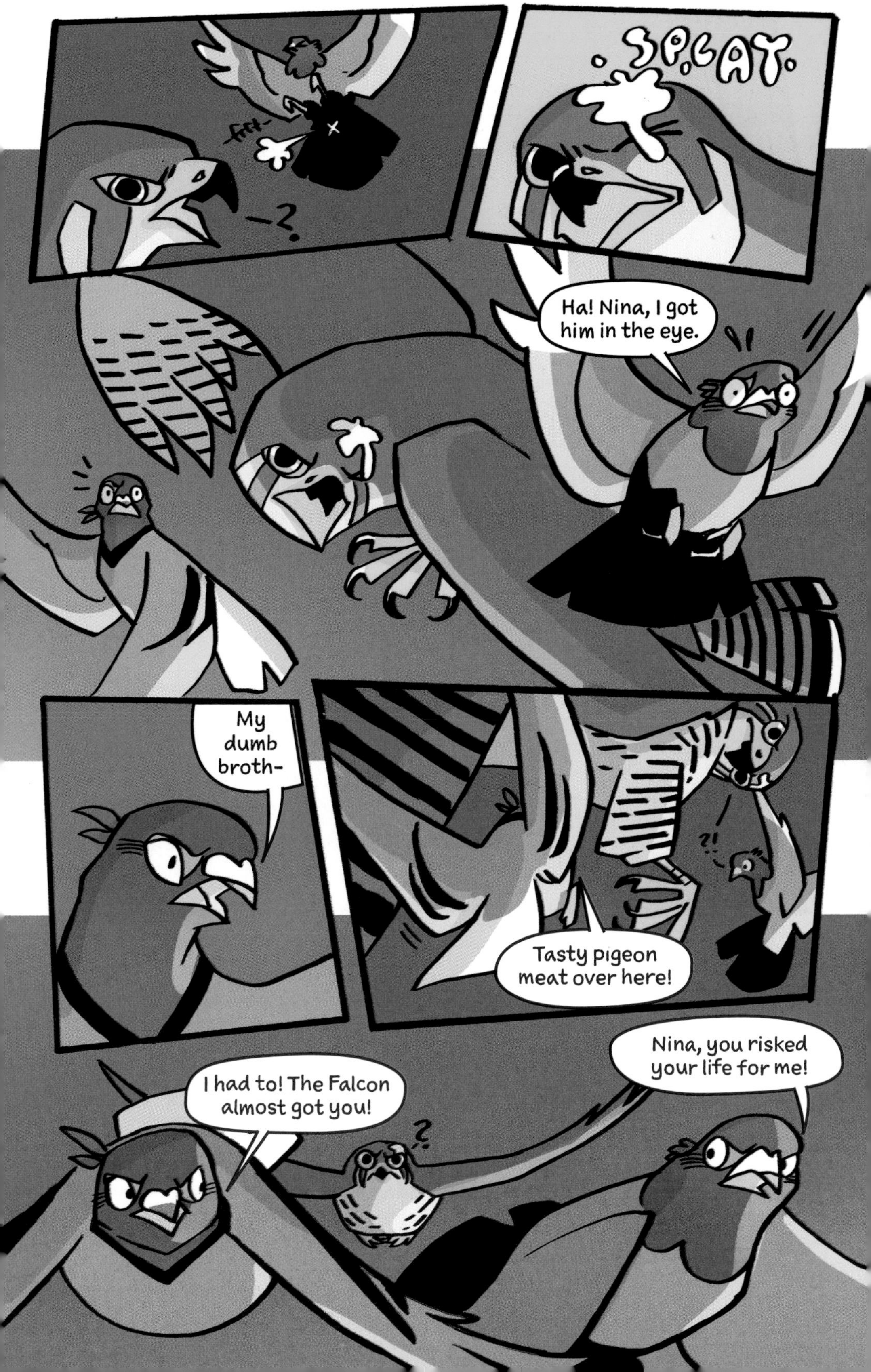

frrt-
-?
SPLAT
Ha! Nina, I got him in the eye.
My dumb broth-
Tasty pigeon meat over here!
?!
I had to! The Falcon almost got you!
Nina, you risked your life for me!
?

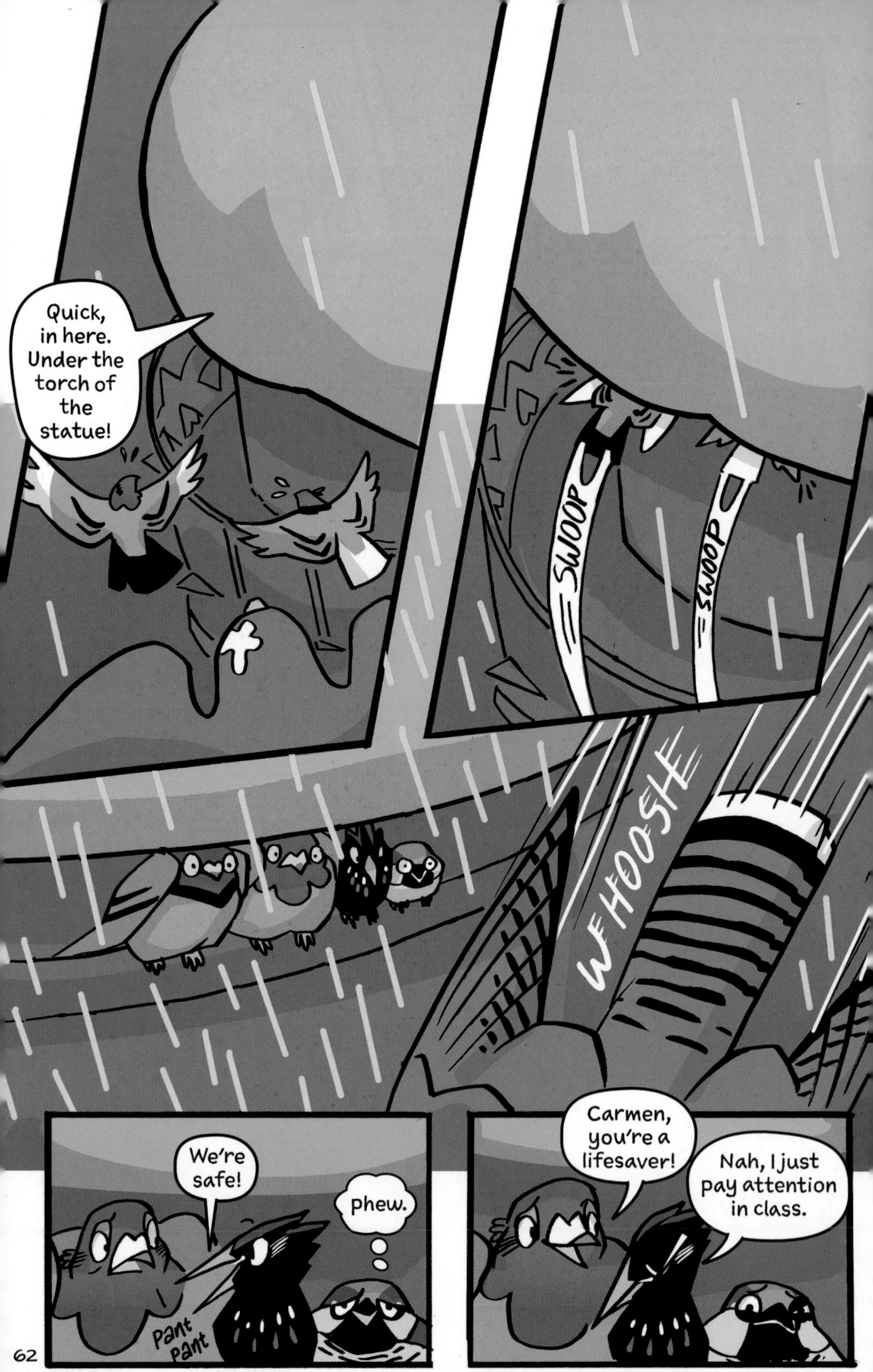
Quick, in here. Under the torch of the statue!
SWOOP
SWOOP
WHOOSH
We're safe!
Pant pant
phew.
Carmen, you're a lifesaver!
Nah, I just pay attention in class.

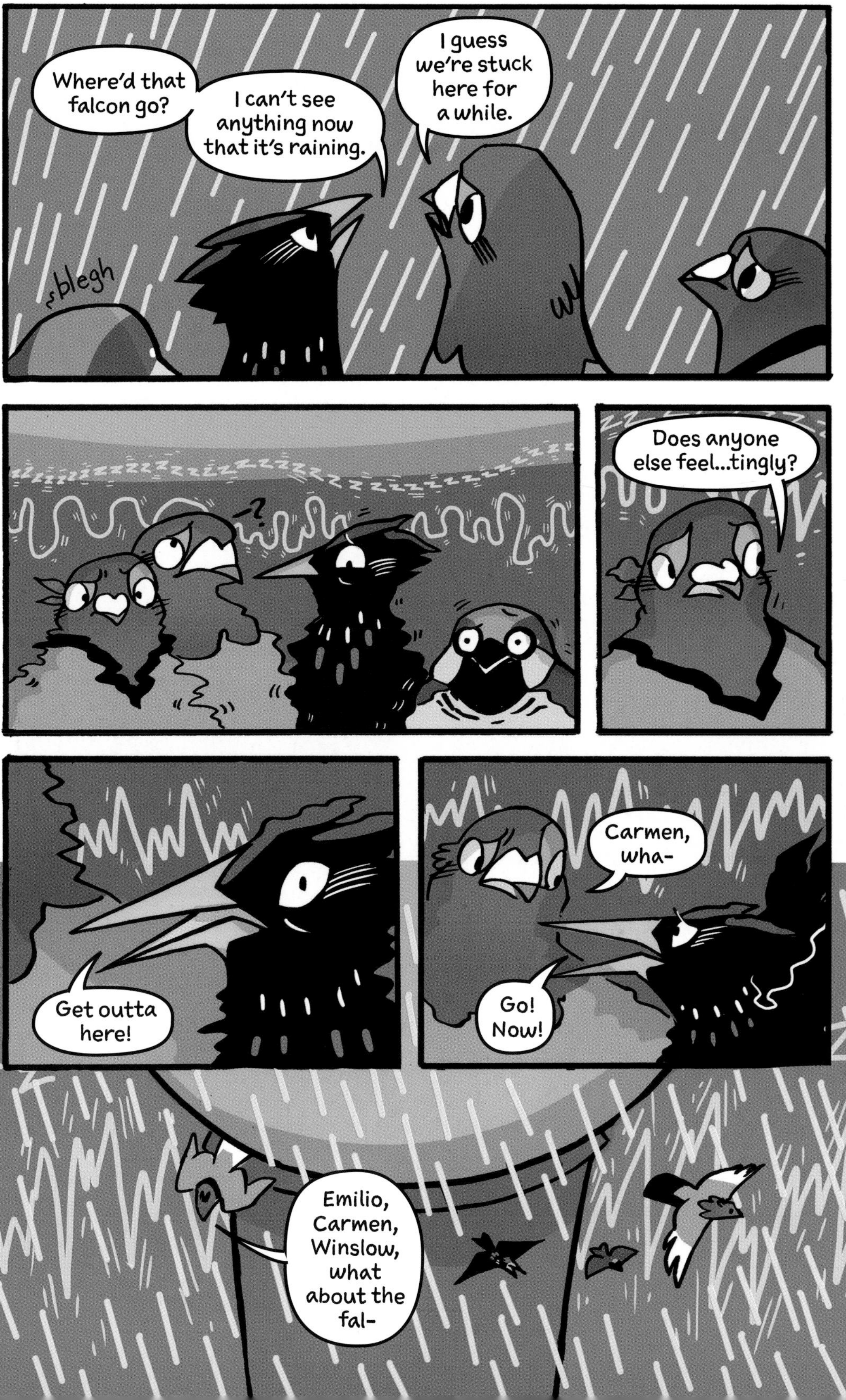
Where'd that falcon go?
I can't see anything now that it's raining.
I guess we're stuck here for a while.
blegh
Does anyone else feel...tingly?
Get outta here!
Carmen, wha-
Go! Now!
Emilio, Carmen, Winslow, what about the fal-

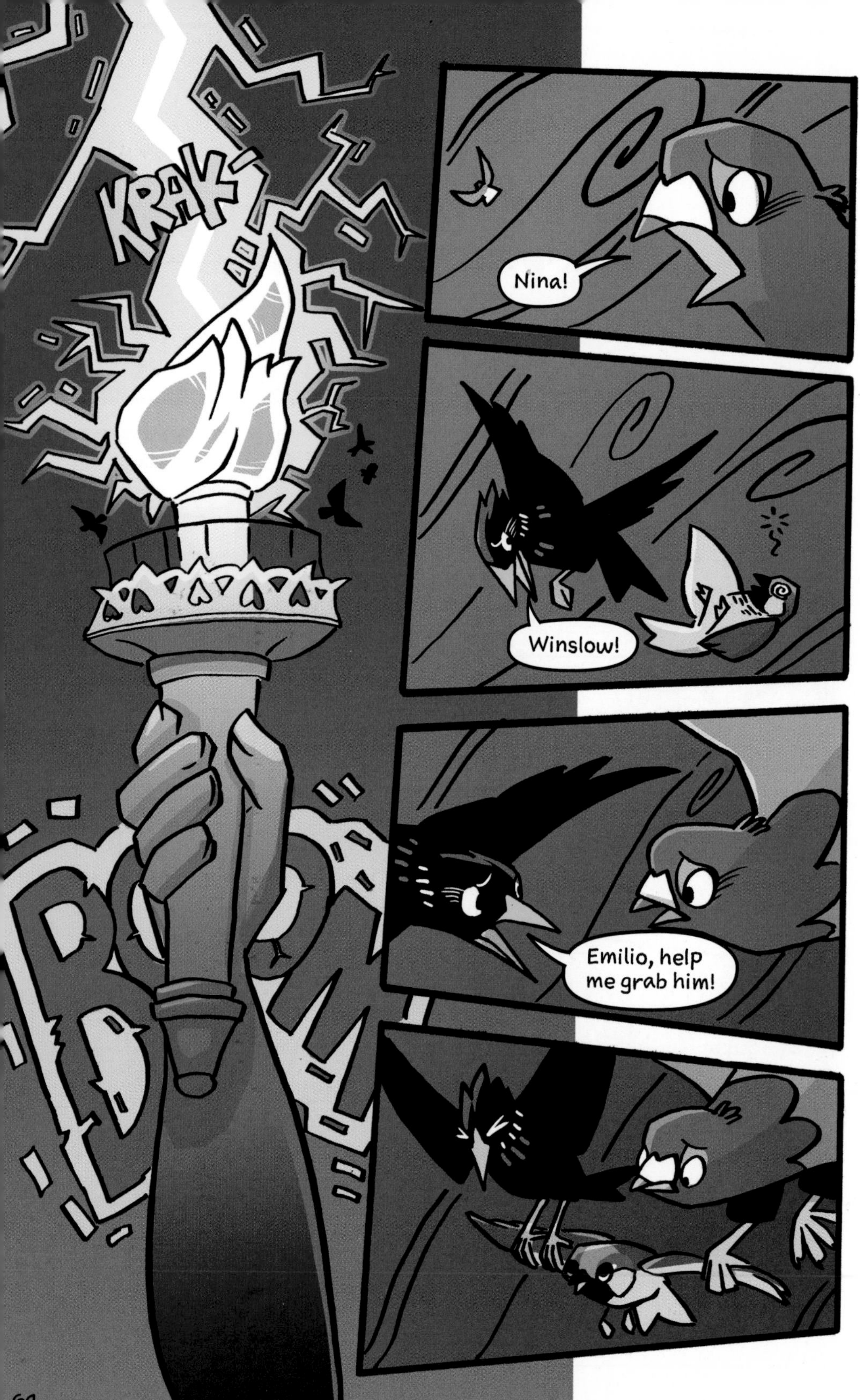
KRAK
BOOM
Nina!
Winslow!
Emilio, help me grab him!

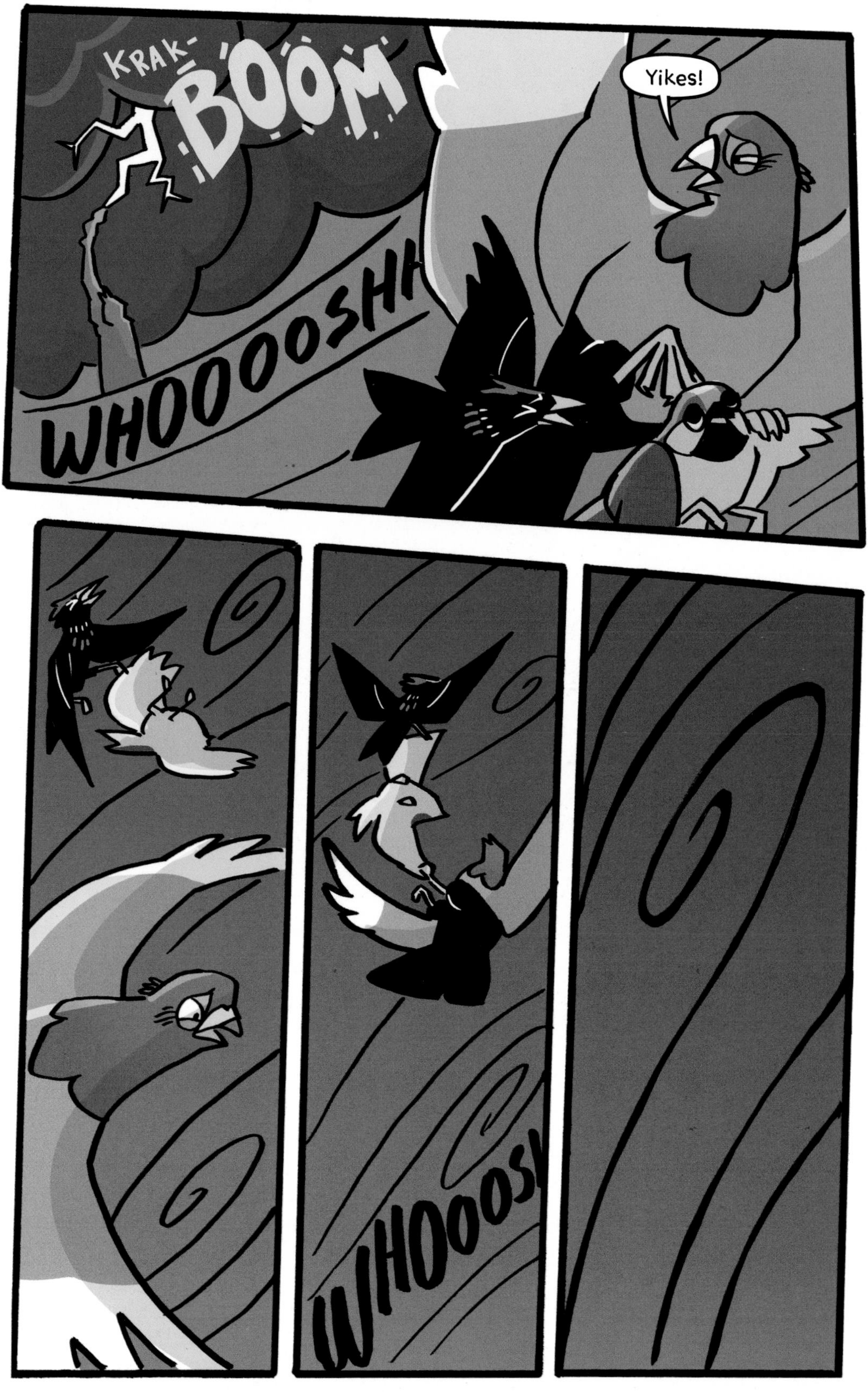
KRAK-
BOOM
Yikes!
WHOOOOSH
WHOOOS

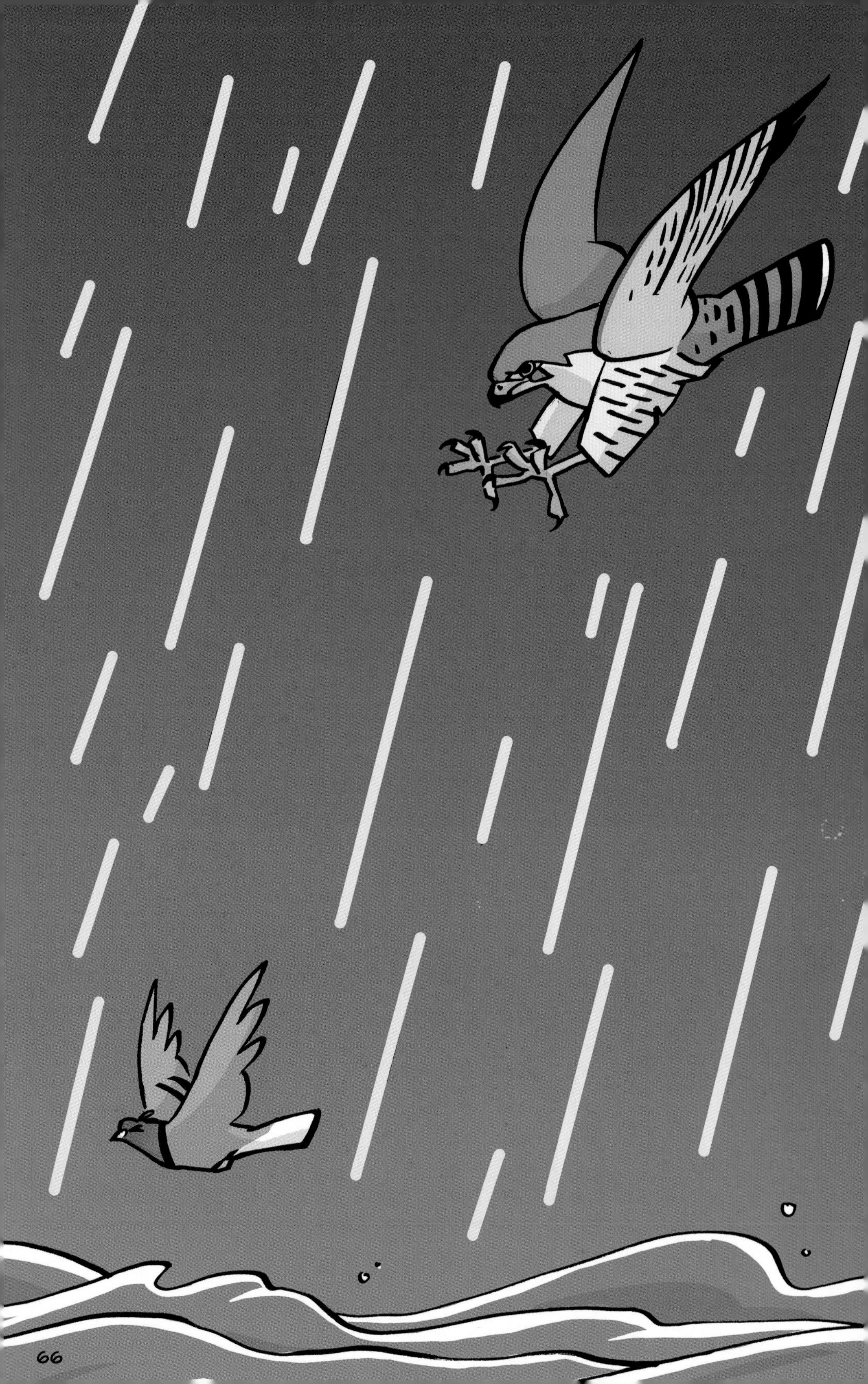

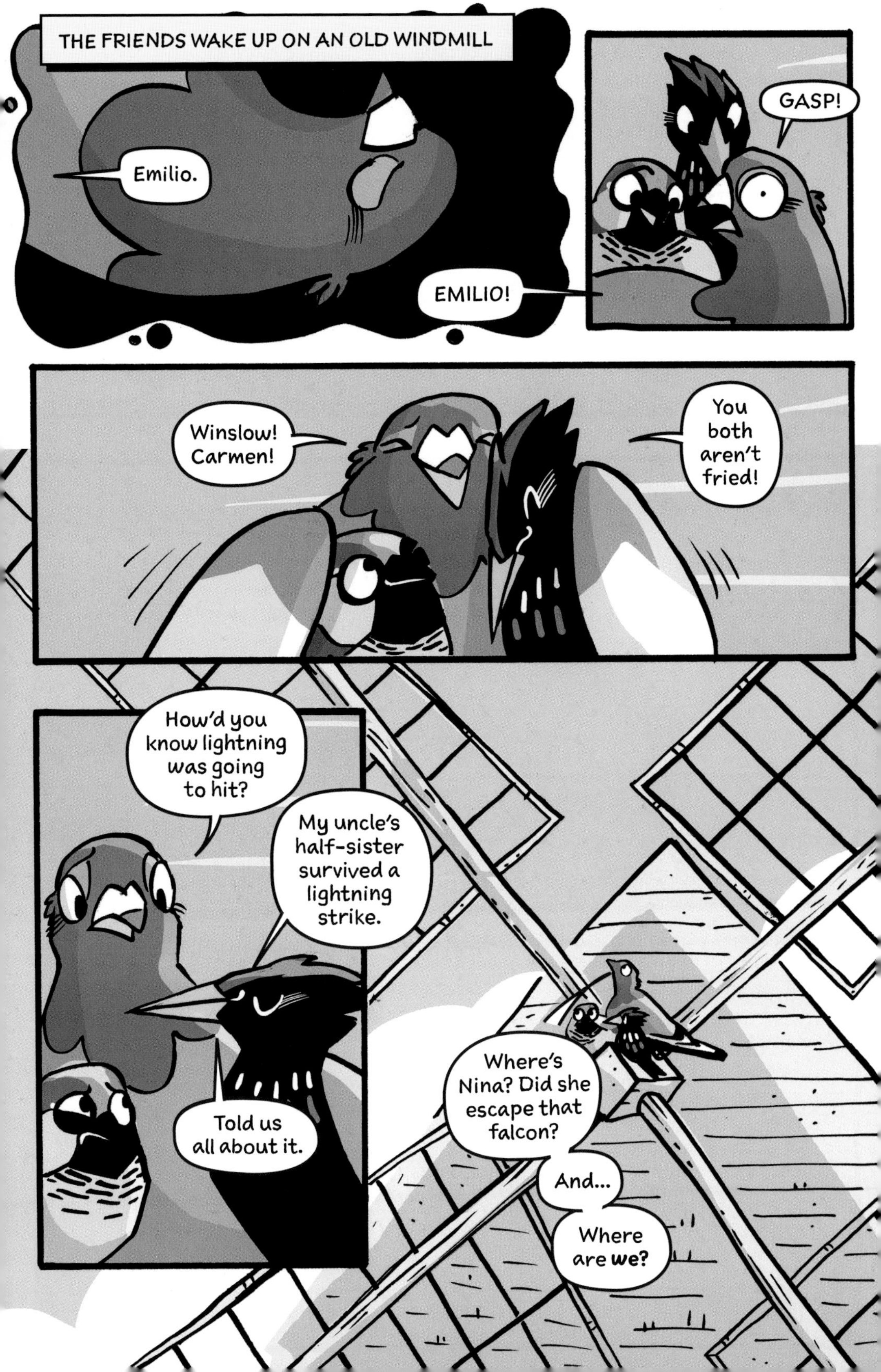
THE FRIENDS WAKE UP ON AN OLD WINDMILL
Emilio.
GASP!
EMILIO!
Winslow! Carmen!
You both aren't fried!
How'd you know lightning was going to hit?
My uncle's half-sister survived a lightning strike.
Told us all about it.
Where's Nina? Did she escape that falcon?
And...
Where are we?

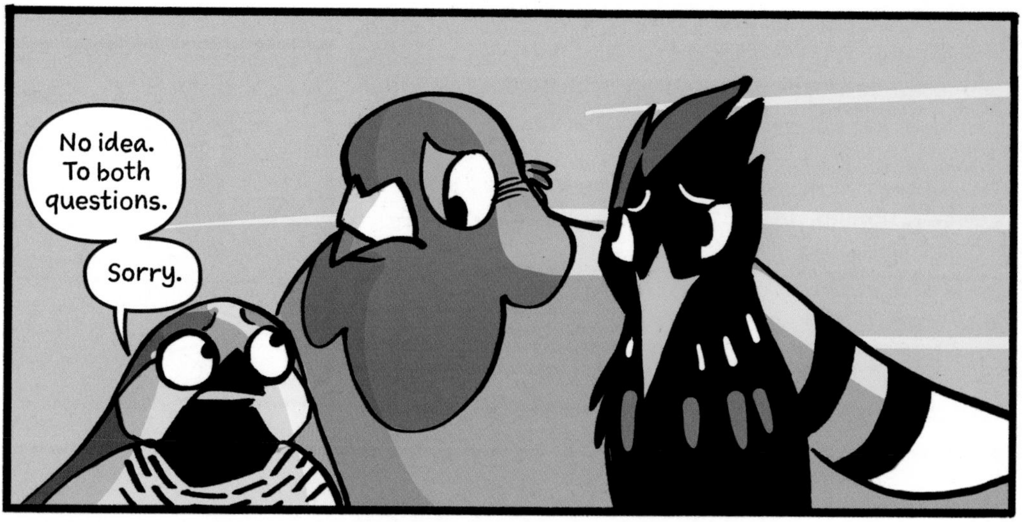
No idea. To both questions.
Sorry.

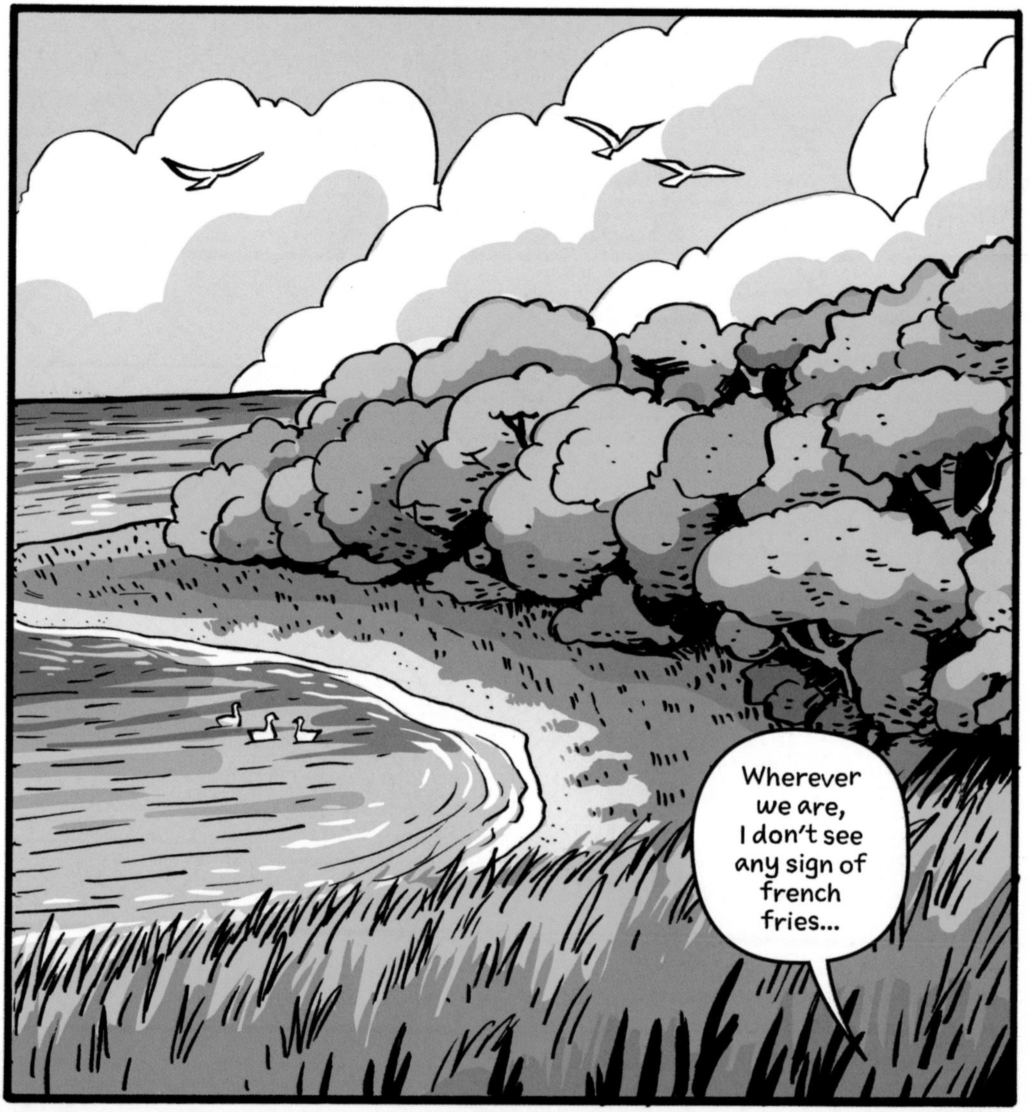
Wherever we are, I don't see any sign of french fries...

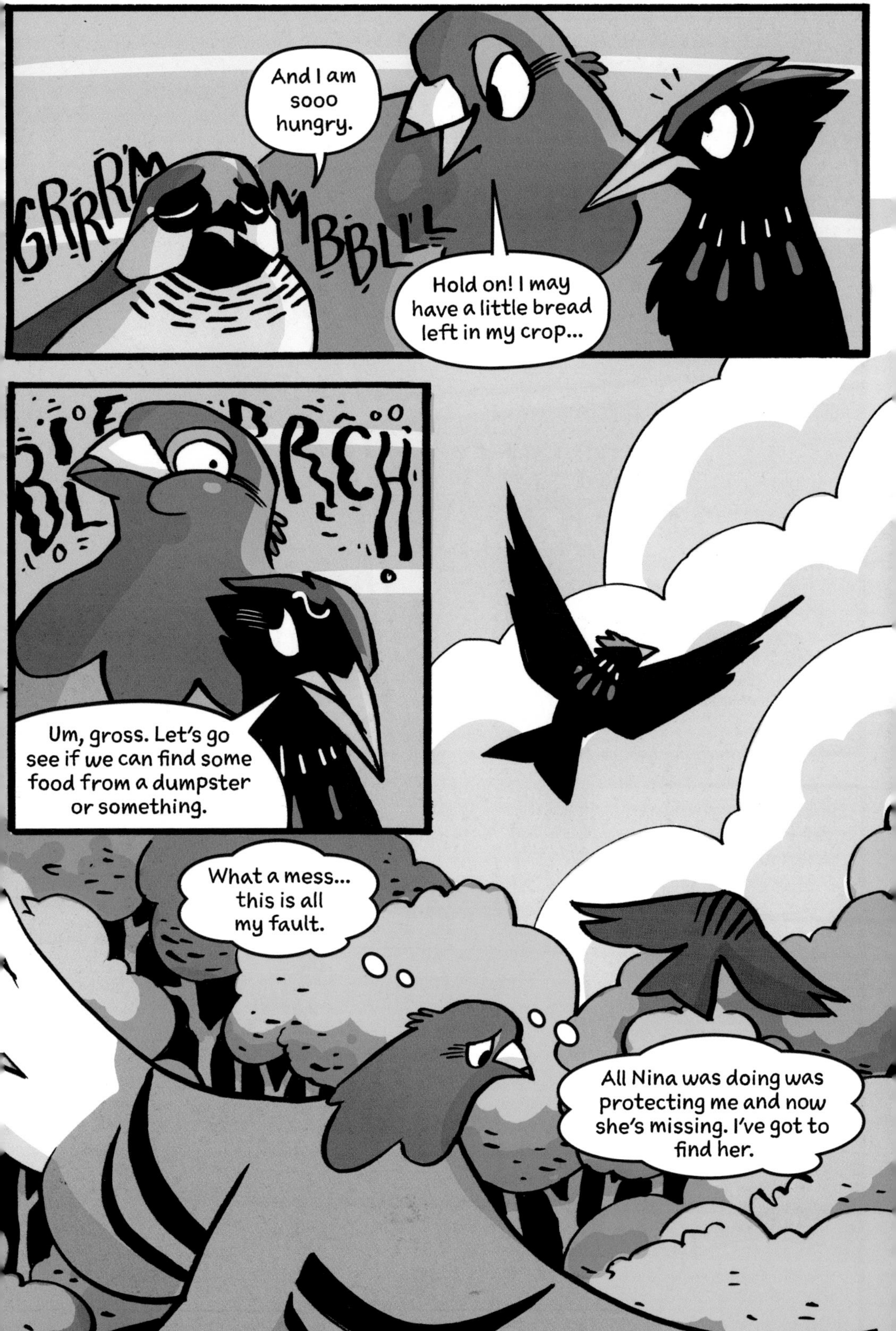

And I am sooo hungry.
GRRRMMBBLLL
Hold on! I may have a little bread left in my crop...
BLOFBRCH
Um, gross. Let's go see if we can find some food from a dumpster or something.
What a mess... this is all my fault.
All Nina was doing was protecting me and now she's missing. I've got to find her.

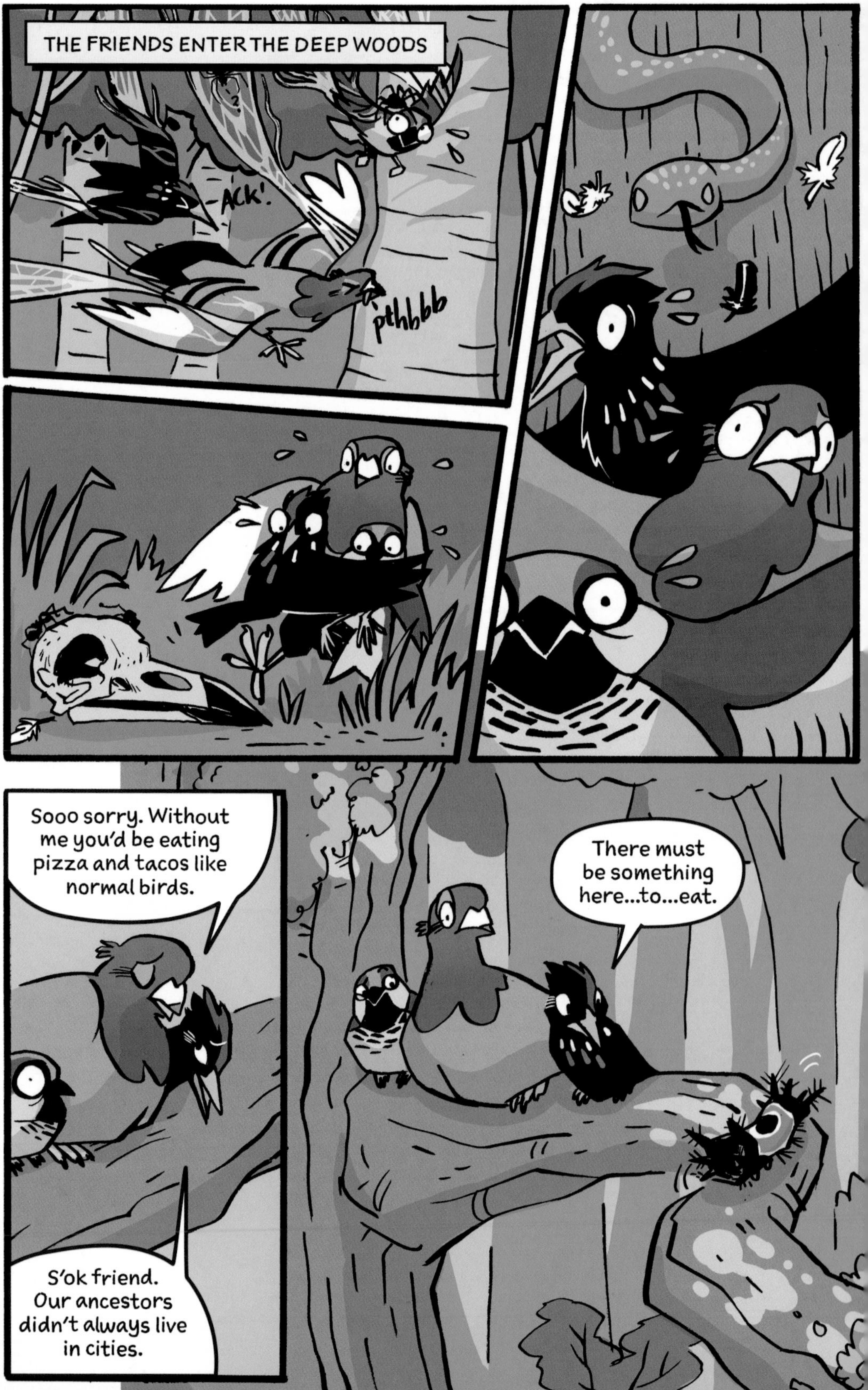
THE FRIENDS ENTER THE DEEP WOODS
ACK!
pthbbb
Sooo sorry. Without me you'd be eating pizza and tacos like normal birds.
S'ok friend. Our ancestors didn't always live in cities.
There must be something here...to...eat.

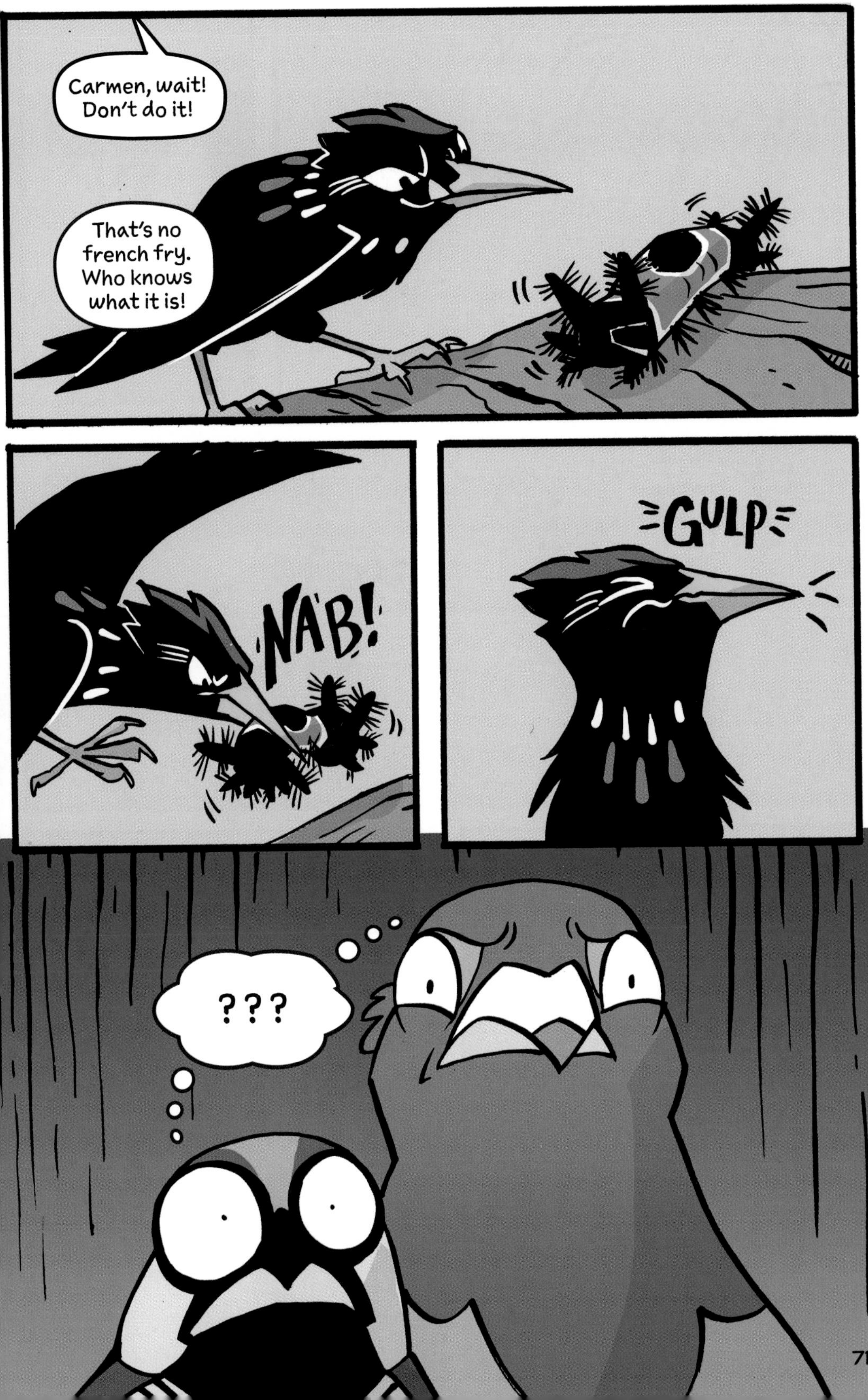
Carmen, wait! Don't do it!
That's no french fry. Who knows what it is!
NAB!
GULP
???

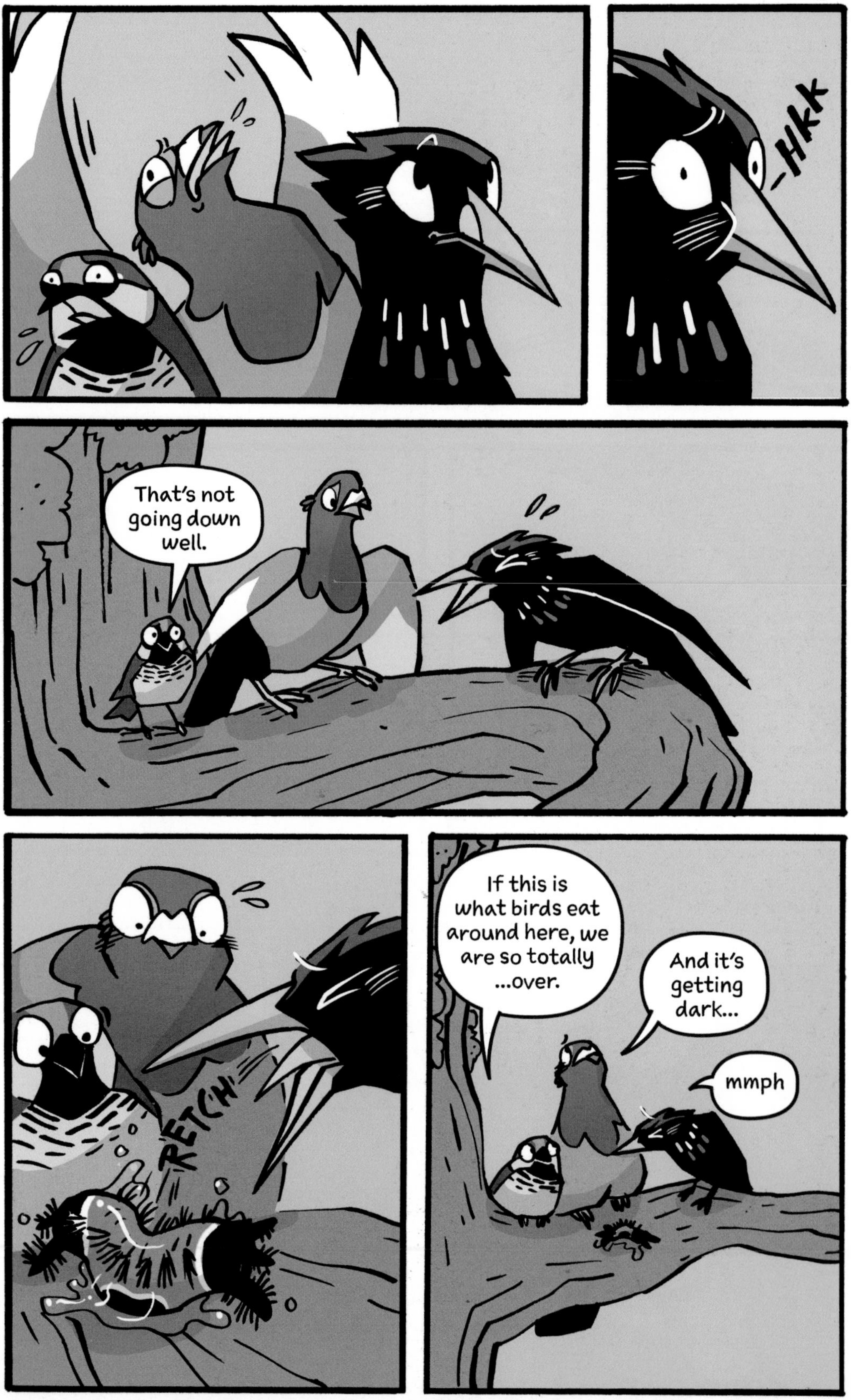

HKK
That's not going down well.
RETCH
If this is what birds eat around here, we are so totally ...over.
And it's getting dark...
mmph

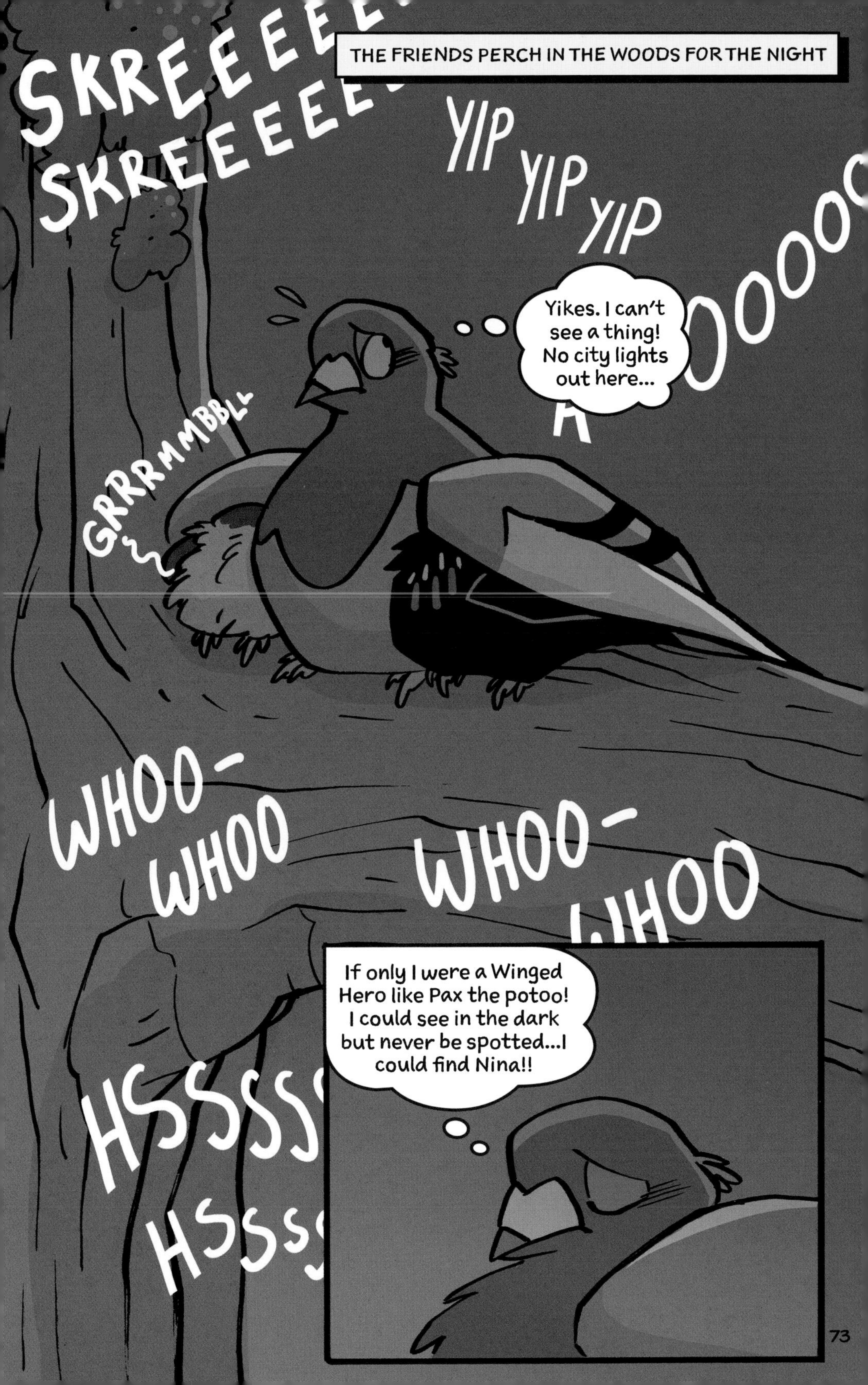
THE FRIENDS PERCH IN THE WOODS FOR THE NIGHT
SKREEEE
SKREEEEE
YIP YIP YIP
OOOOO
A
Yikes. I can't see a thing! No city lights out here...
GRRRMMBBLL
WHOO-WHOO
WHOO-WHOO
HSSSS
HSSS
If only I were a Winged Hero like Pax the potoo! I could see in the dark but never be spotted...I could find Nina!!

WINGED HERO: PAX—THE DECEIVER

PATIENT AND KIND, PAX IS THE GO-TO GUY FOR GATHERING SECRETS.

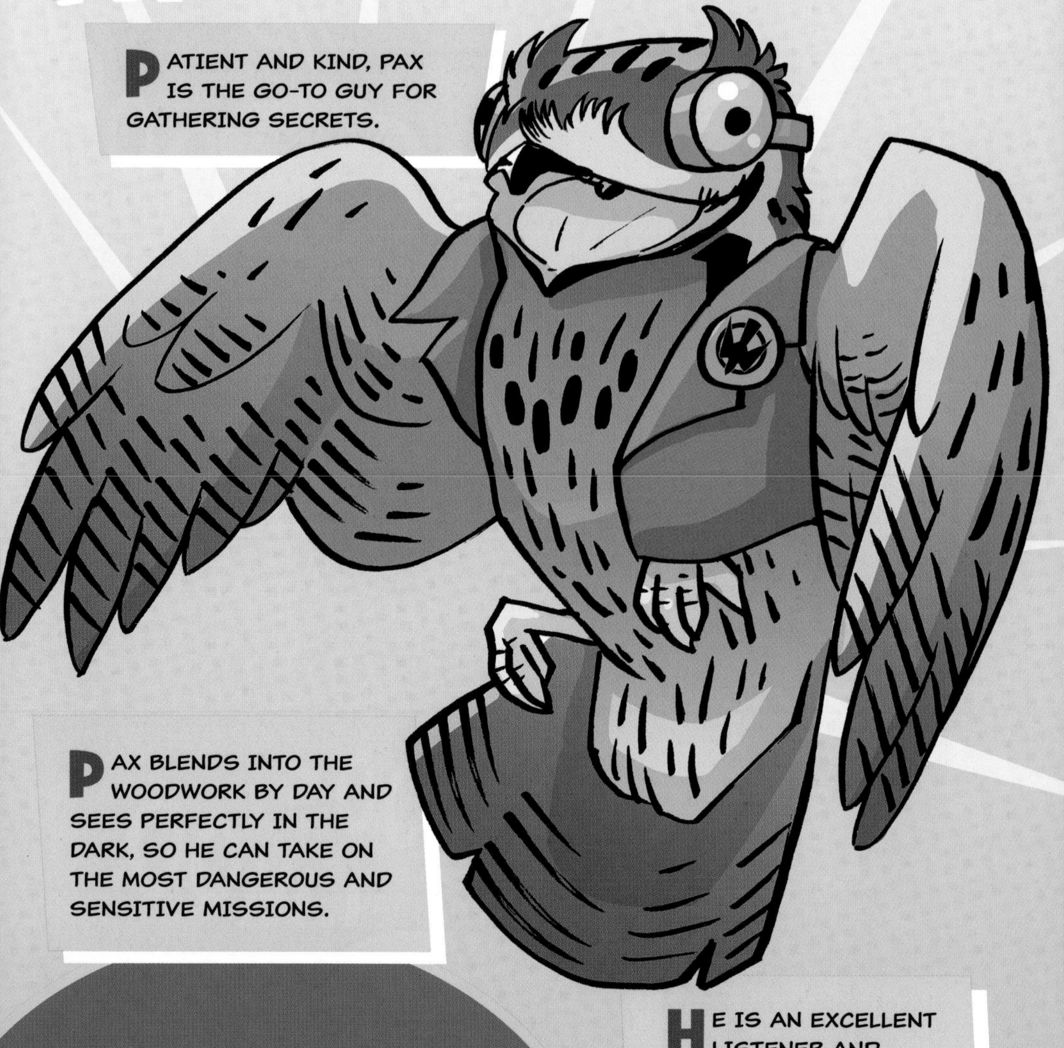

PAX BLENDS INTO THE WOODWORK BY DAY AND SEES PERFECTLY IN THE DARK, SO HE CAN TAKE ON THE MOST DANGEROUS AND SENSITIVE MISSIONS.

HE IS AN EXCELLENT LISTENER AND ALL THE HEROES GO TO HIM WITH THEIR PROBLEMS. RECRUITED FROM THE ZOO BY ARCTICA, PAX IS A VALUABLE FELLOW SPY.

JOB DESCRIPTION

UNDERCOVER AGENT

POWERS INCLUDE

- NEAR PERFECT CAMOUFLAGE
- HIGH-QUALITY NIGHT VISION

WEAKNESS

- SOMETIMES FALLS ASLEEP DURING THE DAY

THE REAL COMMON POTOO

(NYCTIBIUS GRISEUS)

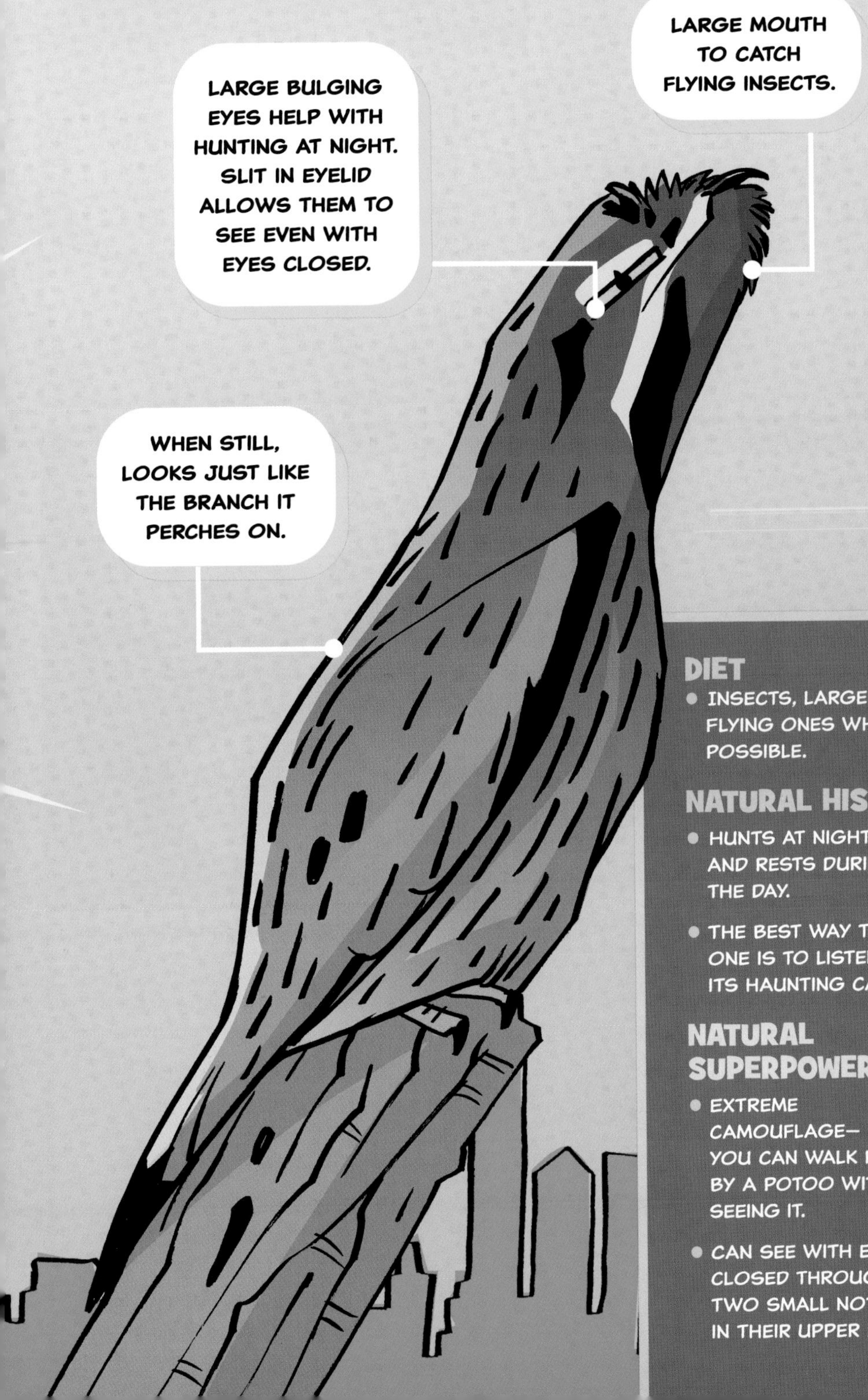
LARGE BULGING EYES HELP WITH HUNTING AT NIGHT. SLIT IN EYELID ALLOWS THEM TO SEE EVEN WITH EYES CLOSED.
LARGE MOUTH TO CATCH FLYING INSECTS.
WHEN STILL, LOOKS JUST LIKE THE BRANCH IT PERCHES ON.

DIET

- INSECTS, LARGE FLYING ONES WHEN POSSIBLE.

NATURAL HISTORY

- HUNTS AT NIGHT AND RESTS DURING THE DAY.
- THE BEST WAY TO FIND ONE IS TO LISTEN FOR ITS HAUNTING CALL.

NATURAL SUPERPOWERS

- EXTREME CAMOUFLAGE—YOU CAN WALK RIGHT BY A POTOO WITHOUT SEEING IT.
- CAN SEE WITH EYES CLOSED THROUGH TWO SMALL NOTCHES IN THEIR UPPER EYELID.

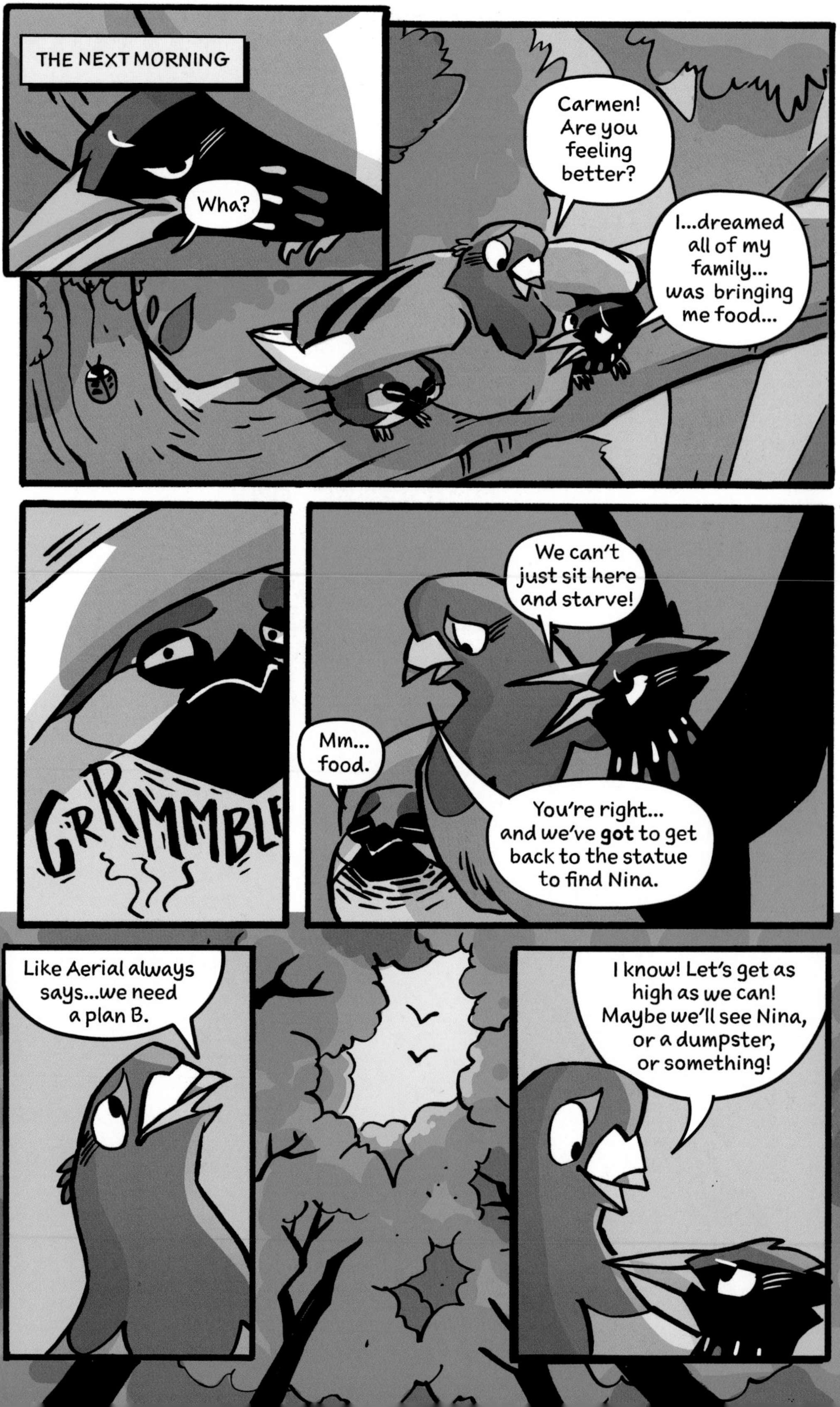

THE NEXT MORNING
Wha?
Carmen! Are you feeling better?
I...dreamed all of my family... was bringing me food...
GRRMMBLE
We can't just sit here and starve!
Mm... food.
You're right... and we've **got** to get back to the statue to find Nina.
Like Aerial always says...we need a plan B.
I know! Let's get as high as we can! Maybe we'll see Nina, or a dumpster, or something!

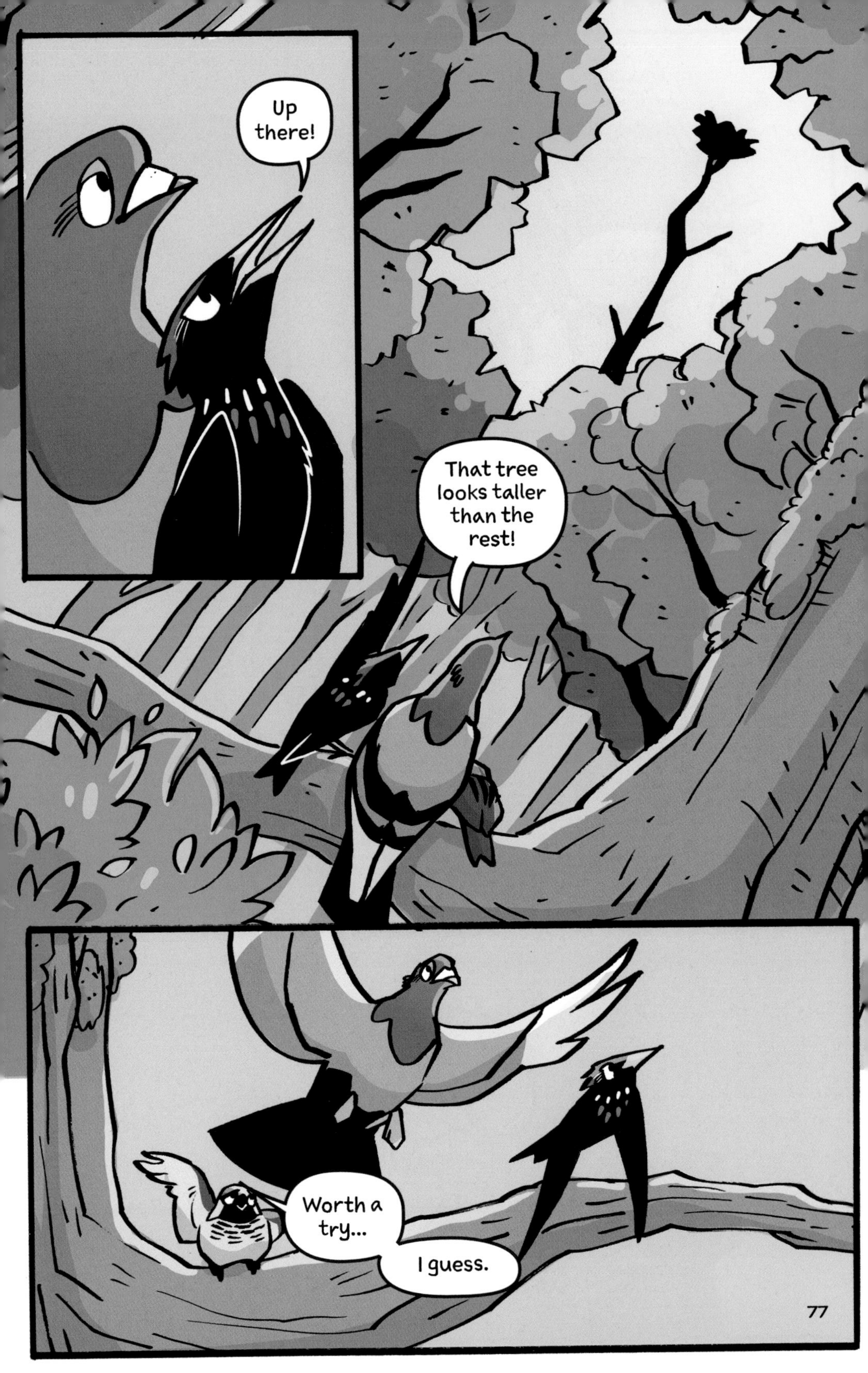
Up there!
That tree looks taller than the rest!
Worth a try...
I guess.

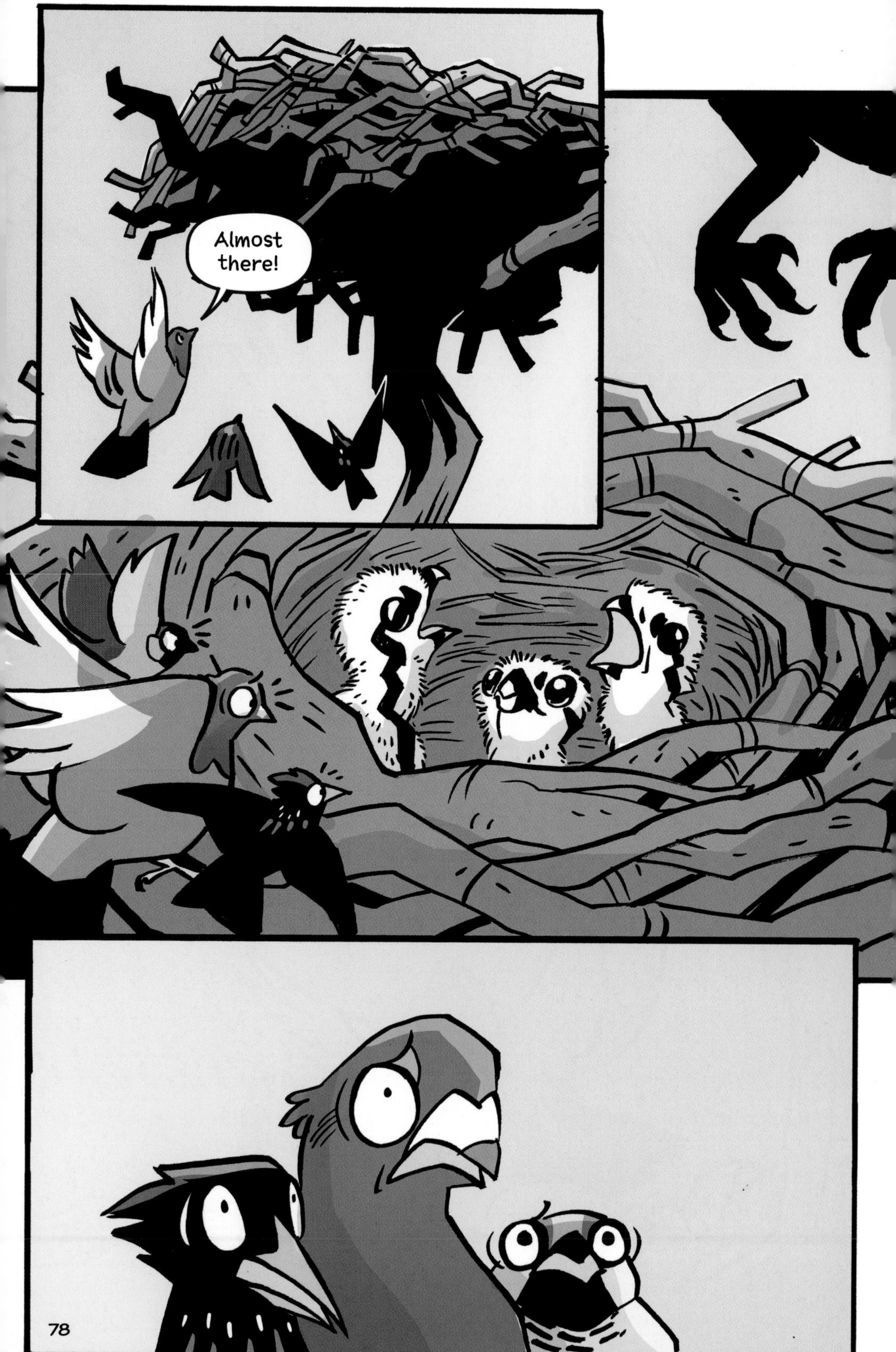
Almost there!

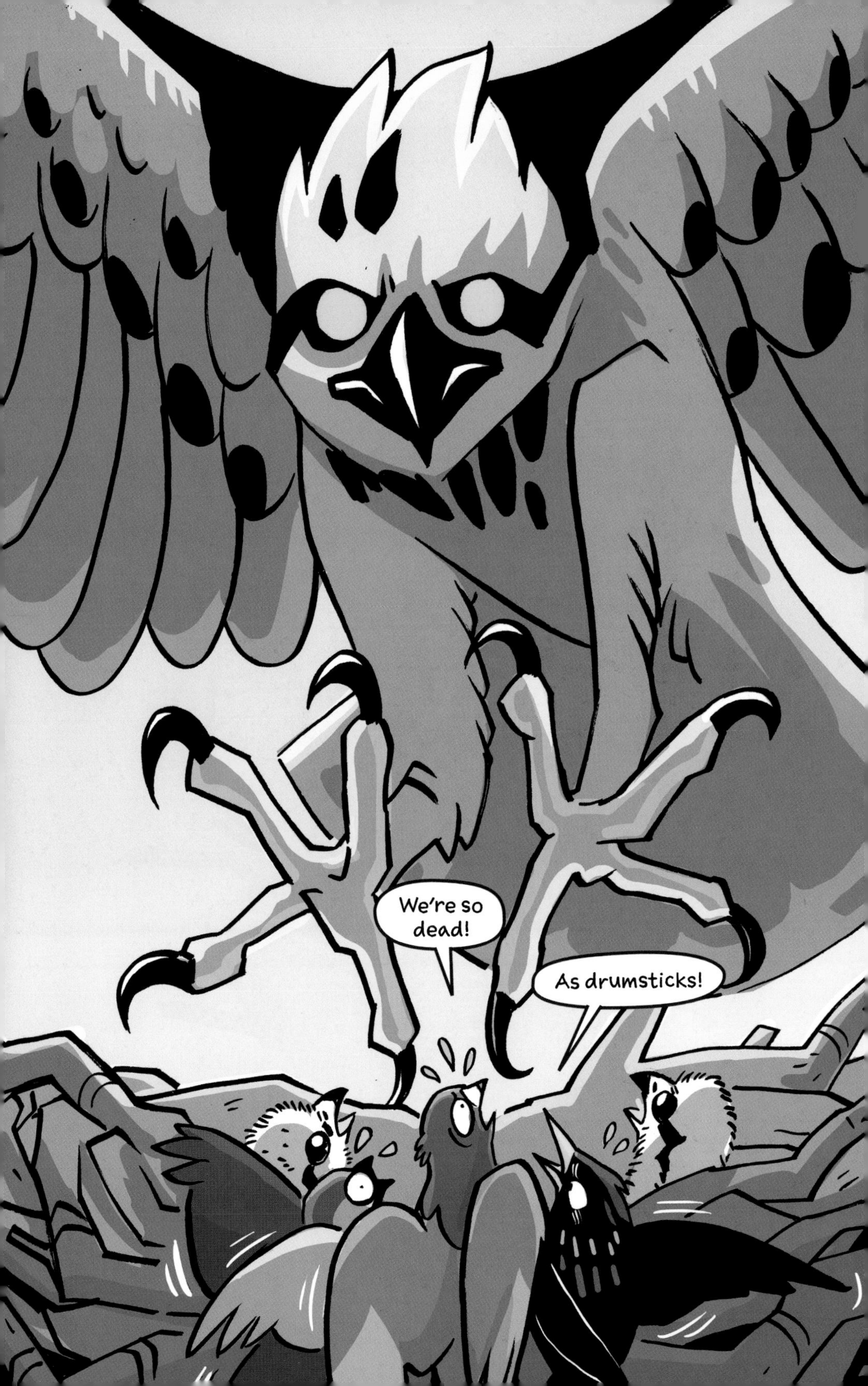
We're so dead!
As drumsticks!

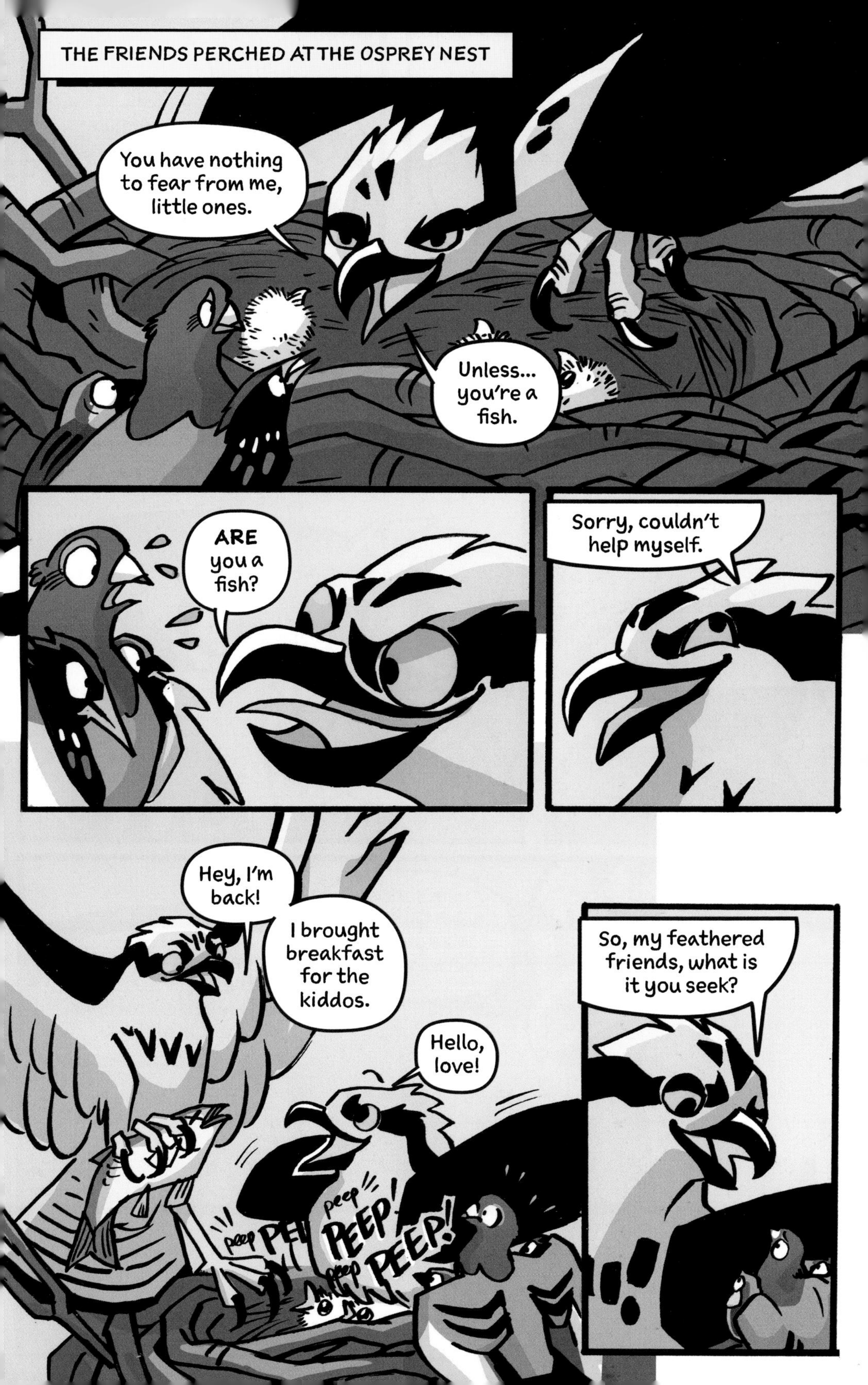
THE FRIENDS PERCHED AT THE OSPREY NEST
You have nothing to fear from me, little ones.
Unless... you're a fish.
ARE you a fish?
Sorry, couldn't help myself.
Hey, I'm back!
I brought breakfast for the kiddos.
Hello, love!
peep PEEP
peep PEEP!
PEEP!
peep
So, my feathered friends, what is it you seek?

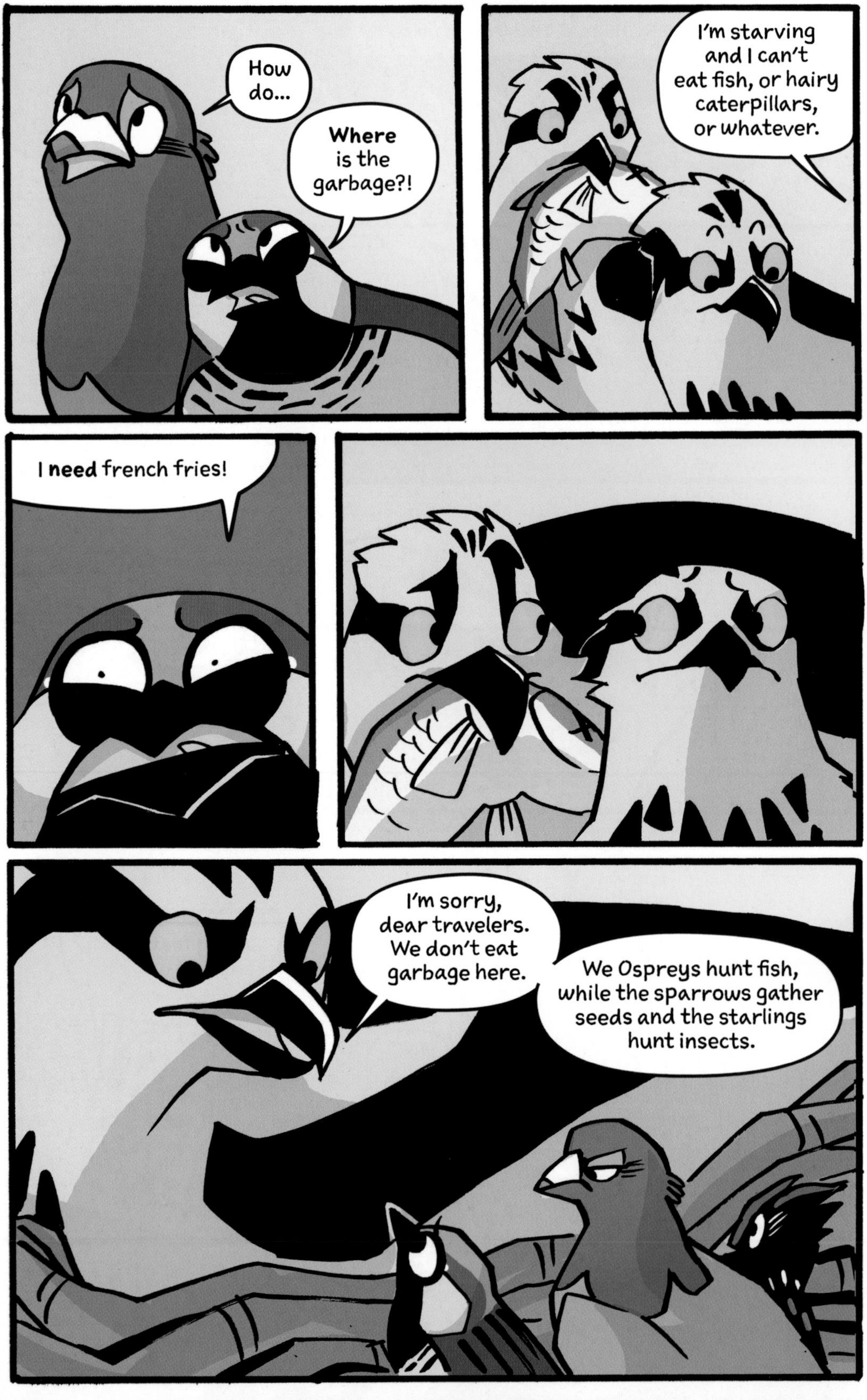
How do...
Where is the garbage?!
I'm starving and I can't eat fish, or hairy caterpillars, or whatever.
I need french fries!
I'm sorry, dear travelers. We don't eat garbage here.
We Ospreys hunt fish, while the sparrows gather seeds and the starlings hunt insects.

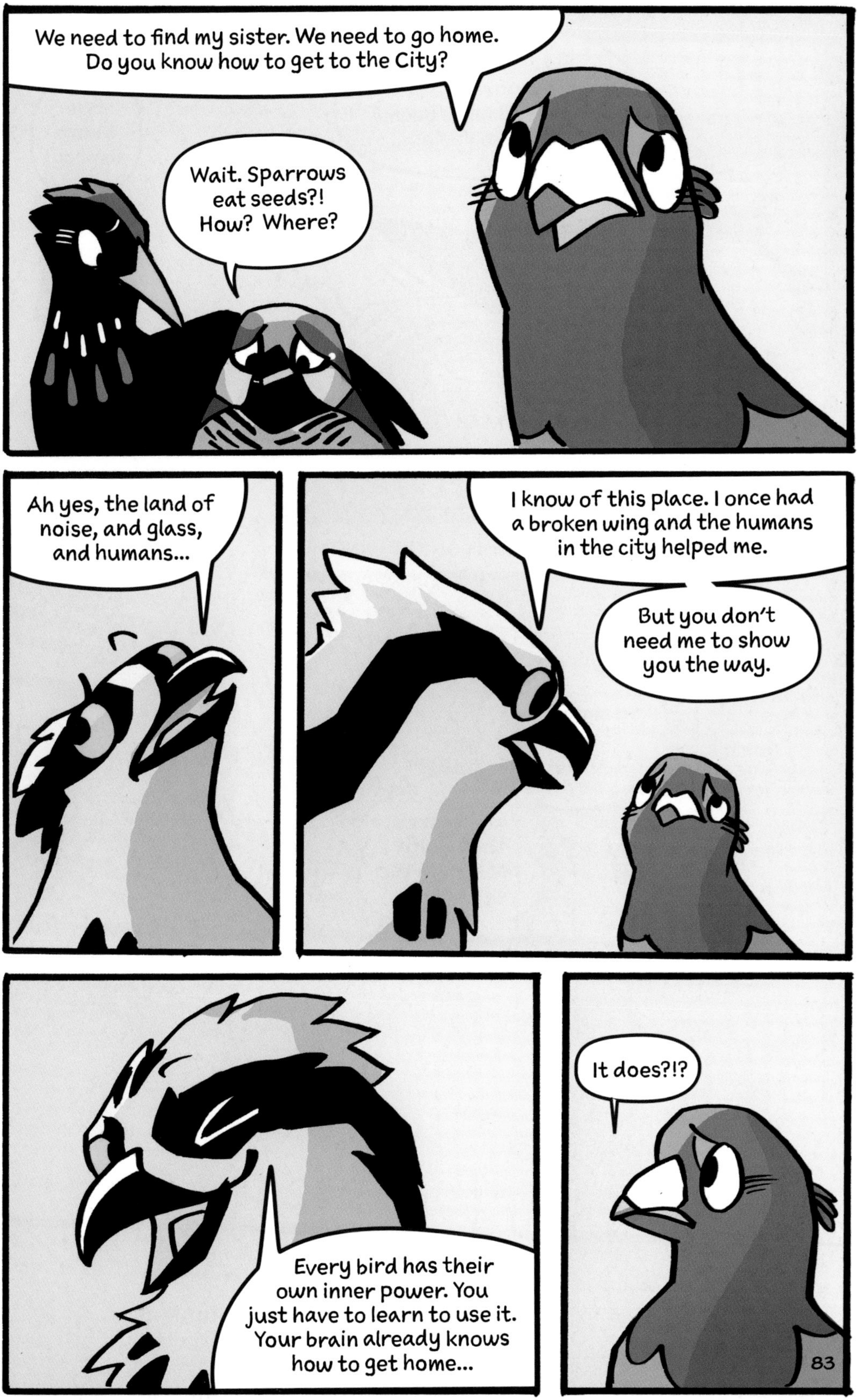
We need to find my sister. We need to go home. Do you know how to get to the City?
Wait. Sparrows eat seeds?! How? Where?
Ah yes, the land of noise, and glass, and humans...
I know of this place. I once had a broken wing and the humans in the city helped me.
But you don't need me to show you the way.
Every bird has their own inner power. You just have to learn to use it. Your brain already knows how to get home...
It does?!?
83

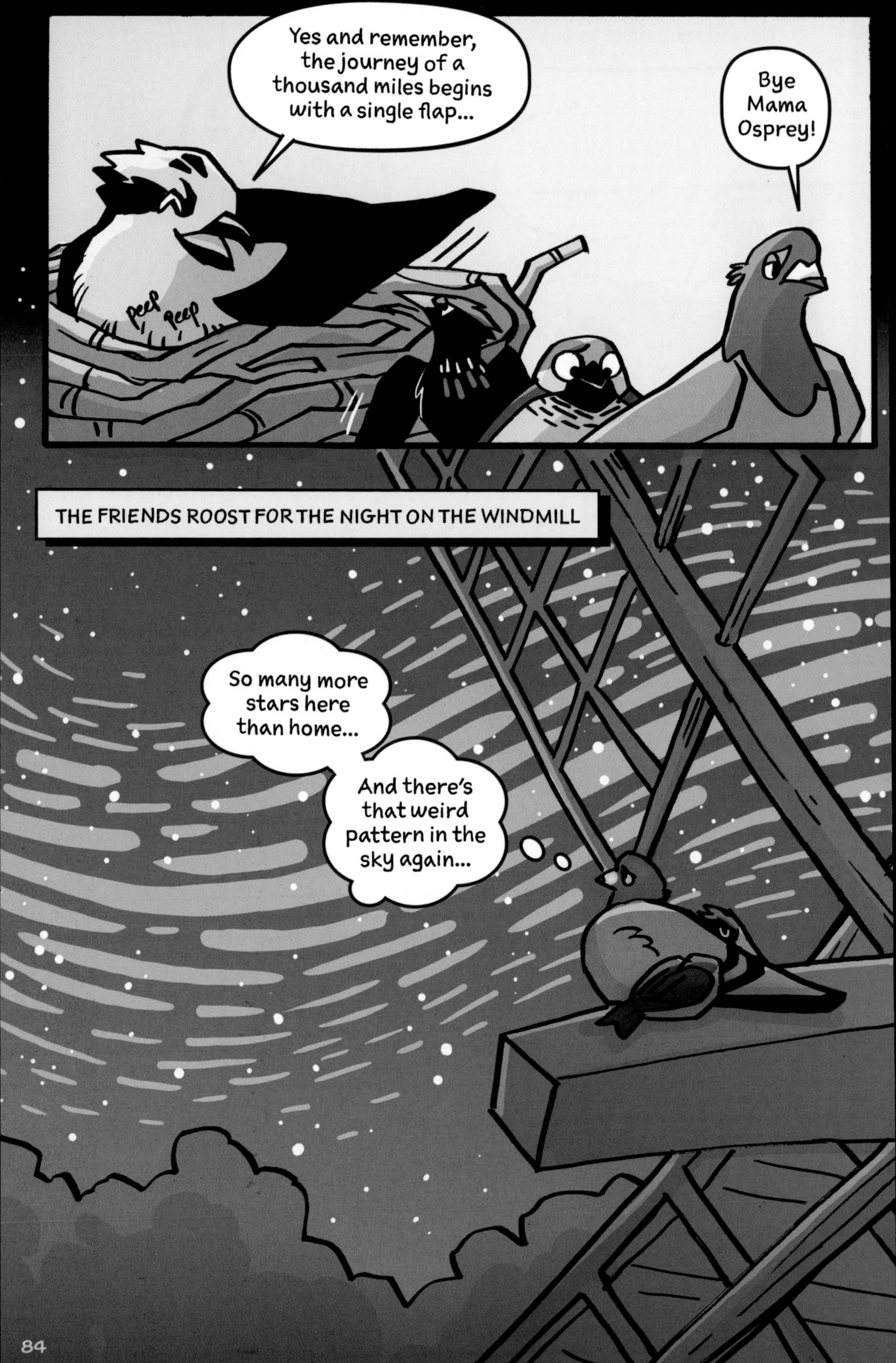

Yes and remember, the journey of a thousand miles begins with a single flap...
peep peep
Bye Mama Osprey!
THE FRIENDS ROOST FOR THE NIGHT ON THE WINDMILL
So many more stars here than home...
And there's that weird pattern in the sky again...

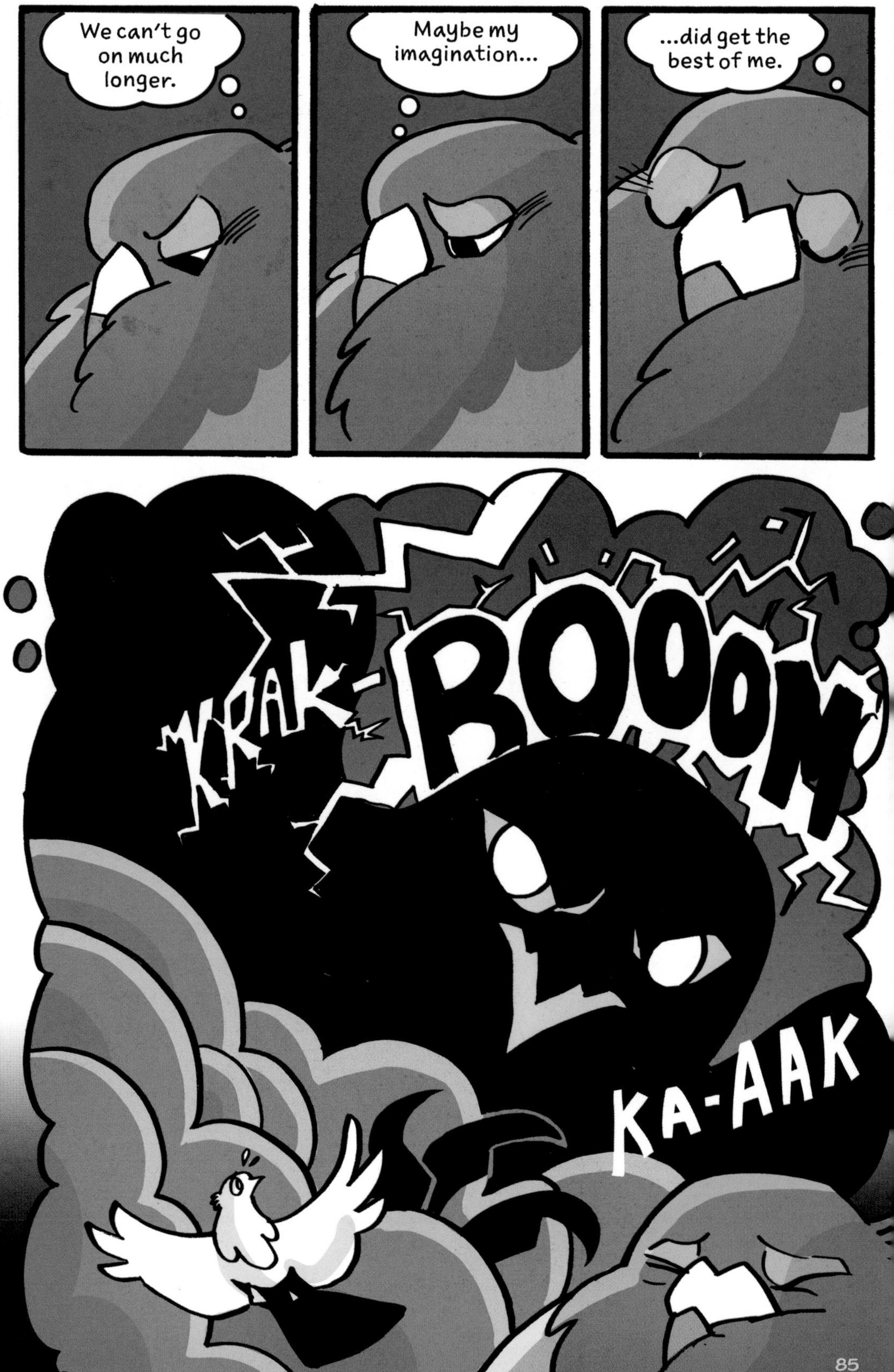
We can't go on much longer.
Maybe my imagination...
...did get the best of me.
KRAK-BOOOOM
KA-AAK

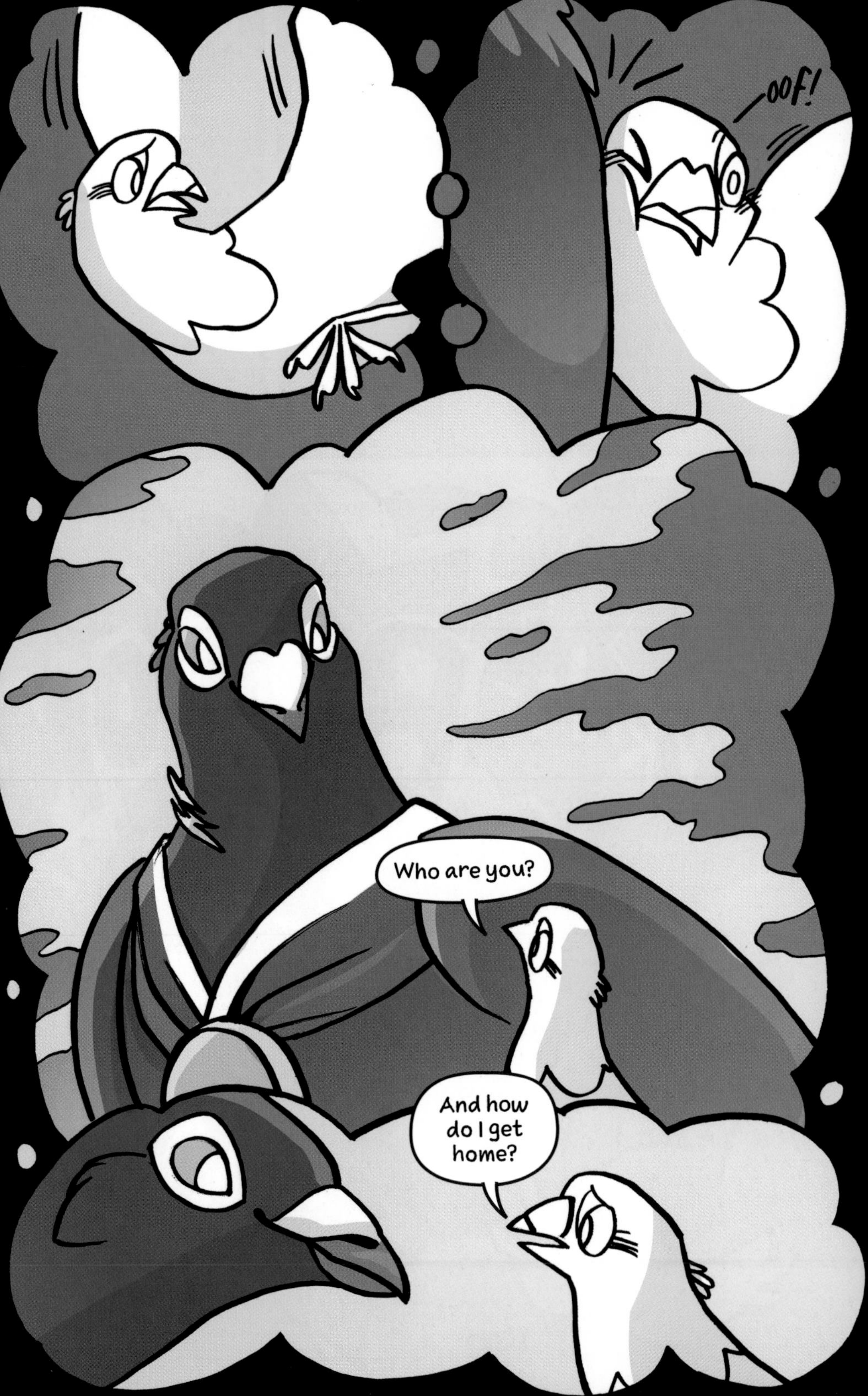
OOF!
Who are you?
And how do I get home?

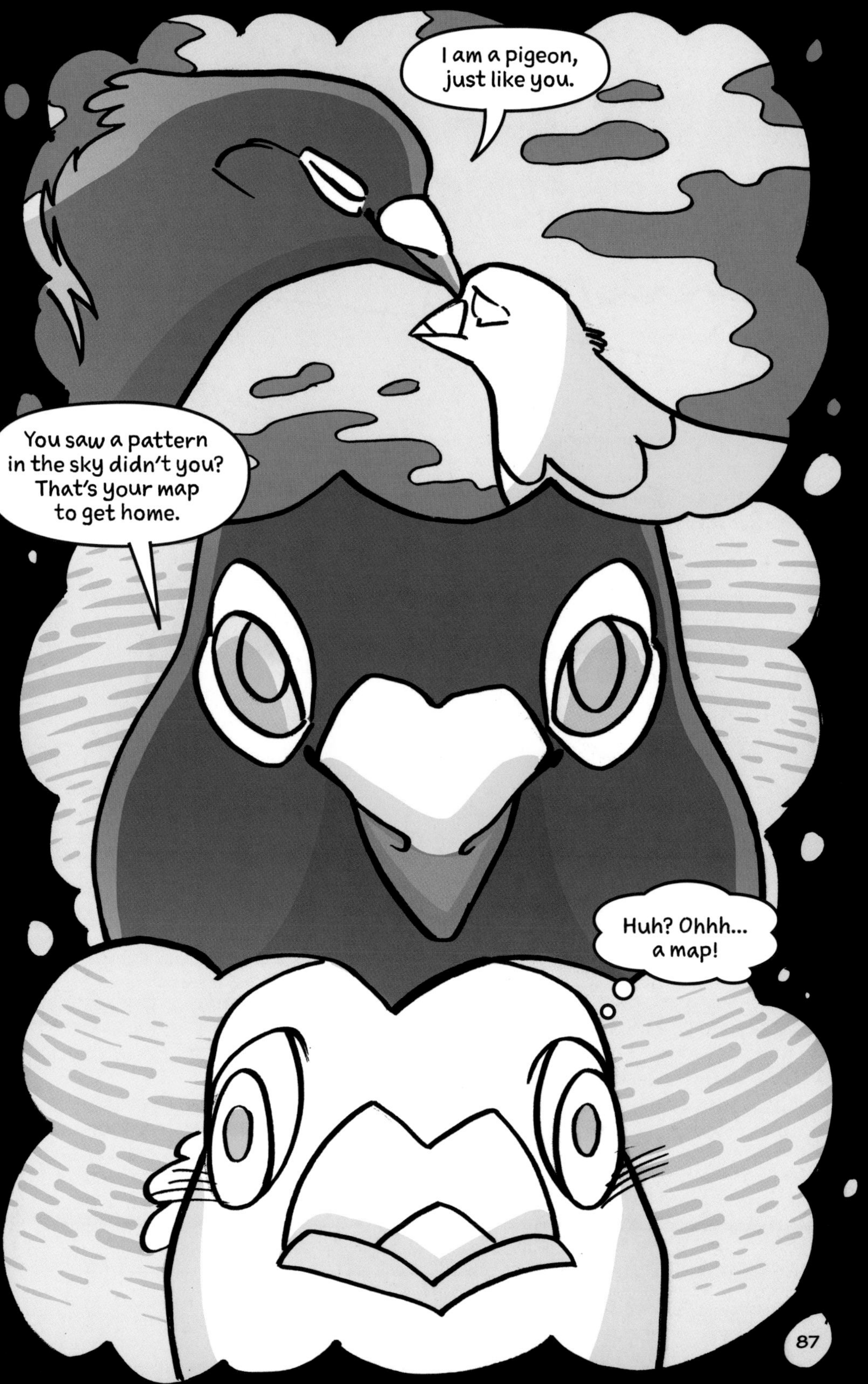
I am a pigeon, just like you.
You saw a pattern in the sky didn't you? That's your map to get home.
Huh? Ohhh... a map!

REAL LIFE HERO: MARY OF EXETER— THE MESSENGER

FACT NOT FICTION

BRAVE AND HARDWORKING, MARY OF EXETER WAS A HOMING PIGEON TRAINED TO DELIVER MESSAGES TO BRITISH SOLDIERS IN WORLD WAR II.

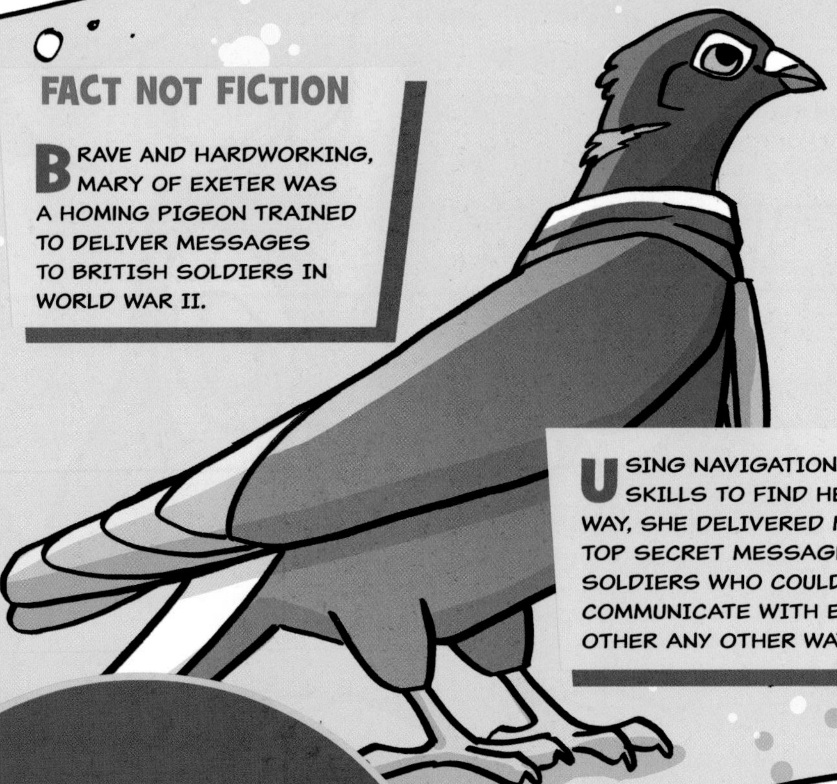

USING NAVIGATION SKILLS TO FIND HER WAY, SHE DELIVERED MANY TOP SECRET MESSAGES TO SOLDIERS WHO COULD NOT COMMUNICATE WITH EACH OTHER ANY OTHER WAY.

JOB DESCRIPTION

WINGED SOLDIER AND REAL-LIFE HERO

POWERS INCLUDE

- ABILITY TO FLY UNDETECTED THROUGH ENEMY TERRITORY
- POWERFUL NAVIGATION SKILLS

WEAKNESS

- MARY OF EXETER HAD NO DOCUMENTED WEAKNESSES

MARY OF EXETER BECAME FAMOUS BECAUSE SHE DELIVERED A MESSAGE AND GOT BACK HOME SAFELY EVEN AFTER BEING ATTACKED BY A HAWK TRAINED BY THE GERMAN ARMY. SHE RECEIVED A MEDAL FOR HER SERVICE.

THE REAL HOMING PIGEON

(COLUMBA LIVIA DOMESTICA)

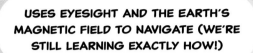

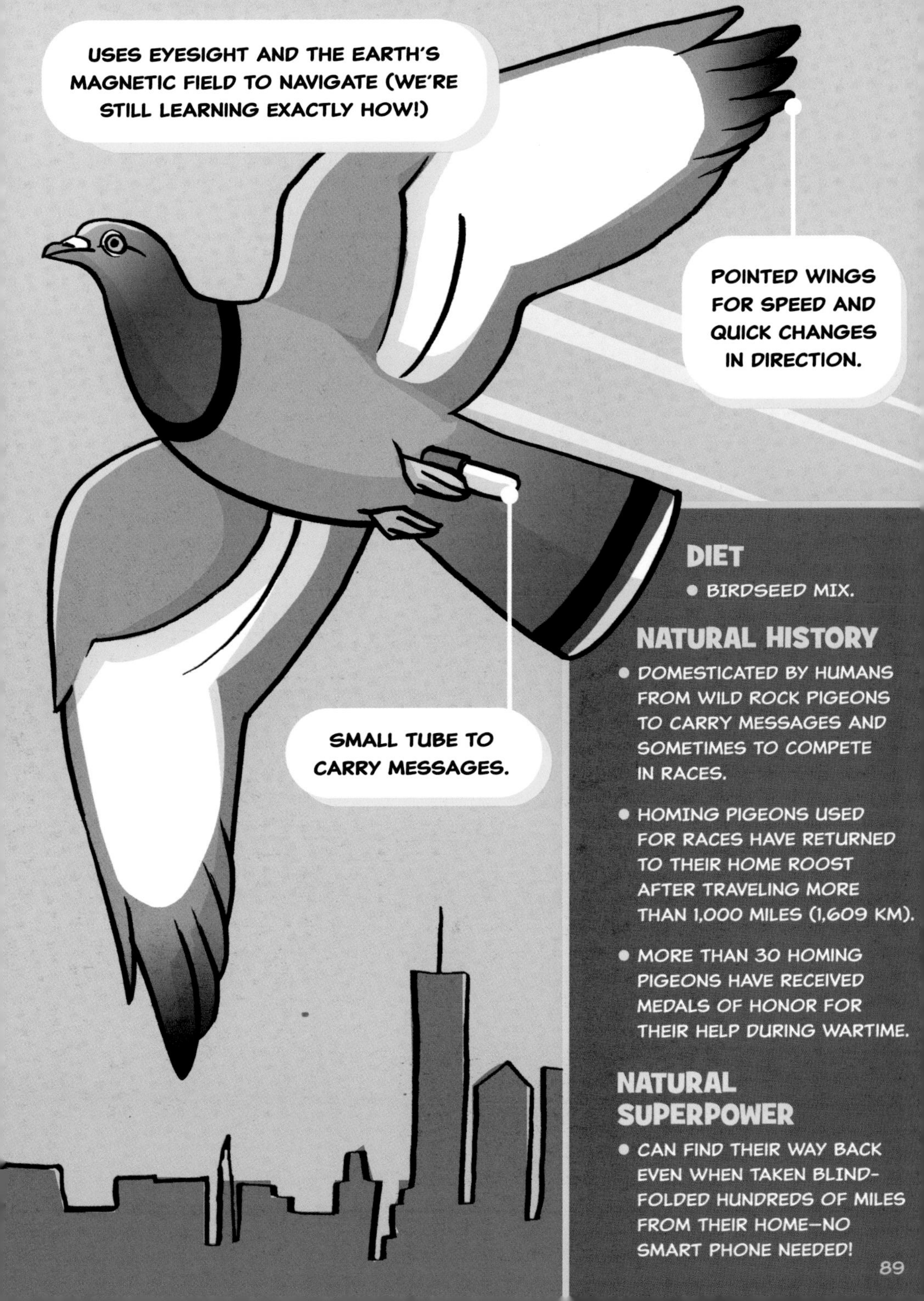

USES EYESIGHT AND THE EARTH'S MAGNETIC FIELD TO NAVIGATE (WE'RE STILL LEARNING EXACTLY HOW!)

POINTED WINGS FOR SPEED AND QUICK CHANGES IN DIRECTION.

SMALL TUBE TO CARRY MESSAGES.

DIET

- BIRDSEED MIX.

NATURAL HISTORY

- DOMESTICATED BY HUMANS FROM WILD ROCK PIGEONS TO CARRY MESSAGES AND SOMETIMES TO COMPETE IN RACES.

- HOMING PIGEONS USED FOR RACES HAVE RETURNED TO THEIR HOME ROOST AFTER TRAVELING MORE THAN 1,000 MILES (1,609 KM).

- MORE THAN 30 HOMING PIGEONS HAVE RECEIVED MEDALS OF HONOR FOR THEIR HELP DURING WARTIME.

NATURAL SUPERPOWER

- CAN FIND THEIR WAY BACK EVEN WHEN TAKEN BLIND-FOLDED HUNDREDS OF MILES FROM THEIR HOME—NO SMART PHONE NEEDED!

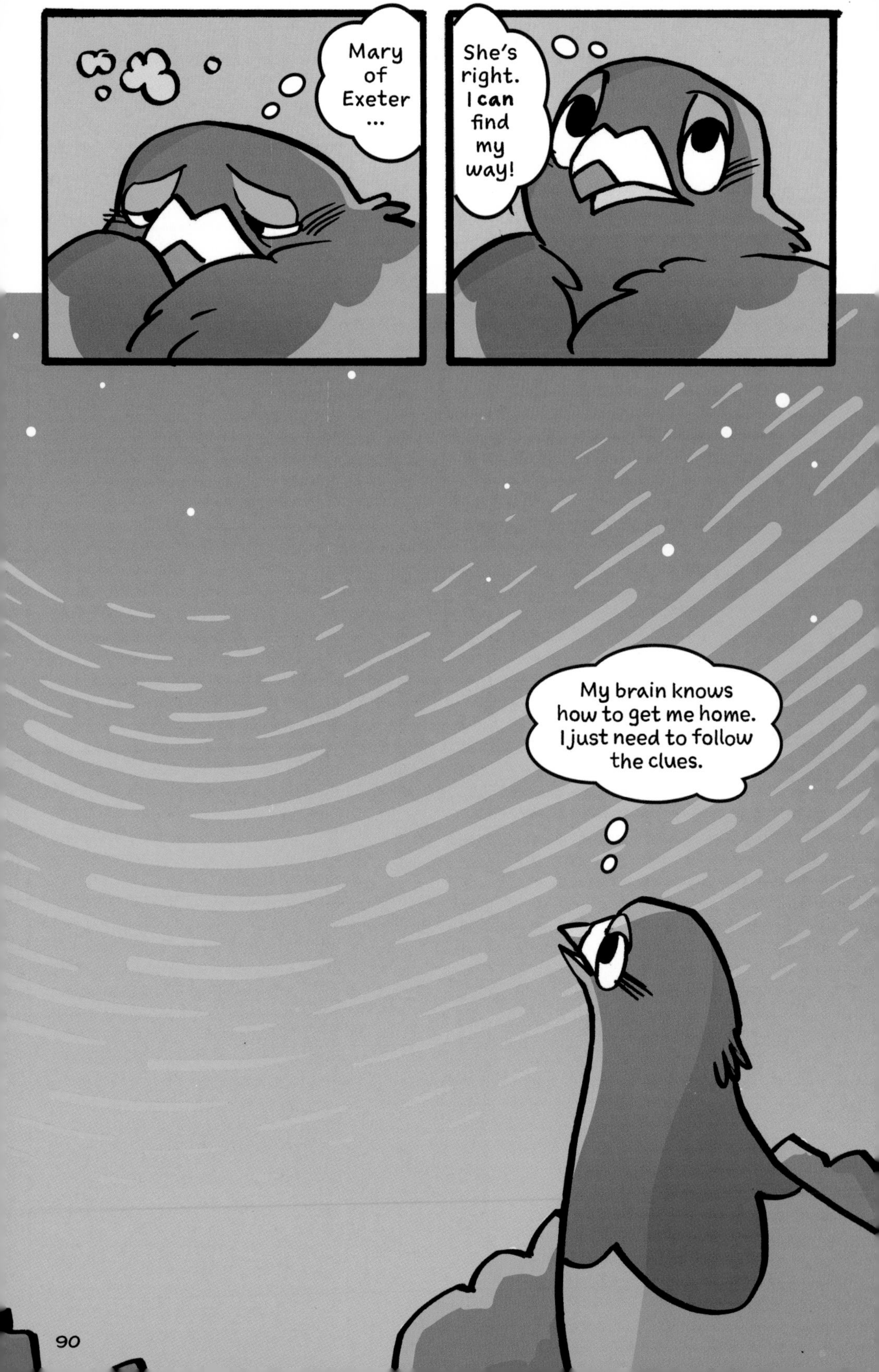
Mary of Exeter ...
She's right. I **can** find my way!
My brain knows how to get me home. I just need to follow the clues.

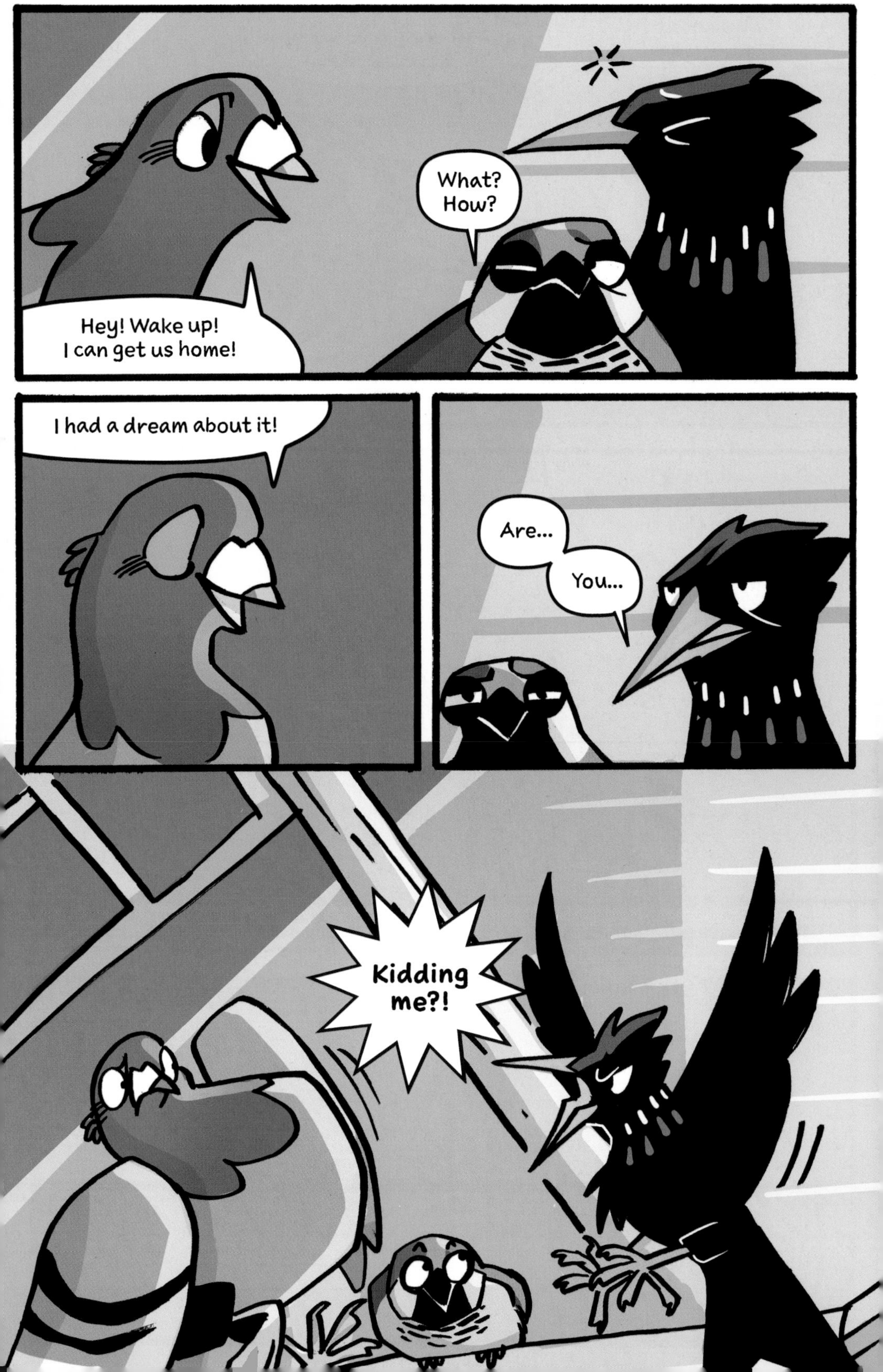
What? How?
Hey! Wake up! I can get us home!
I had a dream about it!
Are...
You...
Kidding me?!

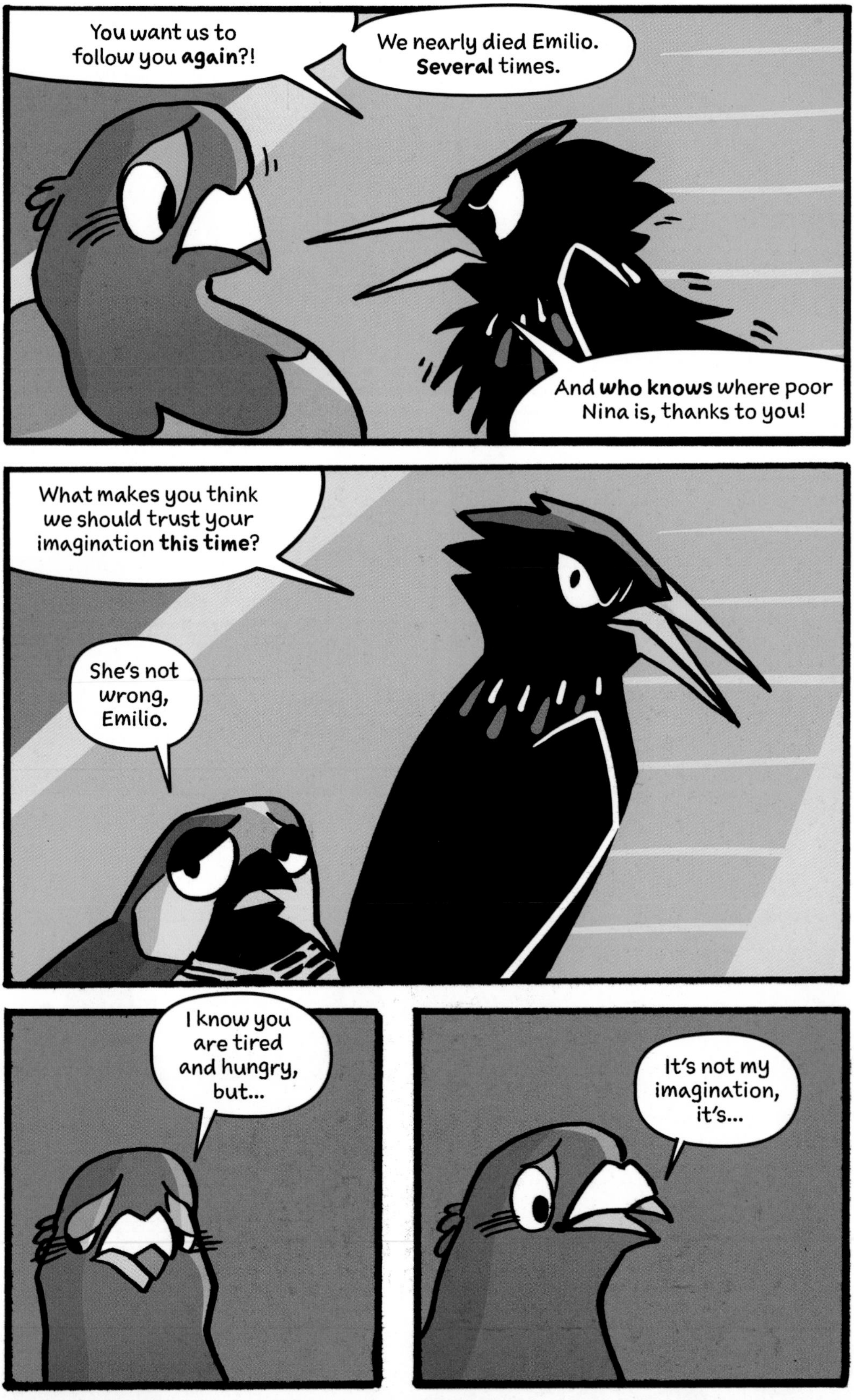
You want us to follow you again?!
We nearly died Emilio. Several times.
And who knows where poor Nina is, thanks to you!
What makes you think we should trust your imagination this time?
She's not wrong, Emilio.
I know you are tired and hungry, but...
It's not my imagination, it's...

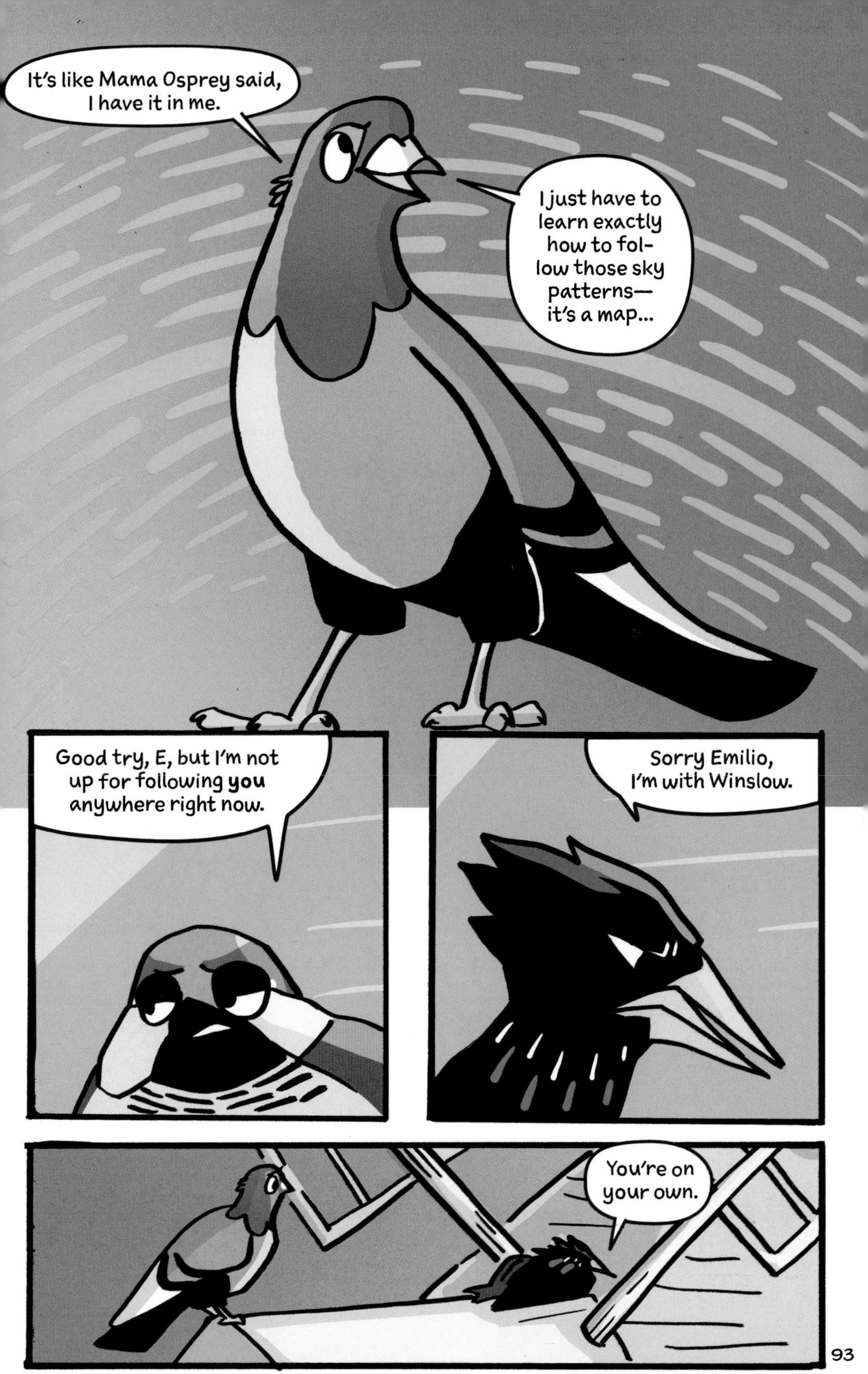
It's like Mama Osprey said, I have it in me.
I just have to learn exactly how to fol-low those sky patterns—it's a map...
Good try, E, but I'm not up for following **you** anywhere right now.
Sorry Emilio, I'm with Winslow.
You're on your own.

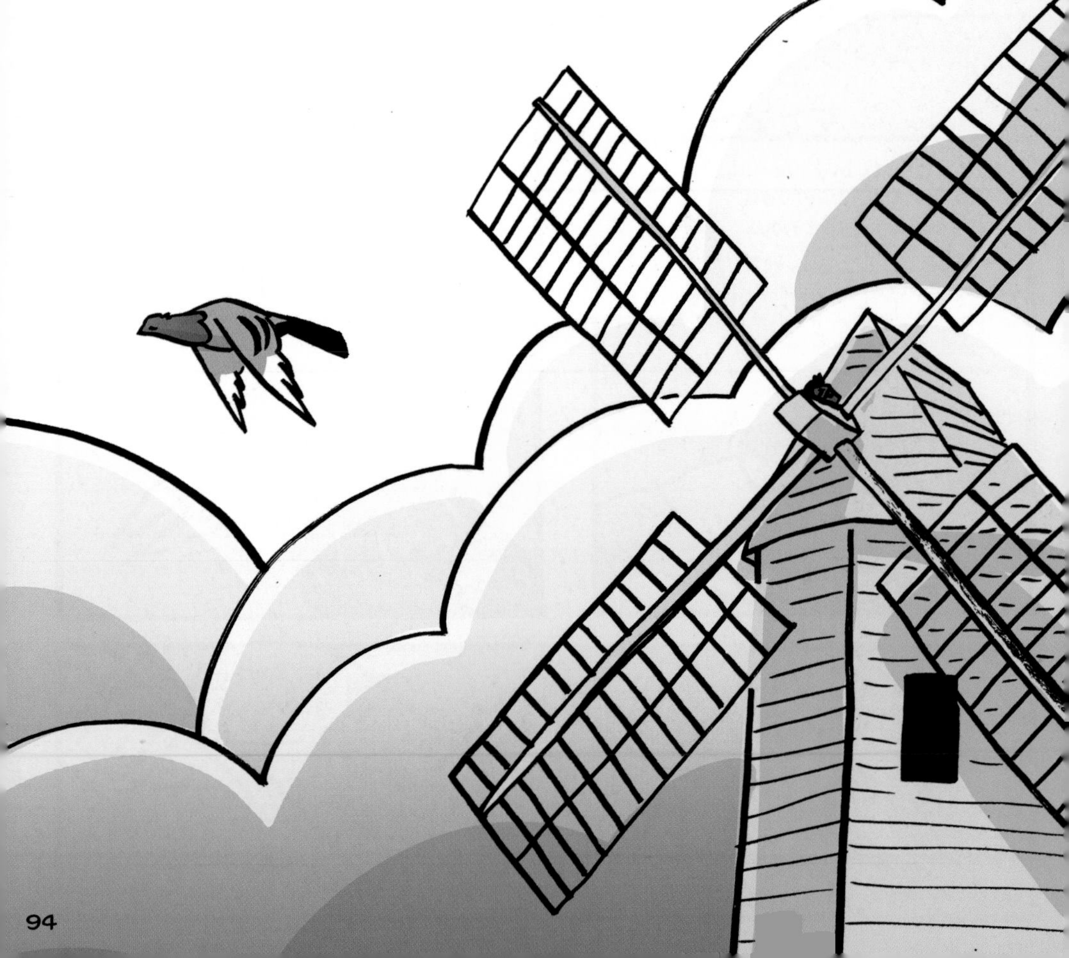

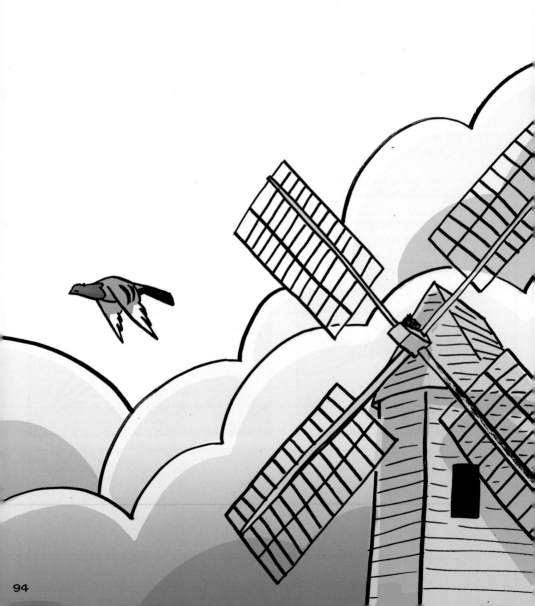

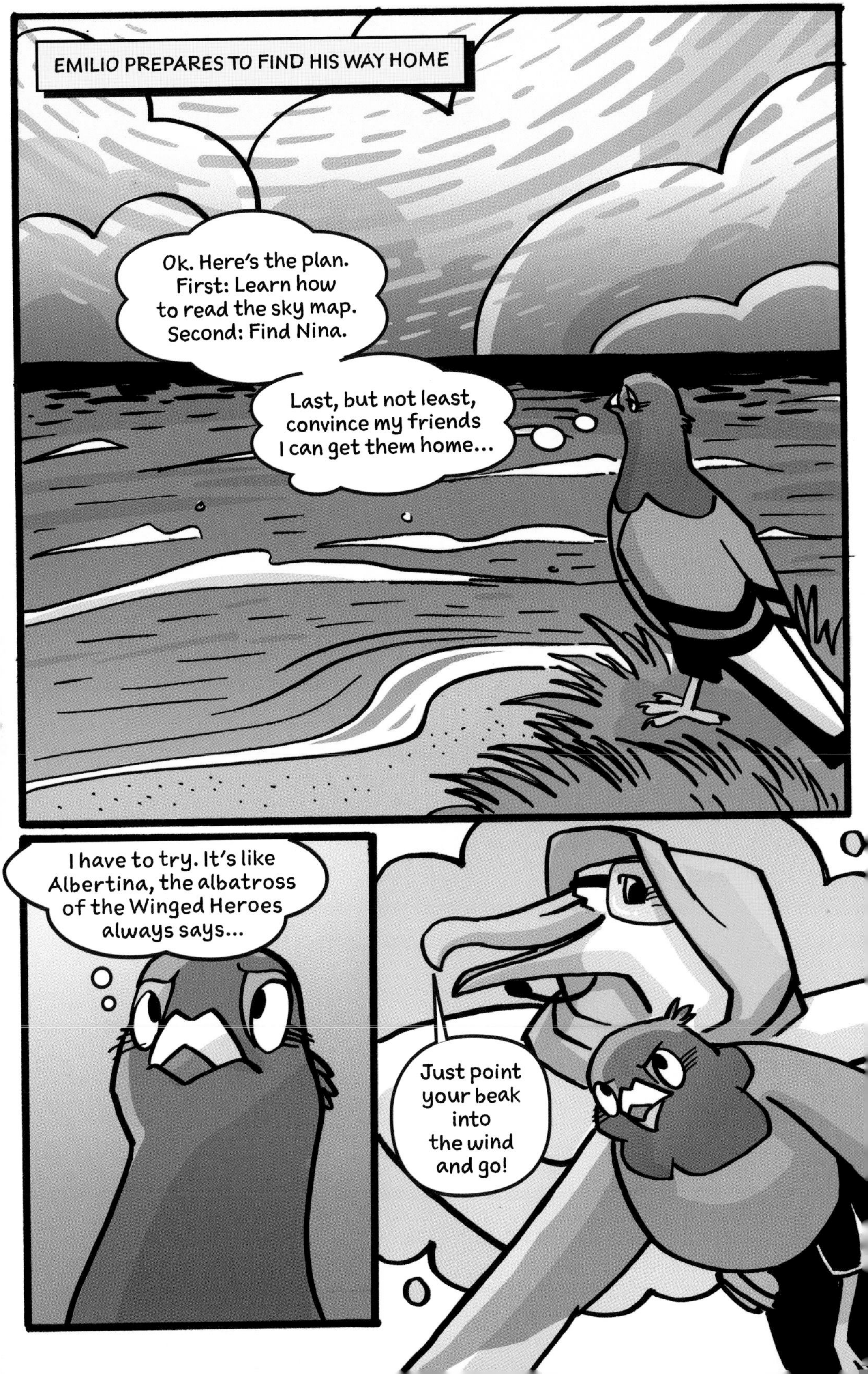

EMILIO PREPARES TO FIND HIS WAY HOME
Ok. Here's the plan. First: Learn how to read the sky map. Second: Find Nina.
Last, but not least, convince my friends I can get them home...
I have to try. It's like Albertina, the albatross of the Winged Heroes always says...
Just point your beak into the wind and go!

WINGED HERO: ALBERTINA—THE FORECASTER

FULL OF INFORMATION AND WELL-TRAVELED, ALBERTINA PROVIDES THE WINGED HEROES WITH IMPORTANT UPDATES ABOUT THE HEALTH OF THE PLANET.

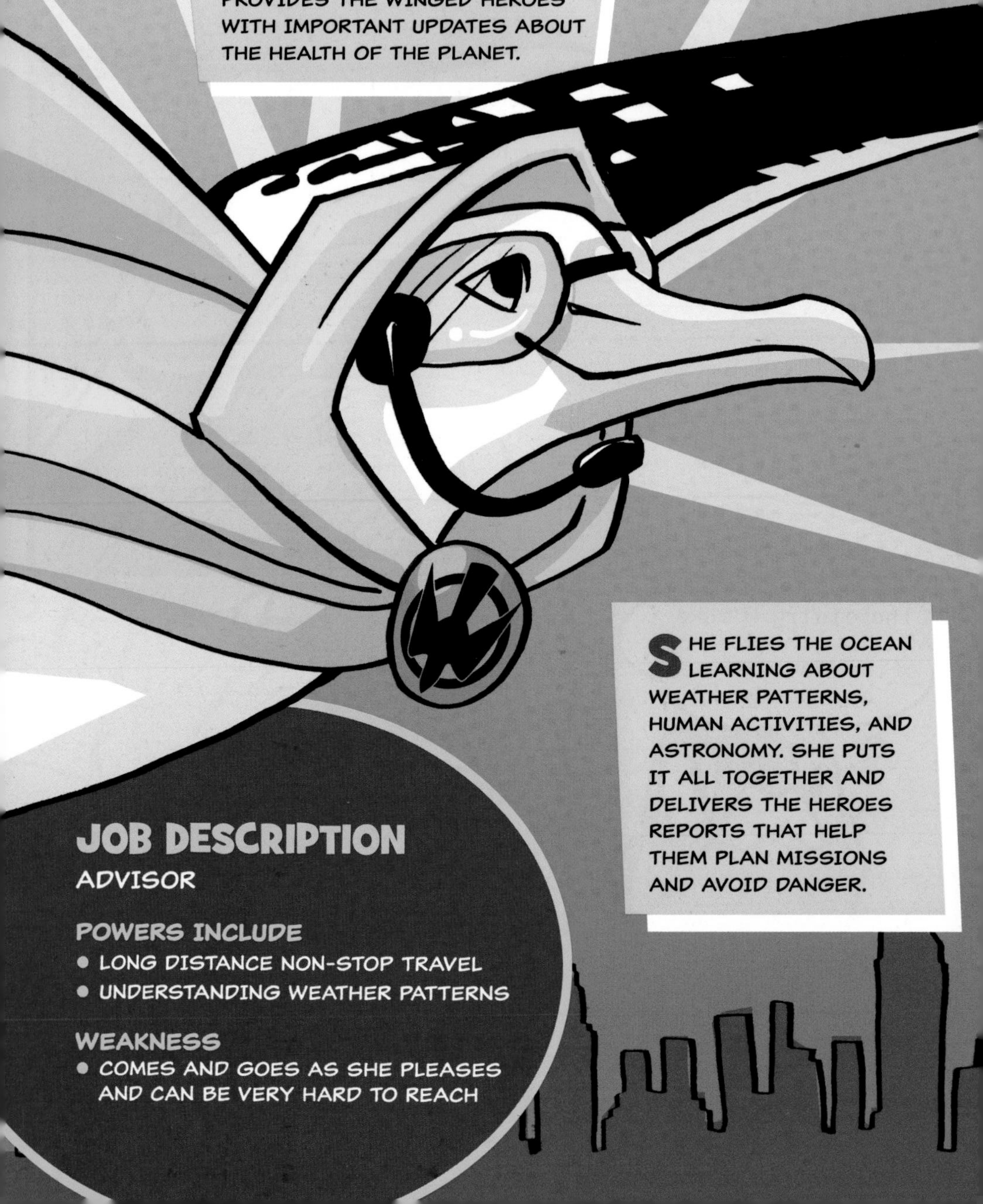

SHE FLIES THE OCEAN LEARNING ABOUT WEATHER PATTERNS, HUMAN ACTIVITIES, AND ASTRONOMY. SHE PUTS IT ALL TOGETHER AND DELIVERS THE HEROES REPORTS THAT HELP THEM PLAN MISSIONS AND AVOID DANGER.

JOB DESCRIPTION

ADVISOR

POWERS INCLUDE

- LONG DISTANCE NON-STOP TRAVEL
- UNDERSTANDING WEATHER PATTERNS

WEAKNESS

- COMES AND GOES AS SHE PLEASES AND CAN BE VERY HARD TO REACH

THE REAL WANDERING ALBATROSS

(DIOMEDEA EXULANS)

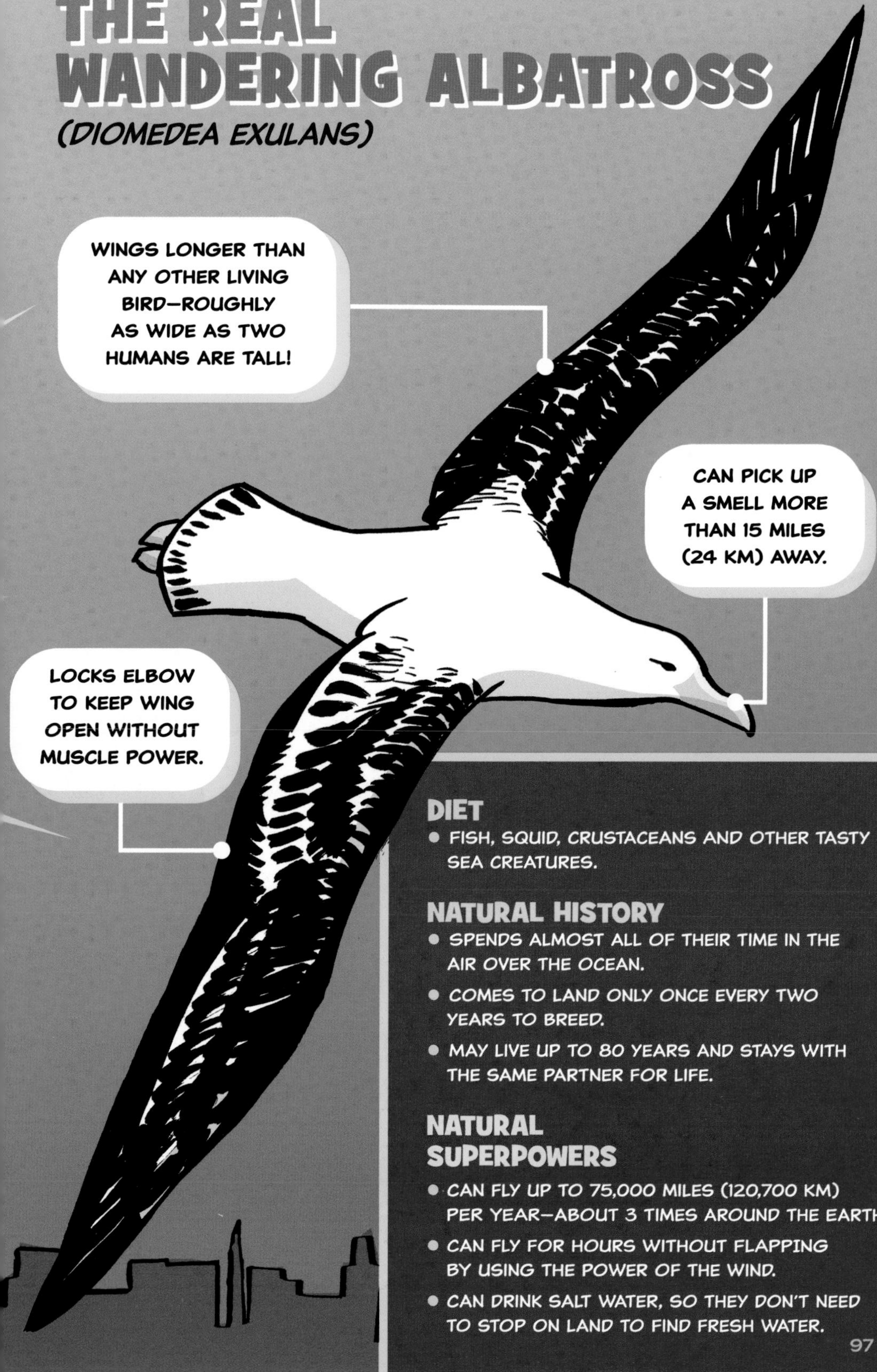
WINGS LONGER THAN ANY OTHER LIVING BIRD—ROUGHLY AS WIDE AS TWO HUMANS ARE TALL!
CAN PICK UP A SMELL MORE THAN 15 MILES (24 KM) AWAY.
LOCKS ELBOW TO KEEP WING OPEN WITHOUT MUSCLE POWER.

DIET

- FISH, SQUID, CRUSTACEANS AND OTHER TASTY SEA CREATURES.

NATURAL HISTORY

- SPENDS ALMOST ALL OF THEIR TIME IN THE AIR OVER THE OCEAN.
- COMES TO LAND ONLY ONCE EVERY TWO YEARS TO BREED.
- MAY LIVE UP TO 80 YEARS AND STAYS WITH THE SAME PARTNER FOR LIFE.

NATURAL SUPERPOWERS

- CAN FLY UP TO 75,000 MILES (120,700 KM) PER YEAR—ABOUT 3 TIMES AROUND THE EARTH.
- CAN FLY FOR HOURS WITHOUT FLAPPING BY USING THE POWER OF THE WIND.
- CAN DRINK SALT WATER, SO THEY DON'T NEED TO STOP ON LAND TO FIND FRESH WATER.

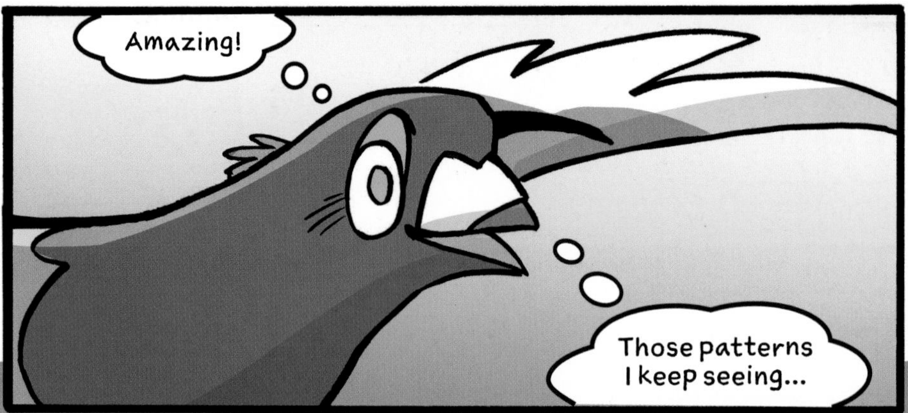
Amazing!
Those patterns I keep seeing...

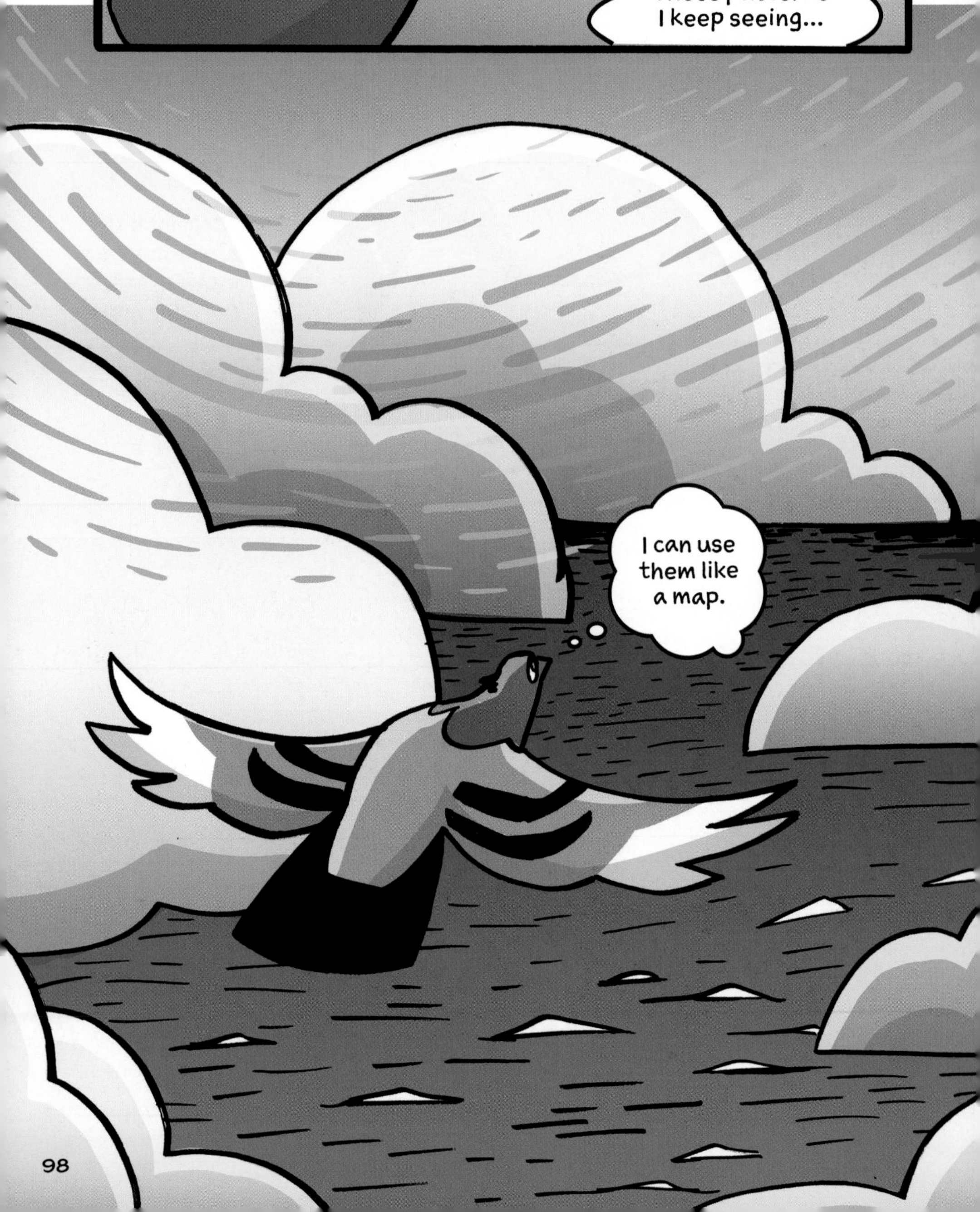
I can use them like a map.

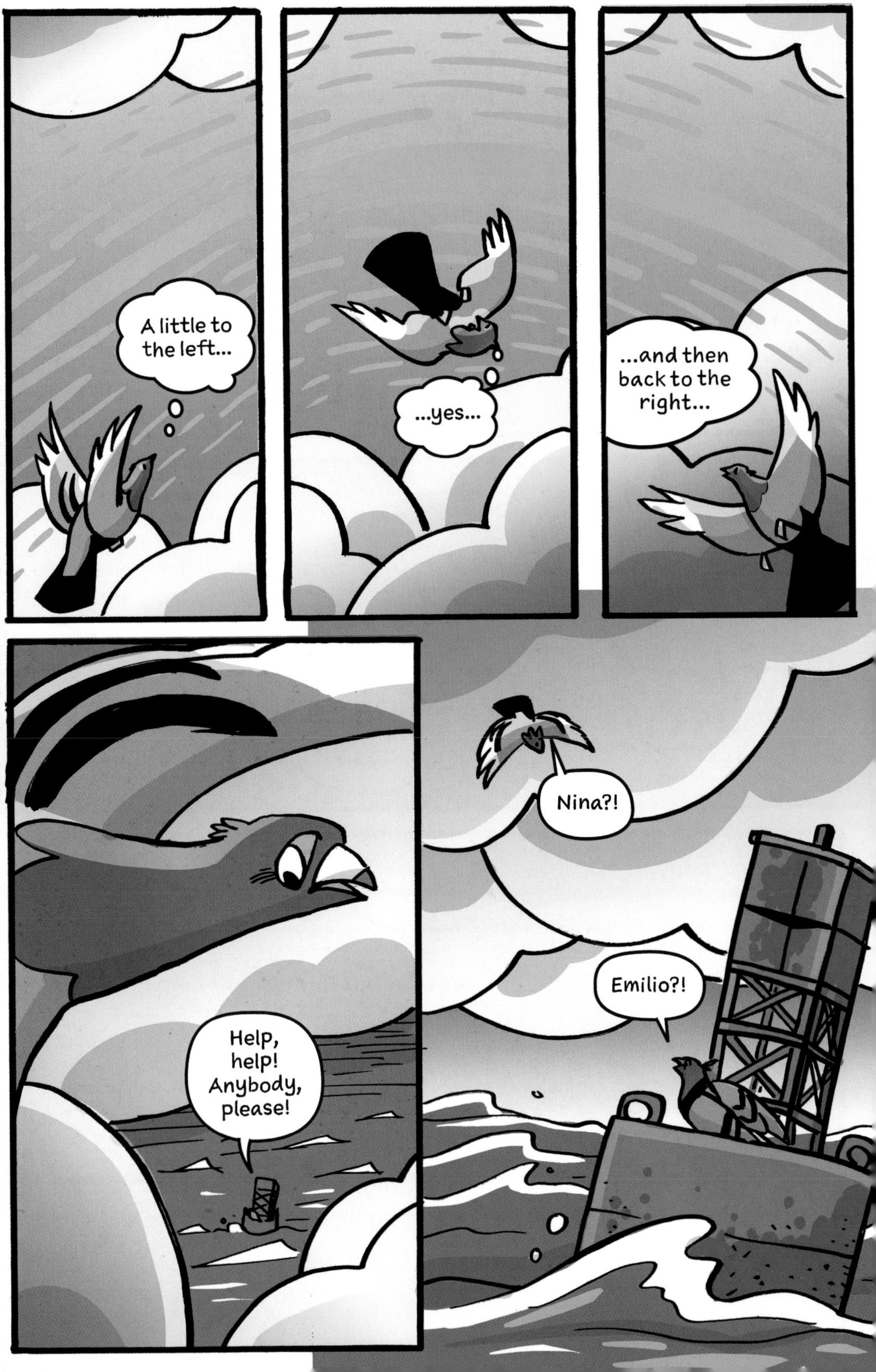
A little to the left...
...yes...
...and then back to the right...
Help, help! Anybody, please!
Nina?!
Emilio?!

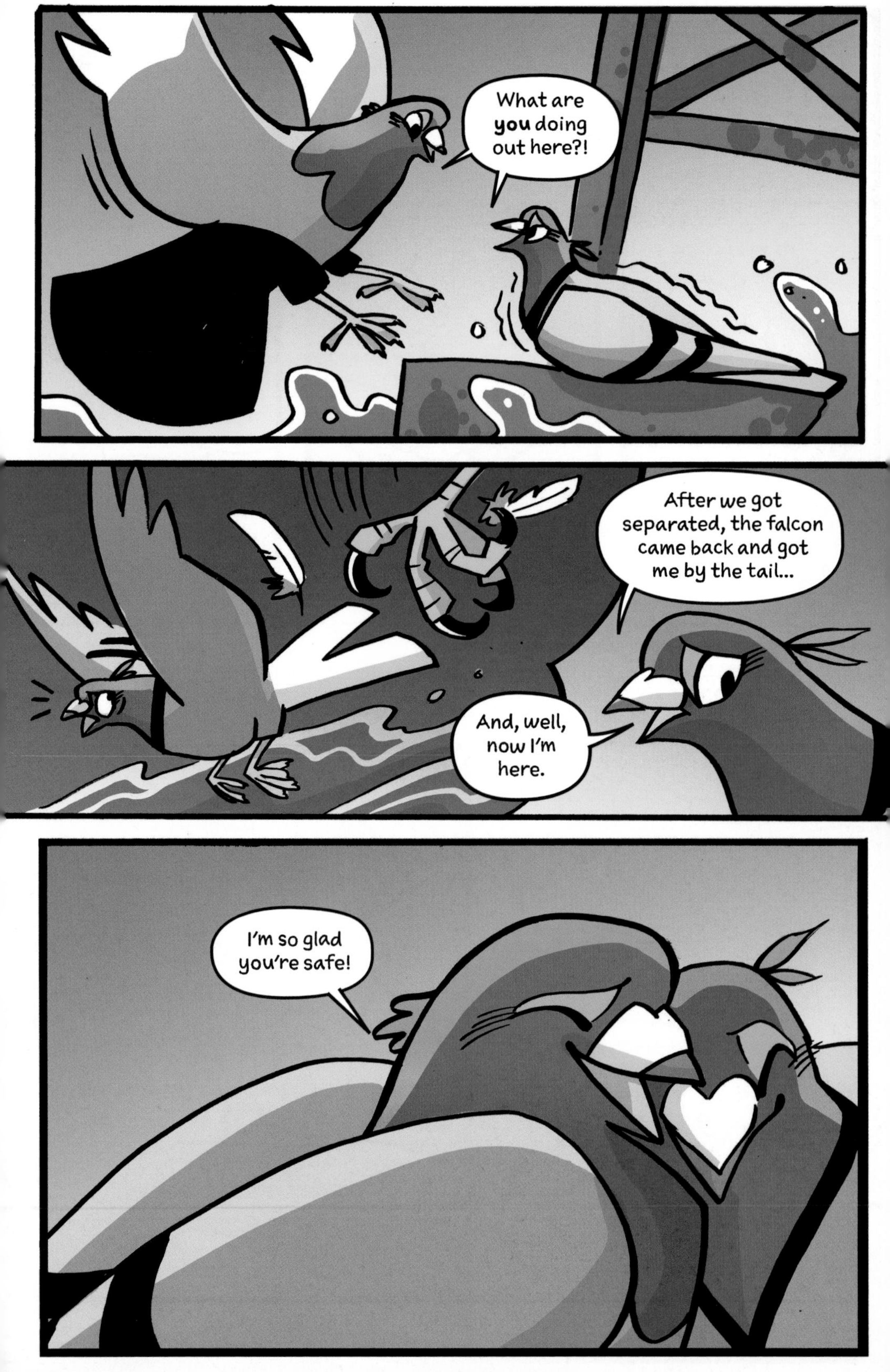
What are you doing out here?!
After we got separated, the falcon came back and got me by the tail...
And, well, now I'm here.
I'm so glad you're safe!

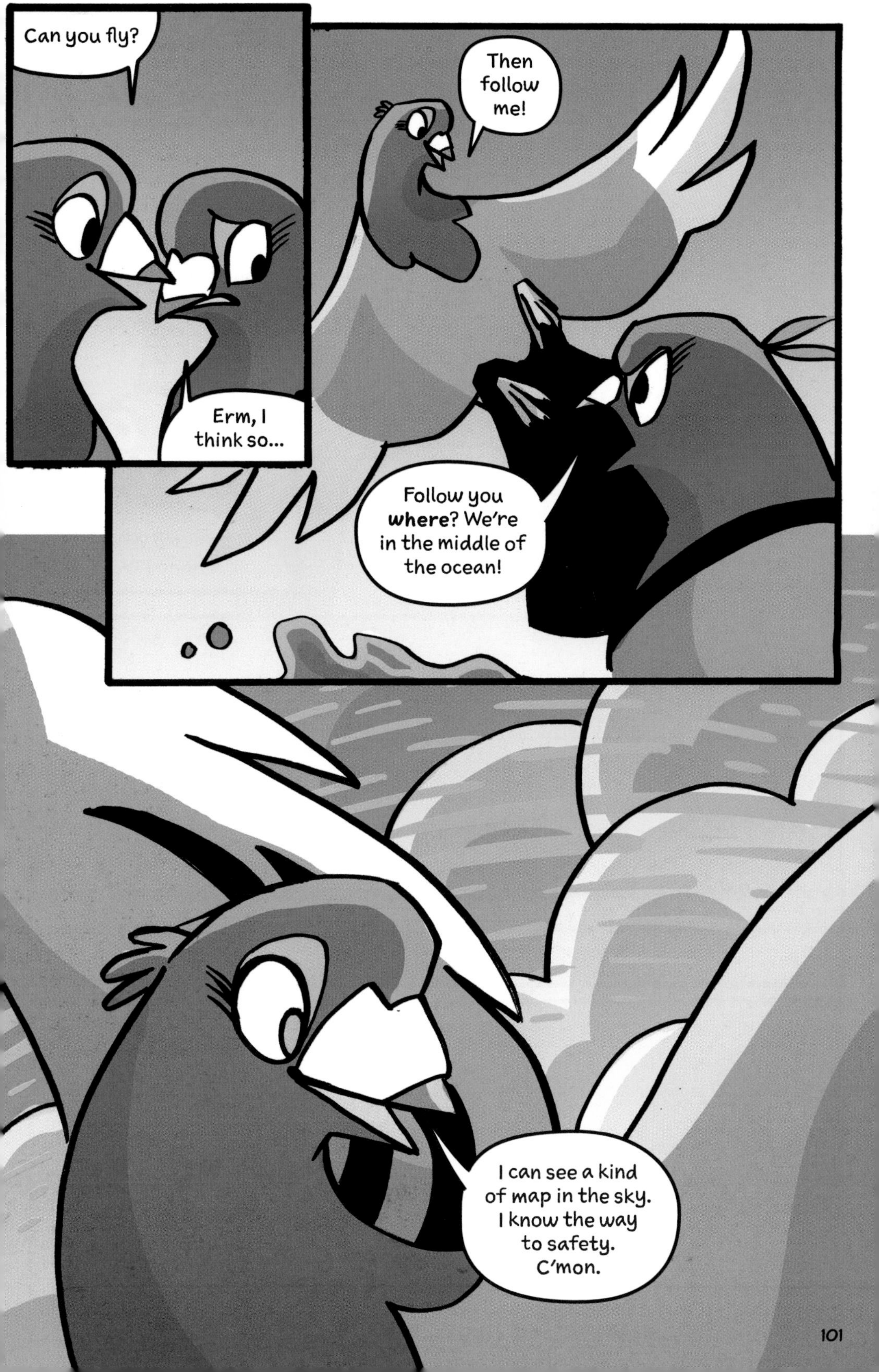
Can you fly?
Erm, I think so...
Then follow me!
Follow you **where**? We're in the middle of the ocean!
I can see a kind of map in the sky. I know the way to safety. C'mon.

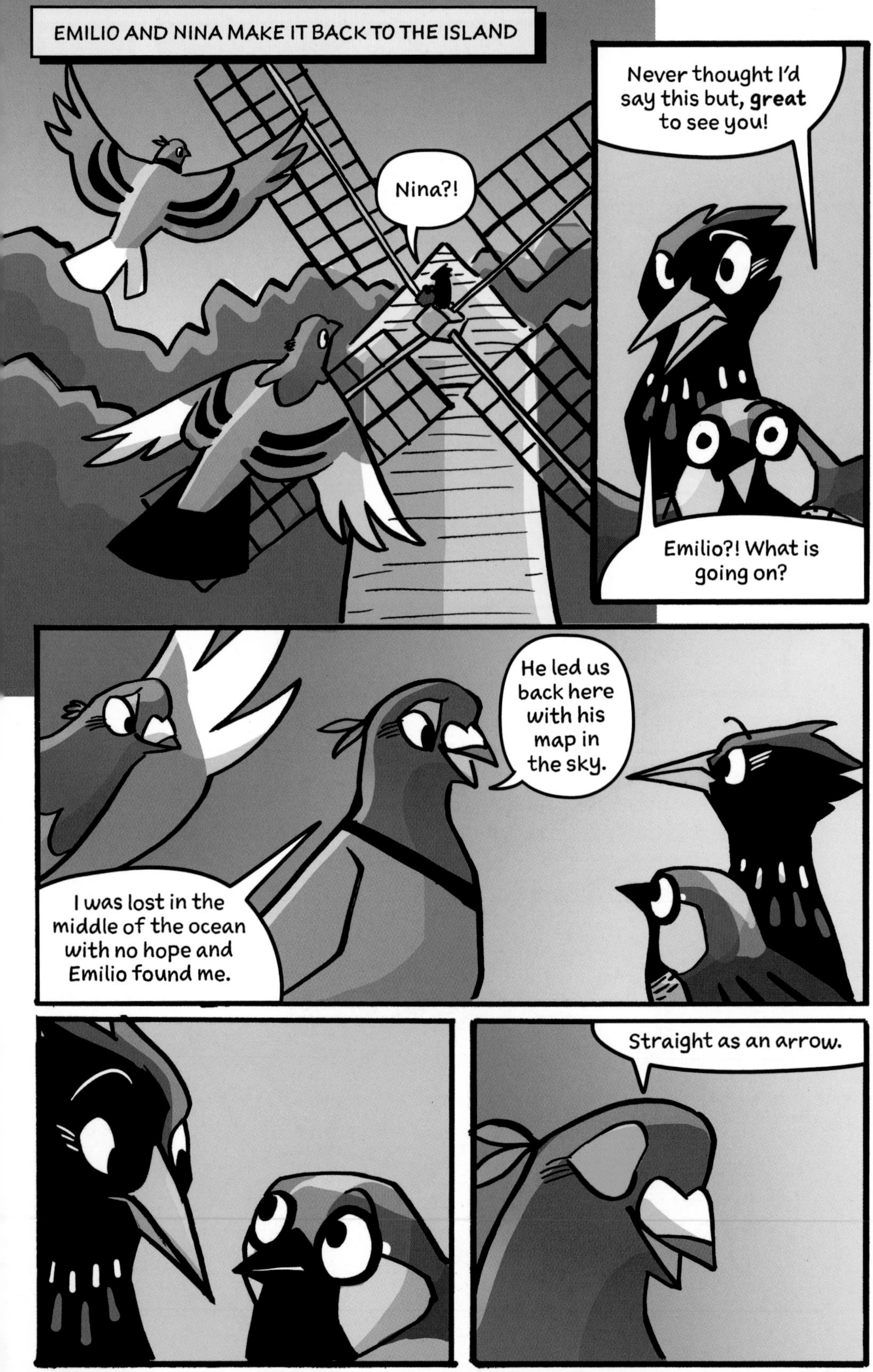
EMILIO AND NINA MAKE IT BACK TO THE ISLAND
Nina?!
Never thought I'd say this but, **great** to see you!
Emilio?! What is going on?
He led us back here with his map in the sky.
I was lost in the middle of the ocean with no hope and Emilio found me.
Straight as an arrow.

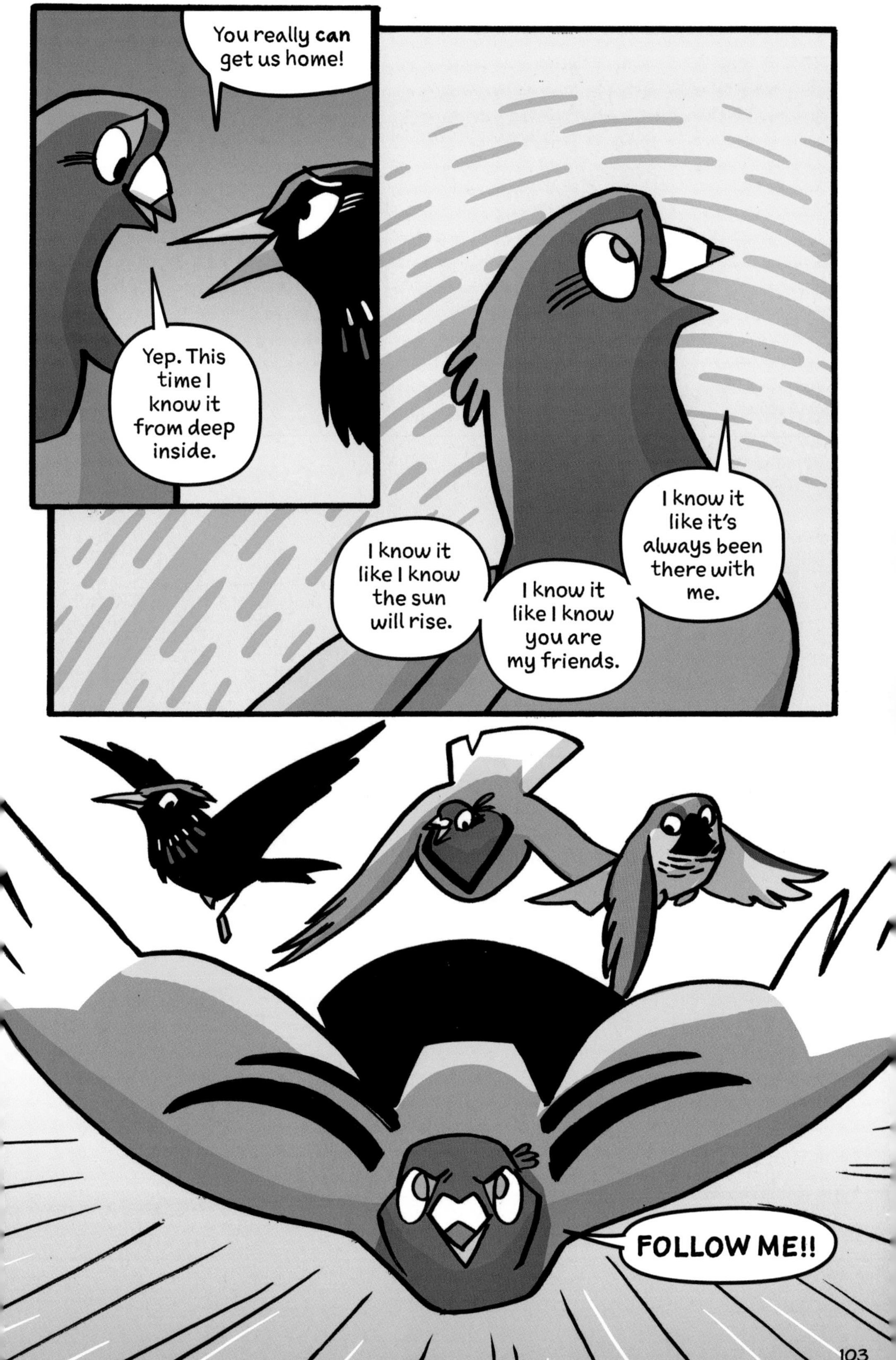
You really **can** get us home!
Yep. This time I know it from deep inside.
I know it like I know the sun will rise.
I know it like I know you are my friends.
I know it like it's always been there with me.
FOLLOW ME!!

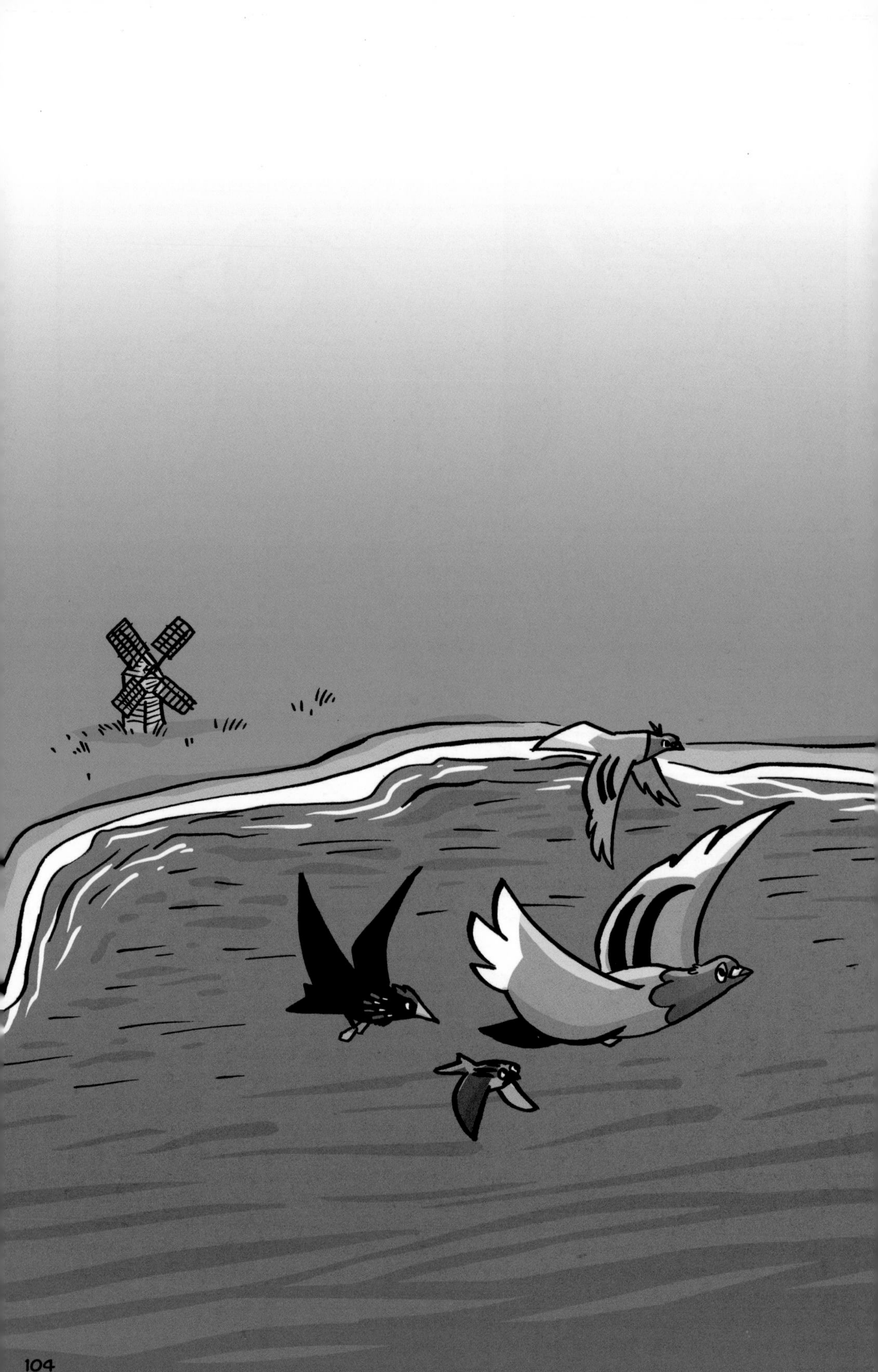

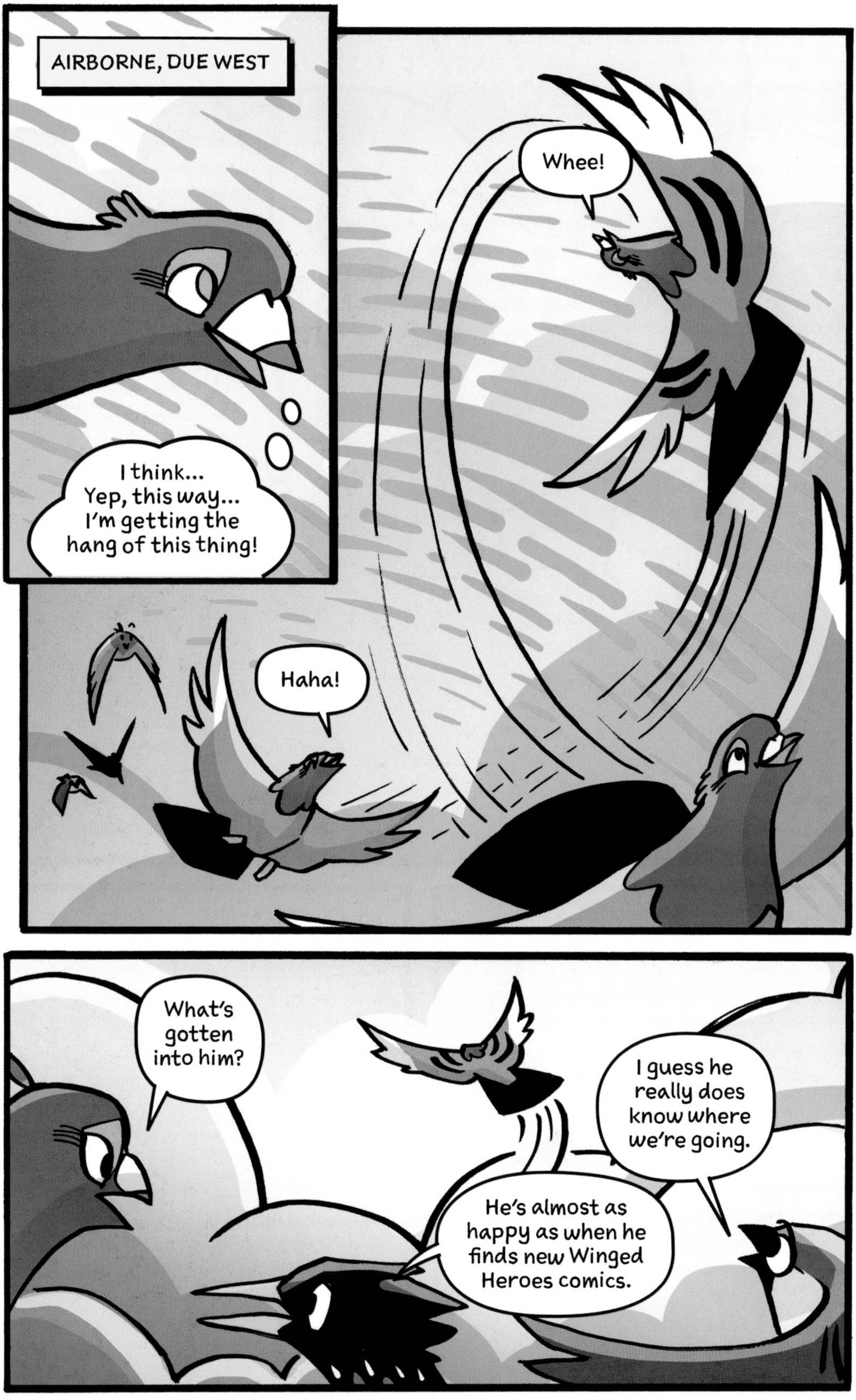
AIRBORNE, DUE WEST
I think... Yep, this way... I'm getting the hang of this thing!
Whee!
Haha!
What's gotten into him?
I guess he really does know where we're going.
He's almost as happy as when he finds new Winged Heroes comics.

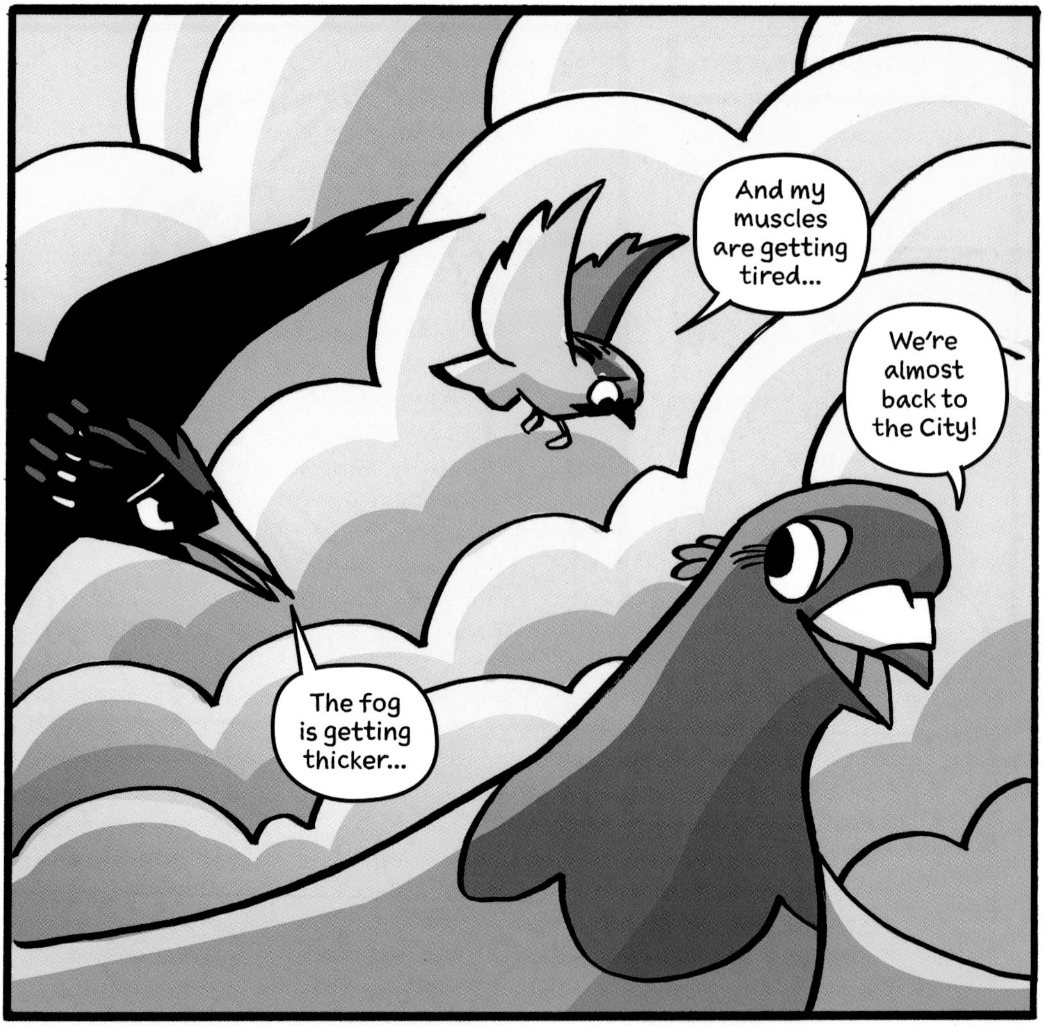
And my muscles are getting tired...
We're almost back to the City!
The fog is getting thicker...

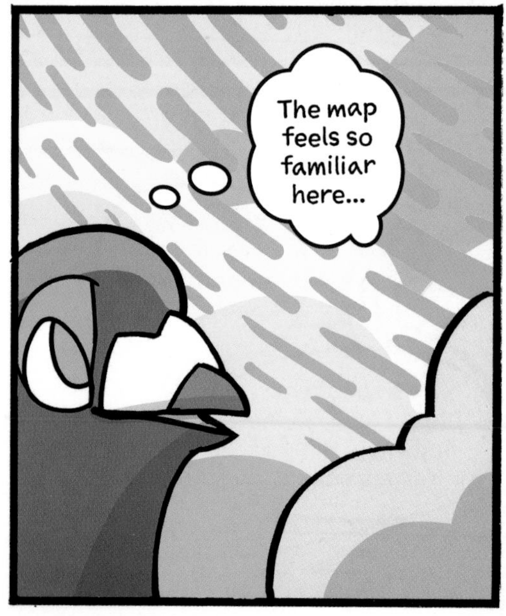
The map feels so familiar here...

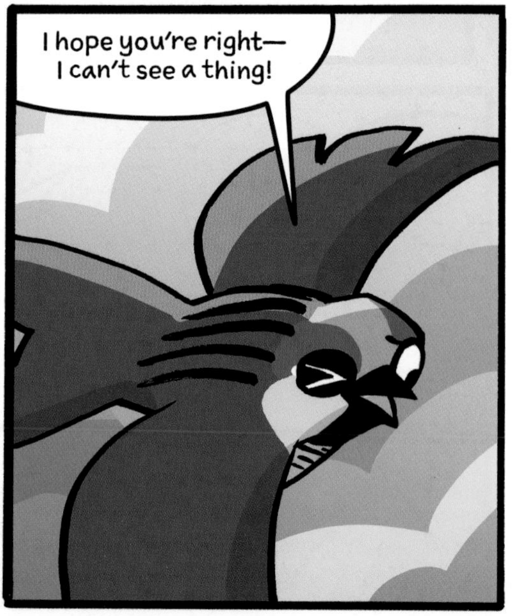
I hope you're right—
I can't see a thing!

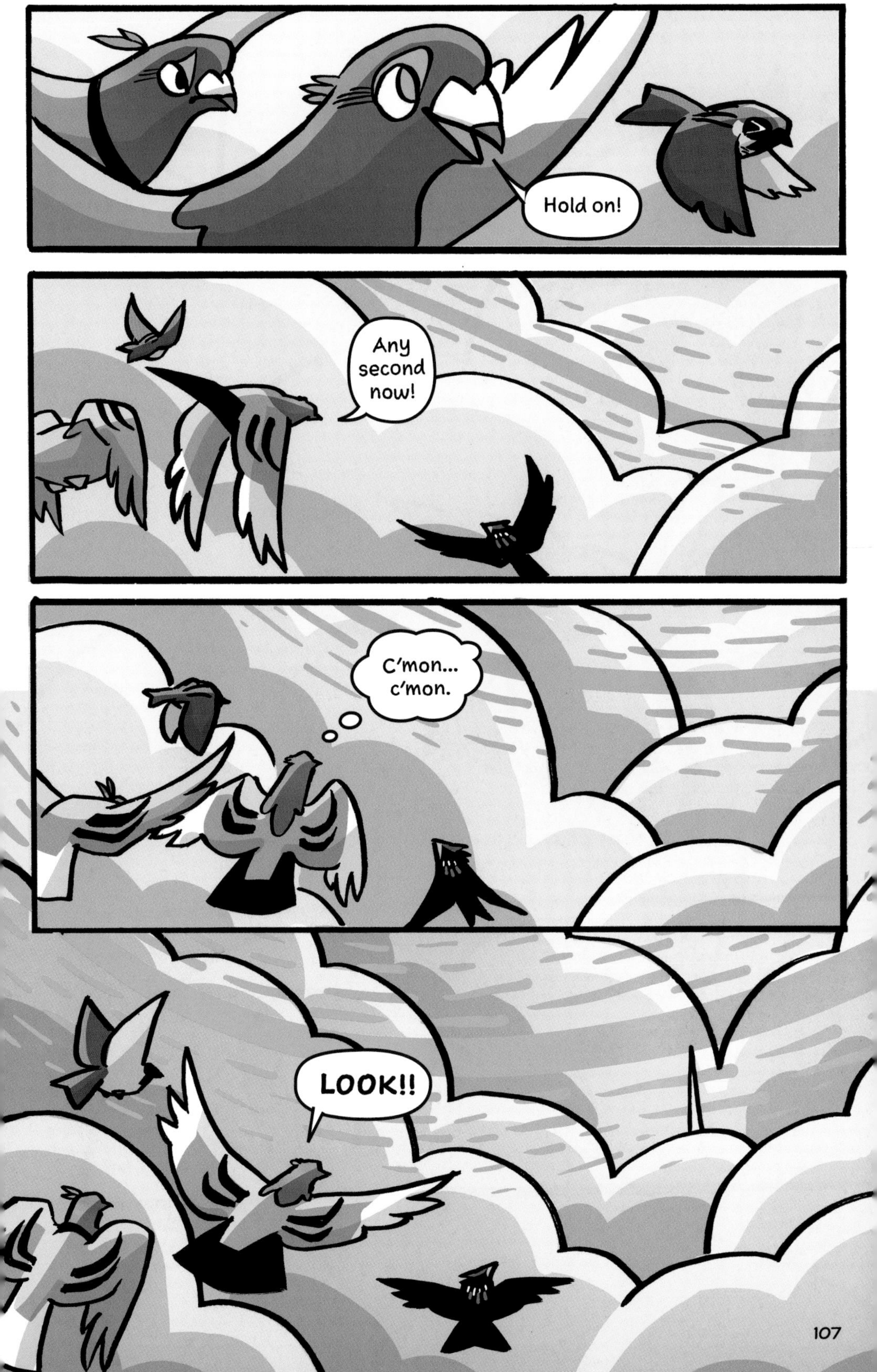
Hold on!
Any second now!
C'mon... c'mon.
LOOK!!

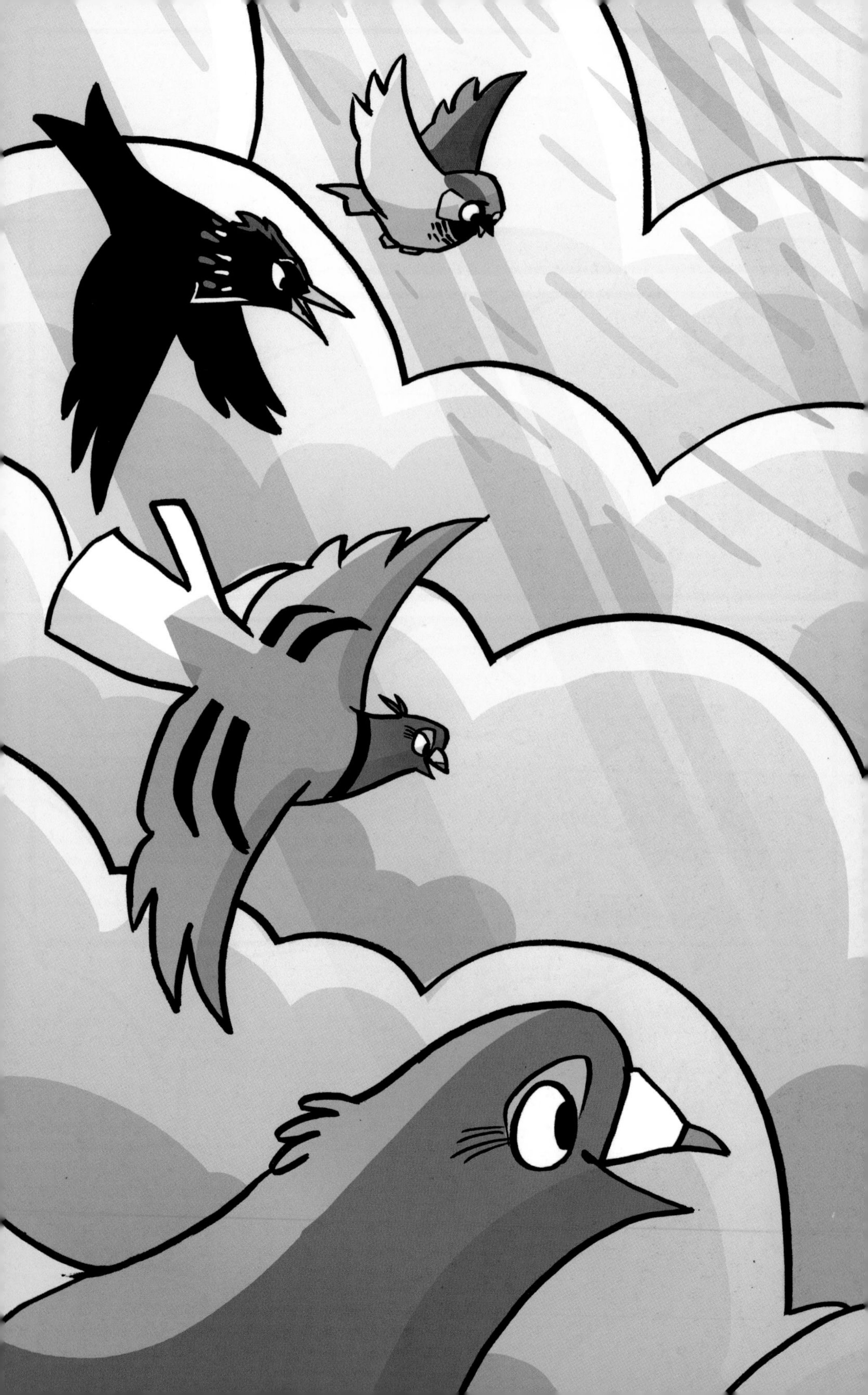

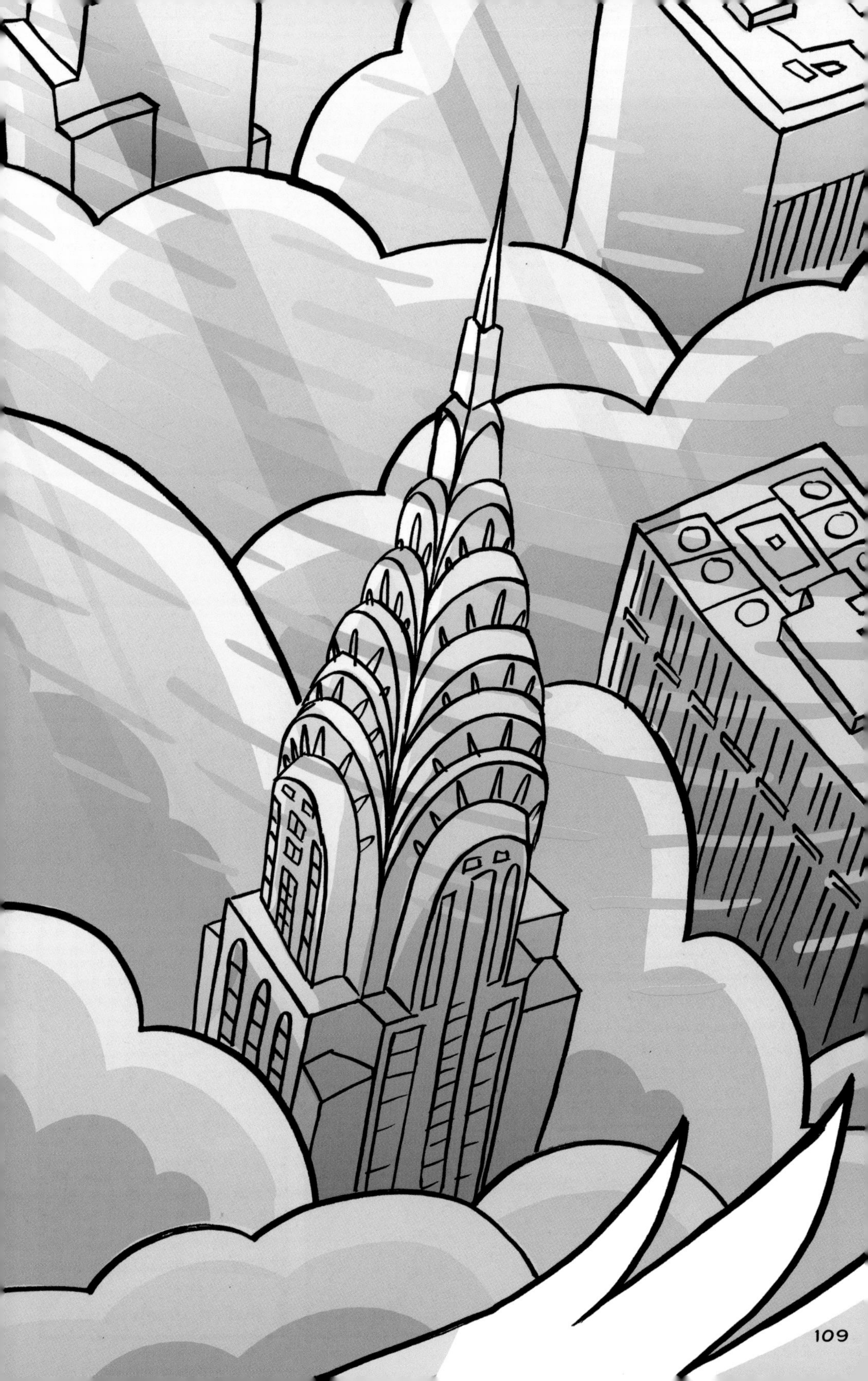

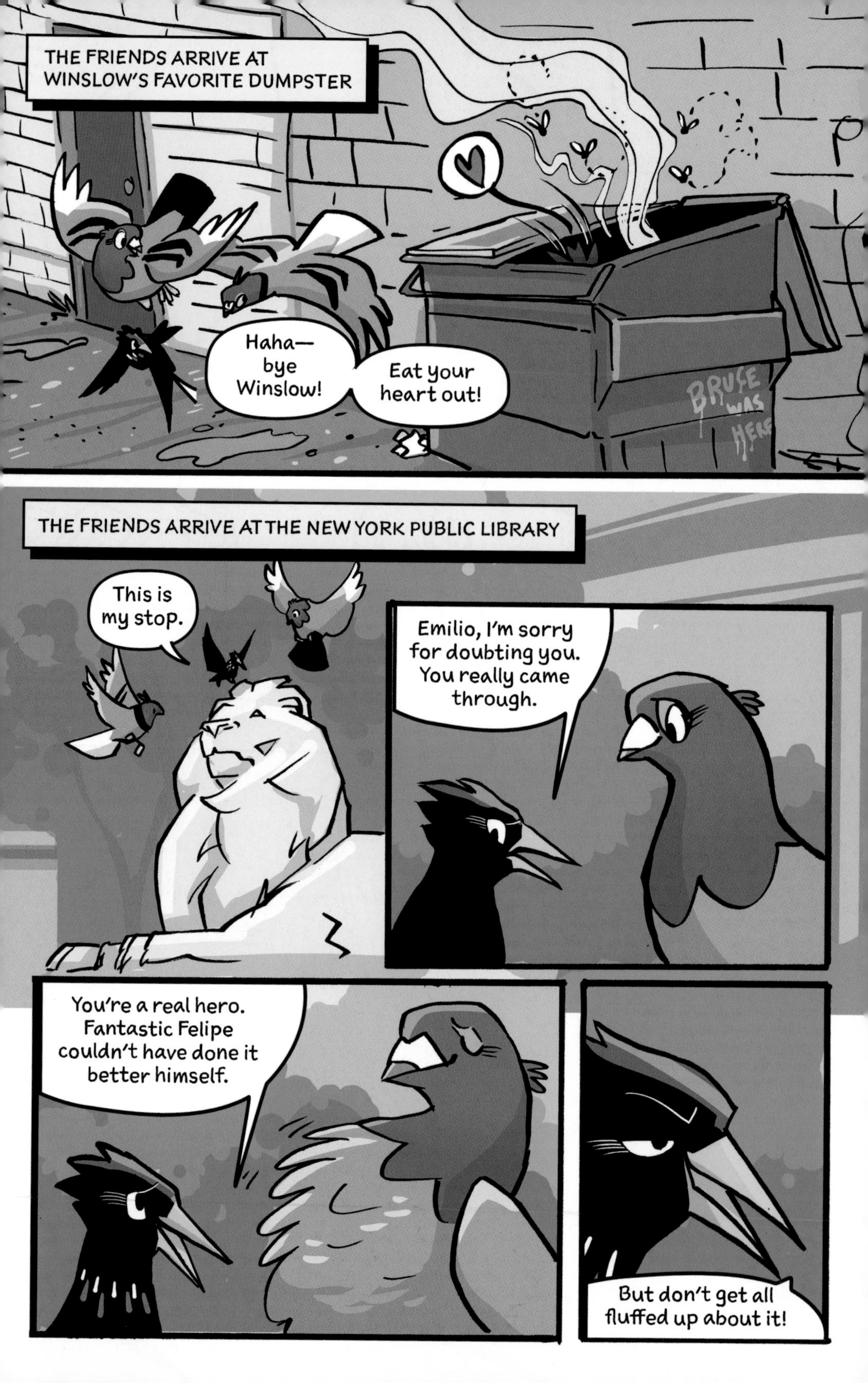
THE FRIENDS ARRIVE AT WINSLOW'S FAVORITE DUMPSTER
Haha— bye Winslow!
Eat your heart out!
BRUCE WAS HERE
THE FRIENDS ARRIVE AT THE NEW YORK PUBLIC LIBRARY
This is my stop.
Emilio, I'm sorry for doubting you. You really came through.
You're a real hero. Fantastic Felipe couldn't have done it better himself.
But don't get all fluffed up about it!

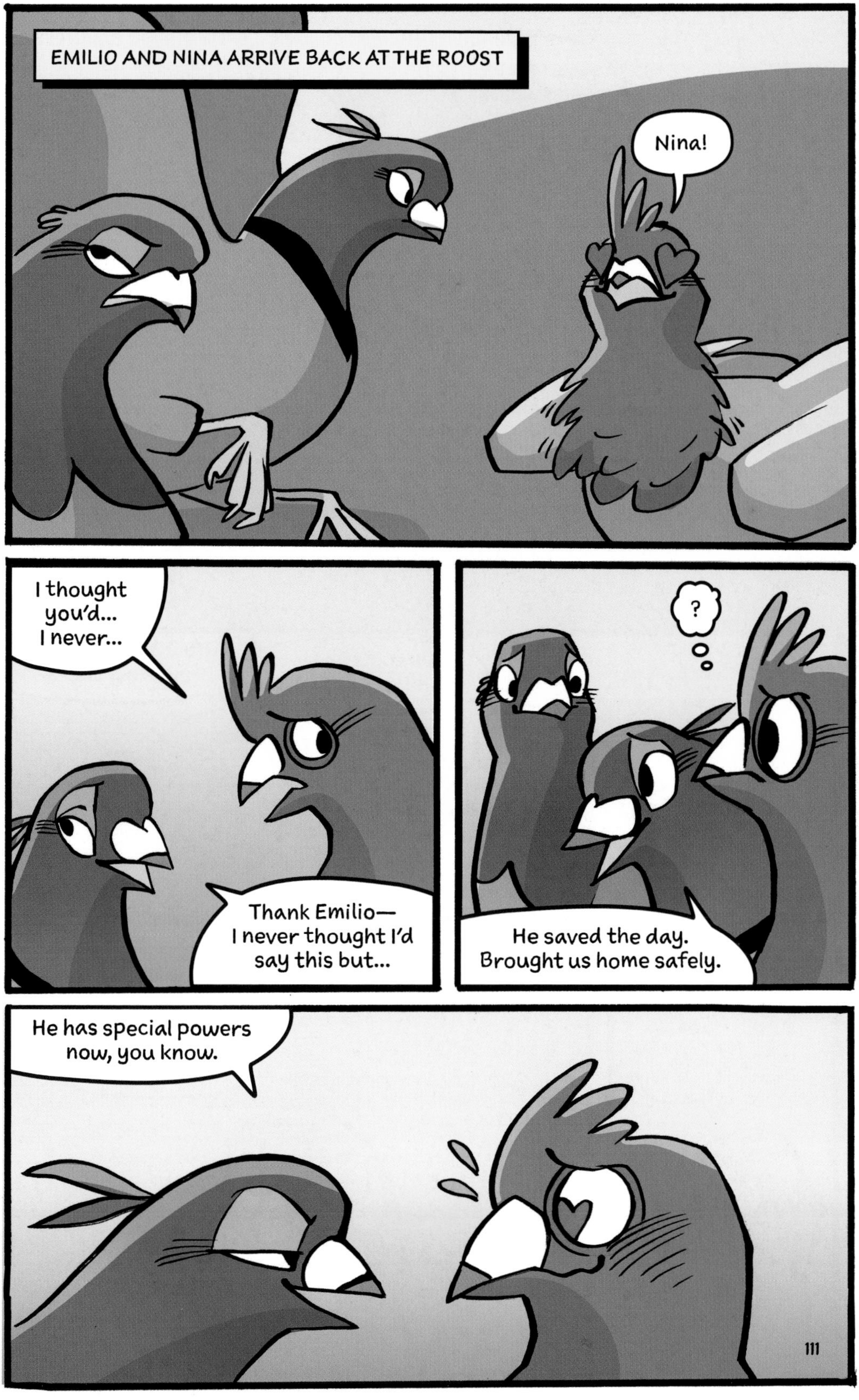
EMILIO AND NINA ARRIVE BACK AT THE ROOST
Nina!
I thought you'd... I never...
Thank Emilio— I never thought I'd say this but...
?
He saved the day. Brought us home safely.
He has special powers now, you know.

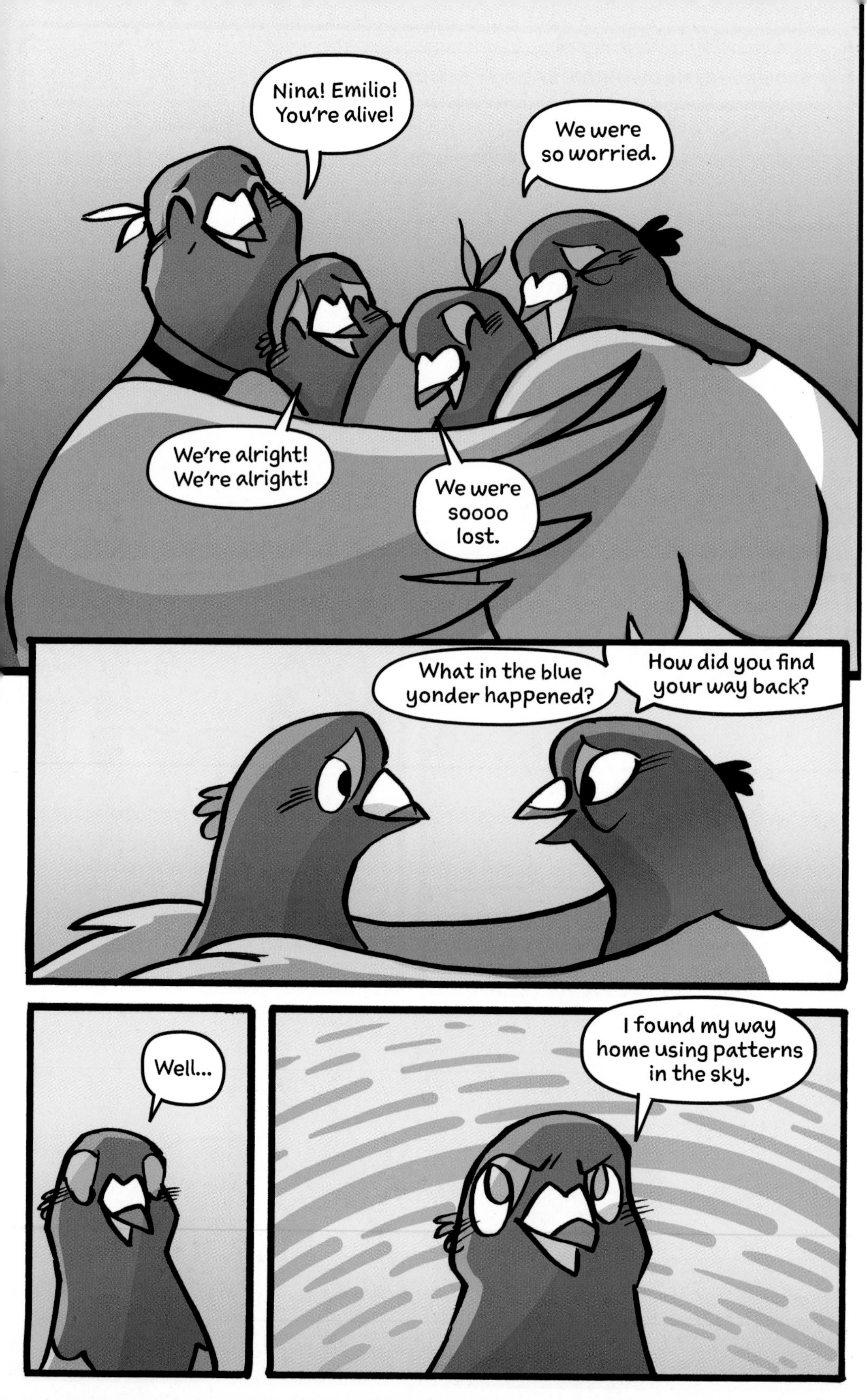
Nina! Emilio! You're alive!
We were so worried.
We're alright! We're alright!
We were soooo lost.
What in the blue yonder happened?
How did you find your way back?
Well...
I found my way home using patterns in the sky.

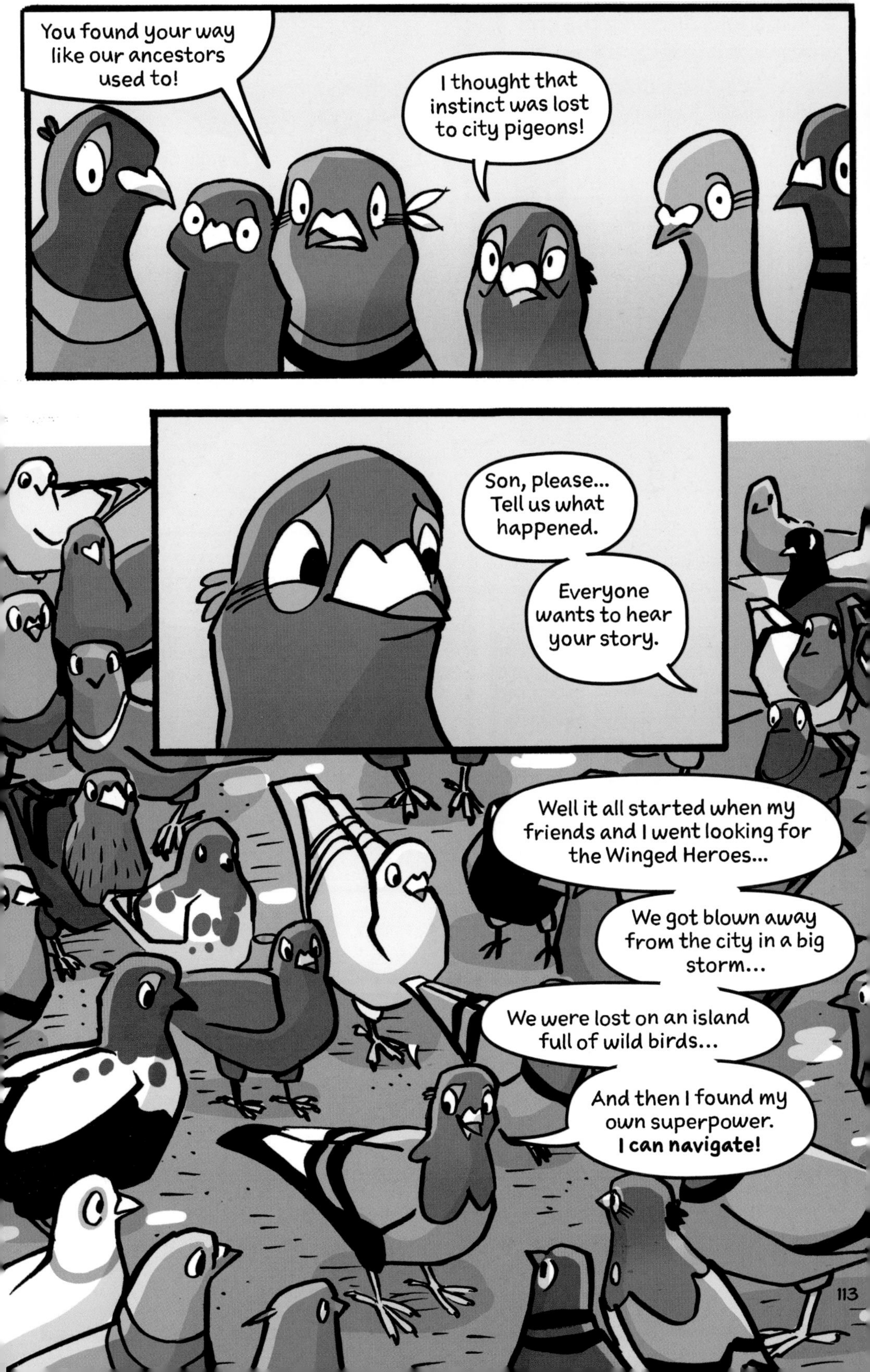
You found your way like our ancestors used to!
I thought that instinct was lost to city pigeons!
Son, please... Tell us what happened.
Everyone wants to hear your story.
Well it all started when my friends and I went looking for the Winged Heroes...
We got blown away from the city in a big storm...
We were lost on an island full of wild birds...
And then I found my own superpower. **I can navigate!**

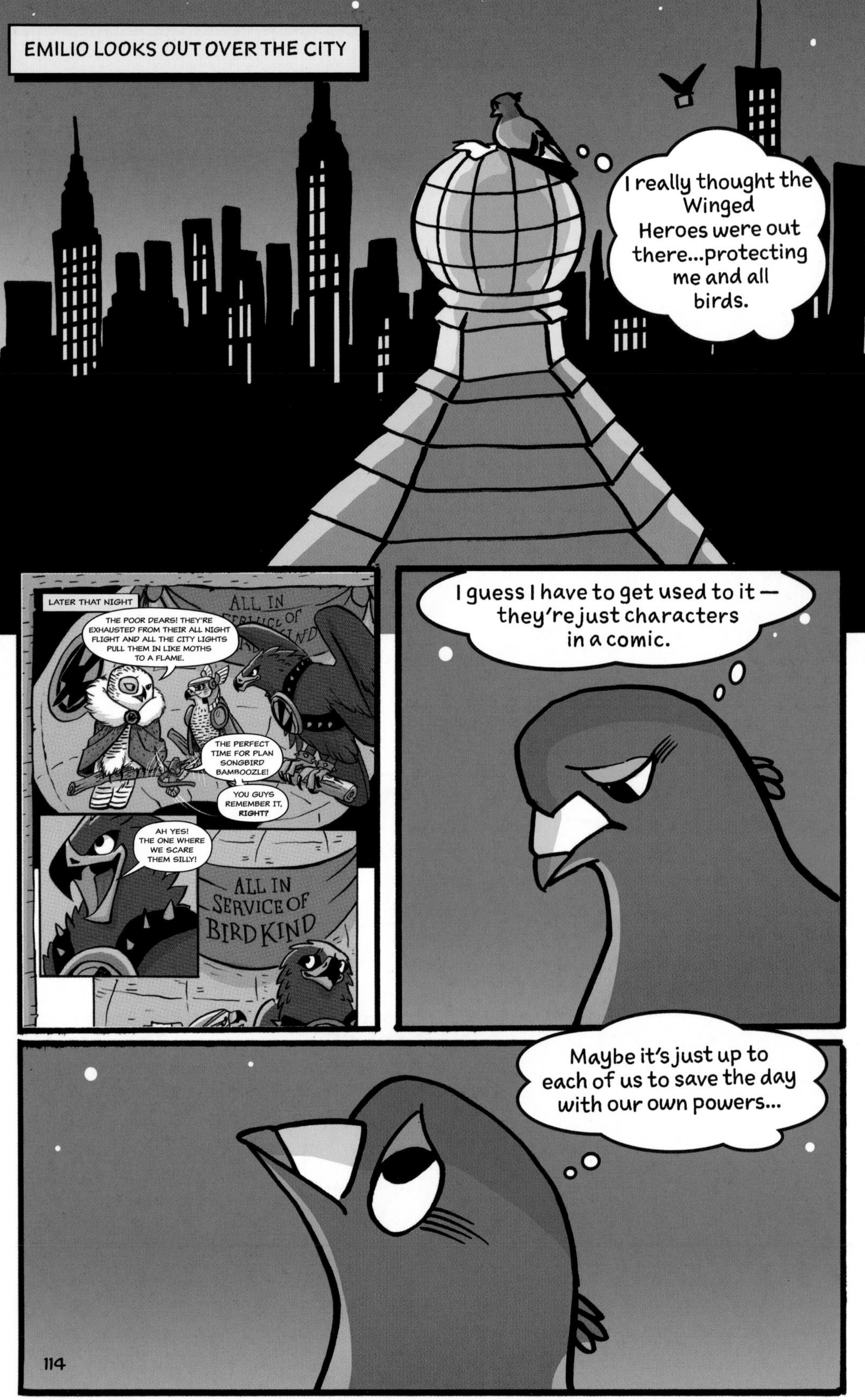
EMILIO LOOKS OUT OVER THE CITY
I really thought the Winged Heroes were out there...protecting me and all birds.
LATER THAT NIGHT
THE POOR DEARS! THEY'RE EXHAUSTED FROM THEIR ALL NIGHT FLIGHT AND ALL THE CITY LIGHTS PULL THEM IN LIKE MOTHS TO A FLAME.
THE PERFECT TIME FOR PLAN SONGBIRD BAMBOOZLE!
YOU GUYS REMEMBER IT, RIGHT?
AH YES! THE ONE WHERE WE SCARE THEM SILLY!
ALL IN SERVICE OF BIRD KIND
I guess I have to get used to it — they're just characters in a comic.
Maybe it's just up to each of us to save the day with our own powers...

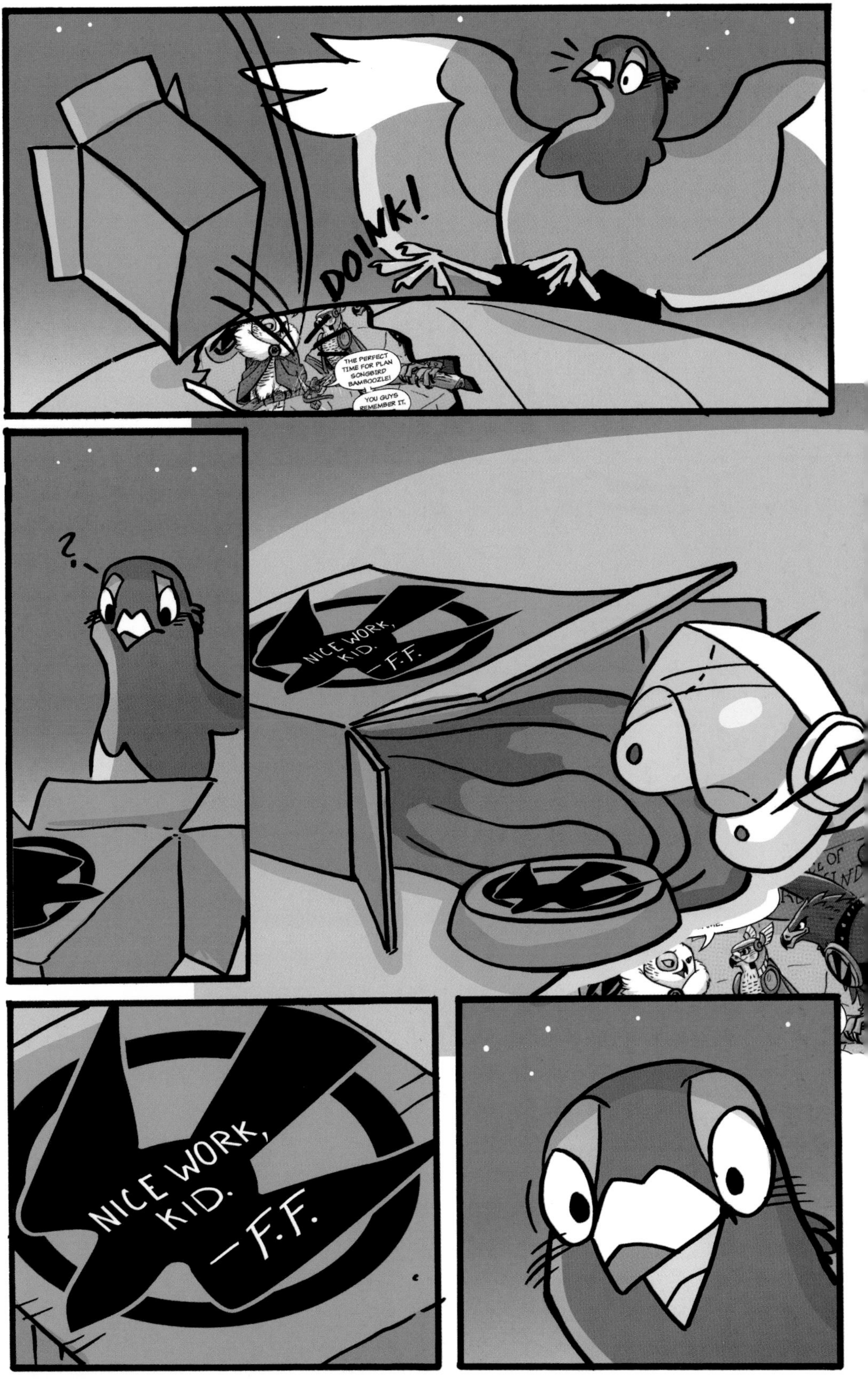
DOINK!
THE PERFECT TIME FOR PLAN SONGBIRD BAMBOOZLE!
YOU GUYS REMEMBER IT.
?
NICE WORK, KID. —F.F.
NICE WORK, KID. —F.F.

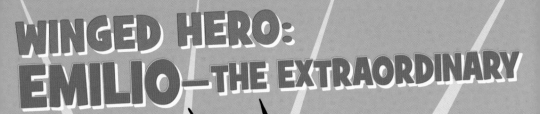

WINGED HERO: EMILIO—THE EXTRAORDINARY

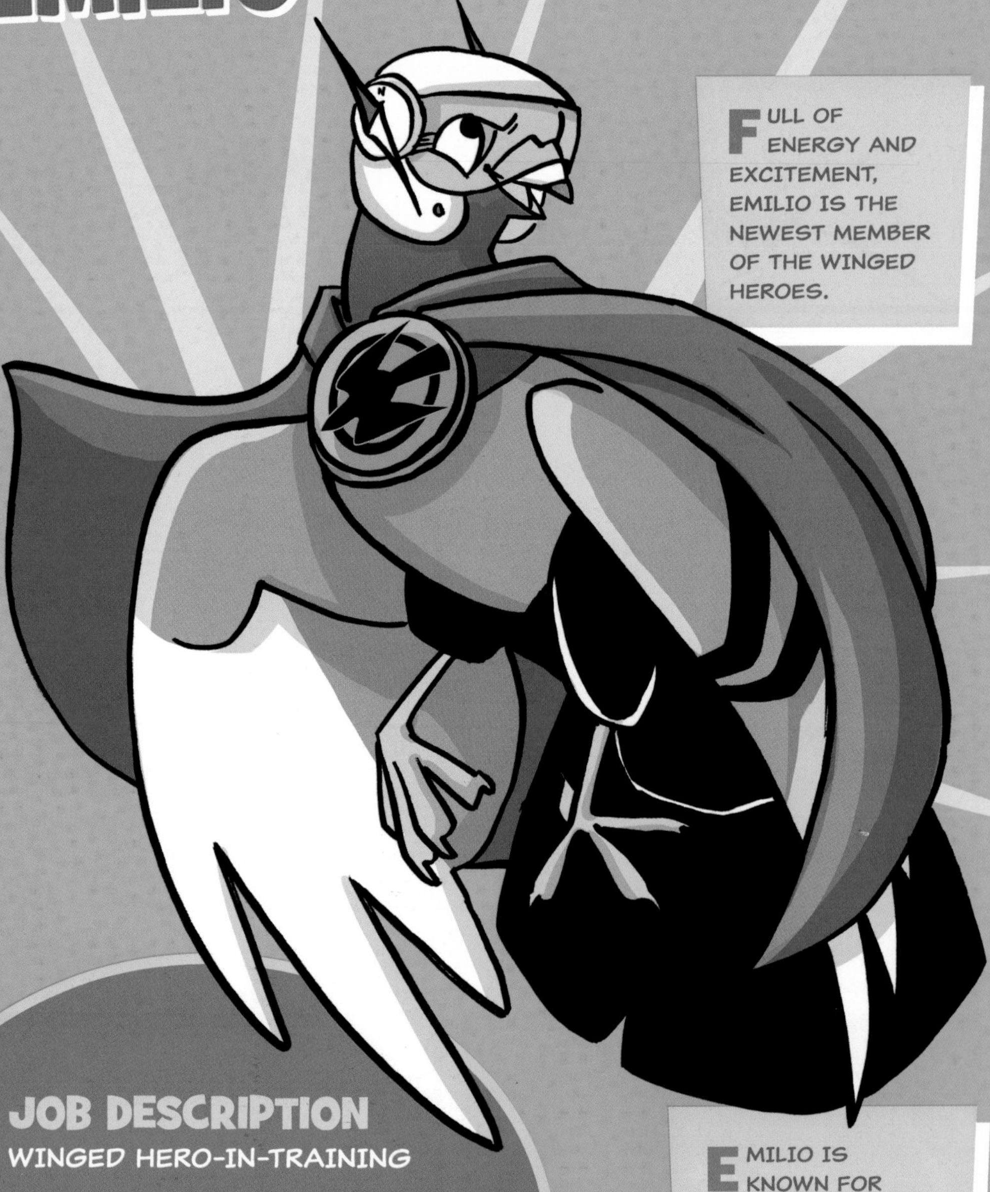

FULL OF ENERGY AND EXCITEMENT, EMILIO IS THE NEWEST MEMBER OF THE WINGED HEROES.

JOB DESCRIPTION

WINGED HERO-IN-TRAINING

POWERS INCLUDE

- ABILITY TO READ THE EARTH'S MAGNETIC FIELD

WEAKNESS

- IF HE KEEPS HIS EYES OPEN AND FOLLOWS HIS INSTINCTS, HE SHOULD BE OK

EMILIO IS KNOWN FOR HIS ABILITY TO NAVIGATE AND FOR HIS LOYALTY. HE'LL SOON BE CALLED UPON TO ASSIST IN MISSIONS TO PROTECT BIRDKIND.

THE REAL ROCK PIGEON

(COLUMBA LIVIA)

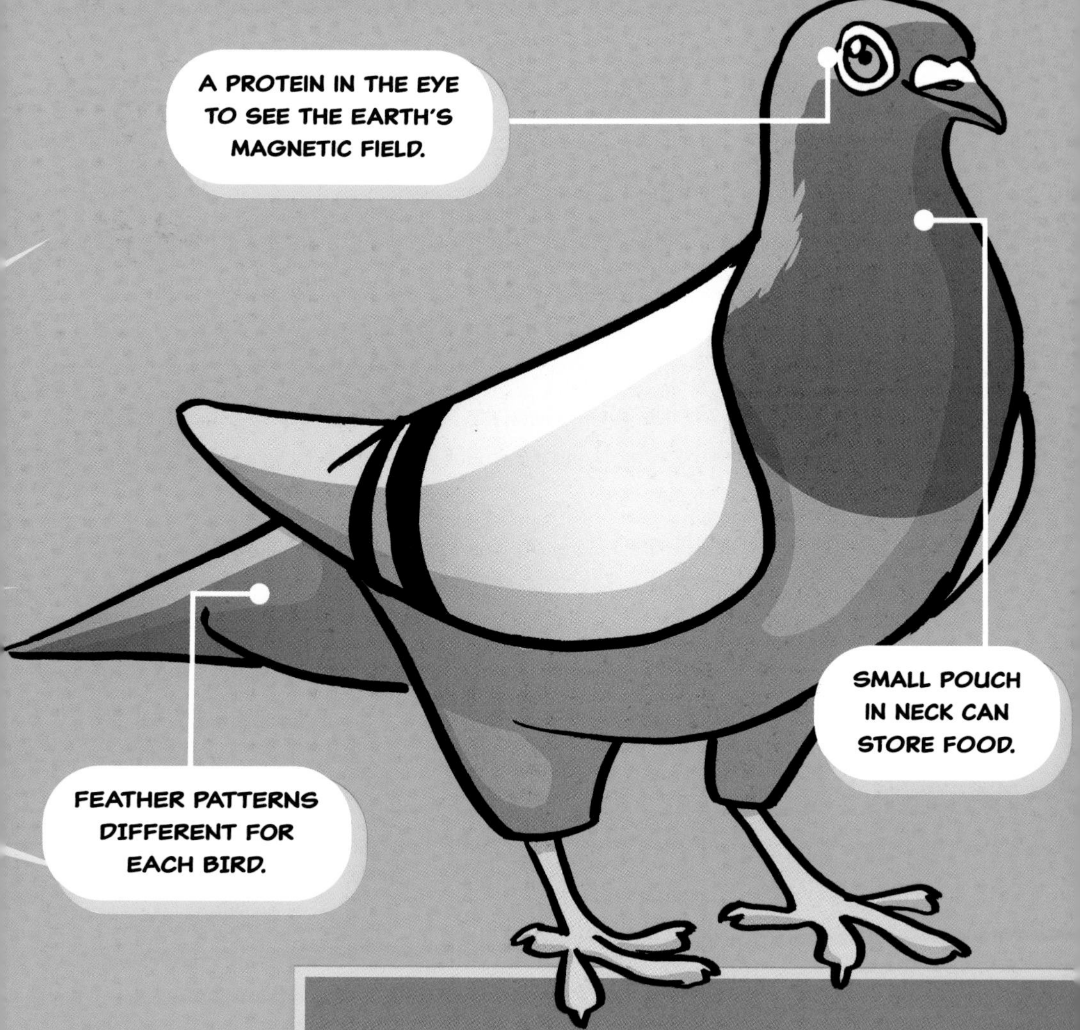
A PROTEIN IN THE EYE TO SEE THE EARTH'S MAGNETIC FIELD.
SMALL POUCH IN NECK CAN STORE FOOD.
FEATHER PATTERNS DIFFERENT FOR EACH BIRD.

DIET

- GRAINS LIKE CORN AND WHEAT, DISCARDED HUMAN FOOD.

NATURAL HISTORY

- BROUGHT TO NORTH AMERICA IN THE 1600S FROM EUROPE.
- IN CITIES, VERY COMMON AND LIVING IN LARGE FLOCKS.
- HAVE MANY DIFFERENT COLORS AND FEATHER PATTERNS.

NATURAL SUPERPOWERS

- AFTER A PERIOD OF LEARNING, CAN USE THE SUN, STARS, AND THE EARTH'S MAGNETIC FIELD TO FIND HOME.
- THEIR NAVIGATIONAL POWERS ARE STILL A BIT OF A MYSTERY, EVEN AFTER HUNDREDS OF SCIENTIFIC STUDIES.

PIGEON SUPERPOWERS

HOW THEY FIND THEIR WAY HOME USING MAGNETIC FIELD NAVITATION

If you were lost in the middle of the woods and could not see the Sun, you might use a compass to try to decide which direction to take. A magnetic compass needle lines itself up with Earth's magnetic field and points north and south: from that, you can figure out east and west, too. Because this works fairly well, people have been using magnetic compasses to find their way for about 1,000 years.

But how do other animals find their way? How do they navigate when it is cloudy? You probably know that many animals rely on their sense of smell to keep track of where they have been and where other animals are. However, some animals migrate (travel from one place to another), regularly covering hundreds or even thousands of miles each year. It seems unlikely that animals could repeat such long trips accurately if they were relying only on their sense of smell, so scientists have been looking for evidence of what else animals may use to navigate. There are scientific studies into how animals use the Sun, Moon and stars, the Earth's magnetic field, and recognition of landmarks to repeat their long journeys.

Homing Pigeons are famous for being able to navigate over extremely long distances. Their "homing" is so reliable that they were used in World War I and World War II to deliver messages to soldiers who could not safely travel. How do Homing Pigeons find their way—even on cloudy days? Do they carry a map and a compass? Scientists have been working on this fascinating mystery for more than 100 years. One really dedicated scientist named Hans Wallraff loaded up the back of his van with Homing Pigeons and drove them 100 miles (160 KM) from home. He placed them in airtight containers with bottled air, turned lights on and off at random, played constant noise, surrounded them with changing magnets and put all of this on a tilting, spinning table. After all that, when he released them, they found their way straight back home! This is evidence that pigeons have some way of mapping where they are even when they are in an unknown location and have no way of retracing the path that brought them there. Wow, that's some map! It's like they have a smart phone in their pocket.

Other scientists have discovered that Homing Pigeons actively use the magnetic field to navigate. Charles Walcott found that he could influence Homing Pigeons by changing the magnetic field around their heads. When he attached magnetic coils to the birds' heads and switched them on, the birds were fooled into flying in the opposite direction from home. When the batteries died, they turned around and made it back safely. After that, scientists got to work figuring out how exactly Homing Pigeons can sense the magnetic field and make it into a reliable map.

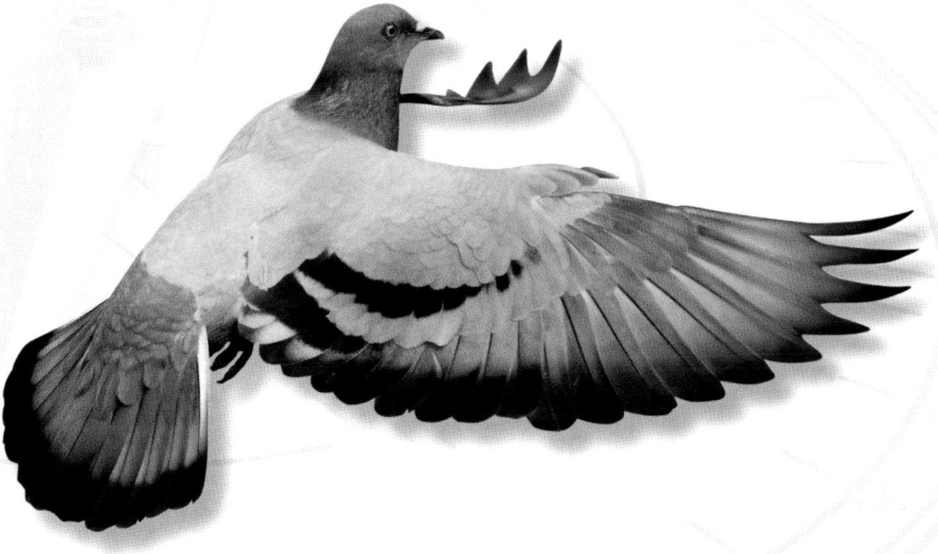

It was only recently discovered that birds have sensors in their eyes that help them actually SEE the magnetic field. In Winged Heroes, Emilio starts to make use of this ability and that's how he finds his way home. To us, it's a hidden world, but scientists now think that birds use this secret sense to travel the globe and get home safely.

Compass image credit: Shutterstock by Sashkin
Rock Pigeon image credit: Shutterstock by Cherdchai Chaivimo

MEET THE REAL BIRDS

PEREGRINE FALCON
(FALCO PEREGRINUS)

POWERFUL AND FAST-FLYING, THE PEREGRINE FALCON DROPS DOWN ON PREY FROM HIGH ABOVE IN AN AMAZING STOOP. THEY WERE ALMOST GONE FROM EASTERN NORTH AMERICA BECAUSE OF PESTICIDE POISONING IN THE MIDDLE 20TH CENTURY, BUT STRONG RECOVERY EFFORTS HAVE HELPED PEREGRINE FALCONS THRIVE IN MANY LARGE CITIES AND COASTAL AREAS.

RUBY-THROATED HUMMINGBIRD
(ARCHILOCHUS COLUBRIS)

EASTERN NORTH AMERICA'S ONLY COMMON HUMMINGBIRD. THESE PRECISION-FLYING CREATURES GLITTER IN THE FULL SUN, AND ARE COMMON AT FEEDERS AND IN FLOWER GARDENS IN SUMMER. IN EARLY FALL, THEY HEAD TO CENTRAL AMERICA, WITH MANY CROSSING THE GULF OF MEXICO IN A SINGLE FLIGHT.

SNOWY OWL
(BUBO SCANDIACUS)

THE REGAL SNOWY OWL, THE LARGEST NORTH AMERICAN OWL (BY WEIGHT), SHOWS UP ON OCCASION IN WINTER TO HUNT IN WINDSWEPT FIELDS OR DUNES. IT SUMMERS FAR NORTH OF THE ARCTIC CIR-CLE, HUNTING PREY IN 24-HOUR DAYLIGHT. IN YEARS OF LEMMING POPULATION BOOMS, IT CAN RAISE DOUBLE OR TRIPLE THE USUAL NUMBER OF YOUNG.

GOLDEN EAGLE
(AQUILA CHRYSAETOS)

THE GOLDEN EAGLE IS ONE OF THE LARGEST AND FIERCEST RAPTORS IN NORTH AMERICA. LOOK FOR THEM IN THE WEST, SOARING OR DIVING ON THE HUNT FOR SMALL MAMMALS. SOMETIMES SEEN ATTACKING OR FIGHTING OFF COYOTES OR BEARS IN DEFENSE OF ITS PREY AND YOUNG, THE GOLDEN EAGLE INSPIRES BOTH AWE AND FEAR.

FROM WINGED HEROES

MEET THE REAL BIRDS

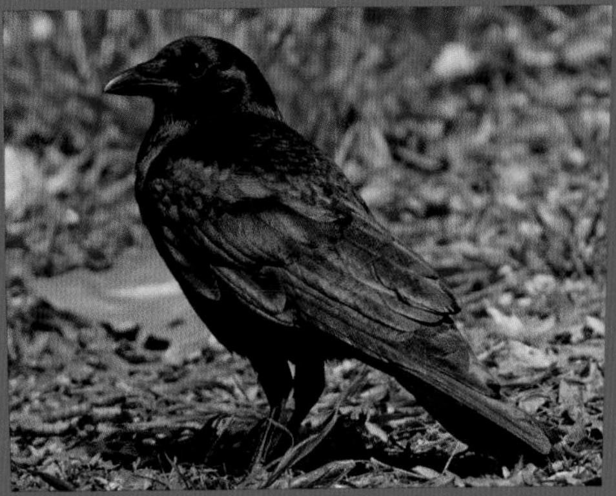

AMERICAN CROW

(CORVUS BRACHYRHYNCHOS)

AMERICAN CROWS ARE FAMILIAR OVER MUCH OF THE CONTINENT: LARGE, INTELLIGENT, ALL-BLACK BIRDS WITH HOARSE, CAWING VOICES. THEY ARE A COMMON SIGHT IN TREETOPS, FIELDS, AND ON ROADSIDES, AND IN HABITATS RANGING FROM OPEN WOODS AND EMPTY BEACHES TO TOWN CENTERS. THEY USUALLY FEED ON THE GROUND AND EAT ALMOST ANYTHING.

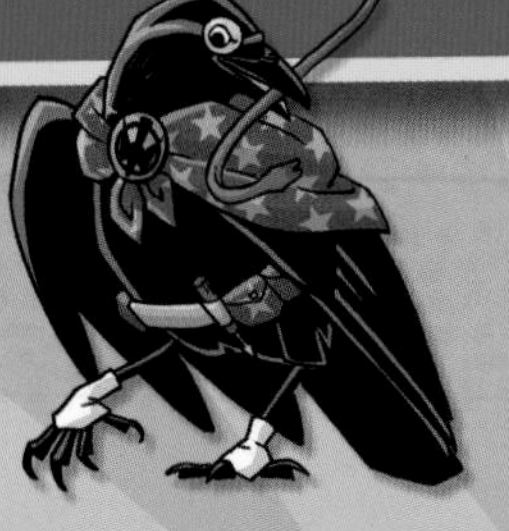

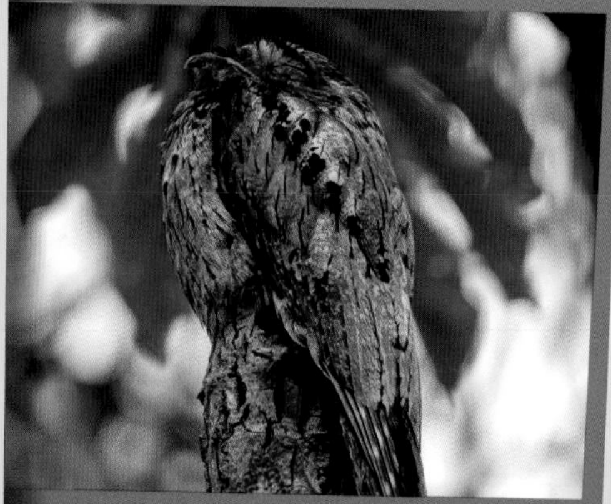

COMMON POTOO

(NYCTIBIUS GRISEUS)

COMMON POTOOS ARE KNOWN FOR BEING ABLE TO BLEND IN PERFECTLY WITH THEIR SURROUNDINGS AND ARE SOMETIMES VERY DIFFICULT TO SPOT. THEY LIVE IN OPEN FORESTS WITH SCATTERED TREES. THEY MAKE A SERIES OF WHISTLES, FROM HIGH TO LOWER PITCH THAT SOUND LIKE: "POO, POO, POO, POO, POO."

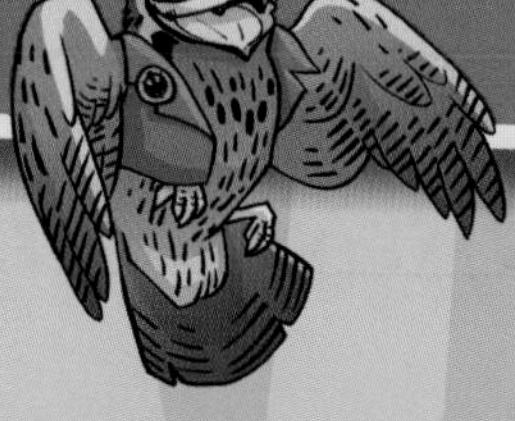

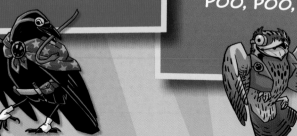

HOMING PIGEON
(COLUMBA LIVIA DOMESTICA)

HOMING PIGEONS ARE DOMESTICATED (BRED AND TRAINED) ROCK PIGEONS WHO ARE ABLE TO RETURN TO THEIR HOME WHEN RELEASED FROM PLACES THEY'VE NEVER VISITED. THEY SOMETIMES TRANSPORT MESSAGES PLACED IN SMALL TUBES AND ATTACHED TO ONE OF THEIR LEGS. THE ROCK PIGEON (LIKE EMILIO), ALSO HAS THIS A HOMING ABILITY.

WANDERING ALBATROSS
(DIOMEDEA EXULANS)

THE WANDERING ALBATROSS HAS THE LONGEST WINGSPAN OF ANY BIRD ON EARTH— AT 11-FEET (3.4 METERS). THEY USE THOSE MASSIVE WINGS TO TRAVEL THOUSANDS OF MILES IN A SINGLE JOURNEY, TYPICALLY OVER OCEANS WITHOUT EVER TOUCHING DOWN ON LAND.

FROM WINGED HEROES

AND THE REAL EMILIO!

ROCK PIGEON
(COLUMBA LIVIA)

COMMON IN CITIES AROUND THE WORLD, ROCK PIGEONS CROWD STREETS AND PUBLIC SQUARES, LIVING ON DISCARDED FOOD AND BIRDSEED. INTRODUCED TO NORTH AMERICA IN THE EARLY 1600S, CITY PIGEONS NEST ON BUILDINGS AND WINDOW LEDGES. IN THE COUNTRYSIDE, THEY ALSO NEST ON BARNS, GRAIN TOWERS, NATURAL CLIFFS, AND BRIDGES.

Images used under license from Shutterstock.com:
Compass by Sashkin / Golden Eagle by Iluta Goean / Homing Pigeon by hrui / Wandering Albatross by mzphoto.cz / Common Potoo by Iguazu Falls / Rock Pigeon (flying) by Cherdchai Chaivimol / Rock Pigeon (perched) by Snehaaaa Patel / Peregrine Falcon by Harry Collins Photography / Ruby-throated Hummingbird by Brian A Wolf / Snowy Owl by Jim Cumming / American Crow by Melinda Fawver

ACTIVITIES

Mama Osprey says, "Every bird has their own inner power. You just have to learn to use it…" This could be said for every animal. Why do you think animals have different senses and abilities instead of every animal having the same powers?

Discussion Questions:

Emilio builds his confidence up through the book. What friends and experiences help him become more confident? What are ways in which you have become more confident as you have grown?

In the end, Emilio gets a special delivery. What do you think Emilio will do with it? How will he use his superpowers to help himself and birdkind?

The Winged Heroes in Emilio's comic book protect a flock of song-birds that are attracted by the city lights from slamming into a sky-scraper. Based on what you know about birds, what other ways do you think birds might be in danger from human activities?

Emilio starts off the book dreaming about how he'd rather be a powerful predator than powerless prey. In nature, do you think it is always better to be a predator than prey or do predators face special challenges of their own?

Emilio started to see magnetic patterns in the sky before he understood how they could help him navigate. Have you ever noticed something in nature that you didn't understand at first? What was it and how did you end up learning more about it?

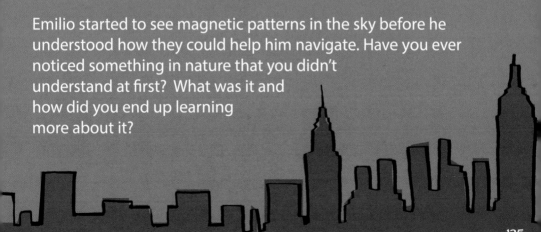

More Discussion Questions

When Emilio and his friends were on the island, they had trouble finding food because they weren't used to the island habitat. How would you describe your habitat? What foods have you observed birds in your neighborhood eating? Are your local birds more like Emilio and his friends in their diet or are they more like the island birds?

Teacher tells the class that to avoid getting caught by falcons they should stay close to buildings. This tip saves them later on when Carmen tells them to hide under the Statue of Liberty's torch. Can you think of something that you have learned in school that came in handy later in your everyday life?

Scientists have been studying bird navigation for hundreds of years and still don't know everything about how it works. The latest data suggests that birds actually see the magnetic field based on special structures in their eyes. How that works is still being studied. Can you think of other things in nature that we understand better now through science but still have more to learn about?

Finish this in your mind:

I used to think birds _____

and now I know birds _____.

Based on superpower, w
Winged Hero wou
you most like to be?

TAKE THE QUIZ TO FIND OUT WHICH WINGED HERO (AND BIRD) YOU ARE MOST LIKE! VISIT:

WingedHeroes.com

...ene for bringing the Winged Heroes to life by drawing birds ...he heart of this story—love, fear, kindness, bravery and all. ...illustration together with the best of cartooning. Thank you ...kin, and Caroline Watkins for all the positive energy and ...ed Heroes grow from an unhatched egg to a full-fledged book. Special thanks to Deborah Lee Rose for your wisdom and science writer's touch and to Ethan Young for guiding us at the start.

Thanks to Cecily Molnar, Mateo Schoenwiese, Anya and Niko Ross, and Nancy Thompson's 4th grade class for your careful reads and helpful ideas. Katy Payne your curious spirit set me on the path and Erika Molnar your creative moral support keeps me going. Zev, thanks for being a great partner. Thank you Charles Walcott for your studies of bird navigation and for the lecture that first got me fascinated with this topic. A big shout out to all the bird nerds at the Lab of Ornithology who inspire me every day. Real birds are so incredible that it's easy to imagine them as superheroes. Thank you to the birds!

About the Cornell Lab:

The Cornell Lab of Ornithology is in Ithaca, New York surrounded by trails alive with birdsong where hundreds of people work to understand birds and nature. We are a global organization that teams up with people all over the world to help restore our planet and protect birds. Our goal is to support people of all ages and backgrounds to connect with birds, participate in science, and become advocates for life on Earth.

Cornell Lab Mission:

Dedicated to advancing the understanding and protection of the natural world, the Cornell Lab joins with people from all walks of life to make new scientific discoveries, share insights, and galvanize conservation action.

35% of the net proceeds from every Cornell Lab Publishing Group book purchase will support projects such as children's educational and community programs.

Learn more at *birds.cornell.edu* and *allaboutbirds.org*